WRINKLES IN SPACETIME

CATHERINE HAUSTEIN

CITY OWL
PRESS

WRINKLES IN SPACETIME
Unstable States, Book Three

CITY OWL PRESS
www.cityowlpress.com

Cover Design by MiblArt. All stock photos licensed appropriately.

Edited by Christie Stratos

For information on subsidiary rights, please contact the publisher at info@cityowlpress.com.

Print Edition ISBN: 978-1-64898-220-0

Digital Edition ISBN: 978-1-64898-219-4

Printed in the United States of America

To everyone who looks up.

PRAISE FOR CATHERINE HAUSTEIN

"Haustein creates her world with subtlety and intelligence which captures the imagination. Wonderfully entertaining, Mixed In delivers a powerful message with an admirable and honest grace. The reader can look forward to more tales from this author with anticipation. Well done!"
- *InD'tale*

"The author introduces an entertaining cast of characters, while warning us of what could be."
- *Author Lee Joanne Collins*

"Catrina bucks the typical trend you see of female scientists in pop culture. While she's a dedicated scientist, she refuses to let people see her as a one-dimensional nerd girl -- she also has aspirations for sex, romance, and having a family. This was a fantastic, sexy read, and the main character's struggles are very relatable for all women. Would definitely recommend!"
- *Book Reviewer*

"Hilarious, life-affirming, politically provocative . . . I loved seeing the world from the viewpoint of a chemist! A page-turner plot and clever writing."
- *Cynthia Mahmood, Book Reviewer*

"From romance to mystery to intrigue, Mixed In offers the reader a little bit of everything. Catrina and Ulysses's unlikely union sets the stage for all sorts of situations that occur throughout the book, keeping the reader interested from start to finish. Love how the author inserts tidbits of knowledge at the beginning of each

chapter! Love the dialogue throughout the book that builds the characters. Loved the book!"
- *Ann V., Book Reviewer*

"A unique love story that will suck you in, take you on a wild ride, and spit you back out on the other side with a smile."
- *Karin A Van Wyk, Book Reviewer*

Isaac Newton said, "A man might imagine things that are false but he can only understand things that are true."

CHAPTER ONE

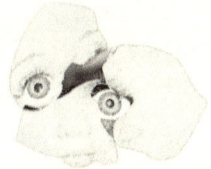

If you know anything about scientists, you know they love working with someone else—a lab partner who can help record data, discuss results, mix up chemical reagents, and share a passion for science.

I had no lab partner.

I walked alone down the halls of the research wing of Cochton Enterprises, groups of two—lab partners—passing by with their carts of corn mash samples or adulterated soybean paste. At times, in the bathroom of my research building, I'd say hello to another scientist as we washed our hands, our lab coats pulled above our wrists. I'd make a friendly gesture, smoothing my hair or laughing nervously, as if I was dissolving a Porkie in acid. I'd worked to develop Porkies, which were bite-sized blobs of pork fat covered in corn meal. Nobody returned my smiles. I'd be left standing there wiping my wet hands on my lab coat because we were out of paper towels again. Perhaps they thought being on the Porkie Team had made me rich. It hadn't. I was clearly a person no one understood and I tried not to fault them for it.

The company itself was not to blame for my isolation. They had over 100 scientists working in one sprawling building, eating together in the cafeteria emblazoned with peppy slogans like, *Don't ask why you have so little but why you have so much!* and *Judge yourself and report others.* I still couldn't tell if I liked working alone or not, but the fact was, I was alone, rambling around in my big lab in the food development division of Cochton Enterprises. All I wanted for my birthday was something I hadn't had in nearly twenty years —a lab partner.

Being alone, with few to relate to, had resulted in me having a crush on my boss, Sir Gotfried, a chubby but distinguished supervisor who had taken me under his wing after I graduated from private college with a degree in food chemistry and development science. I thought he might do something special for me on my big day, my birthday. However, it had been uneventful, as I was at work. It wasn't as though my work made me sad. It didn't. I had my own lab and nothing could make a scientist more content.

My lab was beautiful and filled with light from tall windows overlooking the Cedar River, which was struggling along with silt. Below the window, the citizens of Cochtonville, in the nation of Cochtonia, went about their day with obedient productivity, just as I did. I was content, yes, content, and yet, I wasn't sure contentment was all I needed. I was too young to be this content and too old to be this virginal.

Minutes before I left for the day, Sir Gotfried came into my lab. I was turning off the autoclave when he approached me. He was dressed in his uniform, green with a gold sash and adorned with silver, bronze, and even gold corn kernels—all signs of his utmost loyalty and productive contributions to our empire of Cochtonia. Except for his eyes, he was a small-featured man, with a wide leathery face, a twist of chin, gray-streaked hair, and a tiny smear of sticky candy at a corner of his mouth. He put a hand on my shoulder. I thought this might be it, he'd spill his affection for me and I could say it was mutual. We'd kiss sweetly, thanks to his candy munching habit, gaze shyly into each other's eyes, and rip off each other's clothes in a frenzy I'd never experienced before. I'll be honest, I was withering away for lack of human touch. His steady hand on my shoulder had me dizzy.

He said, "Stella, I'll have a new assignment for you Monday. I apologize, it's something different. I have no choice in this matter, as the Cochtons are all in."

His tone alarmed me. It was dead serious, telling me our founding fathers, Bert and Clarence Cochton, wanted me to do something unusual. I'd been a hard worker, a food chemist with bundles of know-how. I'd helped develop Porkies! In fact, I still had the prototype corn meal we'd used to coat them here in the lab along with some germ-free samples of fat in beakers on my shelves in case we needed to use them again. I'd been solid, dependable. As with all good chemists, stability was my goal.

If only the leaders of my country, also the owners of my employer, Cochton Enterprises, were secure and not like a couple of dried-up bottles of picric acid, which explodes when joggled. Notice I didn't say uranium. Uranium decays but leaves daughter nuclei. Not the two Cochton brothers, they were aging and desperate for heirs. Sons preferred but daughters would do. They had neither, despite the technological advances of our nation. Thanks to genetic engineering, we could produce any kind of person here in Cochtonia—good-looking ones were preferred, even for jobs such as Vice Patrol agent and firefighter. The sticking point was, we had to start with something; we couldn't create a person from nothing. Spontaneous generation wasn't a thing. Somehow, the leaders of our nation hadn't started anything. Perhaps they couldn't.

My boss, my one human connection here at work, averted his large, brown eyes, which were shaded by peppered brows. He reached into his pocket and drew out a handful of candy corn. He held it out to me.

"Want some? This stuff is close to perfect."

"Why you?" I asked, taking one kernel. "And why me?"

"You're a small research group. You can easily be retired."

"Small? I could hardly be smaller. Retired? I'm not old enough! I'll join another group. I can learn to work with others."

"Our projects aren't the future, we could easily go to the pigs!" Being sent to the pigs was a way of saying people were killed, gotten rid of for the good of the nation. We were an agricultural state, after all, and raised and slaughtered 20,000 hogs a day. We grew the corn to fatten them. On days like today, humid and sunny, you could smell them even though they were ten or even twenty miles away in confinements—buildings which housed and raised them until they were market weight, 300 pounds. This took about six months. If there was a wind, their drifting hairs tickled your nose. Pigs don't have much hair, but the nation of Cochtonia had lots of pigs. It didn't need people who weren't contributors, which we were reminded of often.

"No!" I said, the kernel shaking between my fingers. "Not the pigs!"

"Don't be alarmed. What I'm asking won't be difficult. I need you to host some guests." Host and guest had a special meaning in science. Hosts were big molecules that swallowed and held smaller ones and could be used, for example, to spray a scent-trapping host into the air to trap a stinky guest. We needed to do this more often in Cochtonia. It stunk.

"I can be a host," I said, wondering if he thought of me as large. No matter, I was curious and loyal and scared enough to do whatever this was.

"You'll be more of a tour guide or a helping hand. You are small and they are big—bigger than life, you might say, and you will help these, umm, *creations,* set up a lab for an experiment that is both unsavory and unusual. If it doesn't work—and it won't, I fear—I'm off to the pigs and you could go with me."

"What do you need me to do?" My stomach churned as I popped the candy into my mouth. Modified beings always made me nervous, no matter how common they were becoming. Not everyone was modified. There were normal people like Sir and me, who were unmodified. I'd been normal enough to be sent to a makeshift college for a degree in science and be gainfully employed. Normal enough to be floating through life nearly alone.

"They will be seting up a lab. Help them find the proper space."

"Set up a lab for what type of experiments? Give me the specifications. How do I get ready?" I put my hand on his as it rested on my shoulder and scrutinized his face to see if anything would happen. I moved my face a little closer. He slid his hand from under mine, slipped it into his pocket, drew out a couple bits of candy corn, and ate them anxiously. Yes, his teeth were shot to pieces from his candy habit, but he was otherwise a distinguished man with nervous energy able to be channeled.

"The Brothers are demanding something I view as..." He stopped. It was a crime to say anything doubtful about our leaders.

"Sir, I'll do whatever you ask." I considered asking for something in return but wanted to show him how much I would do without asking for anything.

"You are loyal, as were your parents. I'll introduce you Monday."

CHAPTER TWO

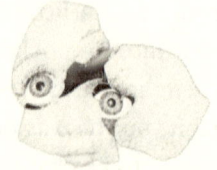

I walked home after work. The roads were privatized and cost by the mile, so I rarely drove. The sidewalks cost too, although they were less expensive. The street was busy today. In addition to autonomous company cars and Vice Patrol vans scanning for deviants to arrest, hog trucks rumbled through the streets, two-tiered haulers driving the inhabitants squealing for their lives. No one would listen. They'd soon be Porkies. All in all, the street wasn't a pleasant place to be, which kept us citizens from going places. This capital city had once been your average midwestern small metropolis until our nation, fueled by agriculture, hateful of environmental regulations, and run by the biggest farm owners around, broke from the United States. I guess you could call this place hog heaven. Or at least hog-lot heaven.

Pain, hot pain, at least was an honest emotion, and the pain of "never" rolled around in me. It was better than no emotion. It was a hunger, an emptiness, rather than a void. No lab partner. No affair with my boss. No passion. Never. Time was running out.

The sidewalk ahead was draped in dense black smoke due to the Pestos starting a plastic bag fire again. The Pestos were displaced farm women, unhappy about the way the Cochtons had gobbled up small farms and modernized them. I went blocks out of my way to avoid the bag burning even though the fires were harmless. However, the women stole, and I wasn't sure where they popped up from when they appeared in town. My turn took me toward the town square and past the Union Station bar. It was right downtown but it had never caught my eye until now. There was a sign in the window.

"Man Show."

This hole in the wall had Crisper male strip shows using genetically modified *erotic* men known as Crispers. Their purpose was to entice workers to put in extra effort to qualify to rent one of the men for a night of passion usually not experienced in Cochtonia. I'd never even seen a naked man. I didn't want to die this way. It was time! I was old enough to know pleasure. I'd check them out now, then demand one after I'd completed my task, whatever it was. With a head full of hedonism, I entered the bar.

Despite the sidewalk cracks outside, Union Station was clean, with glittery lamp shades with colored glass patterns, a bank of booths near the window, and tidy round tables throughout.

I went to the counter, hoping it was what a person did in a place like this.

"Is *this* the Man Show?" I asked, disappointedly pointing to a portrait of a man with a beard above the bar.

The bartender, a woman, who was wearing flowing dragon pajamas and much older than one usually saw in Cochtonia, said, "No, it's U.S. Grant. The Man Show is coming up. Should I pour ya one?"

"Pour me a man? It's that easy?"

"No, a beer. We have the house special on tap today. It's got hints of velvet bean with a jasmine undertone." She was completely serious, eyeing me like I was a pork loin. "How about I give you a free taste? All the ingredients we were generously allowed to import from Wowville since the colony's been such a success." She was purposely playing up an area of Cochtonia outside of the mainstream. Perhaps she thought her mention of misfits would put me at ease. Did I look as misfit and alone as I felt? She pulled a lever underneath U.S. Grant and lightly foamed liquid poured out into the glass she held beneath it.

I took a sip. It was both bright and animally, like swimming in dirty water. The next sip was sweet, diluted nectar. The third sip was bottled emotions. It hit a spot I didn't know I had.

I was tipping my glass for a fourth time when a tall woman in a corn silk suit took the stool next to me. "I'm here," she told the bartender. The bartender didn't look up but pushed a button under the counter.

"Smile," said the woman. "It's showtime!"

"Here's the Man Show," the bartender said to me. She went past the beer cooler behind the bar and opened a door.

A muscular guy, short with a sloping forehead and wearing a furry skin draped across one shoulder like a bath towel, entered the room. His bulging thighs were succulent hams glistening from beneath a small, furry loin cloth. I'd never seen four distinct muscles in a man's arm before. They were like meat on the table. He carried a wooden weapon in one hand—a club, not smooth as if he was a Vice Patrol agent, but coarse, as he was. Some of his silky hair was pulled into a high bun, and the rest cascaded down his back. His brawny chest dove into a tight waist, as if he was a triangle at the butcher shop.

"Who is he?" I said aloud.

The tall woman leaned on the bar next to me. "Have you been living in a closet? He's a high-end caveman for women such as myself with InVitro status. He's going to perform. Hush!" She gave me a dirty look as she spun on her stool, as if I should have recognized her. InVitro status was granted to women who did something extraordinary, such as winning a baking contest by using frosting made from boar fat or devising a technique to make plastic from hog manure. The status allowed them to have a genetically modified baby without the bother or expense of a husband. Even better, it came with money and a house in a classy suburb. This woman looked familiar but without the camera filters and in this dim light, it was hard to say who she was. The brothers picked the InVitros and preferred willowy and buxom. After a while, they all looked alike.

The bartender said, "Neadaen, take us back to a time, a time all of us long for, when all men said was 'ugh.'"

Neadaen swung his club over his head, his beefy shoulders flexing.

"Ugh. Ugh. Wo-man. Wo-man. Oohh, whaa." He pointed the club at a woman sitting at a booth and lunged at her. She leapt out of her seat and ran among the tables as he chased her. Clearly this was faked. Who would run from a man like Neadaen?

The InVitro next to me watched this unfold, her hands in her tailored pockets. Neadaen tapped the woman on the head with the club. She fell back and he caught her with one arm, as hairy as corn with Fusarium fungus. How I longed to touch it.

The bartender called out, "Neadaen, halt! You aren't giving your services away for nothing."

He threw back his head, opened his large mouth. "Aaa uahuaha uaaahhh." His yell bounced around the bar.

The InVitro next to me raised an arm, her hand bulging with a wad of bills nearly as big as Neadaen's biceps. She yelled back, "Aaaha ahaha ah ah aahhhhh."

The caveman rushed to her, tossing tables as he approached.

"Make *me* unconscious, man-slave," she called out. "I'm Lady LouOtta Maliegene and I have everything you need."

Bar patrons, including me, quickly pushed our index finger to our forehead. This woman wrote the national anthem! To put finger to forehead to show you were thinking of Cochtonia when it played was mandatory. Clearly, her name warranted the same reaction.

He lurched toward the two of us as we leaned on the bar. He got down on one knee in front of Lady Maliegene and pointed to his forehead. "Lady, I give you finger."

I wanted him so fiercely my thighs ached to be opened. I wasn't seeking a transformative experience, as I had no aspirations of a higher status. I wanted to rent a Crisper, an erotic expert, for a

one-night policy engagement. It was possible here in the Empire
of Cochtonia. All I needed was cash; surely, I'd get some for my
birthday from my parents. And employer approval. I'd do whatever
Sir Gotfried wanted me to do and then I'd ask for it when my task
was made clear to me. I might not have a lab partner but I could
have a fling. Of course, at this moment, Lady Maliegene was
paying for him. She gave him the bills and he tucked them away
behind his furry loincloth.

Standing, with a swing of his corn silk topknot, Neadaen threw
his club in the air. The InVitro caught it. The Crisper ran his
fingers through his hair and thrust his hips toward her.

"He's all mine," she said.

She was wrong, I would have him! I would rent him after I got
employer permission. I'd ask Sir Gotfried and then I'd be back.

CHAPTER THREE

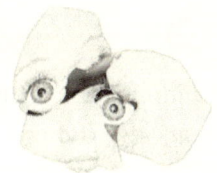

We decorated in shades of white in the one-story, two-bedroom home I shared with my parents—white carpet, white walls, white appliances, and two off-white recliners in front of the CA (Citizen's Advisory) screen, one for Mom and one for Dad. My old baby doll, Jelly, with her bald head and vacant blue eyes, was propped up at the round kitchen table, visible from the living room in the open-concept bungalow. The doll wore a pink polka-dotted party hat with a pink pompom. Mom kept her dressed for each occasion. Thirty some years ago, the old me had treasured Jelly. There'd been many nights where I held her pliant artificial body to mine as if she'd been the last baby in Cochtonia, as well she might have been, for babies were rare here among us normal folks. The hollow plastic doll had been passed from Mom's mother to her and to me. There would be no more passing.

I picked Jelly up. Her painted-on blue eyes stared over her button nose. Her slick plastic lips were open for a bottle, lost long ago.

Dad, in his recliner, called out, "Stay tuned! Hope it's good news."

I put the doll back in her seat and went to join him in the living room, which was only a few steps away from the kitchen.

"Where's Mom?" There weren't many places to look in this two-bedroom, tan and vinyl one story.

"Big message coming on the CA."

"Dad, not what I asked."

"She went out. Could you get me a cookie? I spent all afternoon power washing the car."

I opened the cookie bag on the counter and put the Maize Chip cookies on a plate. "She left you here?"

"Hell, yes."

I nearly tripped over a kitchen chair hurrying to open the door to the garage. The car, an ancient station wagon devoid of modern technology, sat freshly washed, as white as a rusty car could be. My parents had been in the Vice Patrol. They'd worn long white coats and white Stetsons and enforced laws and made some up, too. They were retired and had slowly lost their fondness for a clean, crisp look. The car, however, was Dad's treasure.

"Did she walk?"

"The car was being washed, so, yes."

We were interrupted by an announcement over the Citizen Advisory System on the wall.

"Citizens, activating for important information."

"It's Them! They'll be on the Citizen Advisory." Sure enough, the two brothers who founded our nation appeared on the Citizen Advisory screen. It was the size of a toaster and popped from the wall for our viewing, as if the foreheads of our leaders were rising suns. Bert, short and wiry with big cheeks and small features, almost a doll himself, and Clarence, large and fleshy with flapping lips, zoomed to meet us. Behind them was a living room decorated in gold and white, wherein lurked Layal, the family bastard, hovering as if ready to eat the first uncle who died.

Bert, the smaller of the two, spoke first. "Greetings to our loyal citizens of the proud nation of Cochtonia. We bring good tidings. We plan to live a hundred more years. However, we do not want our nation to despair because of our lack of heirs. Yes, our family was chosen by fate to lead and we take our duty seriously. But we lack children, which is not our fault."

"All they wanted in a dame was looks," Dad interjected. "All the scans and stuff we have here and they couldn't find a fertile Myrtle. They need to invest more in science."

"Hush," I said, putting the plate of cookies on the end table next to his chair. "You should know better." The Vice Patrol could and did listen in. He and Mom had both been in their ranks.

"It weren't a criticism."

"Women of Cochtonia have shouldered a great deal of work as of late. We have rewarded them adequately with our child creation technique known as InVitro. However, the ones we have chosen for our own are not fertile enough to be used in these techniques."

"T'aint the broads. The bros barfed their balls inside out, like I did," Dad said, eating a cookie.

"Dad, stop with the exposition. We need to listen."

"Easy for you to say. You'll never know the pain of vomiting with testicles. It's much worse than erectile dysfunction."

"Dad, hush." It was frowned upon to remember bad times, especially if the leaders of our nation hadn't done much to help when we'd been hit with a vomit virus.

"We have embarked on a new venture—an ascent into history, alchemy, and the search for the homunculus—a little man, a man created from within a man, without a woman. This way, we will have heirs."

"Homo what?" said Dad. "A man from a man?"

"Additionally, we have been influenced by the great dreams of the alchemists. All the ancient dreamers called alchemists knew this little man was possible but disagreed on the ingredients. Some said to mix semen with the blood of a cow, others said to use a mare as a womb. We have, however, come up with a plan, and the two greatest alchemists who ever lived will execute it."

I winced at the word *execute*.

"This project is thirty years in the making. We've raided tombs to bring these men here and our genetics team brought them to life. The State Crisper Facility trained them for our modern world."

"Good thing your mom isn't listening in," Dad remarked. My parents had been replaced by genetically modified Vice Patrol agents. A few non-modified officers were left but most had been forced into retirement.

"Dad, shhh."

"Let us introduce the best known of the alchemists, our old guests in this new century. Alchemy, as you might know, combines the skills of chemistry with the hopes of mysticism."

"I didn't know," said Dad. "They are assuming a whole lot about us here. We don't have hopes."

Two men walked into the frame to join them. They were dressed in ancient clothes, one in a white wig, loose blue waistcoat, buttoned breeches, and frilly jabot. The other, a wide man, wore a ballooning Renaissance robe with a red hat and upturned brim. The clothes didn't have the sheen of our corn-based garments here in Cochtonia. They were dull.

Bert motioned to the one in the wig. "Come on now, come here." He put an arm around the man and drew him close. "Cochtonia, meet the brilliant scientist who discovered gravity and developed the reflecting telescope, the three laws of motion, and love it or hate it, calculus. Did you know he was also gifted with Second Sight—he could see the future—and he made advances in the science of alchemy? Knighted in 1705 and newly resurrected from England, I introduce Sir Isaac Newton."

The wisp of a man in a wig broke from Bert's grasp and bowed, his unease illustrated with a deep frown.

Clarence commanded the screen next. "Paracelsus was a skilled alchemist who developed medicines, pioneered the use of numerous remedies, including laudanum, and gave us the notion of dosage. His greatest work was his promotion of the homunculus. He will lead our project. Fresh from the grave in Austria, having died in 1541, Paracelsus." The second alchemist and Clarence fist-bumped. He waved and blew kisses in our direction.

"Newton I've heard of but the Australian guy, no," Dad said, eating a cookie. Perhaps this was why I had been attracted to Sir Gotfried and his candy habit—it remined me of Dad. No longer. I was going to rent a lean, mean caveman.

The alchemists looked so much like the Cochtons. Isaac was sensitive and fine-boned, Paracelsus ruddy and cocky. How they came to be here and alive hadn't been explained completely. Few in Cochtonia needed a complete explanation and I didn't like being an exception. It was a good way to get executed.

"They will be joining us in the laboratories of Cochton Enterprises with the goal of making a little man," said Clarence.

"Or two," Bert added cheerfully.

"Oink!" I said, using a common swear word in Cochtonia. "Male parthenogenesis? The genetics lab at Cochton Enterprises is going gangbusters." A realization crept over me—these were the guests! I would be called on to assist with an impossible and questionable project—making life from one sex cell without the other. I grabbed Jelly and held her close. This wasn't making sense.

Bert said, "One might say it's the opposite of parthenogenesis. Eggs can reproduce when stimulated with no male as in some bees, birds, and reptiles but we will stimulate the *male* gamete and grow it using ancient ways. Where modern knowledge fails us, alchemy steps in. This dream of ours is possible by combining alchemy with new genetics."

Newton hung back with a surly, arms-crossed scowl. I appreciated his apparent skepticism. The Cochton nephew lurked behind him, larger than life.

"Meanwhile, they will keep you updated on their progress and on special offers from Cochton Enterprises," added Clarence. "Newton, oh Newton."

Isaac flushed as the nephew pushed him in front of the camera.

"What cheer, future humans," he said. "I am here to tell you about this offer. A set of coins commemorating this occasion. As you might know, I worked for the Royal Mint in times gone by." He held up five plastic coins. Four were adorned with the polymer profile of each alchemist and each brother. The fifth was a baby, head on its arms as if in the womb.

As he fidgeted with the coin set, Newton might as well have had a dark cloud over his head. I pitied him, having to sell these trinkets when all he wanted to do was drop things and shove them together to test their attraction for each other. He'd rather look through a prism than hawk these trinkets. Didn't he invent the color wheel? He was one man from the outside who'd been part of my schooling.

"They are solid carbon based, carbon like the relic of fire, but your land makes it from manure, which is a most fecund substance." Striving for accuracy, Newton searched for the word unsuccessfully. "This is all new to me. This structural material bears little resemblance to a mineral. However, as a celebrity who once ran the Royal Mint, I am compelled by those more powerful than I am to endorse them as valuable."

The bastard-nephew shoved himself into view. He was the son of the disinherited Cochton sister, and had been modified to be an escort—a Crisper, like the caveman. His stripper career never got out of the barn. By betraying his mother, he'd won favor with his uncles, and was as close to an heir as we had.

"Plastic. These lush items are made from the freshest of plastic created from raw sewage converted to polyester. Push your BUY NOW button to order." Layal was supposed to be handsome but he'd let himself go. At least he had something to let go of, unlike most of the natural male citizens in this small nation in what was once Iowa.

"We're watching you."

The last thing I wanted right now was a set of coins. My whole life had been skimping, working, living with my parents. I never had enough for anything frivolous. I didn't know what playfulness was. Until I'd gotten a free beer at the bar, nothing had ever been handed to me. We had a cupboard full of Cochton mugs and closets full of Cochton t-shirts. We didn't need anything more.

There could be a knock on the door, would be a knock on the door, if we didn't buy these coins.

Dad rose from the recliner, toddled over and pushed the button on the screen.

Next, the larger alchemist said, "In order to fund our most important venture of creating an heir, I am selling this elixir known as Wonder in a Bottle. Buy today. Buy now."

As Dad pushed the button again, my head spun as I tried to make sense of it. They wanted a homunculus? Why? Why not a clone or genetically modify a baby stuffed with their genes? Oh, those both required a female! The key was, no woman needed. The uncomfortable announcement and the dread of this being the project I needed to help with made me reach for any source of pleasure I could find to balm my spirit. I grabbed a cookie and shoved it in my mouth.

At last, the Citizen Advisory went dark.

Box in hand, plastic bag over one arm, Mom came through the door.

"Mom. You went out and left Dad?"

"He has to get used to it sometimes. Stella, I got a cake. I splurged for your birthday. I got a cake and some Porkies."

Porkies, my Porkies. Bite-sized fried processed balls of pork, salt, corn sweetener, corn bread batter, and preservatives. They were sold by the frozen five-pound pack. All you had to do was microwave. Porkies were dubbed, "The Official Food of the Cochton Empire," and thus, expensive and coveted.

"Yum," I said, with faked enthusiasm. My secret shame was: I'd had enough of Porkies. I'd spent a year in a lab doing a gravimetric analysis of the fat content in an exhausting trial of various iterations of fat content. If you don't know what a gravimetric determination is, you're lucky. To do this procedure, I had to extract the fat from ground up Porkies into chloroform, isolate the fat-laden chloroform, let the solvent evaporate, and weigh the greasy residue. The heavier it was, the more fat. Porkies, in the end, were the right combination of fat with a sweet coating and limited availability to induce binge eating. However, after smelling all the chloroform and having nightmares every night, I was averse to them.

She gave Dad the bag of Porkies. "Give these a zap in the microwave, please."

"I'm not a servant," he said, walking to the kitchen and putting them on the counter.

"Stella, come look at the cake. It has a big four and a big zero." We followed Dad into the kitchen. Mom put the box on the kitchen table and opened the sides.

"It has black icing," I said. "Do you know how much food coloring it takes to make black?"

Mom ignored this, as she'd ignored Dad's comment. She gave me a gift bag. "Open it."

I took out a jar. "Wrinkle cream?"

"Yes! Happy birthday. Did you see how I got Jelly ready?"

"She looks ready for a kid's party."

Mom took a serving plate from the cupboard. She put the Porkies in the microwave. "Oh, you're still my kid. Speaking of parties, I've been thinking of how lonely you must be. Dad and I will be gone someday. You need a bigger family. You need someone to be with you and help around the house. I filled out some paperwork today. If we are approved, you're going to have a Pesto sister. Happy birthday!"

She snatched Jelly, held the doll inches from her face and said, "You'll have an auntie."

I let what she said sink in. My birthday present was a Pesto child. In other words, they were hiring a servant and saying it would be my sister.

"I thought there'd be more excitement about this," Mom said. "I requested a child, an older girl, at Headquarters. She'll be better company than a baby and rehabilitated at the Camp for Pestos." She wiggled Jelly. "Yay," she said in a baby voice. She put the doll on the table.

I said, "I thought the Pesto camp was closed."

"I have on good authority it's not. There are still girls without proper parents. Aren't you happy, Stella?"

Now even my parents were finding me unsuitable company. "My present is a Pesto? Will she have the eyes?"

"Don't they all have the eyes? They're small. It's a mutation. Let's have some Porkies. It's a happy day!" She emptied the steaming bag of Porkies onto a platter and put it on the table next to the cake.

"Speaking of eyes, did you see the announcement?" Dad asked. "A new way to get kids is on the horizon. Maybe I should volunteer if you want another kid. It would be a full copy of myself."

Mom handed each of us a plate. "Yes, I saw it on my device. Shocking! Is it going to work? Women wouldn't be needed at all."

Dad took the plate along with three Porkies, squeezed together with tongs and dripping grease. "Good for them. It's inconvenient —all this InVitro stuff. The contests to see which women are the best of the best and selected to bear children are costly. The winners run around as if their shit don't stink. Lady Maliegene is a prime example."

My ears perked up at the mention of the woman I'd met at the bar. She certainly was full of herself but what did I know? She was a popular celebrity.

"Hush! We'll get a knock at the door with such talk. She's special. InVitros are special. We should respect it. Plus, the contests keep the population amused." Mom helped herself to a Porkie. "Aren't you hungry, Stella?"

Dad went on. "I'm looking forward to this Homo-whatever project. It's time for men to rise again."

There was a beep and a clatter at the front door as a drone dropped the coins on the front stoop. Another thud came as the liquor was delivered.

"Did you get the coins they advertised? Good," Mom said. She went to the door and brought in the coin package—the size of a GoodNCorny candy bar. She handed it to me. "Happy birthday. Gotta say, we do make good plastic here."

"And liquor," Dad said, grabbing the Styrofoam bottle.

I opened the coin box. They were a thin, gray plastic.

"How attractive," I said, in case we were being listened to.

"Time to celebrate!" Dad poured us each a shot of Wonder in a Bottle. It was bitter with a chloroform after taste.

"I can't wait to expand our family," Mom said, dropping into a recliner.

In a haze, I took the gift to my small bedroom, nearly tripping over a basket of clothes I needed to put away. I rammed the coins in my too-full sock drawer and closed it, but not before I took the Newton one and put it under my pillow. In my dreams, he laid with me and offered to teach me to stand on the shoulders of giants, but I told him, "No, thanks, I want to lie beneath a caveman." We all have to stick with our principles.

CHAPTER FOUR

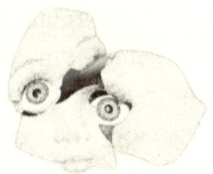

"When the guests arrive, show them our labs, explain what we do here, and help them select a suitable space." Gotfried stood in my lab looking much less sexy to me than he had the week before.

"Space for what?" I knew what he was going to say. I still twinged when he said it.

"The Homunculus Project."

"Sir, I'm going to ask a favor for this."

He looked shocked. I'd always been a content employee, not asking for favors.

"We can talk about it later. Listen, they will be accompanied by a publicity team. This will be broadcast, so don't share confidential information."

"Confidential information? Such as what?"

"Maintain an air of detached professionalism."

I would not, of course, do any such thing. When Paracelsus and Newton entered, followed by camera brandishing sex-pots, I knew I'd do whatever it took to cheer the surly Newton. The poor man's eyes drooped and so did his mouth as if he had a neural lesion. He had a wretched old wig and a cute dimple on his chin. Was it really him—Isaac Newton—looking a bit lost around the eyes? Poor Newton was glum, little more than a prize hog in the barn of

Cochton Enterprises. Resurrection hadn't been cheap and the company would exploit it for profit. A scientist might do something out of curiosity but why would a company do anything but make money? Cochton Enterprises wasn't a person after all. It could expand and progress like something not alive. The family who owned it, the Cochtons, meant to live forever or close to it. Resurrecting the alchemists was just a trial run.

"Gentlemen," said Sir, "meet Virginia."

"Virginia's my middle name. I'm Stella, Stella Smithfailed. Welcome to my lab. Please put on eye protection for the tour of our facilities." I handed Newton a pair of safety glasses. He didn't take them so I slipped them on his eyes, my hand brushing the soft skin of his face. He tilted his head to stare at the ceiling and then the floor.

"Optics," he said. "How I love to see through a glass! Warm thanks to you from your humble servant, Isaac Newton." He bowed stiffly and wobbled back on his heels in a way I found charming. I fished some diffraction grating glasses from a drawer of science novelties I kept for fun—fun I never had.

"Try these," I said, putting them on his eyes, touching him again. The film crew tittered as he wagged his head and examined the lights. They looked like rainbows to him.

"Wondrously lit," he said as he gazed about like a child. "Prism goggles."

"Yes, the diffraction grating disperses the light as a prism would —each color taking a different bend through the lens."

"I was the one who showed white light is composed of many colors—seven in all since seven is a sacred number. The color droplets are dispersed according to their color consistently. Each color has its own refrangibility. Moreover, hue is a property of a material's reflection of color."

The film crew giggled as if he was a buffoon instead of expressing wonder.

Here was a problem with modern science and the employment of scientists—wonder was expected, demanded, and paid for. You were expected to roll out wonder as if it was a product and then the marketers would whisk it away and make it even more magnificent but in a false way. No one was amazed at wonder these days. Wonder and passion were things of the past.

"Yes, we see what is transmitted, the complimentary color."

"These lenses are not prisms?"

"No, they are diffraction gratings made from regularly spaced scratches on a transparent plastic. They behave as prisms but are less bulky and much less costly. You may keep them," I said. "But they aren't safe for the lab. Here, change them out for now." I put them in the pocket of his waistcoat and with my hand so close to the groin of a great man, I felt a surge of new life within.

The film crew zeroed in on his brightening countenance.

"You are here to help us find a location for the homunculus creation?" Paracelsus reminded me.

"Yes. Yes, I am. First, I'd like to offer you the use of *my* lab." As I said this, I saw my lab with fresh eyes. It featured a sink filled with dirty beakers soaking in soapy water, a big, boxy plant growth chamber containing exhaust fans and grow lights but no plants, and a pH meter with a crusty electrode.

"I envision all matters of possibilities here," said Newton.

"We don't have the luxury of possibilities," Paracelsus said, drinking from a flask. "We have to produce a homunculus. This spot is too sunny."

"Let's look at other places. Part of this tour is to help you select a lab of your own. What do you need in a workspace?" I asked the alchemists.

Newton bounced on his buckled shoes as we walked through the halls. I could hear lab doors locking. No one else wanted to share their lab or be part of this fool's errand.

"What do you need to create the Homunculus?"

"Nothing too clean," said Paracelsus. "It involves manure. We will make a bed of manure and allow fertilization and growth to proceed naturally. Or should I say, supernaturally?"

Newton added, "Locked doors without windows. Alchemy rests on secrets."

"How long will this process take?" I asked skeptically.

"Shorter than a pregnancy and longer than hatching an egg," Paracelsus replied.

"The basement has many rooms and the lower level will dampen the vibrations made when people walk. In fact, no one should walk past at all."

I lead the entourage down the back stairs to the lowest level of the Cochton Enterprises research building.

"This space might interest you."

I showed them a storeroom filled with broken equipment, most of which had been mine and was so old I couldn't get parts to fix the stuff. Despite advances in genetics, my area of research, food development, was starved for funds. To make matters worse, a leak from a broken pipe had stained the ceiling and the space reeked of mold.

"The atmosphere is perfect!" Paracelsus announced. He reached into his robe.

Sir Gotfried said hopefully, "Is our task accomplished?"

"Yes." Paracelsus took a drink and a deep breath. "We want this warehouse space."

"Very good." Nearly immediately, Pesto custodians arrived to remove the broken equipment as the PR group filmed.

As I left, Paracelsus bowed and handed me a purple crystal. "My token of thanks. It's enchanting, as are you."

Gotfried and I took the elevator up to our floor.

"Great work, Virginia," he said. "You were a comfort to them and non-threatening. I can't imagine how they must feel, roused from the grave and brought to our time. Newton enjoyed his technical chat with you."

I wished Sir, or someone, would sweep me up in his arms and remember my name. Instead, the elevator door opened and I got out, unsure of reality. They couldn't be the real historical people. If this was possible, anything was possible, and we all know anything is not possible.

I went to the cafeteria for lunch, but it wasn't the usual hot dogs and corn. A fluffy bread filled with shriveled-up plants soaked in alcohol and covered in butter and corn sweetener was the entrée along with a small tube of meat.

"What's this?" I asked in alarm.

"It's stollen and blutwurst—blood sausage," the server said. "We're helping Paracelsus feel at home."

"I thought *I* was in food development!"

"Guess you got scooped," she replied. "How about some ice cream? Haha."

I sat by myself, which was a regular thing. I tended to mention the composition of foods as people ate them, blurting out the high fat content of Porkies when several of us lunched together. Wondering what was in this stollen and blutwurst, I listened for people around me to complain about foreign food. I wasn't sure I'd try it. I didn't want to like it.

Surprisingly, the alchemists came into the cafeteria, escorted by a familiar Vice Patrol security guard, Officer Ursula. She was, as her name suggested, a large, bear-like woman, dressed in a white uniform. She was friendlier to me than most other employees because my parents had been Vice Patrol agents and she understood the tribulations normal agents, as she was, had with the better-equipped modified agents replacing them. They came my way. I hoped I wouldn't have to fake cheerfulness about the new foods. They sat across the table from me and my wishes came true. Newton said nothing, simply stared at his tray in disgust while Paracelsus chatted with Ursula.

"I hope all of your needs are being cared for," she said.

"Almost all," he replied, winking.

"Do you not have concerns about authority figures?" she asked.

"I saw something about your aversion to powerful authority in your profile."

"You are a person as I am," he replied. "And all people are equal."

Equality was treasonous talk, yet she let it slide, taking a bite of her sausage, her eyes on him. He did the same.

The sausage was, in my opinion, darker than meat should be, a stocking bulging with tar-soaked sand.

"Umm, it's creamy," she said. "Like pudding."

"You're not eating any meat." Paracelsus poked Newton with his elbow. "You'll become anemic, if you aren't already."

"It's blood sausage. It's immoral."

"Are you some sort of snob?"

"No, I was born to a wealthy family with strict values."

"What is it?" I asked, favorably disposed since someone else found this new food offensive. "Who approved this?"

"It is animal blood and grain in an intestine," Paracelsus said, picking his up and chomping it. "Tastes like pork blood and corn meal bursting with health."

"Eating it promotes savageness and cruelty," Newton said.

"Newton, am I cruel?"

"It might give you a thirst for blood."

"Newton, do I have a thirst for blood? I'm a lover. Ursula here, might be a different story."

"I crack heads open, but I don't eat the contents."

Newton leapt to his feet. "This is gruesome!"

"Wait," I said, not wanting him to leave me here with these odd foods and company.

He bowed to me. "Good day." He ran off, leaving his tray.

I watched him exit, nearly tripping as he dodged the tables. The other employees gawked, sure I had done something to offend.

I took his tray and mine and put them, untouched, on the conveyor belt. I went back to my lab and washed beakers. Why had I left it such a mess? Sir Gotfried came in. He was eating a blood sausage, holding the thing in his bare hands.

"Did you get a taste of this stuff? So savory! It's great with a chaser of candy corn. It uses up pig blood and guts, which we have plenty of. It's gonna replace Porkies."

"Sir," I said. "I did my duty. I want to talk to you about my request."

"You were a host for a half a day. You'll need something more impressive." He waved the sausage in my face. "Like this. This is impressive." He took a bite. A blob of meat remained on his lower lip.

The air conditioning was cranked up. I shivered. What were my parents thinking? Weren't older people always cold? Dad was at the table. He'd changed out of his bathrobe and into a velvet jacket, knickers, and frilly shirt.

"Oink, Dad. What's going on with the get up?"

"It's damn comfortable. I couldn't afford the wig but otherwise, it's damn comfortable, except for the stockings, and Mom having the cool turned up so high."

Mom wore a voluminous floor length smock with baggy sleeves. "Honey, I'm glad you're home. We were so excited to watch your tour on the Citizen Advisory. I've never seen your lab before."

"Glad to be home. It's been a heck of a day. Humid as a hog snout out there. What's going on here? Why the new duds?"

"We got texts with an offer."

"The deal was too good to pass up. We have to do new things sometimes." Mom twirled in her smock. "We're celebrating the ways of the alchemists."

"While you're up, can you get me a beer?" Dad called.

"We ordered ale to go with the clothes. We're having Alchemy

Day! I worked so hard on dinner," Mom said. "We were sent a recipe and we purchased a box of groceries."

"I hope it's not blood sausage. The texture is off-putting." I hadn't tried one, of course, but I wasn't a fan.

"In honor of your friends, the alchemists!"

"They aren't my friends, I gave them a tour," I clarified. "It wasn't worth anything."

"Come sit down. Look at dinner."

Missing lunch had me famished. I grabbed a can of ale for Dad from the counter and one for me. I plopped down at the table. A bowl in the center contained slices of chicken, bacon, and boiled eggs on a pile of pale grass. It was washed over with corn oil and vinegar and topped with an orange angiosperm, a flower—something that would have been sprayed had it popped up in a yard.

"What's the green stuff?"

Mom beamed. "Lettuce. It's imported. Can you believe it? We imported food because we don't grow this."

"And the flower? Isn't it illegal to have flowers?"

"Not if ordered from Ancient Recipes Delivered. It's an approved recipe and a traditional dish from Newton's time. It's called salmagundi. We had it delivered while you were at work. It doesn't hurt to try new things. There's a whole wide world outside of Cochtonia."

"The Cochtons are getting their money's worth from these guys," said Dad. "New heirs and expensive new products. I don't know how they did it but they did it right."

Except for the expensive part and leaving out women. At this rate, I might not have a job or a lab much longer.

I stared at my food. The salmagundi was moisture rich with a ripped-weed texture. I took a forkful, much of it tumbling back onto the plate. The sweet, salty bacon carried most of the flavor. I scooped up a second bite topped by the orange flower. I put it in my mouth and champed down. The flower exploded with the flavor of mint and pepper gone wild. The burn spread across my palate and up my nose. I sneezed. *Damn, it's good.*

"You don't like it? You're so afraid to try new things."

I wasn't afraid. I was angry and maybe even jealous. I hadn't been in on this new food. I hadn't tested it or even seen it. "No, Mom, I'm not. I like new things. It could be more savory and more filling. Where do these flowers even come from? We don't have flowers here." I hadn't been told a thing about salmagundi. "Also, the mixture doesn't have a coherence. It's incoherent, like it might cause diarrhea." My pride was on the line. I was supposed to be on top of such things. I could taste my usefulness slipping away as a thunderstorm broke. The lights flickered.

"Oh good," Mom said. "The meal kit came with an alchemical glow stick and a tin holder—it's called a candle. No electricity required. Strike these matches and start a fire." She held up a stubby candle, a few inches tall, and pressed it into the holder. "You can make a wish when you light the candle."

That night, in the privacy of my own room, I poured over alchemical texts, available online for a fee. I believed in progress, not this, and yet, the deep, unrealistic dreams held me fast. Elixirs. Magic stones. Chants. It was crazy and had no place in this world. Science was progress while alchemy was a mirage. How had a great man like Isaac Newton gotten drawn into delusion?

I got up to use the bathroom and found myself half drunk from the ale. Science is progress, I told myself. These new developments are progress. Yet the Cochtons had taken it too far. They were seeing progress as economic growth, and seeking out anything they could to push this growth.

The mirror had different ideas as well. Time revealed the enlightenment notion of always moving forward, building on the past, standing on the shoulders of giants, to be flawed. A wyvern, the totem animal of Entropy, had walked all over me; wrinkles were entropy and had no qualms at all about rearranging my familiar face. Alchemists and then a salad? I'd had enough disorder for one day. I needed to hang on to my face. I opened the cabinet, took out the wrinkle cream, and rubbed it on grudgingly.

For solace, I turned to what science had left behind as foolish, the fine art of alchemy. I called upon Venus by lighting the candle. The ancient texts said not to blow the candle or the match. I took out the rock from Paracelsus, purple and crystalline with a hollow. A geode. I set the match on it, letting time extinguish it. I spoke my wish in a whisper: "Let the ships come in, the flower and..." I didn't dare say the rest. And...and what? Respect? No. Sex? Maybe. I'd go for broke. Love. I asked for love. The flame danced about. Perhaps the ancients could understand what it said. Yes. No. There's a draft.

"Is something burning?" Mom was at my door.

"No, I lit the candle."

"Go to bed. Didn't I tell you? Tomorrow we get your sister."

CHAPTER FIVE

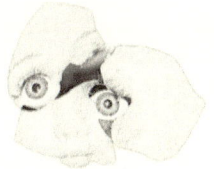

Mom had a delusion of her own—she thought she could drive to the country and pick up a kid at a remote camp, bring her home, and have a new daughter, all in a day. At one time, a camp for orphaned kids had been established in a remote area of Cochtonia, but it had been more gimmick than substance to get people away from the watchful eyes of the Cochton brothers. No matter. Mom was set on going there to find out for herself, and I was driving.

The drive was neither cheap nor easy. First off, we were charged by the mile to use the upkept roads—the ones not gravel. We went in Dad's old car—not autonomous and an ethanol burner with a thirst for the corn-derived fuel. The camp was rural, past several CAFOs or confined animal feeding operations. This was where the nation's hogs were raised, 30,000 or more in a single building, before being hauled off to be butchered. Despite a scent neutralizer developed and sold in Cochtonia, the air around these long and tan vinyl structures had a rotten-sweet odor, disseminated by high-powered fans. If a power failure occurred and the fans stopped, the animals died from the hydrogen sulfide and ammonia rising from their waste products. These waste products were washed into sewage ponds or lagoons. However, since accidents often happened, the urine and feces escaped, ending up most often in the WasteBin, which was a drainage pit, along with carcasses of the dead. The camp of kids was near this place, in the town with the stupid name of Wowville, founded by the estranged Cochton sister, mom of Layal, the shady Cochton nephew.

The two-lane roads were crowded with trucks hauling the hogs away to the slaughter houses. These shared the road with farm equipment hauling vessels filled with sloshing liquid, poisons for either bugs or weeds.

"What about the eyes?" I asked. Pesto kids had been mutated by chemicals applied to fields by their crop duster fathers and had eyes the size of gum balls.

"Just look away. Your eyes aren't enormous pools either. If we get a Pesto, you'll be big-eyed by comparison." Mom arranged her Paracelsus robes on her lap and looked out the window.

After about ten miles, traffic dwindled as the narrow road twisted and became gravel. The road surprised me with a sudden turn left and after a few miles, a right, and right again as if we were in a boxing match.

We turned onto asphalt, newly poured. Despite the new road, the houses were few and far between. Lead paint peeled from their boards, which were baking in the sun. A dump truck with a load of plastic rumbled perilously close, raining dust upon our rarely used car as we rambled on.

We came to a barbwire-topped polyethylene gate flung across the road. Mom held up a communication/identification device and the gate opened. Coarse gravel hit the side of the car as we drove past towering foliage.

"These big plants—they're trees!" I said. I'd learned of them in school. They took up space and had little benefit.

We drove over a creaky bridge spanning a tree-lined creek that rushed beneath us as we left the plants behind and entered a stretch of land bare of all vegetation. The soil was as rocky as the bottom of an aquarium.

"Nearly sixty years ago it was an open pit coal mine," Mom explained. "The coal out here was wet and ashy and not valuable so it closed down before Cochtonia was founded. The land was ruined and not worth reclaiming. That's why it's called the WasteBin. Unfertile land is useless."

I took it as a private offense for no good reason.

At last, we entered the colony of Wowville, with its stupid name. Part of the colony was a Camp for Pestos.

We passed a grove of trees, some with blossoms and some with hanging fruit. Cherries? This had been mentioned in my plant husbandry course but I'd passed over it, as fruit had little place in a nation built on corn. Yet here were fruit trees, short, squat, and evenly spaced, and the ground was loamy. I hadn't expected it from the WasteBin.

"Oh," said Mom. "That reminds me. When you go through the change, you just gush."

"Not now, Mom."

"I am only warning you. Last chance. You could still do something great and get artificial insemination as a prize."

"I'm not pretty enough, Mom."

"InVitro then, and have the baby modified."

"I'd have to do something revolutionary." *And as of now, I'm being scooped by reanimated corpses from eons ago.*

We pulled up next to the Wowville welcome center, an oblong building with a wide porch. A sign read: Camp Cochton Canteen. Sure enough, this place had kids. Campers in uniforms and sunglasses sat at round tables on the new deck eating tree fruit. Shockingly, fluffy chickens pecked about on yellow legs looking like venomous spiders. They waved their wings, drumming the air. Everyone knew hens grew fattest and laid the most eggs when they were caged and kept quiet. This place was a disaster.

"Do we have an appointment?" I asked Mom.

"A golden rule of being a Vice Patrol is to never make an appointment," she said as, robes fluttering, she pushed the door open.

A pregnant woman was behind a counter, a hunky man at her elbow. I could tell by his muscular arms that he was a Crisper, a male escort. Oh, I had to talk to Sir as soon as I could. I needed my rental! I was gushing, but not in the way Mom had alluded to.

"How may we help you?" she said.

I tried not to stare. Pregnant women were rare here in Cochtonia. Mom's voice was as fluttery as her robes. "We'd love a Pesto to take home and cherish."

"I'm sure you've read our materials. We call these country folk Agros, per their request."

"What's in a name? We'll cherish her no matter what she is called. We're anxious for love. There's a hole in our hearts. Besides, my daughter here needs an older, um, Agro. She's forty now and needs a companion for life. She's good with children, you should see how she cherishes her baby doll."

"What kind of child are you envisioning?"

"Her dad and I could use a hand, and Stella, this is Stella, she works so hard at Cochton Enterprises. We can use someone trained in housekeeping. Stella here is not a good housekeeper."

"Of course. Please complete our application." She handed Mom a tablet.

Mom grudgingly added her name and contact information to a form. "I already filled out paperwork in the city."

"We are an independent colony. You are approved to ask for a child. We have no obligation to provide one."

Children came into the store. The sexy Crisper went to a cooler, greeting them.

"We have pig milk ice cream here," he said brightly.

Hot shame poured over me. Since when did pigs lactate enough to be milked? This was yet another food-based scoop. I was falling into the has-been bin.

"Stella, should we try some?"

"No, Mom, I just brushed my teeth," I lied, not wanting to see what I'd missed out on. How ever did this place milk pigs?

"It's a limited supply," the woman said. "We have a small batch of friendly pigs with abundant milk. You're welcome to buy whatever you can eat here. It's not on the market yet."

Yet. I'd soon be more behind the times.

"I'll wait until it's widely available in that case." Mom handed the woman the tablet as she studied the kids. "Oh, so cute! Hello, hello. Who wants a new home?" The children had been taught not to swear at the camp but two curled their lips, as if they wanted to bust out a round of cuss words.

The pregnant woman put the tablet on the counter and went to the door. "Nice meeting you. We'll be in touch, Mrs. Smithfailed," she said, opening the door.

"I can't have one now?"

"We need to check your background." The Crisper handed the woman a scoop of pink ice cream, as if he knew what she wanted. I was jealous—a man who understood a woman!

"I'm the one who does background checking," Mom said, her voice rising and deepening. I took her arm. Now was not the time for her to play authoritarian hard ball, no matter how instinctive it was.

The woman stood firm. "We'll get back to you."

Mom trudged to the car and we drove off.

"Of all things, they're prejudiced," Mom said in a huff.

"Didn't you tell me stories of Dad tossing down Pestos, I mean Agros? He has a reputation for going above and beyond. If they looked up his record, they'd say no." It was hard for me to tell her this. After all, the Vice Patrol had kept us safe; it had given me a mostly on-line education followed by a job.

"Those were bad Pestos and not raised properly. I'd show the world how to raise a Pesto."

"Maybe we don't need a sister. You always complain about Agros interjecting their opinions into our stable society. You yourself said they remind us that the Cochton brothers are oppressive."

"Ours would not light fires or curse or have opinions. She'd be clean and healthy and appreciative. She'd have small eyes but not a small mind. And how did the woman get pregnant? They barely have technology out there."

We passed a sign. *Now leaving Wowville. Thank you for visiting.* Gravel turned to asphalt. Mom turned quiet. Her shoulders slumped. I thought she might be sleeping. Her chin rested on her chest.

"I blew it, didn't I?" she said at last. "I'm losing my smarts. I'm sorry if you won't be getting a sister because of me." She wiped her cheeks as scant tears spattered them. "My whole life was breaking in and busting heads. I guess you can't always get a kid by busting heads."

"Aww, Mom. They said they'd get back to you. Weren't you always telling me to hold fast to my dreams?"

"I don't remember. Did you have dreams?"

"I have a dream now."

"What?"

"I have a dream to hold fast to. I'm going to rent a man. A caveman—a Neanderthal. I'm going to ask for one-time rental since I showed the alchemists around. If I like it, I'll develop a new food product and get a repeat performance."

"New food? I should have pilfered some of the ice cream."

"The lactating pigs would be key to the product. I need something easy to come by."

"What are you thinking of?"

"I have no idea."

Mom rolled down the car window and stuck her arm out, waving her device.

"Mom, what are you doing?"

"Scanning for something edible and easy to come by."

"Mom, food comes from a lab."

"Do you want a Neanderthal or not?"

There wasn't room for Mom in my fantasy. "It's okay, Mom. I've made it this far without a caveman. Do you have your whole gear belt on under the robe?

"Of course. I'd be naked without it. I detect something growing over there. My device suggests flowers."

"They'd have a smell. Pleasant, like jasmine," I said, recalling the beer notes. "When I was at the bar, the bartender mentioned some beer ingredients coming from the colony. There's an idea—native flowers for salmagundi." I stopped the car.

"I'm glad you're seeing the light. I'll scan the area for surveillance." She pressed a button and swiped her device across the hard-packed ground. "It's clean. We can pick them undetected. A patch has been identified. Let's go get 'em."

I backed up back across the bridge, the wooden planks clattering beneath the wheels, and parked by the side of the road.

"Come on, Mom. Let's go for a walk." We got out and stood beside the car. A breeze came up from the small creek meandering under the bridge. Bugs flitted across the creek—insects, which were unheard of in the city of Cochtonia, thanks to generous spraying. Mom swooshed her hand across her face to get rid of them.

"Take charge, Stella. That's my motto. It would be a feather in your cap to get the flowers. And *him*. Whoever he is. Let's see what the microdrone can do." She put her hand in her robe pocket and pulled out a plastic sphere. With one hand, she tossed it in the air. The thing took off like a sneeze, zipping past the trees. I watched it as long as I could. We waited. I wondered what conversation shoe would drop. I tried to take the lead.

"Those flowers can be used for people and animals as well. They can be a food additive, if grown properly in the lab. If I can get a flower and propagate, it could be the start of something big." The thought of Sir Gotfried finally appreciating me caused such hope to rise in me. Like a fart. Uh...no. The air here was fetid, giving me weird thought connections. Hope broke through the dirt like a seed sprouting with promise.

"You know," Mom said, "I read it's much easier now to get approved to be a surrogate mother and even get InVitro status. You need to talk to your boss about these options."

Mom was mentioning sanctioned ways to have a baby. They both involved being in a lab to start the pregnancy and giving the baby to the nation for a pre-assigned job. It was how the new Vice

Patrol agents were made. It was how firefighters were made, even the Crisper strippers.

"I want to rent a man for a night, not genetically mingle or carry something for nine months only to give it away for Cochtonia to raise and modify."

"I hope it works out and you like your taste of man. Back in the day, when men were in abundant supply naturally, we had to get married before any of this was permitted. Sex before marriage —we executed people for less. At the very least, they were arrested and forced to marry. It's a whole new world these days. I imagine one thing remains, you'll do it and doing it will feel like love. It's how I got roped in. Barnabus was husky, had a big gun, and a fondness for making arrests. I was hungry for love. I wanted love more than a plate full of Porkies."

"I've heard enough, Mom. Porkies hadn't been developed back then."

"I was new, working at the prison. We noticed each other. It's how things begin—you enter each other's sphere of consciousness. He confiscated rings from deadbeats he'd detained. He bragged about it. I called his bluff, saying I didn't believe him. 'Show me the goods,' I told him. He was a tad disheveled back then. He made an excuse about keeping the jewelry a secret but kept up the mention of it. In response, I took to buttoning his uniform properly as I challenged him to show me his gold. I'd say, 'How can you be a threat when you can't even dress yourself?'

"After a month of this, he called *my* bluff. We were in the prison. He'd made an arrest—a woman. She had been a teacher. She had a paperback book. I helped put her in her cell and confiscated the book. It was a provocative book, about human sexual pleasure. He watched me put it in my pocket. I straightened his hair, buttoned his coat, and studied his face for a brief moment. Familiarity had made him appear handsome. You'd think a man like him would be brave enough to ask a woman to marry him. Yet, in matters like love, he was nervous. He'd been carrying the rings in his pocket and jingling them when we met. I'd heard the faint clink. He was clinking them at this moment.

"Until I looked into his eyes, he hadn't had the guts to pull them out. The moment we locked eyes, he drew a woman's ring from his pocket, almost like drawing a gun, so fast and with such abandon. He held it up between two fingers. My head swarmed when I saw it. He dared me to put it on. I did." She waved her hand, showing me her ring. I'd seen it many times. It was non-descript, dull silver. The story wasn't adding up, unless he'd been arresting people already betrothed. I wouldn't put it past him. He could have targeted some poor woman because he wanted her ring. He'd have made up a crime. "He took out a thicker ring, for himself. He said he'd get it resized, made larger, if I was brave enough to be the bride of a big man. I always took a dare back then. I did. Well, we did. I was happy for a while. It felt like love. At least you came along naturally." She picked up her device and studied the screen. "I see something, back a ways, where the trees meet the rocky area. We've come far from the Welcome Center. I must say, it wasn't welcoming."

"What happened to the woman with the book? Did you have her killed?"

"No. She was exiled."

"Exiled to where?"

"I didn't ask. I requested it and it was granted. It was granted by my new husband. If it wouldn't have been for her, your dad and I would not have gotten together. My entire life would be devoted to the Vice Patrol."

This was a surprising revelation—that Mom had wanted more than a career. I'd been raised by my grandmother at first but like all old women, she ended up going to the pigs and I'd been alone with my lessons. No wonder I loved science so much. Still, it wasn't enough.

"Let's walk along the tree line," Mom said, staring at her device. "It looks like the easiest path to the flowers."

We hiked along the edge of the trees. They were big and arched menacingly. Anything could hide in them.

"Are you nervous?" Mom asked. "You're gassy. Odor used to help me find criminals in hiding. Of course, I used a gas seeking device and I certainly don't need one today."

"Mom, we're in the country. The country stinks."

She halted.

"Shh." She held up her hand. We stood, listening. The leaves rustled. Things scurried in the litter of dead leaves. Wings beat in the trees. The stench grew stronger, accompanied by a slurping grunt.

CHAPTER SIX

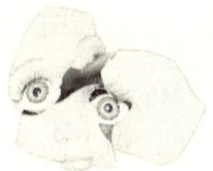

A purple hog burped into view, her snout moving as she came out of the trees. Mosquitos buzzed near her. I took two steps back. I was a scientist, but animals were not my forte. This thing had to weigh hundreds of pounds and everyone knew pigs were smart as a kid.

"Shoot it, Mom," I whispered.

"You think a decommissioned officer is allowed a weapon? I might go berserk from all of those years being passed over for a promotion and shoot myself or someone else."

On second look, the pig was more curious than vicious. Her ears were perked. She wiggled her snout and twirled her lavender tail as mosquitos dodged it.

"Let's back away," I said, queasy.

The pig flapped her ears and sat squarely in front of us on the path. She opened her mouth to smile, pant, or bite. It was hard to tell.

Mom pointed her device at the animal and read. "These pigs were made several years ago but discontinued due to the foul farts. This is a stray, not a wild pig."

The pig flopped down and rolled on her back, showing her flabby nipples.

"Is it sick?" I asked. "Or is it—"

"Trained," Mom replied. "It's one of the milking pigs. Do you want to try to milk it?"

"I'm sure it must be done by machine."

The hog scratched her back on the dirt, sending up a shower of leaf matter and dust.

"Can we go around it?" I asked, stepping forward. The pig struggled a moment and sat up. "It's a trap. It's going to steal something."

"Let's not look at it." Mom kept her eyes on the map sent by the drone as she swiped her arm left to right as we proceeded forward. I checked on the pig. It stayed behind, scratching its back. Being here with an animal terrified me and spurred my step. It was embarrassing to be afraid of the pig, clearly a trained pet, but it would have been stupid not to be, for pigs were smart and dangerous, with their tiny eyes and nearly hairless skin. The resemblance between them and us was uncanny; they even attracted the same bugs as humans. I had the sensation of being naked, as naked as the purple pig with its bristly hair. We walked. It walked. I knew it did.

"Mom, are we almost there?"

"*Almost* is relative."

"How far?"

"A half mile."

"The pig is following."

"With every step," she replied.

"We should run."

"I'm seventy-six. I don't run," she said bluntly.

I'd heard so many stories about Mom and Dad chasing down criminals who had done things such as had sex before marriage, read paper books, or in the case of the Pestos, lit plastic bags on fire and tossed them in public spaces to express their displeasure. The Vice Patrol had permission to kill these lawbreakers, but pommeling them was more frequent. It was hard to believe how long ago all that had been. Mom had a whole half of a life, an exciting hoodlum-chasing life, before she had me.

"Mom, what's it like to have a baby?"

"It blows up your life. Everything you wanted or cared about, your dreams and all you love is shattered, including your vagina, and in its place is a baby."

"Sounds awful."

"It is, but I'd never go back and not do it again. Life is multifaceted, unlike a vagina." She snorted loudly. It was unlike her. "You don't have to snort at me," she said. "I love you with all my heart."

"I thought *you* snorted."

More snorts came from behind us. "Mom!" I grabbed her by the shoulder and hustled her forward. The pounding of cloven hooves, snapping through the undergrowth, grew near. I headed toward a patch of light, hurrying Mom in her robes as best I could. We stumbled into the clearing and onto a mass of vegetation. Behind us, two deer leapt into the clearing, their large bodies hurling over us, leaving a musky smell.

"Oink, I thought it was the pig!" The deer ran past as we panted in quivering heaps. Around us sprung hardy vines covered with white flowers, displaying a pop of ultraviolet, as delicate as the nasturtiums with lingering jasmine fragrance, much like my beer.

"We ditched the pig," Mom laughed.

"And found the flowers!" I ran my hands across them. The wax on the hand-shaped leaves gave them a smooth suppleness with a warmth plastic could never replicate. It was if I was fondling pigskin boots. The flowers were tumbled and allured in various stages of undress—some tight buds, some peeking out a petal, but none in widespread bloom. One wrapped around my wrist before fainting. I wasn't prepared for this foray—I hadn't brought scissors or preservatives—but the calm of the abandoned area, the light on my forehead, the gentle, yielding of the earth beneath my feet rendered me ecstatic. I picked several samples as they bobbled in the cool breeze. It was too early for seeds so I took some cuttings, clumsily pinching the gel-like stems with my fingers.

"I'll propagate what we have. I have growth media—an artificial soil—to root them in. It's a means of asexual reproduction."

"We're asexual here, like the homunculi." Mom grabbed a plastic bag floating across the dirt and used it to store the stems, leaves, and bits of root I harvested.

The sky rumbled. It was clear, breezy, and nearly cloudless. The sound came closer. A small, white plane was right over us. It dipped low and let out a cloud of acrid spray.

"Pesticides," I shouted. "They're killing the plants!"

Mom put her device to her mouth and yelled at the sky. "What are you doing? I'm Officer Smithfailed. Emeritus Officer Smithfailed. Stop at once!"

The plane swooped over us and sprayed again.

"Shit. They don't care who you are."

We made a beeline for the car. As we approached, I could clearly see a person leaning on the car hood, waiting for us. Had we violated some protocol? Was this a secret project? Was the pig involved? Hopefully, Mom could get us out of it.

"Who is that?" I asked, coughing and blinking.

Mom swung her device toward the person. "Not the law. A female in her early twenties."

It wasn't the law. It was a girl in a Camp Cochton uniform, coughing, as we were. I hadn't the breath to interrogate her. I brushed past her, unlocked the car doors, and Mom and I tumbled in. I locked the doors. The person bent over, covering her nose and mouth with her hands. She was an awkward age—not a kid but not a woman, not much fat to her.

The kid tapped on the windshield near Mom's side, her pug nose pressed against the glass.

"Let her in," said Mom. "We can't leave her out there."

"Mom, it's a set up."

"I don't care! We can't leave a child to be sprayed like a bug." Mom leapt from the car and using her device, opened the back door. Covering her face with her sleeve, she swooped the girl into the back seat and sat next to her.

"Poor thing," Mom said between coughs. "Are you hurt?"

"No, I'm only stupid for not taking cover."

"What's happening out there?"

"Spraying for weeds."

"We came for flowers. Cochton Enterprises must have flowers. Those jerks are killing them."

The girl wiped her tiny tearing eyes. "It's happened before. The sons of bitches hate these plants. They're on a shit list."

My heart sank at this. It was much less likely Sir would approve of my project if the plants were on a shit list.

"Are they classified as noxious weeds like quack grass and bull thistle? What the hell are they?" I asked.

"How the fuck would I know? I'm a helpless pawn in this regime. I was out looking for a stray pig."

Mom should have taken offense. Instead, she asked, "Are they edible?"

"Edible? Eat one and find out. Eat one. You aren't pregnant or lactating, are you?"

"No, but thanks for asking." Mom laughed. "I'm here because my daughter wants to rent a Crisper more than once."

"A man? Ooh, juicy. Tell me more."

"You are too young to hear it," I said, eating a leaf before pulling back onto the road.

"Shit. Sex isn't wicked, it's nature. Tell me straight."

"If she brings a new food to Cochton Enterprises, her boss will recommend her for Crisper rental. She's worked herself to a nub and should have been given this long ago."

"Humping and flowers? I don't see the connection."

"Have you ever been to our capital city, Cochtonville?"

"No. Are we headed there?"

"We are."

"Hot damn," she said brightly.

"Pleasure comes only after producing something valuable. My employer will hopefully approve my, um, pleasure if I can find flowers, honest flowers, edible flowers, to adorn a dish called salmagundi."

"Salmagundi? You're shitting me! Mom used to make salmagundi until our country became a nation of grain. Home gardening was outlawed, along with fruits and vegetables, and thus, came the end of salmagundi. Is the Empire suddenly going soft on food, allowing other commodities besides meat, corn, and soybeans to be consumed?"

The blanket of calm surrounding me loosened my tongue. It swung like a rope in the wind. "Indeed. The Cochton brothers have resurrected two alchemists to create a homunculus from their sperm and a load of manure. The investment carried a hefty price. The shrewd brothers saw the alchemists not only as fountains of ancient wisdom but as marketing opportunities. We are embracing the past, old costumes and old foods, including the meat hodgepodge known as salmagundi. It has flowers on top. I want to grow these flowers in a greenhouse and use them to top salmagundi."

"Oh! So that's what's happening with your mom's weird duds. I dig."

"They'll be embracing more old ways if this homunculus works. Like men-only clubs," Mom said.

"Boys will be boys. It's shit. Shit! Worse than shit! Shit's useful. It sounds damn stressful. I'll tell you what you need, you need assistance."

"We certainly do," Mom said. "I applied for a child at the camp. Can you put in a good word for me?"

"I can do better than a good word." She held out her arms. "I'm yours!"

It was unsettlingly easy.

"What?" Mom asked.

"Take me home. Send Camp Cochton a message that I'm no longer available."

"Stella, head for home with your new sister. What's your name, dear?"

"It's NezLeigh with a capital L."

"Stella, hit the gas."

She and Mom chatted as I drove. NezLeigh'd been abandoned as a child and lived in the woods. Eventually she moved to Camp Cochton, where she got wormed and learned to brush her hair. She was excited to get a taste of city life. She was bright, small-eyed, and bushy haired—so young I'd forgotten what it was like.

"Hey Stella, when you get your guy, I need a piece of the action. They'll do two for one I heard."

"In your dreams. You're too young."

"I have a birthday coming up, ya dig? I won't be too young forever."

After a long, chatty car ride, we arrived home. Mom instructed NezLeigh to hang back as a surprise for Dad. He'd changed clothes and was in an XL green t-shirt with gold letters reading I HumP. The irony was too much for me.

"Barnabus," said Mom gently, tugging the shirt down. "Have you been ordering alone?"

"Yes, I have. I'm showing my support of the Cochton's all-man reproduction project. Where's the helping hand?"

"The Pesto? We're on a waiting list," Mom said, crestfallen.

"There's always a catch with them. Always a catch. Well, will you get me a sundae? I'm pooped. I power washed the house again. It's so damn dusty."

"Just goofing, we got one! Here she is."

In this light, NezLeigh looked older than a kid as she sauntered into the living room.

Dad didn't get up. "Hell, it's a beautiful day."

"It sure the fuck is for you. You're sitting here growing a beer belly and stinking up the chair."

"About the ice cream, tiny eyes. You've got a job to do."

"Certainly not, Barnabus. She needs time to get acclimated. We were sprayed with herbicides by a Patrol plane. Have you heard of such a thing? Way out in the middle of nowhere. We all need to shower."

Mom led NezLeigh to my room with me close behind.

"Here's your room. You may sleep in Stella's bed when she's at work. This arrangement will be perfect."

"When will the sheets get washed?" I asked.

"NezLeigh sleeps during the day as I'm sure you know and you go to work. It's called symbiosis."

"Mom, that means working together for mutual benefit."

Mom patted my bed. "Poor thing," she said to NezLeigh. "You've been through so much. Let's take care of each other."

"Shall I prepare an omelet? I once lived in the wild and raided nests for food."

"First let's order you some new clothes. You're in Cochtonville, ya dig?" Mom was trying to use her lingo.

"I can wear what's on the floor," she offered.

"Nonsense. Stella's clothes will be too big. What will it be? Ancient or classical style, sweetie?"

Classical style was hardly any different from her Camp Cochton t-shirt and khaki shorts. Despite this or maybe because of it, NezLeigh chose classical.

"How many hours do you sleep, honey?" Mom asked.

I swear I saw a glint in her tiny eyes. "Sleep? I'd say about ten hours at a crack."

"Let's get you nightgowns."

My jealousy embarrassed me. Of course, Mom needed to feel loved and important. If taking in this person did that for her, I should accommodate it. Still, I couldn't bear to watch them go on and on about the mundane choices of clothing to order.

"I'm off to work to propagate these plant cuttings," I announced. I'd not have to deal with the HumP or my new sister at work.

CHAPTER SEVEN

Luck was not on my side. Displays of obnoxious HumP t-shirts hung on the wall inside the entrance to the building. The Officer of the Guards, Ursula, who had lunched with me briefly before Newton went off about blood sausage, sat at the main entrance. She was wearing white, as Vice Patrol do, but instead of a Stetson, she wore a red cap with a turned-up brim topped with a brown feather.

"Want to buy a shirt? It comes directly out of your paycheck."

I held up my ID and tried not to make eye contact with the shirts.

"Maybe later. I'm in a rush."

Passing people chatting in the halls, I hurried to my lab, eager to begin propagating these cuttings to make them into eventual food. Progress was at my fingertips. These plants were the stars with their mystery, the fireflies with their glow. The new research pulled me like a tide, like a magnet. With science, there was always a future to probe. There was adventure brewing, and it could all be done in a room or two, in the lab, alone if need be.

I unlocked my lab door and spread the plants on the lab bench. They hadn't wilted too much. I got a spray bottle and misted them with water, then I opened the sash to the growth hood. I turned on the sterilizing ultraviolet light. Digging in a drawer, I found a bag of growth culturing media. I added water, set it in the instaclave, and pushed the button. It would pressure-cook the mixture and cool it nearly instantly. When it was done, I'd set the plant fragments in the growth mixture, but I'd have to work late. The work day was nearly done.

The Vice Patrol agent came to the door.

"Ursula. What's up?"

"I must ask the same of you. Someone filed a complaint about you being gone all day and now working even though it's almost closing time."

"I took time off to work outside. I went to the WasteBin, risked my life, captured plants, and escaped a pig doing it. I need to get these cuttings in growth medium before they wilt. It will take less than an hour."

"Aren't you brave? What are you getting out of it?"

"Man rental."

"Oh ho! The scientist caves to the ways of the flesh." She relaxed her shoulders, as if in relief.

"Experimenting is a way of life."

"Do you know what you're getting into? Sex leaves you vulnerable, and even under controlled circumstances, it's risky. It's why the homunculus project is so appealing for some—reproduction without sex has a wide appeal. You know how I got my kid? I picked her up during a disturbance. Her mom committed suicide because she was pregnant again. Ironic, isn't it?"

I wasn't sure what to say. All my mom had ever confiscated was a sex book.

"I'm planning on the flowers being a salmagundi topping."

"I'm not seeing many flowers."

"These have to grow and produce flowers. It will take a while."

"I got to admit, salmagundi is almost as sensuous as blood sausage. When was the last time we had new food in Cochtonia? Are these flowers as snappy as nasturtiums?"

"More mellow, I predict. But all ours. They can be patented, modified, and privately owned. Let's hope the flowers asexually reproduce. This could be the start of something."

"Need any help? I'm developing a love for science."

I wanted a lab partner but would have preferred one trained in science. However, I couldn't be too picky at this point in my life, could I? "Um, okay. A lot of it is pretty routine. Hand me the plastic bottle to your right if you want to be a part of things."

I held a cutting with forceps as she pulled a diluted mixture of bleach and ethanol from my shelf.

"Sterilization is key here. We don't want to propagate surface impurities." I was happy to be able to talk to someone about the intricacies of my project.

"The homunculus project is all impurities," she said.

"You don't say?"

"I'm supervising the homunculus project. I didn't tell you a thing."

"Have you seen it? Is it..."

"Made of hog shit? Sure is."

She put her hand in her pocket and slipped out her screen. She popped up a photo of a sculpture on a pallet in the reconverted storeroom in the basement—a feces sculpture in the shape of curvy, reclining women with flowing hair and open legs. She was voluptuous, her lips slightly parted, and her wide-open eyes without lashes.

I was taken aback.

"How? Why?"

"She's made from manure. Paracelsus sculpted her."

"People sculpt manure?"

"Yes. Does she look like anyone you know?"

"I don't know anyone made of shit."

"It's me. Paracelsus used me as the model. It's slightly larger than life."

"Oh, it's beautiful." I didn't like to lie, but it seemed to be the proper thing to say. "Does it smell?"

"Not as much as when it was fresh."

"Is it moist?"

"If not, it will be after the Cochtons' visit. I hope it's not too much information. I gotta tell somebody. Since you mentioned man rental, it opened the door for me."

"Are you saying they'll be doing things with the sculptures? Ugh, my stomach aches as if I've eaten blood sausage. How can a man be attracted to a feces sculpture?"

"He will be if he does his duty. If they want their own homunculus, they have to seed it. I'm curious, I'd love to watch but it's men only."

"I'm glad. I want nothing to do with this. Ack! Disgusting!"

"Imagine what you wish. It's just them and the manure."

"I need to get back to this plant propagation," I said, afraid to say more. Vice Patrol were known to lie to get incriminating information. "I'm going to position the plant in this growth material. It takes the place of soil."

"Wonder if we could've made a woman from your stuff. It would smell better."

Sir Gotfried came into the lab, his hands in his pockets in a casual way that reminded me of cash in a loincloth.

"There she is. I've been searching for you," he said.

"The feeling's mutual," I answered, hoping he'd get my meaning. "I have something to show you."

"I'll leave you be," said Ursula, touching the brim of her hat and tossing me a sly look as she left.

Clearly my boss, Sir Gotfried, and I, were on the same wavelength at last.

"I wanted to let you know the Cochtons are thrilled with the homunculus project. Thank you for your small part in it. "

I leaned forward, wishing my lab coat was cut lower. "I'm eager, as eager to please as an employee can be."

"Why did you take a personal day today and then show up at work?"

"I took a day to help my mom."

"Is she alright?"

"Yes. She had this idea about picking up another kid. However, work was on my mind. I can't stay away."

"What's on your mind now, Virginia? What are you doing so close to closing time?"

"Mom had an errand in the country. I came across these plants out near the WasteBin. I collected specimens and am propagating them. They have flowers. At one time, flowers were considered worthless trivialities and they attracted insects. As you know, flowers have been banned here. It was a mistake. They're an edible commodity."

"Hasn't this been done before? We must consult the past records. I'm sure I heard there was a flowering plant considered previously and abandoned for a valid reason."

I said, "We can learn from the past. Have you tried salmagundi?"

"Yes. It's delightful."

"It's got flowers on top, foreign flowers. We need a native dish with our own flowers. The Cochtons invested far too much in the resurrection of the alchemists to let marketing opportunities slip away. You want to support the alchemists, don't you?"

"Honestly, no, I don't. This project has been forced on me. What's in it for you?"

"Rental status."

His eyes widened. He smiled and ran his hand through his bushy hair. Did I detect a rising in his groin? Despite my lust for him, he'd never thought of me, little old me, hard-working old me, as deeply sexual. To him, I was a worker bee or a wingless worker ant sprayed with BuzzOff. I wasn't going to be that arachnoid. I was going to be a hairy, groping mammal full of lust and abandon. At least for one day.

"You want a man?"

"Yes, a caveman with primitive lust. I'm begging you! Never before have I had such powerful emotions. They gush from me like blood from a slaughtered pig." I wasn't an eloquent person, being a Midwesterner with speech as pleasant as a saw cutting vinyl siding.

"I'll do my best to get it for you."

I stood up. I had to pee.

He texted rapidly. "I'm putting in the request. You must keep it to yourself. I'm not mentioning the caveman part. It's kinky. Have you considered a businessman or a cowboy? Or a sexy candy chef?"

Trying not to wet myself, I ran for the bathroom as smoothly as possible. I turned the corner and crashed into someone who smelled like oil laced with mud, mud being loam, and loam being clay, sand, and vegetable matter. He smelled both old and wild. I put my hands out to break the force of our meeting, touching the smooth material of his coat before pushing him away.

"Oh," I said. It was Newton. His mouth fell open as he tumbled back. He caught himself on the wall; his wig was askew.

"ME ATHWART A WOMAN? Go hence! I'm a celibate intellectual and must not be touched."

"I'm a scientist," I said, angry and hurt. "I helped you with your project."

Our eyes met. His face was as pale and gasping as a carp with hypoxia—low oxygen. We had a lot of hypoxia here in Cochton Enterprises. The whole place was oxygen deprived because poor ventilation kept costs down. One thing I hadn't considered was the lack of restrooms in the basement. The alchemists had to come up to my floor to use the facilities.

"Behold our tour guide," he said. "Forgive me. I try to maintain purity."

"It can't be easy, given your project."

My bladder swelled uncomfortably and leaked like a badly sealed piston. I twisted to keep myself dry. He grabbed his bladder and I grabbed mine.

"I fear being touched," he said, with his accent unlike anything Midwestern.

"I want to be touched, but not by someone who experiments with mud. I'll steer clear of you."

"The mud was not my idea. I'm a chemical alchemist, strictly."

We each turned and walked to our restrooms. I had to stop

letting this homunculus project bother me. Yes, what Ursula had shown me was horrifying, but it wasn't going to affect me at this point in my life. I'd grow these plants, rent a real man, and maybe even bed my boss as an encore. As I peed, I thought more about Sir Gotfried. I'd undress him slowly and get him naked while I kept my clothes on. I'd stroke him, kiss his bare chest, and teach him all I'd learned from the caveman. Maybe it was my bladder, but oh the throbbing! I pulled up my panties. I walked out of the restroom and as if in a dream, Sir was standing there.

"Your idea about the flower propagation has been approved, and so has your man request. One time only."

"I'm so happy! I don't know how I can repay you." I tried to sound open to anything sexual.

"Try to get something to work out for once," he said with frustration. I thought it was mean of him, given the success of Porkies and my alchemists' tour.

Despite his brush off, I rushed home, filled with enthusiasm. I pulled Mom into my bedroom. "I got it! I got it! I get to rent a man." Perhaps I was being too open about it, but sex was success and Mom needed to hear of me being a success.

"Let's buy you a new outfit," Mom said as she pulled up a catalog. I let her indulge me. After all, NezLeigh was sleeping in my bed, her face buried in my pillow, the lacey collar of her pink nightgown poking above the covers.

I selected a yellow dress with pink corn cobs, pink in a fanciful twist, something Bohemian to match the beer I'd had at the bar. I was returning, as I had vowed, and I'd at last get satisfaction.

CHAPTER EIGHT

My legs burst free on this warm day. The pink corn cobs floated on the smooth, swirling skirt. My work uniform of a polo and khaki pants was shoved in a bottom drawer at home.

I pranced into the bar. Patrons loitered about. Two women played pool beneath a flickering neon sign for Rainy Day Ale. Well, it wasn't a rainy day today—more like my lucky day. Where were the men? Where were the men? The harsh wooden blinds shut out the sun's continuous spectrum, leaving crisp lines on the tables and patrons. Of all people, LouOtta was near the pool table, chatting stiffly with a caveman Crisper—the man I lusted for. My jealousy hit 101 degrees Celsius. He was supposed to be mine! Was she leasing him again?

I strode to the bar. "I'm here to rent," I said. "I have the identification." I held out my wrist certificate, ceremoniously attached by Sir Gotfried. It was designed to dissolve within a week, so I had no time to waste cashing in on my reward.

The bartender was the older woman with a long, white braid. "There's going to be a brief wait. Most of them were sent to a retreat for rehabilitation and recalculating."

"How much of a wait?"

"Minutes. They're being released as we speak. Your place or ours?"

"How do I know? I've never done this before."

"Extra for here. Housekeeping's a bitch, but we go all out to put you in the mood.""How much extra? I'm already in the mood. I can't do it at home. My parents live there with their nosey Pesto. They'd be asking about it and commenting for the rest of my life."

She scanned my wristlet. "You must have done something. You've got a voucher for all you want for a day and free use of our Illusion Room."

"I worked my ass off for the Company."

"Good for you," she said with flat enthusiasm, as if working my ass off didn't impress her. "Worker bee, it's your turn to be queen. What do you want? Who do you want? Care to see some of them before the final decision?"

She pressed a screen on the bar, and it sprang to life with photos of nearly naked men. We hunched over it, scrolling through the images as a drip of my drool fell on the smooth plastic. A patron peered over my shoulder, trying to get a peek for herself. I did my best to block her view. This was all mine. A plethora of options popped up —Space Odyssey, Stranded with Robinson Crusoe, Rawhide and Seek. The bartender handed me a stylus, dipped from a jar of alcohol. "Use this to select. It's disinfected, lots going around right now."

The possibilities danced in front of me. Sexy. Tantalizing. Bare. But not my first choice. "Caveman," I whispered. "Lust at first sight. I don't see one on here. There's one near the pool table, though."

"Neanderthal Nights. You're in luck. We've got one back from training today. He's rehabilitated. He converses like a modern man and he smells less like urine. Totally rehabilitated for a pleasurable experience. He hasn't reported in today. I'll track him, he's chipped."

A wave of disappointment hit me. I didn't want conversation, I needed a savage brute from 100,000 years ago.

I swallowed my disillusionment. "What does a caveman converse about?"

"Prehistoric pillow talk. Could be wild. Are you sure you want the caveman treatment? They have spots you know, skin spots here and there, dark pigments, like a leopard."

"Where are the spots?"

"Various places, along the side of the forehead, the back, and yes, the penis. It's part of being a Neanderthal."

"Spots don't bother me." I couldn't see any spots on the Neanderthal near the pool table. No, there was a dark, irregularly shaped blob on his left shoulder. It was a little like skin cancer. LouOtta put her hands in his animal skin. Was she feeing his nipple? I needed to feel his nipple, and have him stroke mine.

"I want the caveman in the corner. Neadaen."

"So sorry. Don't mean to break your heart, but let's face it. It's not like you wrote the National Anthem. Lady has him wrapped up. Or will have him soon enough." Here it was again. I was getting disappointment instead of what I worked for. "I'm not saying you're not the greatest, you've done something great. Honey, you'll get our second-best caveman." She scrolled the screen to a blonde brutish type. "How about Bigg Gib?"

"Might as well settle."

"That's the spirit. Have a seat here at the bar. May I get you a drink? Kills germs."

"Do I need to kill germs? I thought these guys were safe."

"Safe as a sunny day," she said. "The Company sends only its best. I'm talking about the rest of Cochtonia. A lot ails us."

"Do you have Citric C?" I said, asking for a health drink made with corn derived citric acid, plus synthetic Vitamin C. I was taking her at her word. This was safe but there wouldn't be anything wrong with boosting my immune system.

"You're asking for a screwdriver without the liquor?"

"Yes. Only the basics."

She went to the back of the bar, twinkling in the cut glass from the light fixtures and scooped a powder into a glass. "You say you have a nosey Pesto at home? How's it going?" She added a squirt of water to the crystals in the glass.

"I can't say she's helpful."

"This drink looks kind of plain. Let me pop a fat raspberry in it."

Raspberries were a commodity here.

"It never hurts to have a Pesto on your side," she said. "They know people and things." The frozen raspberry floated atop the cloudy drink.

"This one acts like she's a queen."

"Maybe she was a queen before her rehabilitation. A bit of advice, they like to be called Agros."

"Oh, that's right."

Even with the fruit, the drink was blandly acidic. I had to search for flavor. Back near the pool table, LouOtta willowed over her caveman and massaged his protruding skull. They were a study in contrasts, she with her long neck and he so squat.

The raspberries sunk and pink appeared in the liquid surrounding them. A stocky guy came in wearing a suit, denim, like a working man, since white fabric was reserved for the best of people. He wore a gray V-neck under his jacket. Chest hair curled up and fell over the edge of the fabric like tassels on corn. Half his silky blond hair was pulled into a high bun and the rest cascaded down his back. His chin sprouted sparse stubble while his eyebrows popped forward like mustaches. He had a constellation of brown spots along the side of his pale forehead. I caught my breath—it was a caveman, dressed in modern clothes. The whole When Worlds Collide scenario had my head spinning.

He strode up to the bar. "Here for work."

I popped the raspberry chunk into my mouth. The powerful explosion of flavor opened my senses. The small oral pleasure unleashed a beast. The beast was me.

"Bigg Gib, meet Stella. She's your first renter since your rehabilitation."

"Nice to meet you. How may I put you at ease?" His voice was a rumble of thunder.

"Yes," I said, wiping raspberry from my lips. "You may."

"How can I make you comfortable? Shall I clean your lips with my mouth?" He leaned forward and gave me a delicate, lippy kiss, tender enough to bring tears to my eyes. "What else do you need?"

"Where's the dinosaur skin?" I asked, feigning shyness. Shouldn't I be shy at a time like this? Yes, I wanted a man, but on my terms. He looked like some sort of businessman gone broke. Despite my efforts at keeping to my standards, yes, I wanted a businessman gone broke. Or any man gone anything. But since this was my one chance, I thought I would go for broke and ask for all I wanted.

"I would be comfortable if you looked like a primitive man from the Neander region."

"My costume is unsuitable? Yes, of course. Cognitive dissonance. The Company doesn't want me walking about skins in public. People must work for what they want. This suit is a new issue. I assure you, I'm totally Neanderthal. Would you like to help me change into something more pleasing to you?"

"Oh, would I!"

The woman said, "Take her up to the Illusion Room. The code is 100,001."

"I remember the code," Bigg Gib said with mild defiance, as if he was my kindred spirit.

"Give her a breathtaking treatment. She's done great things for Cochtonia."

"I'm bringing salmagundi to the masses," I added proudly.

"Did you say asses? Ass rubbing is part of our culture."

"Yes, I say we rub some asses."

"My name is not Bigg Gib for nothing."

At first, I thought he meant his nose, which popped from his face like smut on corn. Yes, it was frighteningly large. I sucked in a breath. It wasn't his nose he was referring to. His pants were expanding like a cumulous cloud.

"I am proud to have such an accomplished woman as a customer. Shall we talk together of your salmagundi? What is it?"

"It's wet," I said. "Wet and juicy."

"Yummy, I can't imagine better! We must not linger here. Escape to my cave and I will come to yours."

For the first time, I wanted something bone deep. If he was buried fifteen feet under, I'd have dug a thirty-foot tunnel to get to him. Fortunately, I didn't have to dig a hole. We walked up a set of stairs and took the second door to the right. Silky hair fell from his topknotted skull like a golden shower. Bigg Gig pushed a keypad. The door became a stone that cracked open to the roar of a beast.

"A saber-toothed tiger," he explained, taking my hand. "Stay close."

"It doesn't seem safe."

"Being afraid and being aroused are easy to confuse. Can you tell me if it is fear or awakening?" he said, brushing my ass with his hand, which was the size of an oven mitt. I was excited to the point of tossing off all caution. If I was an atom, I would have come close to ionization.

"We have been having sex with your type for at least 90,000 years. I know what I am doing." He pushed the door with his shoulder.

We entered a cave, dark except for a fire flickering. I thought about mentioning carbon monoxide but it was, of course, a mirage. There was no fire and there was no carbon monoxide, although my head was light and my heart racing. This was exciting. I'd have to try them all—all of the Crispers—and experience each habitat, each mirage. I'd need more status, and with more status, more mating would come. Maybe next I'd try sex in space. Ground control to Major Tomot.

Gib came up behind me. "That is a beautiful skirt. It is perfect for the rubbing." His deep voice could carry across the ages. He lifted my skirt and pushed his groin into the stretchy panties covering my ass. "This is good for both of us."

It was like the rumbling of a thunderstorm in the night, a

mixture of power and excitement. With each rub, the static charge of storm-struck air surged with the rain spattering before the downpour. I didn't know I could throb so, like having to pee, but better. Much better. The metallic slide of a zipper was followed by sensational insertion.

"You are the best. So tight and new." Being called new gave me a gush of happiness, maybe even love. "Thank you for your rental, thank you, ahhhh." The rubbing split the charges, the positive ice, the negative hail, all happening in a cloud of billowing proportions, the separation of the charge, the stoking wind, building, ever building, a bolt of lightning, and then glorious rain came, so to speak. He slumped onto me like a ladder on the side of a hog confinement shed. I fell forward, slightly smug and pleased.

"What happened?" I asked breathlessly.

Bigg Gib was assuring. "Don't be concerned, I can do it more than once."

His words sank in. That was it? "I hope so. I earned caveman sex, not back door sex with a businessman. I earned all I wanted for a day, not a minute."

The room was dark and the stars were out. His breath was on my neck as he muttered, "You said you worked your ass off. I found it. Should I pound my chest?"

"It's the least you can do."

He thudded himself as he stood behind me. The dim light of the cave had me discombobulated, frozen in place. Desire, however, was thawed, after so many years. The back door had done nothing but pour oil on it.

"I'll pound *your* chest." He put his arms around me and massaged my breasts. "Pounding like a gentle rain. Sit with me on this mastodon rug, we can chat while I recover."

We tumbled together onto the rug. In the flickering flames, our shadow stretched ahead of us like a two-headed beast.

"This room is fascinating. Can it give the impression of any time period?"

"Yes, it's in the code. Is there a time you desire to visit?"

"Middle Ages? I might enjoy seeing you in some tights."

"I don't know what it is. Let me tell you about my era. Long ago when the world was new, only 4.4 billion years old, my people lived communally and shared what we had. We shared freely, even of ourselves."

"Lots of sharing."

"Many men, many women. This way, no one was left alone. There were chances to mate limited to no more than your own ability. We rolled together like pups. The children were what nature chose. Anyone could have been the fathers and we cared for all. We were an intimate community. We belonged to each other."

"Like the Pestos, um Agros, but kinder."

"It was a utopia. We had no agriculture. We hunted. We ate. We made love on skin rugs." He bit my neck gently. "We wrestled our prey to the ground."

I giggled, something I hadn't done since I'd played with my doll, Jelly, as a kid.

"Nonetheless, you did not pay for talk."

"Do you talk with all of your clients?" I wanted to feel special.

"If they desire it."

"Keep talking." If we talked enough maybe he'd fall in love with me. I was somewhat in love with him after our encounter, no matter how brief. "We are together in the past. Tell me about it."

"Imagine."

"What do you mean?"

"Imagine? It's as a dream when awake. Dream for me. It is cold. We lay on a hide made of shaggy elephant. The stars peek through the mouth of the cave. Our soft silky hair keeps our heads warm."

I touched his hair. "How do you know this?"

"Genetic memory. Memory of us together. It is inside of us. It is in the blood and in the bones and at the tips of our hair." This was not true, I'd never been a cavewoman. We'd not been together. He was acting and mixing eras at the same time. I longed for the not-truth, anything to break the loneliness that was living in Cochtonia.

"I pull you onto my lap. No, you leap onto it. It's you who wants me." This much was true. I hopped onto his lap. He moved rhythmically. I liked it, I was a real woman.

"I'm grateful. For your rental, so thankful," he said.

"I feel you. You're touching me. Again. Oh, the power."

"My name is Bigg Gib for a reason. It's not my height. It's my girth. And you, you're hotter than fire. You're a star. Your breasts are tumescent—as I am, engorged with arousal. Your nipples are erect. I have been taught to serve you. You must approach me. Touch me, see for yourself what you do to me."

Slightly afraid of this eloquent caveman but intrigued by his story, I placed my hand down below, onto the pulsing beast, so much like the flowering plant that for a moment, I wanted to tissue culture it. How silly. There wasn't room for more than one Bigg Gib.

"Are you really a caveman? You're still wearing the suit."

"I don't know what I am. Like all of us, I was called into existence and recall little of it happening. For a short time, I exist. I'm happy we overlapped in time." He coughed. "It's allergies. Our immune systems overreact."

"Overreaction is your middle name," I said playfully.

"It can't be. My name must be a palindrome according to law."

"I'll take you forwards since I have already had you backwards."

He grabbed my face with his wide hands and smothered me with his lips until I was dizzy. He dropped one hand to caress my breast. I melted like a candle beneath his touch. He put his other hand up my skirt. His wide fingers touched me with a promise I never dared give myself. I forgot he was wearing a cheap suit, forgot everything except his hands. An animal roared in the distance. He tensed.

"Don't stop," I begged.

Obtrusive knocking came from somewhere.

"No," I said. "Yes! Yes!" A pleasurable convulsion took hold of me." What's happening?" I asked breathlessly.

"Another couple wishes to join in. Are you up for it? I can be."

My first inclination was no. I wanted him all to myself. But curiosity took over. When else would I experience all of this? "Let them in."

To my shock, it was Lady Maliegene and her caveman. Lady was tall, statuesque if you will. She wore a suit woven from corn tassels. These things cost a fortune.

"I'm here to help you with your first Crisper experience," she announced.

I giggled. She'd arrived too late.

"I'm not an amateur when it comes to Crispers," LouOtta explained. "I'm pampering myself with this thick Neanderthal hunk. But what's this amalgamation you have here?" She tugged at Bigg Gib's lapel. "This business-tacky won't do at all."

"He got back from rehab today," I said defensively.

"Let's shed some clothing and get into some comfortable prehistoric skins."

"It's called a leisure suit, Lady."

"Take it off."

"It's what we're here for," Bigg Gib said. "We are all you need."

He ducked behind an illusionary boulder in what seemed to be a needless display of modesty. Then, it struck me. He was going into a closet. "What skin do you want to rub?" he called out, over the slip of hangers on a rack.

"Reptile," I said. "Something scaly."

In a move that made me uncomfortable, LouOtta, I could call her by her first name at this point, couldn't I? LouOtta, the famous penner of our National Anthem, pulled her blouse over her head. Her bra was beautiful and sparked a jealousy deep within me.

"Oh, a cold choice, so cold. I like it. Good thing it's hot in here," she said. "You can have a taste of my first-rate man. Yours can't even undress quickly. These guys come from a sharing culture and I normally don't like sharing, but I'll make an exception if I get to watch and have a taste of yours if he ever gets his clothes off." She stripped off her pants to show matching panties. "He's slow for someone so primitive. I'd think he'd be impulsive."

"I assure you, he's not." I was defensive for the poor guy in his cheap suit.

"The suit is tight in the legs, Lady." He sneezed twice. "I might be allergic to the fabric."

"Cover your mouth and tug off the suit. Commence your primitive grunting. Come on, take a peek." She wiggled her butt. "Ookie bookie, caveman. Do something crude."

He rushed out from behind the rock, wearing a reptile skin, grabbed her and began his preliminary rubbing. "Ooogie boogie."

The illusionary fire flickered. I was sprouting horns. I should have been honored by Lady Maliegene's tutoring. Instead, the seed of envy popped through my soil and shot down roots.

I tugged Bigg Gig's skin. "Stop! You're mine!"

He gave me a blank look. "Group rub. We do." Despite his objections, he released LouOtta and stood back, puzzled at my change of heart.

Going with the flow, I, too, shook my rump, calling up my inner Bohemian. "Oh, my thunder, strike once again. Ookie dookie." He stepped forward to embrace *me*. I was more ready this time and twice as charged. I lifted my skirt. And as the fire popped and flared, I saw it.

"Hold on a minute. What's all over you?"

CHAPTER NINE

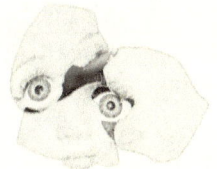

I took a step back. He was splashed in gray. I thought at first it was his spots scattered over his legs. No, his skin was tinted blue, as if starved for oxygen, particularly around the legs, groin, and bulging arms.

LouOtta screamed, "Infection!"

"No, I'm fine. I've been tested and scanned."

"Blue skin is *not* fine! I don't feel safe!" LouOtta reached for her clothes.

"They did this to me at the rehab center. They must have. It's not catching, I was cleared." He ducked behind the boulder.

LouOtta pulled on her shirt. "Neadaen! Take care of this!"

Neadaen rushed to the boulder but couldn't get around it.

"Keep him in there, Neadaen!" Neadaen screamed and pounded on the boulder.

Panic ran over me. The last outbreak had been enough to leave me with trauma. I thought only one thing: *save yourself*. I ran to the wall of the "cave" and felt over it with my fingertips. It had the smoothness of plastic with spots of dried grit, as from spills. Desperately, I searched for a button, a switch, anything to turn off the illusion.

LouOtta yelled into her device. "Send a containment crew!"

My hands touched a panel. My fingers searched for something to press.

"That's right. Union Station. Upstairs. Hurry! We have him sequestered."

I ran my palms across the panel. It was a smooth plastic cover.

"Yes, I *am* Lady Maliegene! I've been exposed. Get a hospital bed ready, I'll need a full evaluation!"

The premier caveman banged his head on the boulder. The boulder rattled like a door. I wanted to turn off the illusion. I couldn't even see my exit. This place was dangerous.

Neadaen turned toward us. "Agh!" He smacked his forehead with his fist and lunged at LouOtta in anger. She shoved out an arm and pushed him back. "Turn around and focus on the boulder or you'll be next in line for rehab, you brute!" She spun him to face the boulder and gave him a shove. "He's there. Block him in."

I felt along the edge of the panel, seeking a latch. The panic switch had to be here. There wasn't a switch on the panel. I pried the edges. I could feel two panels touching, but prying did nothing. My heart beat out of control. I put both hands on the panel and pushed. Nothing. I pushed down. Nothing. I pushed up. It slid. Yes, it slid up! I groped for a switch. There it was. I threw it. The room was flooded with light. No boulders. No fire. A smooth walled room, a bed, an exit, and Neadaen pounding his fists on a narrow door.

LouOtta was half dressed. "This place is a dump," she said, brushing her toes across a clump of dust and hair.

The exit was to my left. I reached for the door, pausing at the sound of footsteps coming up the stairs. Two white-clad officers burst in, nearly knocking me over.

"Hold her for scanning," said LouOtta, pointing to me. "She had sex with the infected!"

An agent beamed me with a NoRegrets device. "She's clean."

Her Vice Patrol partner said, "Don't mean much if it's something new. We couldn't detect it but let her go. Apprehending the hoodlum is the important thing right now."

"He's in the closet," LouOtta said.

I staggered downstairs, through the bar, and out the door, onto the cracked sidewalk. Fear had me blind. At one point, a group of kids followed me calling, "Hey, Blue!" and "The sky is falling."

By the time I got home, my joints ached as if I'd been run over by a driverless combine. My head swam. I opened the door slowly, soundlessly. The parents were sleeping in their recliners. NezLeigh was in the kitchen, her head deep in the refrigerator. If I got to my room, if I opened the window, they wouldn't catch this. I swirled into the room and with my last bit of effort, threw open the sash to let in fresh air. The bed came up to meet me as I fell into it. This wouldn't be like the last time, when men vomited until their nuts were numb. This virus affected all of us. A shower of fragments, like glass, danced in front of my eyes. A head loomed over me.

"Stay back," I moaned.

"You're in my bed. I was getting a noon snack, not awakening. How was it with a Crisper? Your confidence is gonna attract them like flies now."

"You're too young to be asking."

She put her face up to mine, risking infection. "My birthday's coming up. Not to mention, it's day and my turn in bed."

"Get back. The sky is falling."

"What the hell? Are you delirious? The sky sure the hell isn't falling."

"I'm sick, I caught a blue skin disease from the Crisper. A blue skin disease! It's probably from your neck of the woods. It's on my legs and it's spreading."

NezLeigh ran off, leaving me to roll and whimper in bed. A short time later, she came back and handed me a glass of water.

"Maybe you're dehydrated?"

"Or diseased."

"Diseased? Screw that! Let me see those legs." She pulled back the covers. "What a mess! There is so much more to this sexuality than solo practice."

"The blue is abnormal. Lady Maliegene screamed when she saw it and shut down our orgy because of it."

"She was there? Hard to imagine frolicking with the common folk would suit her. And an orgy? Holy hell."

I took a drink. "It was a coincidence of timing, we rented cavemen at the same time. She got the primo caveman and mine was fresh from rehabilitation. We never had the orgy because of the disease outbreak."

She whistled. "The skirt is a total loss. What filthy beast did this to you?"

"He's called Bigg Gib."

"The names are getting stupider and stupider."

I moaned in pain and embarrassment. "Why did I have to be so curious? I'll never touch a man again."

"Are you feverish?"

"I'm dizzy and I'm blue."

"It's getting all over the sheets."

"It is?" I took a gander. The blue disease was rubbing off my legs and onto the bedding. I splashed water on my blue thigh to see if the color would wash off. The "disease" slightly dissolved in the water, sitting on my skin in a blue-tinged puddle.

"Could you get me alcohol, rubbing or otherwise? And some corn fiber pads, menstrual or otherwise?"

"Do I look like a fricking servant?"

"As a friend. Please?"

"You're using the F word on me?"

"Please! My head is spinning and I don't want Mom to ask a bunch of questions." I fell into a faint, my mind racing with images of my body being fed to pigs.

She came back with a bottle of rubbing alcohol and a menstrual pad. "Good to know where to find this stuff. You see me as a kid, but I'm active in the woman department."

"Hand them over, I need to disinfect." I soaked the pad with rubbing alcohol and rubbed it across my legs. The pad sucked in blue. The color was slightly soluble in a solvent like water and fully dissolved in a disinfecting alcohol.

"It's not a disease. It's a dye!" I got out of bed. "How stupid! I should have known. He had a new, cheap suit and he rubbed it all over me."

"Bet it was a good time."

"As a matter of fact—"

"Damn, look at your mess. Take off your skirt—I'll wash it—and get in the shower."

"You'll do my laundry?"

"This one time. We're kin now."

I stood in the shower, the water screaming at me as it hit. I'd been so stupid. I, of all people, should have recognized the blue as a dye. With the help of a soapy scrubbing, the last of it swirled around the drain. Ironically, my wristlet fell to pieces and slipped away as well. I wrapped myself in a towel, the darkest color I could find, an ugly maroon, and went back to the bedroom. NezLeigh had my sheets off the bed. She held the skirt at arm's length, inspecting it.

"Maybe I can fix this. But if I can, it's mine."

"It's all yours. What's going to happen to Bigg Gib? He's innocent. Lady called for the Vice Patrol. They took him away."

"Back to rehab I imagine. Or maybe, to the pigs."

"I can't let this happen to him."

"He was that good?"

"No. Yes. He was accused unfairly." I stopped. This was nothing new here in Cochtonia. Why did it bother me? "Can you help him? You've got to know an underground way."

"Me? You think I have some sort of folk wisdom? No, it's not up to me. *You* know people. Newton and his friend are closer to the top than anyone."

"What are you saying?"

"Your friends can request a diseased caveman for a miracle cure. How many can there be?"

"And then what?"

"I get seconds."

"They aren't my friends. I barely know them."

"Make nice with them. You owe it to the poor caveman. Besides, threesomes might be fun."

"It wasn't fun the last time."

Mom came in. "Is everything alright?"

"Stella's growing a spine and a heart. F'ing A. Mom, excuse me, I have some laundry to do."

CHAPTER TEN

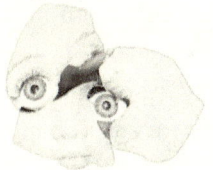

I didn't want a spine or a heart. Such things could be dangerous. A mob of media women swarmed outside of the Cochton Enterprises research facility. One swooped at me. "Do you work here? What's your opinion of the homunculus project?"

I stammered. I couldn't say a discouraging word. It would be a crime. "I just work here."

"Did you see the Cochtons?"

"No. Yet I felt their immense presence." This was such bullshit. I hadn't felt anything except maybe dread and later revulsion when Ursula showed me the feces sculpture photos. I resented her for drawing me in. Ignorance had been bliss.

"Will it work? What's your scientific opinion?"

This was nearly a trap. We didn't have opinions here. The truth was, I didn't think it would work, nor did I want it to work. Science was my all. Alchemistry couldn't and wouldn't get in its way. The pseudoscience had been overthrown for three hundred years.

In the face of my silence, she babbled on, filling the dead air. "Tell us, will this solve the problem of limited reproductive options?"

Several office workers walked by in HumP t-shirts. We'd gotten a memo approving them for office attire and both men and women were sporting them. I couldn't give an unpopular opinion. I'd go to the pigs and these folks would drag me there.

"The proof will be in the manure, I mean pudding. In the pudding, bursting with high fructose corn syrup produced right here in Cochtonia." I pressed my forehead and sang the anthem as a cover up for my conflicted feelings before dashing up the stairs to my lab. I was early and didn't run into anyone else. Despite my cooled enthusiasm for strippers, I was excited about my new plants and didn't want any other employees to scoop me. A win for the plants would be a win for science and science had never let me down. I regretted telling Ursula about them, although I rejoiced to see the plant stems standing straight, erect, and growing longer than the day before, roots filling the transparent beakers holding them.

Inspired, I set up a run-of-the-mill experiment to see if their growth was affected by the greenhouse gas CO_2. I measured each plant, then put a fourth of the plants in a specialized plastic balloon and added carbon dioxide from a portable tank propped up on a ring stand and clamped in place, using a regulator and a silicon-PVC plastic tube. The bag puffed up.

"Hello. What Cheer." Newton stood in the doorway.

"Come in," I said, flustered. "Why are you here?" I didn't mean to be rude. I hadn't expected him, of all people, to walk into my lab with his frilly shirt and shorts with tights, his thighs bursting forth and his dainty shoes. I hastily attempted to tidy up without being too obvious. I picked up a ten-milliliter pipet and suction bulb sitting out on the lab bench, knocking over a fifty-milliliter graduate cylinder by mistake.

"I'm seeking refuge from the overpowering manure smell. It reminds me too much of being dead." He watched the bag expand like a racoon corpse on a country road. "You have an interesting setup. What is it for, pray tell?"

I righted the cylinder, pretending I hadn't knocked it over by keeping my eyes on his. "I propagated some new plants. They are growing in a cultivating mixture, a liquid containing nutrients they need for proper development." I did my best to sound precise and scientific without any of the superlatives the alchemists appeared to use to embellish their work. "I'm testing to see if carbon dioxide increases the growth or decreases it. You'd think it would always accelerate the growth, but this isn't the case. It depends on the plant. Growing more in carbon dioxide gives plants an edge these days. Beans for example, grow increasingly large in higher carbon dioxide. These look like beans, don't they?"

He leaned forward and made a show of examining the plant, jutting out his large chin with a dimple in the middle. "Yes, beans. Grandmother told me a tale about an enchanted bean."

Our scientific conversation had been too good to last. Here it came: enchantment, secret powers, magic, alchemy, all the stuff I didn't believe in.

"I didn't like Grandmother much," he added.

I could feel myself relaxing. "These aren't enchanted although they grow fast." I put a randomly scattered pipet and bulb in a drawer before I knocked them off the lab bench in my nervousness. When I was fixated on a project, I didn't see the mess. With this new person in my space, I recognized how disorganized I looked to others. I had to put six dirty beakers in the sink to look less haphazard but there wasn't time. Newton was at my elbow.

"Carbon dioxide is in the transparent bag?" he asked.

"Yes. It won't kill the plants. They use it to make sugar. They need fertilizer to convert it to other building materials."

"This world has much carbon, it appears."

"Yes, it's life's scaffolding."

"Carbon dioxide appears to be what I'd call the element air."

Oink! I'd forgotten. He didn't know about elements beyond air, earth, fire, water, and a few metals such as gold, lead, copper, and zinc.

"Air is not an element, it's a mixture of gases. And not all gases are in air. Gas is a state of matter. Substances without much attraction to each other form gases at room temperature." I spoke gently, not wanting to offend the great man, since although this was new to him, he wasn't dumb. He'd pretty much founded modern science, he and Galileo.

"Attraction is something I know much about. Are these molecules small?"

"Yes," I said. *How about you? Large, small, or in between?* I was embarrassed to have such a stupid thought pop into my head. I'd invite him to assist me today, to keep things professional between us. Maybe I could later bring up the need to free Bigg Gib. "Um, would you like to help me set up the group with extra fertilizer?"

"Nutrients?"

"Yes. Sometimes nutrients help plants grow under increased carbon dioxide and sometimes they hinder. Plants are complex and sensitive beings. I've got a lot of enthusiasm for this shaggy greenery and I need to study every aspect moving forward. They will be used for salmagundi. They could represent a new crop. Would you like to add fertilizer to the media and I'll mix it? Unless you want to mix. If you mix, you can use a machine to mix."

"New crop? Yes! Let me help. I'd love to mix in as I am an outsider, still learning your modern speech and mannerisms, but I'll leave it up to you to mix. I'm a measuring man."

"Measuring man? Of course! Be my guest. Use this." I handed him the plastic graduated cylinder, much like a measuring cup but long and erect. *I'd like to see your cylinder.*

I was appalled by my intrusive thoughts. Was this a by-product of the ill-fated but in retrospect pleasurable moment I'd had with a Crisper? Fortunately, Newton was unaware. He picked up the cylinder and looked at the graduation lines indicating the volumes. "This is a well- crafted device. I thank you for allowing me to handle it. I can assure you, I have skill in this area. Furthermore, I'm so idle I sense my blood settling, watching nothing happening and selling coins and trinkets on occasion. I am in your debt for this opportunity. There is nothing like a lab to provide refuge for a lost soul. This fertilizer is a liquid?"

"Yes, let me get it for you." I almost tripped over myself as I fetched a bottle of nutrient from the shelf. I gingerly placed it next to him.

"The propagating broth is already in there. Each container needs fifty milliliters of fertilizer."

"I'm used to drams, but I do see the fifty. Seems to be a little over ten drams. Where is the dip to measure the volume—the meniscus?"

"It has none. It's plastic. Water isn't attracted to plastic. It's made of something different than plastic. They don't care to mix."

"As with fat and water."

"Exactly. Like dissolves like."

"Mutual attraction," he said. "They have none."

"You're getting the hang of modern chemistry quickly."

"You're an excellent teacher. I was a mathematics instructor. I wasn't suited for teaching. I had two bouts of extreme nervous agitation. I couldn't enjoy having the rapt and longing eyes of a pupil upon me." He stared at me and I wasn't sure if it was unintentional or to prove his point about pupil eyes. I even doubted his story. How did he remember these former things after being dead? He loved talking about himself. In any case, it didn't bother me. I almost liked it.

I stared back at him. "Perhaps it won't happen this time around. Having a break down might not be repeatable. The conditions are different after all. You could be in a better place."

"I have no rivals here, it's true. The collapse came after arguing with Leibniz about calculus. He plagiarized me."

"I'm not a plagiarist. I have a hard time lying." Our eyes met again. I thought I shouldn't look away or I'd seem like I was lying. He wasn't bad looking. He had new stubble on his chin. How did he shave? Where did he shave? Didn't old-time dudes have barbers shave them? I wanted to touch his face and see if it was scratchy. *What about your chest? Hairy or smooth?*

"I endure something nearly as odious in this life. Making these advertisements is torture in front the mechanical portrait device." He shuddered, possibly for effect. I realized I needed to answer him, not simply stare back into his brown eyes.

"Oh. The mechanical portrait? The camera?"

"Yes, it's harsh. A good artist portrays the soul of a person, not simply the physical form with glaring imperfections, but the truth within."

"An artist interprets?"

"Yes, it took time to have a portrait painted, a fortnight in my case, and was only for the well-to-do or well-known, but the essence came through. The setting was perfected. Imagination combined with what could be seen. Now, I must have my flaws flung to the world instantly as I stand in starkness. I am going to become nervous again, I can feel it coming on."

I can't say I'd ever been moved to compassion before. It's not what we were in Cochtonia. We were sacrificing individualists— the nation-state first and us second. We only gave in order to receive and we sacrificed because we were afraid not to. Now, something bubbled from within me, like carbon dioxide in syrup, at the sight of his helpless masculinity.

"How can I help you?" I asked. *May I help you undress?*

He straightened his back. "It's I who am here to help you."

I snapped back to reality. "Add fifty milliliters of the fertilizer solution to each of these flasks I have laid out here," I said, being as professional as I could.

After he filled a flask, I mixed it using sonication, labeled it with tape and a marker, giving it a number. This was easy enough for me to do alone, but it was all I could think of to have him help with. It was nice to have someone assist with this mundane ritual of science, someone who understood that the setup took much longer than the eureka. *Someone sexier than I'd imagined him to be at first glance.*

"Numbers are so comforting," he said. "Numbers and measuring. They were my children."

"These plants are my children. I nurture them and care about them and study them. Next, we'll take cuttings." I pulled a scalpel from a drawer. "How do you feel about cutting?"

"I'm not in favor."

"It's the way to get new plants at this point. We'll cut the long vines into sections of equal length, add them to the nutrient mixture, and get them to root. We'll see how they survive in the high carbon dioxide atmosphere."

He touched his neck and frowned. Had I offended him? He was known to be touchy and had mentioned bouts of nervousness. Was this it?

"Alright, I'll do the cutting. Don't worry, they won't be harmed. Only propagated."

"I must go back," he said abruptly. "I'm on a privy break and it's over. My solitary life is a jag from one room through a corridor to the next. Our collaboration today has been a pleasure. We should have tea sometime. In fact, please visit me straightaway. I must get your scientific opinion. It's urgent."

"Meet you where?"

"The most cloistered place you can think of."

My mind raced. Besides the bathroom, what was private? There was no sequestered place in this whole nation.

He waited, watching my face, for a suggestion. Where could we go to be alone?

"I'll walk back with you, we can check the gas tanks. They're in a closet."

The closet was right next to my lab and was filled with gases a scientist might want—nitrogen, helium, hydrogen, and in my case, carbon dioxide—all stored in metal tanks with screw off caps protecting their valves. If a tank fell over and the vale busted off, the gas would flow out and propel the tank with enough force to smash through a wall. There was barely room for two people in here and we squeezed in, closed the door, and stood close in the dark.

He took a breath. Was I touching him? He gasped. "There's no homunculus."

At first, I was overjoyed. The dumb t-shirts and the dirty mud, the dismissal of women.

"Why did you think there would be one?"

"It was not my idea. As you recently witnessed, Paracelsus is a barbaric optimist. However, the idea has merit. Life comes from manure. You see crawly things."

"Crawly things? Those are maggots. Flies lay eggs and the eggs hatch."

"Into worms?"

"Yes."

"As with birds? I've never seen a fly incubation or an egg."

"They are too small to see. You use a microscope."

"I should have taken my eye from the telescope."

"The manure heats them. You must have heard that sealed vessels produce no flies. More importantly, humans must lie together to produce babies."

"Paracelsus claims it is not necessary. Being wed to celibacy, I deeply wanted to believe him. I was looking under my own rocks, not searching for truth. Alas, there will be no homunculus and we'll be hanged as frauds, won't we?"

"Possibly thrown in a private prison. Hanging isn't big here. We poison people more often." I felt bad for him. I needed him to help me find Bigg Gib, but I also wanted to help *him*. I was tired of being selfish. He was a great man, or had been. I didn't treasure the thought of the father of Modern Science hanged or in one of our many rehabilitation facilities, as prisons were called.

"I've always despised the wicked. Now I'll be a criminal through no fault of my own."

"It could happen to anyone." I considered how I might console him. "We're scientists, we solve problems. We take our knowledge and extend it. There must be some way! When does the shit hit the fan?"

"A fan?"

"I mean, when do you have to produce these babies?"

"I was told there would be a festival. I didn't ask to be here and now it proves so inhospitable. I didn't devote my life to studying natural laws to have your capricious dictators idle me."

"Keep your voice down. They are our founders!"

"This horrid society of yours uses science but doesn't appreciate its beauty. It's perverse."

"You're overreacting! We'll come up with a way to get a baby."

He fell back, knocking into a nitrogen tank, fortunately not pushing it over. In the dark, my adjusting eyes saw his face pale. His mouth hung open at my suggestion. He was so soft and surly. My heart broke for him a little. His frustration at his impossible task reminded me of Bigg Gib and possibly, of all of us. I had to admit to myself, our leaders were incompetent.

"Cool down, I didn't mean I'd have the baby. I have an idea. I'll get an idea, I just need time."

"Time is the ultimate tyrant."

"I'll help you." I was going to say, "If you help me." I didn't. I left it at *I'll help you.*

CHAPTER ELEVEN

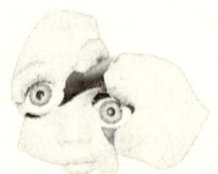

By the time I got home, it was raining. Something plastic sat on the kitchen table. It was about the size of a bar of soap, some sort of decoration, a pink resin harshly cast. A person with a big, bald head resting on his arms crouched inside a drop, like a big teardrop. The thing was nude, with crossed legs. I tried not to be afraid, as if it was some sort of demonic signal. It was a homunculus.

Why, I asked myself, *Why?*

Mom and Dad were in their recliners. Mom was back to her classic clothes with a t-shirt reading *I support the HumP*. Dad, too, was declaring *I HumP*.

"What's the thing on the table?" I asked, trying not to look at their chests.

"You know what it is."

"Homunculi are not real and they aren't going to be real."

"Oh Stella, jealousy is an ugly thing. We all have our talents. Your sister's such an entrepreneur. She made homunculus figurines to sell. Without her, you'd be facing a future alone with Jelly. You needed something alive, more than the treasured baby doll."

"I don't need Jelly. She represents everything I'm not going to do. I won't be alone or I won't care."

I grabbed the doll from the kitchen table and tossed her to the floor. She hit with a hollow thump and scraped across the vinyl. The party hat she still wore skidded until it hit the refrigerator. "She's a thing. Old plastic junk. As worthless as the trash on the table!"

"Are you worried about the competition? I have room in my heart."

"No one can compete with a homunculus," Dad said.

I opened the refrigerator. I had the worst appetite after work, as if I needed to eat away the stress. "Where's the salmagundi?"

"We had it for lunch. It doesn't go far, all that watery lettuce."

"How about thawing some Porkies?" Dad said. "Porkies will make you splorkie."

"I never understood the meaning."

"They'll make you squeal," Mom clarified.

Dad corrected her. "No, they make you poop."

Mom leaned over and poked Dad playfully. "At least something does."

Defeated, I picked up Jelly and went to my room. The entrepreneur was asleep. I sat on my bed. What was I doing? How was I going to help Newton when I couldn't even keep my clothes off the floor at age forty? Jelly. Damn, why was this thing in my life? I needed a couple of real babies and I needed them quick, not some dumb doll, old as the hills.

"Newton," I said. "You can't explain *this* attraction. Why am I doing this for you?"

NezLeigh, waking up, kicked at me. "Are you so goofy you can't tell day from night? I'm supposed to be asleep for another hour."

"Do Pestos have boy babies?" I asked her.

"You wake me up for this? Not much. And call us Agros, damn it! Pesto is an insult. You want a boy baby? Gonna take in another one of us and civilize us? No, nobody is gonna give you one."

"It's not for me. I'm wondering if there are spare boy babies anywhere."

"You know the answer, dope. Babies come from an InVitro

clinic or the State Crisper Facility, wherever it is. If you want a boy baby, any baby, you've got to do something great and get a treatment. You can have a Crisper son. Even I know it and I've been living in the woods. You wasted your fame on the blue skin caveman. Go big next time and ask for what you deserve. Was he any good?"

"The caveman? Not as good as I'd hoped. The blue dye ruined the mood."

I could hear the rain. In the living room, Dad cursed the spatters. "This is going to get mud on the house."

"Oh, you know you like to squirt it off with the powerful hose," Mom said.

"Was it a powerful hose?" NezLeigh asked. "The caveman?"

"If you want to find out about hoses, *you've* got to do something great. And grow up!"

"At least I'm not forty years old and holding some bald ancient doll. That's the only baby you've got."

I should have been mad, but, no, instead I had a vision, a vision of two babies, two Jellies. Yes, she could be passed off as a homunculus. Her head was big. She was old enough to make it unlikely there would be another one like her out there. Nobody would recognize this doll. I simply needed another one of her—like her, but alive.

"She's precious, one of a kind. Anyone would be happy with this type of baby. There's far too much emphasis on filling up the world with DNA," I said. "Tell me, how did you make those homunculus statues? And in such a clandestine manner."

"You like 'em? Pretty low tech." She watched my face eagerly. I didn't pretend to like them.

"How did you make them?"

"I used the coin as a model. I whittled a prototype from a bar of soap and cast it. They're damn ugly. They sell well though. I sold a bushel downtown this morning. I put them on a blanket in the square. Dumbshits bought 'em! Cash money, too. But I'm pooped now. Let me sleep."

"I wonder if other things would sell. Maybe something less ugly?"

"Nothing will sell like those. They're so f'ing easy to make, too. City life is the bomb."

"How do you do it? Where'd you get the materials?"

"Your dad had the materials from a prior confiscation of a low budget pleasure pals operation. The inspiration was a craft project back in my Camp Cochton days. We made handprints."

"Camp project? I thought you lived mostly in the wild."

"When it suited me. I told you, I also lived at the camp, along with my sister, when we felt like it. You're being too snoopy. Snitches get stitches."

Sister? I backed off. I had a plan and I needed her cooperation. "This doll, she doesn't have to be one of a kind. Can we make molds of her, too?"

"Why would you?"

"I'd like to try. What if something happens to her?"

"I'm not believing this new affection for the doll. I know crap when I see it."

"You're right, someone I know would appreciate a couple of dolls. If I help this someone, the person will help me find the caveman. They are an experienced sleuth. I won't feel so guilty about running away from his blue legs."

"An adult needs dolls? Baby dolls? Some people!"

"More like homunculus stand-ins. You could say the person is a fan, a collector. Don't you think the doll can be a homunculus metaphor?"

"Yes, if you market it the correct way. People here don't need a lot of evidence."

"Exactly. I'll need your advice. You make these in the basement?"

"I'll help you if I get seconds," NezLeigh said. "No questions asked about your perverted friend."

"Thirds. You can have the third doll. I want two molds," I said, elaborating as little as possible. My idea was this: I'd use the mold to fashion two babies from the vines. Plants have genetic plasticity and adapt to their environment. Under the right conditions, they could fill the molds with gel-like protoplasm and provide a living "baby"—not a vine but a copy of Jelly. About ten years ago, I'd tried this technique to make a molded pudding out of soybeans. Soybean pudding didn't have enough fat to satisfy the average Cochtonian and never made it past trials. However, if I added material from say, an air plant, they would have a defined shape and resemble the inside of an aloe stem. My plan wasn't perfect but as long as the "baby" didn't look or smell like corn or soybeans, it wouldn't be immediately recognizable and it would buy time.

"You can make all the dolls you want, I'm talking seconds on the man."

I couldn't implicate Newton in this. I might not even tell him. It would help him and keep Sir and I from being fed to the pigs. "What makes you think it's a man?" I said slowly. "Women can be homunculus fans. Look at Mom."

"I want seconds on Mr. Blue Legs. I'll share his pain of being unfairly judged based on appearance."

"When I find him, I'll introduce you."

"I'll help you cuz we got shit in common. We're two lost girls— I'm ugly and you're ditzy."

I was mad, taken aback. I covered it up. "You're not ugly and I'm alternatively organized."

"Oh, yeah. How stupid do I look? One more thing—you owe me a favor in the future."

"Okay, but tell me why you're here? You jumped into our car. Why?"

"I was getting sprayed like a weed. Currently, I'm observing. If I knew why I was here, I'd know what favor I needed. On the bright side, this place is full of suckers and I'm making a fortune."

"Keep it on the down low or some law making your craft illegal will pop up."

"How bad does this place suck? Listen up. We need a box bigger than the doll. It's gotta surround this homely toy. The formula is in the basement. I'll meet you down there after I get your parents a nightcap and me a cup of breakfast beverage with extra caffeine."

I got a shoe box from the closet, tossing my shoes on the floor. I put Jelly in it and crept down the stairs, easy for me as I had light footsteps. NezLeigh served the folks corn liquor and raspberry syrup before coming to join me in the basement.

It would be easy to hide a project in the basement. The washing machine was here and the top of it was packed with bottles of different detergents since Mom appreciated new scents. The laundry was in baskets, folded by NezLeigh but not brought up the stairs to be put away. Two shop vacs were in one corner next to a crate of old incandescent light bulbs. An exercise bike sat beside a planter full of fake greenery. Tubs of my old toys lined the walls. I'd liked plastic building blocks and, embarrassingly, fashion dolls. I'd dreamed of being fashionable but never got the hang of high heels and form-fitting clothes. I wasn't willing to put up with the discomfort. Several tubs held my old clothes starting with baby booties all the way up to old sweatshirts. Board games were piled on wire shelves. Another shelf held toilet paper and bathroom cleaning spray, things that had been stockpiled since the virus days. A shoebox and a doll would never be noticed. I could probably assemble a monster down here.

NezLeigh tiptoed down the stairs.

"They won't be asking any questions after the double shots," she said. She went to a sink in the corner and pulled out an old ice cream tub.

"First step is to mix up the molding compound." She opened a jar and scooped a powder into the tub. She ran water into it and stirred it with a used paint stick.

"Aren't you worried about a lack of precision?" I asked.

"Hand me the box and I'll show you fucking precision."

She put the box on the floor and poured it half full of molding gel. "Where's the ugly-as-sin doll?"

I cuddled Jelly. Maybe she wasn't bland. She fit into my arms perfectly with her smooth soft plastic, open eyes, and unjudgmental face, her mouth ready to accept whatever she was given. "Plastic today is made from hog sewage," I said. "*She's* made from a puff of oil. She's something from almost nothing. She's special!"

"It won't hurt the doll. You'll get it back and then some. Grease her up so the casting shit doesn't stick to her."

I sprayed the doll with the cooking spray she tossed to me.

"Lower her slippery ass down."

I stuck Jelly face up in the mud.

"We gotta pass the time," NezLeigh said. "This half of the mold needs to harden before we can pour the top. Tell me, are you all hoarders of this shit?"

"It's mostly Mom's stuff. Or I should say my stuff that she kept. She's sentimental, but Dad stockpiled the light bulbs." I didn't even want to tell NezLeigh about the attic above the garage. More stuff was up there, things never accessed but apparently still valuable to Mom. "This place is pretty small," I added defensively.

"You come by it honestly then, the disorder gene and the lack of emotions."

It was a smack in the head to have her say it aloud again. Not about the emotions, I hid them well and was proud of it, but about the disarray. My mess was supposed to be my own private embarrassment, not a public shame.

"I'm not bragging, but if ever you need someone to find a needle in a haystack, I'm it."

"We should tidy up down here."

"Maybe for your sake. I don't need things organized and neither does Newton. Nature has secrets, but they aren't in files. They are scattered about like pebbles on a beach."

I opened a plastic tub sitting in a corner. It was full of Styrofoam cups. They'd been popular once but phased out when Cochtonia began producing its own plastic made from animal waste. NezLeigh went to an old chest of drawers and picked up a plastic can from the top that once held caffeinated corn breakfast beverage.

"Stella DNA," she read. She opened it. "Oh gross! Anyone could make a voodoo doll from this." I went over to look, trying to act calm and collected, not uncontrollably curious. I peeked over her shoulder. The box held a tangle of hair and small teeth—my baby teeth. "It's your old dirty teeth and hair."

"You shouldn't be poking around," I said. Her grotesque finds had me questioning how plants would pass a DNA test looking for humans. I'd have to cross this bridge later.

"Girls, what are you doing?" Mom stood at the top of the stairs, wobbling.

"Mom, what are you doing?" I called in alarm.

"Stella's helping me cast more big-ticket items. We're gonna be rich, Mom."

"It's only a hobby, no moonlighting. The Cochtons control the purse strings."

"Mom," NezLeigh said. "How can it be moonlighting when I don't have a job? Mom, what do you need? Why are you standing there ready to fall down the stairs?"

"How about some slurpies? Dad wants something cold to drink. I can make some for all of us."

"Oink, I don't want her to see this," I said quietly.

"Mom, I thought I made the food? Why don't I make the drinks?" NezLeigh dashed up the stairs.

I sat for a painfully long time while the casting resin hardened around the doll. NezLeigh brought down the frozen corn syrup brightly dyed with Red 40 in disposable glasses with straws. I took a sip and got a brain freeze so I put it on an abandoned coffee table. "Newton wouldn't approve, the slurpie looks too much like blood."

"You've mentioned him three times since you rudely woke me up," said NezLeigh.

"You told me to kiss up to him."

"An interesting choice of words."

"He's a celibate intellectual."

"Hmm. Challenges are fun to overcome."

"He helped me in lab. I haven't had a lab partner since college."

"Two nerds vs. everybody. How cute. Makes me want to touch myself. What'd ya do?"

"We propagated those plants from your waste area. I plan to use the flowers on salmagundi."

"Have they flowered?"

"Not yet."

"They are kind of weeds and, well," she paused, "hard to handle at times. They're sensitive to assholes."

"Like an anus?"

"Kind of, you ditz I wanted to know if you and Newton made out or grabbed each other."

"Did you ever consider that swearing and cursing and talking about sex are your way of flinging yourself on people?"

"Swearing and cursing? You're fucking redundant! Focus on our project. We need to make the indentations in the mold," NezLeigh said. "When we pour the next layer, it'll know where to rest." Jelly stared at the plastic tiles in the ceiling as NezLeigh used a screwdriver, conveniently resting near an old bentwood rocker to take a divot from each corner of the plastic the doll floated in.

"Something's missing," I mused.

"Shit, she's dickless! Homunculus-things are all male. It's okay, we need an open spot where you can pour in the plastic to make the dolls from the cast. It can do double duty as a dick. Damn straight!" She held up her thick one-use straw from the smoothie.

"A little longer than I'm used to," I said.

"These are magic beings. You're going to need a funnel to transfer in whatever you're filling this with. Pour it right through the dick. Are you using my plastic?"

"No, it's my own formulation. I have plenty of funnels at work. Plenty of filling material, too."

She put the thick straw on the doll's pubic area. "Hold this for me." I did as she ordered, posing the straw in approximately the correct spot. She sprayed Jelly, the straw, and the bottom layer with pan spray, then poured casting gel on top of the doll, burying it with the tip of the penis rising above the gel. "This should cast as well as I can manage. Can you hold the straw a little longer?"

"Okay." I contemplated the thick casting gel. It flowed enough to cover the doll but wasn't so runny that it slopped all over as water might.

"Tell me more about the caveman."

"He was a nice guy, chatty, an eager beaver to please. We went to an illusion room set to pre-historic times. He told a story about Neanderthals being really friendly with each other. Lady LouOtta had been in the bar with a high-end caveman and they asked to join us. Bigg Gib had on a denim suit. He went behind a rock to change into his animal skin but when he came back, his legs were blue from the dye on the suit. We thought it was a disease. When LouOtta called the authorities, I fled. I should have investigated and helped the poor Neanderthal."

"Your story is consistent. What caused the blue legs is of no consequence to her. He killed the mood. It was enough to have him taken away. Powerful people can do what they want."

And I'm faking them out.

CHAPTER TWELVE

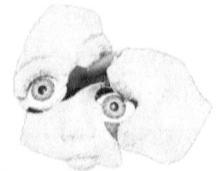

I entered the Cochton Enterprises building with one set of floppy molds rolled, duct taped, and hidden in my bra, giving me a matronly look. The other two added extra padding to my behind. My pants were uncomfortably tight. I'd regrettably purchased an extra-large HumP t-shirt the day before to wear over it all since my own clothes were too tight. I asked myself once again why I was doing this. What did I expect to get out of it? I walked through the sensor and the guard said, "Let it all hang out.

I went upstairs and through the hall to my lab.

"Hi," said a person from the microbiology division as she strolled past me with a cart full of petri dishes.

"Stella, how are you doing?" said someone from synthetics. She smelled slightly like acetone.

"How's your system?" asked a person from IT. What a time for people to be noticing me. My boobs and my ass were sweating like a virus pouring from a hog snout as I rushed into my lab.

Feverously, I took the molds from their hiding places. I put them in a sink of warm water and adhesive remover until the tape released. *Now to fill them.* One plant was particularly robust with a long tendril shooting out. I'd use that one. A second one was long but ventured out an erect, scraggly shoot. It wasn't quite lengthy enough to easily insert into the doll mold. It would have to be clamped in place.

I rinsed the molds with alcohol, coated them with some warmed up fat from my Porkie project, added growth gel, and rinsed the insides with waxase, an enzyme to promote cuticle growth in plants. I'd done a test using this with corn. It had been a flop. Waxy corn was too difficult to harvest. I then added some rootinhibitase to the molds. This had been a suggestion when corn rootworms were at an all-time high. Yes, the plants lived with shallow roots, but the corn had blown over during a derecho. I still had the chemicals, though, and maybe being a chemical packrat would pay off at last! I added a growth accelerator called Bean Stalk to the mother plants and rinsed each mold with some Crassulacean Acid metabolizer booster, found in succulents, to the template. The plants would possibly absorb it as they grew. For a final touch, I added one of my baby teeth, dipped first in alcohol, to a mold.

I got a water bath, an oblong steel vessel much like a doll bathtub, and put it in the growth chamber, the boxy structure with sterilizing lights and fans. I'd hide the molds and the plants in the vessel. There were such advantages to being haphazard. No one would suspect anything was out of place because it all was out of place. When Alexander Fleming carelessly left his lab window open when he went on vacation and came back to find mold on his petri dish, which killed the bacteria he'd left there in his hurry, he wasn't ashamed. He was curious. He didn't discover penicillin in a day. He worked on it. Yes, I'd work on this project.

I rinsed the vessel with alcohol to sterilize it. I didn't want the pink slime of bacterial biofilm to get a foothold. When bacteria band together to form a slime, it's almost impossible to get rid of them. I took out a doll mold and washed it copiously with alcohol to sterilize it. I put a mold in the growth chamber and gently wiped the tendril with an alcohol wipe. I then inserted it into the hole made by the straw. It would grow in there and fill the mold. I carefully tucked the form in the water bath to hide it. I put the water bath into the growth chamber and turned on the grow lights.

I repeated my procedure with the second tendril. However, now I had a problem to go with my solution. Sir Gotfried might drop by and peek in the water bath. How would I explain it? I was trying a new way to grow them. Yes, I'd tell him confinement operations worked for animals, why not confining plants to stainless steel tubs? Fortunately, on the outside, the molds looked nothing like a baby. They looked like rectangles. It wasn't Sir Gotfried who came in, however. It was Newton.

"I've arrived to assist and measure the progress," he said, as if it was the most natural thing in the world for one of the most famous men ever to exist to stride into my lab. I was flustered and flattered. Also, pleasantly reminded of his unplanned apple drop inspiration. Yes, he'd seen it fall, he'd wondered why things fell down and not up or sideways. Yes, theory said they desired to be part of the earth but he'd watched the planets move and devised experiments. I was at the apple drop stage of this experiment. It was an experiment, wasn't it? It was an experiment and not a scheme. He stood in the door, pale, clearly lonely.

"Come in and close the door," I blurted out. "I'm making babies for you."

A normal man would have caught this as innuendo but it flew right over Newton. "I'd be delighted and grateful. But how?" he said endearingly.

I turned on the sonic-mixer in case eavesdropping devices were present.

"I am molding these plants. I made two molds and inserted a tendril in each. As the plants grow, they will expand to fill the containers, much like air. In fact, I added an air plant enzyme to the container. They should grow quickly."

"How fascinating. Yet, a plant is not a baby."

"They will be floppy like babies and be alive. How much do people expect? If nature worked well this way, we wouldn't have sexual reproduction."

His face was stony, revealing no emotion.

"It's all I could think of on short notice. Hopefully it will buy time. We'll put the formed plants in the mud woman and they will resemble babies until real babies can be located. They'll even have penises."

"I see. Plants fancy light, do they not?"

"They do. Without light, they won't last forever. I used the amorphous propagation technique. It's being done with the flowers. We have to keep the initial plants sterile but once they have established, they can be put in the belly of the mud woman."

"Will this counterfeit be plausible? I have seen people hanged for as much."

His words burned through me. Of course, this would be sedition. I could be executed. Nevertheless, this didn't deter me. Curiosity about my process had me in its grip and certainly Sir would be executed if I didn't at least try something.

"The best kind of bullshit is both true and false. People lap it up. It's how Cochtonia survives."

"The combination is, however, ultimately false, as the lie taints the truth."

I was frustrated that my efforts weren't appreciated while knowing he was correct. "Are you going to let me help you or not?"

"I'll consider it. I'm not closed minded. You said you wished to visit the mud woman. Come."

The mud woman and details about the alchemists had been kept a secret from all but Officer Ursula—where they lived, for example, and what they did during the day when they weren't being used for advertisements. We took the stairs together, down to the basement.

The storage room was nothing like it had been. A platform, a couple feet high, had been built from plastic and took up most of the front half of the room. On it, as I'd seen in the photo, rested the mud sculpture, the sickly-sweet smell of damp manure rising from her. What Officer Ursula's snaps hadn't shown clearly was the raw nakedness of her, including the prominent genitals, and the faint, maybe even imaginary outline of two bodies on the sculpture, as if the Cochton brothers had pressed themselves down. I averted my eyes. The image was too repulsive, even for someone who'd sampled caveman sex.

The far end of the storeroom was partitioned off with shower curtains. Someone sang from behind the partition, "As is above, so be below. Help us now, oh divine unknown."

"What cheer," Newton called out. "Show yourself, man."

Paracelsus came from behind a partition at the far end of the storeroom. He held a flask in one hand and a blood sausage in another.

"We have company," Newton told him.

"I see," said the alchemist. "We've met before, I believe."

"Yes, I'm Stella Smithfailed, from the laboratory above you. I gave you a tour and we had lunch together once."

"Stella Smithfailed, thank you for your help in securing our laboratory. How do you like our bier?"

"I haven't tried it," I replied, confused. "I do like Bohemian beer."

"He means the platform."

I couldn't manage another lie. "I'm shocked, to be honest."

"As any moral person would be," Newton said. "What has been seen can't be unseen."

"Where is the science?" I blurted out. "This is proto-science."

"Alchemy is as much art and religion as it is science. As above, so is below is our motto, calling the heavens and earth to join together to transform. Hope gives us power."

"Oink! Even hope bows before Mother Nature. You need her permission to succeed."

"You are correct. We have failed to transform the mud and the seed from our leaders into homunculi. Our beliefs were not enough. All is lost. There's no sign of life. Newton, it will be back to the grave for us. We'll leave all of this glorious food." He bit into the sausage nervously.

"What's gotten into you, man? This isn't healthy."

"I know, but it is delicious. We'll be hanged or worse. All is lost!"

"It's not," I said. "I came to review the site and the sculpture. We'll add the infants. They are forming as we speak."

"You have homunculi?"

"In a certain form, yes."

"Newton, this woman has the alchemical spirit. She believes in the miraculous. Such a ray of light in this dreary existence of ours."

I wasn't used to being overtly appreciated. It made me uncomfortable. To add to the discomfort, Paracelsus grabbed my hands and bobbed up and down.

Someone knocked on the door. "Open up!" The door unlocked and Officer Ursula and her kid came in.

"I sensed a disturbance. Are you safe?"

"As safe as one can be making merry," Paracelsus said, dropping my hands and pouncing on her gleefully, grabbing her hands. "Join in and follow me. Dance with me!" She was ambushed by his boisterousness. He pranced around the mud woman, pulling the officer along.

"Mom," said the daughter. "Stop having fun."

"Jump on my back!" he called to the girl. "There's plenty of room." I was reminded of a game I played with Dad, Catch the Crook, where I'd leap on him. I'd grab his neck as he spun around, playing the part of the crook. At last, he'd tumble gently to the couch, my captive. The girl did the same. Paracelsus tripped and his red cap fell to the ground.

"Angel, easy," her mother said, as the Vice Patrol agent swooped to retrieve the cap.

"You are light on your feet for a woman weighed down by utensils."

"And you dance well for a man dodging a mud woman with a child on his back."

"I'm great at many things."

"As am I."

The trio lurched past us, Paracelsus humming a tune. Angel accidently, I think, kicked me in the face as they passed.

"Yow!" I held my cheek. The smell of manure on top of the mild pain was overpowering. I was going to faint.

"Sorry, loser! Not my fault."

"Angel, legs down. She's not a criminal."

Newton put an arm around my waist. "Here, hold on to me. Put your hand on my shoulder. Take my other hand. I'll move your body while we move. Dancing is wrong, it's a sin, but it's safer this way. We move when they move." He took my hand and pulled me close enough to create an attraction, a combination of nervous energy and familiarity. I'd not experienced anything like this since riding Dad's back. At first, I tripped and resisted his embrace. It seemed like something to struggle against like a chute in a slaughterhouse. I stiffened.

"It was only a suggestion," he said, holding me less tightly. "Would you like me to release you?"

No. No. I'm not used to closeness. "No, hold me."

He swayed and walked through the room carrying me with him. I clutched his hands and stepped when he did, turned when he did, clung to his warmth, my eyes closed slightly to banish the emotions. I buried my face in his frilly shirt to keep away the manure smell. How could this poor man live like a captive here? He was less perfect than a caveman but closer and more intelligent. I clung to this moment of touch and warmth. It was pathetic how I worked and strove here at Cochton Enterprises and all I'd wished for was one day of rented touch after which I'd come back to work and do it all again, yearning for a moment of warm flesh and a flash of intimacy. It made the deception I was working on less evil, didn't it? Or was I deluding myself?

The mood was broken when Sir Gotfried came in. We stopped our frolic and stood apart from each other.

"Great news! The babies will be featured on *Cochtonia Today*. How are they coming? Have you detected a heartbeat?"

"Yes," I said. I was referring to my own heartbeat so it wasn't a lie. "Hold off on the feature. It's too early for an announcement."

"Yes, bad luck," Paracelsus added.

"Inviting the evil eye," Newton added.

"I'll need to bring in officers for security,'" Ursula said. "It will take time."

"When will the public be allowed to view the project?"

"A month," I said, immediately wishing I'd said nine months. "Two months. They can't be disturbed at the embryonic stage."

"I appreciate your enthusiasm but this isn't your project, Smithfailed."

"She is correct," Newton said. "They can't be disturbed."

"Why are so many people in this space gallivanting around if these babies are so delicate?"

"This isn't *any* project," Paracelsus said. "It requires what you might call magical thinking. We are here, doing a special dance to promote magical thinking, not, whatever you call it, gallivanting."

"It's entertaining. This should be recorded for the public." Sir popped candy corn in his mouth.

"Eating in front of us is bad luck if you don't share," Ursula's kid said.

Gotfried put his hands in his pockets. "I don't believe in luck. In a month, we need to have evidence of a homunculus or two or we will suffer the consequences."

CHAPTER THIRTEEN

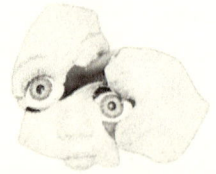

Over the next few weeks, Newton hung around my lab each day. I'd block the door with a chair and we'd reach in the water bath and each pull out a rectangular mold with a tendril poked in, still attached to a mother plant growing inside the chamber. Newton was utterly joyful with a childlike wonder about the project. At his insistence, we recorded the diameter of each tendril inserted into the mold and made observations on its color and turgidity. The tendrils got thicker, longer, firmer, and greener until I too was overcome with enthusiasm for our venture. Thick stems would mean the plant material had filled the molds. I treasured Newton's daily visits to see the project. If this was the hill I'd die on, I'd die happy. I'd found my lab partner. He was out of my league but I'd found him, and I hadn't even been looking. And he had no idea.

The end of the month approached too quickly. It was time to sever the connection between the babies and their mothers and get them growing on their own, ideally in the mud of the sculpture. This was a dangerous moment. They could die, they could be formless blobs we'd have to pass off as molar pregnancies, or we'd mess up the sculpture by inserting them. The first step would be cutting the cord.

On the day of the cut, I waited a bit for Newton to show, in case he wanted to be part of this event, but when he didn't come at his usual time, I removed a mold from the stainless-steel tub I'd hidden it in. It looked like nearly nothing on the outside, like a stone, but so light. I put the mold on the black work bench surface. The tendril stretched between the plant and the mold. Something was in the mold, growing. I had to set it free. I moved to the tool drawer in the lab. Scissors or scalpel? Scalpel. I used this, on occasion, to cut a length of rubber tubing. I poured some ethanol into a beaker, grabbed a scalpel, and swished it in the alcohol. It seemed pointless when all I was going to do was put whatever was in the mold into manure, but habits were hard to break—nearly superstitions.

The scalpel was old but had a new blade. It was smaller than a knife, with grooves on each side for the thumb and forefinger. The handle fit just right in my hand. I hunched over the tendril cord tethering the plant to the growing homunculus. *Cut close, cut long, cut in the middle.* Cut close, or the penis will be comical. My hand shook. I sliced down, severing the stem precisely two inches from the mold.

"I find you attractive."

My hand shot up in an involuntary startle. A man yelled. I swirled around, still holding the scalpel. It was Newton, applying pressure to his right middle finger with his left hand.

"Newton, what are you doing? Are you hurt?"

"It's a scratch. I shouldn't have scared you."

"You're bleeding!"

"Much is pouring from me. Have you a rag? I'm leaking."

"Put your hand on the work counter while I get a bandage. I've got a first aid kit somewhere." I rummaged through the nearest drawer and then the next. *Wrenches. Vials. Electrodes.*

I dug under a drawer of old data charts, totally useless paper things. I might have gotten arrested if the Vice Patrol had seen them. Paper was frowned upon for being too secretive. Beneath them were several compasses, a knife, and a wrench. There was the rectangular box under it all. The first aid kit. I opened it and took out an aerosol can. By now, his blood was all over the chamber. "Hold out your finger. It's a spray-on bandage. I aimed and sprayed. More blood spattered across the chamber, some landing all over the plants. The bleeding stopped.

"There," I said. *What was it you were saying?*

"I made a mess for such a small cut."

"It's easy to clean. There's a hose right here on the faucet and drains on each end of the work space."

"You cut the baby free!" he said, noticing the mold, slightly blood spattered.

"We need to make a move," I said. "Science runs on extreme patience but it's no virtue at the moment."

"Yes. The time dials short." We gazed at each other. A shiver ran through me.

"If the stem holds firm, we need to open the mold," I said.

"Here's to a firm stem. Forgive me for intruding on your cutting."

"Forgive my unwarranted reaction."

"My balls say reaction is inevitable. There is no action without a reaction."

He was talking about a Newton's cradle device, which used firm balls to demonstrate conservation of momentum. "Inevitable. I'll keep it in mind. What were you saying when you came in?"

"I'm attracted to your...to your stability."

"So stable I jumped out of my skin and cut you?"

"I'm sorry I surprised you."

"You did in many ways." Was I having arrhythmia? My heart was losing its mind and flapping like a flat tire.

"You can tell how much attraction bodies have for each other by observing their travels together. It's the inverse square law. Have you heard of it?" Did he draw closer, or did I imagine it?

"Yes, but hearing it from you helps me understand it so much better." I was sure I was flushed by now. Was he coming on to me? It would be a dream come true.

"The more attraction, the more time spent close."

"Close can be pleasant."

Yes, he came close but didn't touch me. It was maddening, as if I was involved with Midas. "Stella, you've given me something to do, something to ponder, something to measure, something to look forward to. Now, you might be saving my life. Is there anything I can do to repay you?

Help me find my... I should ask for help finding Bigg Gib. It's why I started this helpful task. Now was the time.

"You mentioned you were good at finding missing persons," I said.

"In my past, I found a notorious coin clipper."

"Did you relearn all your memories?"

"I'm uncertain. Perhaps some remain buried in obscurity. In any case, you are helping me. How may I help you?"

His eyes were so deep and brown. I couldn't ask for the favor now. Maybe I never was going to. I understood why this was called falling. *Is this guy for real? And is he really Isaac Newton? Do I even care?*

"Newton, I need help finding..."

I was being buried by his eyes. I was covered over with their softness, their depth.

"I need..." *A kiss. A warm, wet kiss.* A horrible realization hit me. I was not good enough for the real Isaac Newton.

"I need help cutting the stem." *And a kiss, I need a spontaneous, impulsive kiss, launching me on a journey of no return.*

"Certainly," he said. Did I detect a hint of disappointment or was I imagining it?

Newton ran his hand across the stem. "It's firm." He measured its diameter. "An inch and a half round. Three inches long. It's grown slightly and has good turgor."

I ran my hand across the stem. "No matter what its units, indeed it's full of life and succulent in appearance. I must conclude it's safe to cut. Now, where's the scalpel?" The scalpel was flung down on the work space where I'd dropped it when Newton yelped. I cursed myself for my carelessness. On the other hand, I'd found it.

"I concur. It's the hour to make another slice. May I do the honors?" Newton asked. "If you trust me."

I handed him the scalpel. "I trust you."

"Thank you. I've missed the hand work that comes with experimenting. Science is really the whole ball of wax—mind, body, concentration, daydreaming." He held the tendril and made a slanted slice far from the mold. Clear liquid dripped out of both ends. He inspected the end of the cut on the mother plant. "It's nearly transparent inside without any organization, like gelatin." He touched his cut finger to each end of the cut plant. "We share a bond, dear shrub, although you have no muscles and no form. The deed is done. I've released you from your umbilical state. How wonderful life is in its many forms! Thank you for your contribution." He turned to me. "How did you stimulate the growth?"

"I added a growth accelerator called Bean Stalk and some enzymes from fast-growing mustard seeds. I also added some Crassulacean Acid metabolizer. It should help them live with less water. I put some enzymes in the molds. Enzymes are catalysts, but they are sensitive to temperature and chemical environment. A catalyst helps molecules get over an energy hill and into the valley of reaction. It makes slow reactions speed up."

"You're brilliant! I love hearing those words roll off your tongue. You're superior to Shakespeare. I've been lonely here, surrounded by small minds."

"It's an honor to work with you."

"I worked alone more than I should have. I was misunderstood and I misunderstood others."

"When you were repelled by the blood sausage, I knew we shared a bond."

"And now what?"

We kiss. We embrace. No, we are strictly lab partners. "We need to open the mold."

I took the silicone rectangle in my hands. "This is it. I'm terrified. Should I pull the mold apart quickly or slowly?"

"Slowly I'd say or you will crack off the erect portion."

"I was thinking the same."

"I'll hold the bottom, while you raise the top."

I gave Newton the mold. "Here goes."

I ran my hands around the seam in the mold, the place where the two halves met. Only the marks I'd made in the bottom mold, where the top had flowed in, were holding them together. But what if by taking off the top, the baby ripped apart? What if there was no plant growth inside? I wanted to help Newton and equally as much, to impress him. My pride was on the line. With trepidation, I seized the top half of the mold, working to keep my hands from trembling. My nerves screamed to yank it up and get it over with. Slowly, I carefully lifted the top mold, my guts churning at the thought of breaking off part of the casting and from being near Newton, so close I could feel his warmth as he stared at me intently. He smelled like dust, or maybe like stardust, the stuff of which we all were made.

The first half of the mold came off more easily than I'd planned. It lifted and there, beneath it, was a copy of Jelly, pale protoplasm, a smooth, solid gel, covered with a thin coat of wax, a green tinge and a blush of red on the cheek. Except for the featureless straw penis, this was a perfect cast. I giggled in relief.

"Eureka!" Newton gushed, "It's beautiful." He ventured a finger and stroked the cast-baby lightly on the arm. "It's solid and sturdy! How did it get the rosy cheek? It looks like blood in an egg."

"It's yours!" I said excitedly, like a child. "Your blood spattered in the chamber and somehow got into the pulp. It adds a human touch."

He laughed. I hadn't seen him happy before, had I? "You did it! An expert forgery. For better or worse, I appreciate the desperation and craft going into forgery now."

The perfection of the plant homunculus added a new layer of worry—how to not mess up this accomplishment.

"I'm at a loss about removing the second half. Should I flip the baby over? I'll have to lift off the mold. What sort of surface should we rest our baby on? I don't want to crack anything off," I said.

Newton was fixated on our project. "I'll hold him, you can pull off the mold."

"Alright, I'll flip the rectangle into your hands. Are you ready? Catch."

He took the baby in both hands as I tipped him face down. As Newton cradled the Jelly doppelganger, his straw between Newton's fingers, I gently removed the bottom of the mold to show the tiny rear end, the hint of a spine, the bitty ears.

"Ahh," I said in relief.

"We have a homunculus. No one promised what the composition would be. It's a male child and alive."

"I suppose we must plant it in the woman and pull it out when asked. It's what I planned, but it's so adorable." He handed me the baby. It was firm, yet the arms and legs and neck were floppier than the dolls. "I want to wrap it in a blanket." I pulled it to my chest instinctively. *And hold it to my breast. Wow. What a weird thought.*

"Mother will keep him warm. If we insert it into the sculpture, we might as well do both infants at the same time. It will create less disturbance," he said.

"Yes, good plan."

"You know," he said, "reproduction is somewhat of a scam. You feel it is your purpose in life, but the result is more generally miserable human life forms. We start in shit and dust and end in it as well. I commend myself for not reproducing. I applaud you for doing the same. We've improved on humanity with these plant infants, don't you agree? No suffering. No betrayal. Life raw and without complications. Ecce innocentes. Behold the innocent."

But we are not at all innocent. We're frauds. "I hope they pass inspection." I wasn't at all convinced of my plan, but being near Newton had me high.

"We will convince everyone of their worth. No one has experience with a homunculus. The expectations should be wide open. The demand was for a tiny man-child. Here he is. Shall we unlock the second infant?"

I took a deep breath. "Yes, I'm ready." I'd be lying if I didn't say I wasn't a little sentimental about this next baby, the one from the stretched tendril. Opening these babies was so intimate. It made me close to Newton in a way I hadn't been with other people. This would end our time together and mark a turning point—continue as a pair or part. "This one is from a shorter tendril."

"As am I." *It's why I am so attached to it, and him.*

We wrapped the first baby in my lab coat and repeated our procedure, me removing the top mold first. The baby stared up at us, much like the first. Maybe he was a little smaller and greener but there he was, endowed and open eyed at his birth.

"Another triumph!" said Newton.

"Let's get him all the way out."

Newton palmed the baby while I gently tugged the mold.

"It's stuck!"

"Shake the mold ever so slightly."

"Jiggle the mold," I said under my breath as I shook the mold.

"Peel the edges slowly," Newton said nervously.

My hands shook. "We only need one baby, yet I so much want two."

"Yes, I prefer to outdo myself if possible."

The baby plopped out of the mold into Newton's waiting palms as a shaft of sunlight beamed through the window. The back of his head was missing a chunk. It wasn't a huge chunk, the size of a few kernels of corn but alarmingly imperfect.

"Ick," I said. "It's so ghastly! We can't use this one."

"Nonsense, science gives us hope for remedying the wrongs nature inflicts upon us. I'd say to cover it with milk snow—cream stirred with a willow branch in the cold. However, you have little cold here."

"Hold on to him, I'll give him a temporary plug." I searched through the lab for something to put over the divot, rummaging through drawers until I found an old package of chewing gum. I opened it and took out a stale stick. "Open your mouth and chew this." My fingers brushed Newton's lips as I inserted the gum.

"It's like sap with mint."

"I'm going to use it to cover the dent. I'd do it myself but want something with male-only saliva. These need to be all-male. Let me know when your stick is soft."

"It might take a while for softness to reveal itself." For a man who had warned me not to touch him, he stood close, chewing, the imperfect infant dangling in his hands. "It's masticated."

"Let me have it, if you please." I put my hand beneath his mouth. Timidly, but skillfully, he pushed the chewed gum into my hand with his tongue. I stretched a portion of the gum into a semi-translucent membrane that blended pretty well with the rest of the head. Carefully, I affixed it, covering the dent. Surprisingly, it stuck like putty.

"Fine work. The best tailor couldn't have done it better!"

"It's on solidly," I said joyfully. "Ah, he looks more complete now with the head dent covered."

"They are marvels of science and imagination. Should we introduce them to their mother?"

"Yes, it's time."

CHAPTER FOURTEEN

I unwrapped my lab coat and exposed the first baby. Paracelsus took him.

"Wondrously made and delightfully waxy. I am in awe!" He put the floppy plant infant on the belly of the woman.

Newton carried in the weaker baby, the one with the patched head. He tenderly drew him out of his jacket.

"Two! Two miracles!" Paracelsus was joyful.

They rested on the mud, maybe they moved some, yes, they reached, as a weak animal might.

"Ho, are they animated?"

"Fully living," Newton said, beaming.

The doll-shaped plants were my pride and joy. "I hate to bury them, but I'm sure they need some nutrients." I froze. "We need dirt to put over them! I have a growth mixture but it's clear. Have you extra manure?"

"No, it was removed after I completed my work. This is all we have. Perhaps Mother can lose a leg?" Paracelsus offered. "Or even her head?"

My vision hadn't extended far enough. After all this work, the final step was marred by an imperfect plan. "No, this place lives for ceremony. We can't present a headless mother. I must get manure or, even better, have some brought in covertly."

"Where there is meat, there is manure." Paracelsus stated the obvious.

"Too bad there aren't horses handy," Newton mused.

Someone's stomach growled. Paracelsus patted his belly. "I could eat a horse. Ever done it, Newton?"

"Good Lord, no! How churlish to mention such barbarism."

"I'm not anemic."

As I listened to the talk of meat, an idea presented itself. "There's one place nearby with meat—the cafeteria," I said. "We must get blood sausage at lunch. I can grind it, sterilize it, mix it with growing compound, and it will resemble mud enough. I can't think of anything else. Newton, will it offend you?"

"As long as none passes our lips, I support the plan, although it's hasty and undignified. Everything about this project is degrading."

As soon as 11 a.m. hit, we hurried to the cafeteria.

"I'll take ten blood sausages and a serving of salmagundi," I said, trying to be casual.

"The same for me. *Bitte*," Paracelsus said.

"I'm ravenous. How about a dozen?" Newton added.

"Two sausage per person, max," said the server, dishing up our trays.

We sat together at a table, hoping no one would notice as we slipped the sausages in our sleeves.

"This won't be enough," I grumbled.

"We can order some for supper," Newton said. "We are brought a light meal before being locked up for the night."

"Locked up?"

"Yes, totally sequestered."

"How do you—?"

"Chamber pot."

"And—"

"Doors unlock at dawn. There's a vacant laboratory at the end of your hall where we pull a chain and water rushes out."

"A safety shower? Those are to be used for chemical splashes or fires."

"It's invigorating and I urinate down the drain sometimes," said Paracelsus.

Other employees walked past us. The alchemists were an everyday presence now, less sensational than when they'd first arrived. We ate alone.

"Spend more time with us and you'll be called our Altotus, or our guide," Paracelsus remarked.

"I'm going to be ill instead of illustrious," Newton said, standing. "People are too close and watching them chew the blood sausages is like being in the midst of a plague of grasshoppers."

We took our trays to the conveyor belt for dirty dishes. They were swept away, into a hole where a worker would put them into a dishwasher. Newton and I hurried off, the hidden sausages rubbing our arms, as Paracelsus stood watching the conveyer belt.

Newton was irritated. "Make haste!"

Paracelsus grabbed a half-eaten sausage from a tray and hustled after us. I lead them to my lab and put our six and a half sausages in a blender. My idea was to grind them and disperse the particles in the growth gel. I wanted this to look as much like mud, or mud with stretch marks, as possible. I whirled them into a sausage smoothie. I'd add this to the transparent growth gel I'd used for the propagation.

"We can only get six whole sausages, but there are abundant sausage fragments," Paracelsus said joyfully. "We must get more. We want deep, dark mud, after all."

"You're right, and we don't have nearly enough." I grabbed another autoclave bag. "Let's get some more."

We took the stairs down a floor.

As we approached the cafeteria, Paracelsus stopped. "Newton and I are too obvious. Stella, you'll have to snatch the sausages."

"Okay," I said, pulling on some plastic gloves. I wasn't going to handle half-eaten blood pudding with my bare hands.

"We must keep watch," Newton said, "and give some sort of call if danger approaches."

"An owl hoot," Paracelsus suggested.

"No, my good sir," Newton said. "Have you looked out the window? There are no trees. Thus, no owls. You'll have to sing one of your songs."

"Brilliant! You must give one of your lectures about laws of motion, and if anyone comes to investigate the sausage stealing, I'll burst into verse."

"There's the plan," said Newton. "As we distract, Stella will purloin the used sausages. As revolting as that sounds, we lack the time to conceive a better strategy."

As they entered the cafeteria, I ducked into the conveyor belt area behind the three pillars. I lurked near the pillars, the bag slung over my shoulder, pretending to be deeply engrossed with my device. The first people to dispose of their trays were "clean-platers." I could feel my shoulders slumping. I cheered up when the self-starving media crew came along. Yup. Each had taken only one bite of the sausage. I grabbed four sausages before the trays went into the hole. I stood back, leaning on a pillar, as Newton gave a lecture.

"During my life, the great ocean of truth lay its pebbles before me. As I was isolating from the plague, I had time to ponder and I saw that the Earth and an apple and the Earth and the moon were tethered by the same force. The force diminishes as the objects grow distance according to the inverse square law."

Someone from accounting came past, leaving a nub of sausage on her tray.

"And yet, the most mysterious of all was the secret world of chemical matter and the wonders of alchemy."

Several Sirs strode past, leaving trays with tiny bits of sausage.

"In alchemy, each planet has a symbolic element. Jupiter and tin are interchangeable, for example, and are cheerful spirits, hoping to both cure and preserve."

A pack of advertisers left trays and I snatched several half sausages.

"Copper is the looking glass of Venus, with a deep allure, and tinctures can be made to promote both love and lust."

The IT crew only picked at their food. I seized the leftovers as fast as I could as the trays zipped past. I put a nibbled sausage in the bag as Paracelsus burst into his song, "As is above so become below."

Warned, I headed back toward my lab with a bulging autoclave bag full of food scraps.

"Hold up! I've gotten complaints about you stealing food." It was Officer Ursula, with another agent by her side.

"I'm not stealing food. I'm-I'm taking samples." I hoped my face didn't reflect how startled I felt. "I'm a food scientist. I want to study when people stop eating these blood sausages. We could make them shorter and save money if people aren't eating them all."

"Great idea. Need any help?"

Help from the Vice Patrol was the last thing I wanted. I had to get this done quickly without them—or anyone—seeing the plant babies sprawled out, uncovered on the mother.

"It's so mundane. I don't need assistance, but thanks."

"It's a trap," said the other agent, a woman with twinkly glasses. "I detect a ruse of some sort. No sane person collects sausage scraps. These are suspicious sausages."

"Sausages aren't suspicious," Ursula said, irritated. "Plenty of women want to study sausages."

Paracelsus and Newton came around the corner and rushed to my rescue.

"Come, we aren't done talking about the planets," Paracelsus said, taking Ursula's hand.

"Can you put it on ice while I escort Stella to her lab? We don't want the sausages harmed."

"Hurry back. Saturn is fascinating and it has a ring around it."

We all took the elevator to the second floor. The smell of sausage spice permeated the car.

"I know more about sausages than you think," Ursula said as we walked to my lab. "Although these are not true sausages. The texture is different, as well as the firmness."

"Kind of like when a rendering truck turns over," said the agent with glasses.

"We mature women are talking about sausages, not meat by-products," Ursula said. "You're making the case for Crisper Vice Patrol painfully clear."

The agent pushed up her glasses and blinked at me. "Are you going to have us help with the sausages?"

"No, I need to concentrate," I said, using her chattiness as an excuse. "Alone. Excuse me, Officers." I was taking a risk refusing them as I stood next to my lab door.

"We need to check in on this concentrating," she said. "Right?"

"Briefly," said Ursula. "I must get back to Saturn, after all."

They followed me into the lab. I'd left the tape measurer sitting out, but, to my horror, the baby molds were still in the hood inside of the stainless-steel tub. Fortunately, plants grew in front, obscuring the tub.

"I swear I've seen those plants before," Ursula said.

"Let's measure the sausages over here by the window," I said, moving them as far away from the growth chamber as possible. "The light is beautiful and you can see the river. Here's a box of plastic gloves you can use to keep your hands clean."

Sweat popped up on my neck. Ursula was friendly, but friendship didn't stop the Vice Patrol from turning you in. I tried to make this task as dull as possible.

"Each of us should measure the same sausage. The results will be averaged."

"It's overkill," said Ursula.

"It'll take forever," said the agent.

"It's science," I said. "It bears repeating. We need precision and accuracy. Newton and Paracelsus were pioneers in measurement. No one-offs."

"If they say so," Ursula replied.

"How about you read the numbers and I'll record them? We'll also need to measure whole sausages. I've got some here. Let's get started before we get any shrinkage."

Ursula held up an unevenly chomped sausage. "Do I measure to the far end?"

"Measure the close end and the far end and report the average."

"I'll need a calculator."

"Science is too complicated," said her partner. "Who thought studying sausages would be so boring?"

"I've got to get out of here before my love of sausages is killed completely," Ursula said. "If you were attempting to put us to sleep, you've done it."

"I guess I'm on my own, saving Cochtonia from sausage waste," I said, waving good-bye. "Give Saturn my regards."

The few minutes they were with me had been torture. Alone at last, I dove for the blender on the counter. I popped in a batch of sausage fragments, ground them, then repeated with more sausage until I had more brown mush.

After time in the autoclave to kill any germs and an impatient half hour cooling on the counter, I mixed the mush with growth gel—the same stuff I'd used to propagate the plants. The "manure" was ready to be applied.

I used a beaker to scoop the sticky moist crumbles into a cast iron pan, left out from an experiment I'd forgotten. I put it on a laboratory cart and wheeled it to the basement. It resembled chocolate cake batter. No one looked at me with the slightest curiosity. It was like every day. I tapped on the door. "It's me." The alchemists weren't yet back, even after nearly an hour. Things were always way more complicated than they should have been. I felt like a corncob in a hog's jaws.

In frustration, I pushed the cart into the door, tapping it, making a sound a little louder than a knock. The door responded with a faint tick, like a latch being thrown. I tapped it again. Click. And again. Click. I turned the knob. It opened. I didn't have time to wonder why. I pushed the cart in and locked the door behind me.

The babies were beautiful as ever, resting on the mud, snuggling in slightly, possibly sprouting roots on their heads. Reluctant to dig into the woman, I poured sterilized "manure" over the first baby, starting with the feet. I dumped more on the belly and at last, buried the head with the unblinking eyes and puckered mouth. I did the same for the second covering him, as if planting a seed. From the front, he looked as passive and thoughtless as the other homunculus. I smoothed the mounds over with my gloved hands, uniting them and creating a "belly" on the mother, stretched over the two homunculi. *Now to destroy the molds.*

My gloves were dirty from my sausage concoction and they smelled slightly of sage. I put them on the cart, opened the door, and peeked out into the hall. Sir Gotfried strode down the corridor, a team of women, one with camera, one with an umbrella light, and two extraneous ones on his elbows. They were well groomed, attractive and aware of it, pleasing to the Cochton brothers' eyes, survival savvy, and Sir was eating out of their hands.

I closed the door. *The publicity team is coming this way. Why am I here? I'm not supposed to be here.*

I grabbed my cart and shoved it into Newton's bedroom as the team burst through the door, Newton and Paracelsus close behind the camera operators.

"Halt!" Newton yelled. "You'll disturb the process."

He and Paracelsus looked amazed to see me, my hands behind my back, in front of the woman's swollen belly.

"You've interrupted the caretaking," Paracelsus said. "Clearly the woman is in confinement. The infants will be born in due time."

"Who is the interloper?" someone asked.

"It's our Altotus," Paracelsus replied.

Newton pulled me close. "She's our escort, our guide."

The camerawomen zoomed in on me, then cut to the mud, the belly. A second woman held the umbrella light over the "mud".

"Her belly looks silty. She is expanding," stated the interviewer. "The woman is larger and has a pleasant, earthy scent. How did it happen? Alchemy is miraculous!"

The interviewers peppered the alchemists with questions.

"Is there one homunculus or two?"

"Will they be fed formula or have a wet nurse?"

"When will we see more?"

"When will they be born?"

The abdomen quivered. The room was silent. The soil heaved as if taking a breath. It shuddered. It cracked. A tiny hand, white with a greenish hue, peeked through the mud and reached out with a wave. The videographer fell back in surprise as all in the room gasped. I gripped Newton's arm. Paracelsus took a drink of laudanum. "God help us."

The videographer moved in. The hand waved with a cupped palm. Next to the hand, a foot kicked to the surface, toes straining upward, stuck together as Jelly's were.

Newton sprang into action with quick thinking. "I forewarn the citizens, the infants will resemble frogs at first, as with any homunculus. With careful training and a proper boarding school, they will become boys, and then heirs."

"How will they be born? Will they bust out? Will they be delivered?"

"You'll find out when we're ready. Now get out, you foul harpies," Newton said, grabbing the umbrella light and hurling it at the door.

"Enough!" Paracelsus removed his cap and waved it at the interlopers. "You'll dry the mud with your hot breaths. Get out!" The publicity team backed away and Paracelsus slammed the door behind them. "Can you imagine—women wearing heels?"

"I apologize for my outburst. The untrimmed eyelashes were

disturbing," Newton added. "In my day, women removed the eye hair. These added to it! Why is beauty so fickle?"

Gotfried sobbed. "It's true, you did it! What a miracle!" He moved to hug Newton who dodged him. He embraced me as consolation. "Stella, I'm sorry I so often overlooked you. It's a winner! The babies will be presented at the festival. The Cochtons have ordered you alchemists to birth them in front of a live audience. Birth them in real time so all of Cochtonia can experience the event."

"I've helped women in childbirth many times," Paracelsus said cheerfully. "Never one made of mud."

"You're saying we appear in public, with this batch of mud, and pull the infants from it."

I knew this day was coming, but the immediacy of it now hung heavy upon me. "Can't this be done remotely? These are infants. They haven't got developed immune systems."

"I'm uncomfortable with crowds," Newton said. "It might disturb the fabric of the universe to make this into a show. It's delicate work, alchemy."

"Alchemists, you're not alive by your own choice. You owe life to the Cochton Brothers. Your continuation depends on keeping them happy. They are big into pageantry. We will celebrate the arrival of the babies with a festival with the entire town in attendance, or at least, invited. Prepare them for the event, Stella, and help the alchemists get ready."

The mud mother was prone on her back. Pale green wiggly toes poked through her belly. We looked at the mud, smooth but punctuated with an occasional bump from a kick.

"Newton, brilliant mention of their resemblance to frogs," I said.

"It's one way to explain their color, clamminess, and vacant stare. And Stella, once again, you're a genius." Newton embraced me in a non-Newtonian way. "Your surreptitious mud saved the day!"

"Today is saved but what about tomorrow?" I remarked. "They

aren't going to stay inside much longer. They're searching for sun."
I poked a set of toes back under the "skin."

"How will we keep the babies alive once they are removed from
the womb? They will be like crops torn up after a war," Paracelsus
was frantic and intoxicated.

"They will at least be able to be taken out to show the public.
We can arrange some way of parading them about." My mind
scrambled for a solution. A doll. A stroller. I had one, didn't I?
Unlike Jelly, which represented lost motherhood to Mom, the doll
buggy had been considered too bulky to store in my bedroom once
I was too old to push my doll up and down the driveway in it. It
was in the basement, wasn't it? No, I hadn't seen it. The attic.
Surely it was too filled with memories to have been discarded.

"I'll get a pram with some dirt in the bottom," I said, thinking
aloud. "I have one for my original baby doll and I can get a little
mud from the side of my driveway."

"How long can they remain removed from their soil?"

"They'll need to go back somewhere to get nutrients and water
and live as normal plants eating the sun."

"Eating the sun? As if the sun were drops of energy?" Newton
said.

"Yes, it's called photosynthesis."

"I knew it! Another one of my predictions is truth."

"Yes, you're a genius," Paracelsus said wearily. "I am a plant
expert; my knowledge of their ways is renown. They'll grow. How
can they keep their shape?"

"They won't, they're a hybrid and what they'll become is
uncertain. They might keep their shape and not need the soil, but
otherwise could revert to vines." I locked the door. "In case the
worst happens, we must insist on the display as soon as possible.
But after that, I don't know. You'll have to escape in some fashion.
We'll have to escape. They'll have to catch a disease and die once
they're sent off for training. You're geniuses, after all. You'll find a
way."

I went to Sir Gotfried's office. He was popping candy corn.

"Have some."

"Thank you." I took a handful and ate one. What did candy corn taste like? Vanilla? Marshmallow?

"Good stuff, not offensive. A safe flavor. It's like ice cream without the fat." Sir wiped his mouth. "What's on your mind? Do you have something to get off your chest?"

I was scared to say what I needed to say. I was afraid to have the babies in the public eye, but I couldn't wait, either.

Sir wiped his mouth again. "By the way, thank you for your work. Your redeployment to help with the babies is coming at the perfect time."

My fist clenched the candy corn. He'd kicked me in the sugary teeth. "What are you saying?"

"Thank you for your service."

"You're firing me after all my loyal success?"

"Fortunately, you have a gig lined up."

"A gig?"

"As the caretaker for the homunculus. It will be both a thrill and an honor to watch them grow and prosper. Now, what else were you going to tell me?"

I saw red. Blood rushed to my eyes. I was not only fired but stuck with the fake babies.

"I plan on coming back to work, right here, as I have for decades. I'm developing salmagundi. I know nothing about babies. You heard Newton—these infants need to be put into the educational system immediately."

"Virginia, I'm sorry to stick you with this, but it's an order. The Cochtons saw you on the broadcast and said you'd be perfect. What did you come here to tell me? How can I help?"

How will I be executed? "I've consulted with the alchemists. The birth is imminent. We must have the christening as soon as possible."

He picked up his phone. "I'll get on it." He motioned to the candy. "Take some with you."

CHAPTER FIFTEEN

I pulled down the rickety set of stairs to the attic. They were so steep I climbed up with my hands on each stair instead of standing up. Like the basement, this place was packed with worthless memories. The only difference was the attic was harder to get to and hot in the summer, cold in the winter, with four feet of headspace.

Stooped over, I surveyed racks of old clothes, the door wreaths decorated with corn and little pigs—plastic of course—and a forgotten plastic ear-of-corn-shaped bucket used to hold popcorn on Cochtonville Days. Shafts of light from where the rafters didn't meet the floor stabbed through. This house was one of many tossed up quickly to house the population taking refuge as the rural areas came under the spell of the Cochton family.

I pushed aside a rack with Mom and Dad's old Vice Patrol uniforms—black bomber jackets. Dad's jacket still had his old name: Barnabus Smithfield, from back in the days when we were still the Smithfields. We had to change our name due to copyright violations; we couldn't have the same last name as a famous brand of ham.

It was difficult to imagine Dad as a man who traveled beyond the safety of his recliner. He was like a pilot who wouldn't fly once retired. Dad's always been a big guy but the virus hit him hard. He retired soon after, as did many Vice Patrol agents. The nation was fortunate to have already invested in Crisper Vice Patrol agents. They weren't the smartest but neither was Dad.

I tried on Mom's jacket. She'd been petite back then and probably strong, as the thing weighed as much as a couple of month-old piglets. I plunged my hands in her pockets, wondering if I'd find a weapon. Beneath a bloom of used tissues was a silver device—an old-school version of the personal scanner known as No Regrets. It detected if people were sexually active, pregnant, or diseased. I scanned my forehead, hoping it would declare me a deviant. The device didn't work anymore, just like me. It would be an easy enough fix – a battery. I'd bring it to life and scan virginal Newton for Sexually Transmitted Infections. We'd see if he was the real Isaac Newton.

My face tickled from dust settled over the clothes. Sweat sprang from my forehead. I put the jacket back on its hanger, next to Mom's old bathrobe. It was a shimmery white. I always teased her it looked like a space suit. I felt in the pockets. Another device, pink in color, oblong. *Just BU* it read. I pushed the button on the front. It vibrated with a faint hum and a fresh charge as a stinging insect might. I pressed a series of buttons until, at last, the frightening thing turned off. I should have left well enough alone but I couldn't. I felt in the other pocket and drew out a tube of something. Personal lubricant. *Intimate moisturizer for genital area.* Mom and moisture? I let it sink in. No! I'd found Mom's sex toy and lube. Weren't these illegal back in her day? No. These weren't old. This was her stash in real time. I had to get out of here!

Stepping away, I stumbled over a wooden rocking chair. A box filled with old socks fell off the chair, the socks tumbling with a snap and a clunk. A snap? A mousetrap lay at my feet. It had been in the socks and set like a booby trap. Or was it there for mice? It was true, being a farming nation, we had a lot of mice.

I righted the box so I could toss the socks back in. It was

weighted down. I looked in. There was something rectangular and made of paper under cardboard. Was this a paper book? Such non-digitized information was able to be read in secret and for this reason, it was illegal! I took it from the box. I read the nondescript gray cover. *Virginia Guru's How-To Guide to Human Sexual Response.* I opened it to a spot near the middle, grateful for my eyes' adjustment to the dim light. *Factors in Orgasmic Achievement. Adequate stimulation is required to initiate sexual tension.* I flipped further back and read, *Near the plateau phase, the penis increases in circumference at the corneal crown, the sensitive bulbous region at its end. At the same time, the vagina becomes constricted with a fifty percent reduction in size. The pre-orgasmic labia may turn red and the penis can take on a purple hue due to vasoconstrictive reactions. Males and females may become flushed in response to sexual tension. Involuntary spasms of pleasure will soon follow.*

A flush of shame and excitement rushed through me. How technical and yet, titillating. It explained my pleasurable convulsions at the hand of Bigg Gib. Such a book was high level contraband. Mom must have confiscated this and kept it for herself. Hadn't she mentioned a book when she was trying to describe Dad as some sexy hunk? The pages were dry and yellowed. Sweat dripped from my nose to the page, across the words *orgasm is inevitable.* I startled. The buggy. I was here for a buggy. I put the book back in its place, vowing to return for more, either on the page or in person.

I found the doll buggy behind the rack of clothes. Nostalgia and reading about human sexual response made my eyes sprout tears faster than corn in June. Additionally, I was terrified. I wanted to live. I wanted to see a penis take on a purple hue. I wanted to grow flowers. I wanted a long life of pleasure spasms. I was nervous and filled with desire. My earthly existence would have been so much better with less apprehension and more plateau phases. I was relying on this old pram to help save my life.

"What's going on up there? Why are you poking around?" It was Mom.

I put the book in the box and went to the top of the stairs.

"I was looking at my old toys. The buggy in particular." I stood there with Mom's earnest face below. I could barely make eye contact after what I'd discovered.

"Do you have anything to tell me?" Mom asked.

"Can you give me a big picture? What kind of thing should I be telling you?"

"Silly, I saw the live event today. It was announced afterwards— you have a new job!" She said it excitedly, as if this was a promotion, and not the loss of my lab and a huge chunk of my identity.

"Oh yeah. I'll be moving on to child care, I guess."

"I never thought I'd see the day. Are you looking for Jelly?"

Jelly had a new meaning for me, as in lubricating jelly. Mom had named the doll. She was kind of a pervert.

The pervert prattled on. "I wondered if you'd thrown her away. I haven't seen her recently. Have you?"

"Yes, Mom. I *have* seen her recently. She's in the basement. In fact, um, I'm planning to take her for a ride. I found my doll stroller and I'm taking it for a walk."

"That old thing? It's got to be filthy."

I was too clumsy to consider coming down with the pram alone. "Get NezLeigh to help me get the buggy down."

"The buggy?"

"Yes, Jelly's doll buggy. The stroller. The pram. I want to push her in it."

"NezLeigh's too big."

"The doll. I want to stroll my doll for practice. Get NezLeigh."

"She's asleep."

"Well, I'm afraid of falling head first, so I guess I'll have to rummage through the old clothes until she shows up."

"Stay right there," Mom said with urgency. "I'll wake her."

Waiting for NezLeigh, I hunched under the one bare bulb, opened the book and read.

Physiologically, most women can achieve orgasm once societal pressures against it have been removed. Within 10-30 seconds of becoming aroused, a female will lubricate herself in readiness.

I closed the book nervously, but curiosity got hold of me and I opened it within seconds. I read in an entirely different spot.

Testes will enlarge and elevate. A male generally achieves two or three explosive occurrences 0.8 seconds apart, often followed by two to four more events. In contrast, the female orgasm persists for a longer time and consists of a series of total pelvic contractions 0.8 seconds apart, with an onset of four to eight episodes followed by two to four events. The male will undergo a refractory period while the female can remain in a state of stimulation.

No wonder LouOtta wanted an orgy. I closed the book again and opened further back.

Although there may be a slowing of response, properly maintained individuals can continue their pleasurable reactions into their eighties.

I laughed. There was still time!

"Why did you need me, Ding Dong?" NezLeigh was being sarcastic from the bottom of the stairs. I hustled the book back into its box.

"Give me a hand, will you?"

"You look damn stupid stuck on top of the stairs."

"I know."

"Tell me why?"

"I'm the new caretaker to the homunculus babies. I need a buggy for them."

"There are babies? That's messed up."

"They are life forms."

"You are a life form nanny."

"I suppose."

"You know what happens to nannies when the kids grow up, don't you? They get sent to the CAFOs."

"It's all I have right now. I have to present them at a ceremony and then, who knows, I'll be out of a job."

"Fuck!"

Once we wrestled the carriage down the stairs, Mom fluttered around it until Dad rose from his recliner and took it outside and washed it with his power washer, set to low.

"It looks so much better, but shouldn't you practice with the one the Cochtons will provide for the real babies?" Mom asked, rinsing off Jelly as Dad gently squirted her.

"Mom, they are strapped for cash following this big project."

"I'm sure they'll appreciate your effort to keep costs down," Dad added. "Put in a good word for my power washing abilities."

"Why was Jelly slippery?" Mom asked. "I found her in the basement totally naked."

A prickle of alarm ran through me. I hadn't covered up my evidence, nor could I easily explain it.

"Mom, why were you naked in the basement?" NezLeigh asked. "It sounds kinky."

"Next time you are naked in the basement, call me," Dad added. "You still got what it takes. I don't think I do but it might be worth a try." He squirted the shape of a heart on the smooth cement driveway before turning the hose on Mom and drenching her in his version of playfulness. She ran to the house to escape, taking the doll with her.

We left the buggy to dry in the end of the day sun and went in to a dinner of blood sausage, which I couldn't eat. Jelly sat on the counter, clean and in footed pajamas. I took her to my room and put her on my dresser, next to the purple crystal from Paracelsus.

I woke at 3 a.m. with a thought pressing with the urgency of a pending orgasm. I had to get rid of Jelly. I had to destroy her. She'd be too obvious once the babies were revealed. I needed to destroy the molds. They were evidence of the deceit. I'd simply left them in my lab like a space cadet.

The smell of bacon hung in the air. NezLeigh was cooking in the kitchen. I couldn't wait until dawn to get rid of the doll. I pulled on my work clothes, took Jelly from the dresser, and walked softly through the living room towards the front door.

"Why are you up, dingbat?" Framed by the doorway, NezLeigh stood, watching me, a plate of meat in her hand. The bacon was at least 40% fat and since she'd arrived, NezLeigh had put some flesh on her bones. She no longer looked like a kid. She'd added womanly cargo to her cargo pants.

"I can't sleep, I'm walking to work early. I've got too much to do. I need to clean out my lab since I'm fired." I tried to hold Jelly low and behind my back so NezLeigh wouldn't see her.

"You should leave it up to the person who fired you."

"I have projects...and it's not up to you."

"I see," she said, as if she knew I was guilty of something. "You and your doll. Is she going to be your lab assistant?"

"I don't need a lab assistant."

"The best people are up now. Enjoy."

I went into the garage, fetched the buggy, tossed Jelly in, and pushed it down the sidewalk. It was smaller than I'd remembered. It was made for a kid to push a doll. I hunched over as it rambled down the sidewalk. My eye twitched as a street light shone on my hair. How would I get rid of the doll surreptitiously? The city was quiet except for the hush of a fan, rumbling over the town. The nearby cereal plant, a wing of Cochton Enterprises, was drying grain for a batch of sweetened corn loops. I'd tested the dye used to color it green, detecting how much of it leeched into a bowl of milk.

I went out onto the bridge. The Cedar River flowed, silty beneath me as I stood looking down, my head as muddy as the water. I'd drop Jelly off the bridge. Would she float if I tossed her in the river? I was afraid of the bridge, scared I'd trip. I didn't even have the guts to throw the doll in the water because it would mean going up to the edge. To make it worse, the bridge railing was wet with dew. *What am I doing? What should I be doing?* Seeking came naturally to me but hiding, sneaking about tossing dolls off bridges, wasn't a part of me. Why was I brought to this bridge by my discontent? I was as empty as a new page in a lab notebook.

Despite the glare of the street lights, a couple of Agro kids joined me on the bridge. They were barefoot and one had a plastic tub with fishing gear and the other a tackle box. "What are you up to, Daytripper?" They danced dangerously close to the edge. The bridge had a railing, but it was open enough they might have slipped through. It made me dizzy to be near them.

"Strolling along with this doll in her carriage, Fly by Nights."

"How about we push?"

"Maybe later. How about you step away from the edge?"

"Damn it, we're not babies! Are you buying or selling?"

This last idea caught my interest. Maybe if I played it right, they would steal the doll. What had Newton done to catch the coin clippers? He'd pretended to be one of them. These people didn't like their kids, and I for sure, didn't like the doll. I was almost one of them.

"I don't need this doll. I'm looking to get rid of her in secret. I was hoping to toss her off the bridge when no one was looking. But now you are here, looking." How easy it was, not even a lie!

"We don't like the Washers," they said, using slang for the Vice Patrol. "You're safe with us."

Damn, how worthless were these kids? They couldn't take a hint at all. At least they'd be seen with me on any sort of surveillance. They'd look guilty even if they weren't. The best I could hope for was some sort of an accident with them and the doll to deflect suspicion from me. Or should I get rid of them? I was paralyzed with indecision, as if a knot had been tied in my brain.

"Why would I care about Washers? It's not illegal to not like your doll."

"Why not toss her in the garbage?"

"It would break Mom's heart to find her there."

"Are you gonna throw the doll over or what?"

"Unless you want the doll. She needs a good home."

"Washer Van's coming."

"Do you want the doll or do I pitch her?"

"We don't take dolls for free."

I pulled out all the change I had and showed it to them. "I'll pay you to steal her."

"This would do for a rental of the doll," one said "You need to cough up more to find it a permanent home."

"A home far away," another added.

"I want the doll destroyed," I said, my eyes on the van as it drew near. Was it Ursula driving? "You can cut her into ribbons and use her for bait. What you catching?"

"Turtles. They won't eat a doll. They want meat and fingers."

It was Ursula with her kid next to her in the front seat.

"Here's a kid who will take the doll," I said. "Your last chance." One girl took Jelly, the other took the money, and off they ran to the bank of the river.

The van pulled up. The side door slid open. Ursula's kid leaned out of the window.

"Get in. You're needed at the office."

CHAPTER SIXTEEN

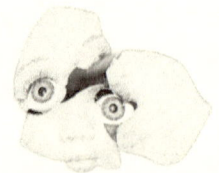

I wasn't sure I wanted to take orders from a child. Yet, I did. I pushed the doll buggy into the van, then sat in a bucket seat, hoping not to have to talk too much. It was early morning, when only crazed workaholics might be out. This wouldn't explain why I was strolling an empty doll pram.

"Sleepwalking?" Ursula asked matter-of-factly.

"I couldn't sleep. There's too much happening at work."

"I'll say!"

"Why were you on the bridge? Were you going to throw that thing off the bridge?" asked her kid. "Were you getting rid of it because it's crap and was too big for the garbage can?"

My stomach clenched and then relaxed. I was relieved to understand she was talking about the doll buggy, not Jelly. This life of deceit was taking a toll.

"No, I need it for the homunculi. I was seeing how easy it is to maneuver."

"You have a stroller for them? Why hasn't one been issued?" Ursula asked.

"I don't know. I'm trying to help. The whole project is a lot of orders without a lot of communication."

"You probably shouldn't have gotten involved to begin with."

"I know."

"You never had a lick of sense anyhow," the kid said, echoing what I'd heard too often in my life.

Ursula turned toward Cochton Enterprises. "When did you leave the house today?"

"About 4 a.m."

"Anyone see you?"

"Yes, my sister. Why? Is something wrong?"

"Would things be right if I had to come in at this hour and take my kid?"

This was it. I'd been busted.

"Has anyone made you do something you didn't want to do lately?" she asked. "Have you been uncomfortable?"

I had to take the blame. The hokey scheme was my brainchild.

"No, it was all my idea."

"You aren't angry about anything?"

"Only at myself."

We parked in front and entered the Cochton Enterprises building. Life-sized statues of Bert and Clarence stood guard, as did a bulky Crisper patrolman.

"Have you any new information?" Ursula asked him.

"No, the crime scene is as you left it," the patrolman said. "The security cameras do not show him leaving for the night or anyone entering."

"What is it? Is it the alchemists?" I could barely take a breath. They were the only ones who lived here 24/7 as far as I knew.

She pushed the *down* button for the elevator. "No, I'd be sobbing if it was them. Get in." We dropped to the basement. The door opened. She shone a light from her device down the hallway toward the former store room, now homunculus incubating station, at the end of the hall.

My mind raced through all the possibilities and I clumsily gave voice to them. "What's happening? Are the homunculi being born? Do they look like frogs?"

"Born? How is that even going to happen? Is the mud woman

going to push them out? Maybe they will pop out? Is the jolly fella going to perform a cesarean? No! But yes, this relates to them."

My heartbeat ticked up further. She scanned the door with her device and it unlocked. She pushed the door with her shoulder and her kid and I followed her in.

A person was on the floor, motionless. I flipped on the lights. It was an older man in a Cochton Enterprises dress uniform.

"Sir! Why?" My worries gave way to an incredulous numbness.

"Appears to be an assault—by him. He had a knife." She held up my scalpel, the one I kept forgetting to put away.

"It's not a knife. It's a scalpel—lab equipment, but why?"

"There's barely a mark on him, but look, his pockets are inside out." He lay on his back, blank eyes on the ceiling, mouth open darkly, a drizzle of blood on his bottom lip, his pockets inside out.

"He's dead?"

"Or he's ugly sleeping," said her kid sarcastically.

"No pulse. No breath," Ursula confirmed. "Angel, run to the van and get the body bag."

I moved closer. Yes, he had a weird empty look. Sir Gotfried was, indeed, dead.

"Oh, the poor man! He didn't deserve this! What happened?"

Ursula scanned the corpse. "Heart attack did him in, but it's not your run of the mill heart attack. The tip of his tongue is missing, as if he bit it off before dying. He appears from the scalpel, to be the aggressor. However, the tongue and the empty pockets are signs of a struggle and a robbery. Did he have any enemies?"

"No, he was the sweetest man. He taught me almost everything I longed to know."

"Secret projects?"

"No. Besides the homunculi, we were propagating salmagundi flowers but it's no secret."

"And you? Do you have anything to tell me?"

"No! How are the infants?" If he'd come to kill the babies, we'd be free of them. I rushed to the mud woman. Her surface was broken, as if she'd been punched. Had the babies been taken? "What did the thief want?"

"They're there. Or at least, something is there. It's got human DNA but doesn't scan as human. Do you have anything to tell me?"

"I didn't rob Sir Gotfried, I adored the man. I've been home rummaging in my attic for the pram. It's in your van."

"Yes, I'll get it to you. I'm not asking about the robbery. Can you tell me about that life form in there? The mud is disturbed. Was he protecting a dark secret hidden in the belly of that creation?" Her words were a snowball on my face. This stupid lie! However, I couldn't betray the alchemists. I'd already experienced Bigg Gib hauled away and I didn't care to see it happen to Newton.

"These are innocent babies, despite their unnatural creation. They have male-only DNA. Officer, your scanner is looking for male and female markers, as found in average humans." I barely knew what I was talking about, so I said this with as much authority as possible. Science always leaves room for doubt based on new evidence, yet I couldn't display doubt right now.

"Nothing is truly innocent, is it?" she said. "Particularly not babes, the helpless parasites."

"Where are the alchemists?" I ran to Newton's curtain-clad bedroom and flung open the drape. He was sleeping, his head back, his arm flung out, revealing a loose white shirt and thin, pale arm. His wig was on a stand, the diffraction-grating glasses I'd given him neatly placed on the forehead. He wore a pointed cap, hiding his hair, although a hint of brown curl poked from one side. In one corner of the space, his clothes hung on a hook. It was so bare and plain, enough to make anyone depressed.

I ran to his side and tapped his arm. "Newton! Newton! What happened?"

"They're drugged," Ursula said. "According to my device, they've been asleep since 9 p.m."

"What? Why? Are they involved?"

"Not unless they were sleepwalking. This guy is more newly dead. He never left after work. He met the alchemists near the bathroom about 8 p.m. and offered them candy. He stayed in his office until midnight, then took this elevator to the basement. He walked down the hall to this laboratory. He held the scalpel. This much we know from cameras."

"There's no camera on the woman?"

"No, the doors are locked. He entered. No one left."

"The alchemists are locked in at night."

"Like animals."

"You don't think..."

"I wouldn't blame them for losing their minds but no. *He* must have been after *them*. He drugged them, and went for them with the scalpel, possibly, but he fell, sparing their lives but taking his own. The only thing out of line is the pockets." She was convincing herself as much as she was me.

"Perhaps he pulled something from the pockets as he stalked the poor men," I said. *What do people have in their pockets? Spare change? Tissues? Devices? Candy*. "He always had candy in his pockets. He ate it when he was nervous. He was eating and stalking."

Her daughter came in with another agent. "I've got the body bag, Mom." These kids were so precocious. This child hadn't even lost her baby teeth yet, and here she was hauling a neatly folded PEVA bag. She tossed it next to the corpse, spread it out, and unzipped it.

"A natural man? There aren't a lot of these fuckers left!"

Gotfried had been after the babies, hadn't he? He'd cut the mud mother and slipped to his death. It was obvious that she'd been disturbed. A smudge of mud dusted the floor. He'd been right, the project was doomed from the start. My head was buzzing. I had to go to my lab, it always made things better. I could think there.

"May I check my lab?" I asked Ursula. "It appears Sir had gone in there for his weapon."

Without waiting for an answer, I rushed to the elevator and

hurried to my lab. It was obvious that Sir, or someone, had been here. The plants were drooping and near dead. The water bath was on its side, the molds shredded into strips on the floor as if chewed by a pig. I fumbled as I grabbed for the limp plants.

Ursula came in. "Find anything?"

"He destroyed the salmagundi project. I don't understand, it was meant to help Cochtonia produce flowers."

"What's the connection?"

The plants. He knew something about the plants.

"Do you have any ideas?" I asked.

"Yes, Smithfailed, we checked the records. *You* are the connection! Did he have a vendetta against you?"

"Not that I was aware of. If anything, he did his best to ignore me."

"The building is no longer safe for the homunculi. They're being presented to the public tomorrow. As soon as the alchemists wake up, you and I will help them get ready."

CHAPTER SEVENTEEN

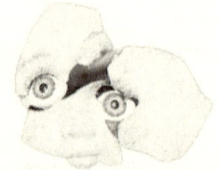

The ceremony began with a parade around the town square. The alchemists sat in a convertible, perched on the edge of the backseat while I sat in front beside the Vice Patrol driver. Newton clutched the back of the seat. Paracelsus waved enthusiastically to the crowd, filled with old dudes in HumP shirts and seed corn caps. My parents were somewhere among them. I strained to find them. NezLeigh, of course was in the crowd selling her trinkets. I focused on the most positive outcome I could imagine. The babies would be welcomed, they'd live a while, then they'd die suddenly and tragically. *After which, I'll be executed.*

The Cochton brothers' limousine, the Corn Burner, was in front of us, their nephew Layal waving to the crowd. The brothers didn't go out in public, they were too old, but they'd be watching remotely. Before them, a contingent of Vice Patrol carrying the Cochtonia flag, which prompted people to press their fingers to their forehead to show they were thinking of Cochtonia. Behind us was a flat-bed truck hauling the mud woman. Following this, an exhibition of corn on a flatbed, a cavalcade of Vice Patrol agents, all in white, and a playful display of male citizens in PVC hamster balls for humans.

The presentation of the babies was held in the open in

Cochtonville square, two blocks wide and two blocks deep across from the Pavilion of Agriculture. The pavilion was a squarish building decorated with kernels of corn, giving it a golden hue. The double front plexiglass doors were flanked on each side by bundles of corn stalks. I thought nervously, *the corn would burn well and release plenty of smoke. This city has no safety laws for building for workers or for anything else. Everything is disposable.* As my ride pulled up to the concrete stage in the center of the square, Mom burst from the throng and waved to me. I blew her a kiss and put my hand to my heart. I might not see her again.

We were escorted from the convertible to backstage. The air smelled like distant hog lots. Vice Patrol, directed by Ursula, guarded the mud woman, who was carried through the crowd on her bier, her platform, and deposited gently center stage.

I was nervous as heck and trying not to show it. We stood behind a billowy gold curtain, held up by three concrete hands. A vivid paragraph from the Virginia Guru's book popped into my mind. *The penis consists of three tubes of erectile tissue.*

We were joined by Vice Patrol guards and, uncomfortably, by Lady LouOtta Maliegene. I hoped I was nondescript enough that she wouldn't recognize me from the blue leg incident and happy day, she didn't, as I stood there in my lab coat. Even without being acknowledged, her presence injected me with shame. What had happened to the poor Neanderthal Crisper? He'd been so sensitive and misunderstood.

LouOtta didn't notice me but this didn't keep her from lobbying the alchemists for attention.

"I love your brain," she said to Newton, revealing orderly teeth in a practiced smile. "Let me take your wig off sometime and get a closer look."

"Can you make me a homunculus baby next?" she asked Paracelsus. "I don't like reproducing, it's bad for the figure."

None of us spoke to her. We were too agitated to be able to focus on banalities. Newton rubbed his neck.

The Cochtonia manager, Norman Allen, a figurehead because

he was the last male conceived naturally, held up a microphone and spoke to the assembled crowd in his slow Iowa drawl. A mosquito landed on Norm's head as he said. "Today is one of anticipation. We are revealing the infants who will rescue us from obscurity and chaos. But first, a rendition of our anthem."

We all pressed our foreheads to show we were thinking of Cochtonia. I panicked. Was he going to announce us right after this?

"I'm privileged to present our master of ceremonies, who will sing the anthem in a duet, the honorable nephew of Cochtonia, the Crisper known as Layal."

Layal sat on a gold-colored plastic throne and addressed the audience.

"Men of Cochtonia, now is your time! You've been run down, you've been lied to. You've been made fools of!"

Sweat poured off my forehead and along my neck. My hair stuck to it. He knew. He knew about this fraud. Again, Newton rubbed his neck, plastered with wet wig material, and a river of perspiration ran from Paracelsus's cap. I did my best not to bolt from the stage. I would be captured or killed if I tried. In a way, I wanted to get it over with, the fear and uncertainty were killing me, but I couldn't end it all with my parents in the audience.

Layal went on, "I am in sympathy and solidarity with you. Today will be a turning point. We will now be free of the burden of female-based reproduction. No more disappointments or rejections. We're taking the fickle out of fucking."

"It's my cue!" LouOtta rushed forward onto center stage. "For women, the advantages are obvious. No matter how we try, pregnancy and childbirth aren't risk free or pain free and those blown-out personal areas and saggy bladders are clear reasons to transfer your burden to the Homunculus Project. Let us begin our precious time as we start a new era."

Layal rose from his golden throne and took the microphone from Norm. Together, he and LouOtta sang the national anthem, "Bombs and Tassels." I peeked through the space between the curtains, watching them gazing into each other's eyes as if they were planning a tryst. I'd heard this anthem many times, but never with a sultry undertone, the pair as erotic as a skeleton making it with a pumpkin. The song was ridiculous enough without this false provocative display. It was about corn tassels, apt enough, but also about bombs and fighting some sort of enemy that we were to be ready for. It had not arrived. The enemy was, of course, from within: the disregard for the collective will of the citizens, the fawning over these founding fathers, the worship of idols like LouOtta, and the ridiculous demands made of scientists. A list of grievances poured through my mind but none of them would do me any good. Being grieved was almost as bad as being stupidly optimistic. Newton and I held each other with our eyes. He, too, was horrified by the display. He was my kind of pessimist.

"Our version was delightfully fecund," Layal projected his voice, "as is appropriate for this marvelous moment where we witness a cultural transformation, a birth which symbolizes freedom for the tyranny of nature. Thank you, LouOtta! You may leave me now. It's time for the alchemists to deliver the heirs."

LouOtta came backstage as hurt as a freshly castrated hog. "I'm not used to being pushed off so quickly. I represent all women who support this project. You'd think I could be a witness! Yet, it's you he wants. What an ass! He doesn't have an appreciation of beauty like his uncles. Why are you standing around? Get out there!"

Newton put his hand on my back. "Please come with me, I can't do this alone." We walked through the curtain together and faced the eager crowd.

The mud woman was worse for the wear following her ride on the flatbed. Her neck was deeply cracked and the rest of her was punctuated by squarish cracked patches, as if she was covered in plaid. The parade in the sun had created some sort of hardpan. Flies landed on the sculpture and walked across the surface. What kind of monsters lurked within?

"Gentlemen, begin the ceremony of birth." Layla forced his

enthusiasm. Who would be happy with being succeeded by a homunculus?

Paracelsus came forth and gave an oratory as Newton stood on one side of him and me on the other. "Behold the silent bearer of children, crafted from the hands of man, who has born our seed. Mother, it is time for your departure from our realm. Your task of nurture is complete.

"These offspring bear no stamp of any mother. Of woman born but man created, solely from the brothers, uninfluenced by others. These are the heirs who will carry the future. The future of Cochtonia. Arise!" He elbowed me and said in an aside, "Take one out and show the citizens."

"Me? It's your job," I whispered back.

"You know them."

It was true. My knees grew weak. It was more than I'd signed up for, yet I had to take responsibility for my creations. I stumbled forward to the woman. I wasn't superstitious, but what I'd done to Jelly was against reason. I shrank back. No, I couldn't go along with my own ploy. Pushing through my fear, I pulled nitrile gloves from the pocket of my lab coat. Yes, I had to continue. I was used to plants.

They couldn't be cut out as if hoeing or yanked out as if weeding. But where were they? I viewed the belly with the vertigo one might get standing on a burning roof and viewing a net below. My life as a scientist had been a pleasant day to day tedium that morphed into flow. Science was a flow, not a leap. That was it, I'd take it slow.

I bent over, placed my palms on the dirt, and brushed it to each side with slow, small strokes. It flew across the belly and onto the cement stage. I let myself feel the sterility of the soil. It was as hard as beef jerky and smelled slightly like beef jerky as well. It was a quiet moment as I knelt, my lab coat slightly open, my hands searching for signs of life. The crowd grew restless. The surface was too hard to puncture.

Newton came to my side to help. "What do you need?"

"The soil is as hard as if a tractor rolled over it. I thought it would be easy, plunging my hands in manure." I picked at a crack across the belly, but it didn't give way.

He pulled a buckle off his shoe. "Archimedes would say, there's little a leverage can't achieve." He pushed the buckle into a cracked seam and twisted his wrist. An irregular rectangle of dirt flew across the stage. The audience clapped. He repeated his flick of the wrist, this time with more flourish. The dirt flew across the stage and into the crowd, where it caused a tussle.

A pale eye came into view, startling me. I suppressed a scream. Newton diligently flicked away more crust. A foot shot up.

"Eureka, we've found them!" said Newton. He released a large square of crust. It fell to the cement and broke into small bits. The plant babies sat in the belly, much as we'd left them. Perhaps one was a little fatter.

I lifted the smaller baby as dirt fell off him. Newton did the same. The life forms were translucent with pale green skin and dangly arms. A tangle of new roots or aspiring tendrils sprouted on their heads. Their slick lips wetly puckered for a doll bottle. Their "straws" added a grotesque touch. A murmur went up from the crowd. "Aww!"

"Behold!" Paracelsus shouted as we held each kid aloft.

Layal reached out and grabbed the flawed baby from me.

"Come to uncle." The baby, light green with red streaks as if veined, lifted an arm and swiped at his face. The crowd cooed.

"You look so much like your father. Citizens, give the alchemists a round of applause!"

The applause sounded like rain, which we needed. It washed over us. People were so happy. If only it was real! The alchemists bowed to the adoring crowd, then Newton grabbed my hand and we bowed together. It was all cheering and bowing and fake smiling. Newton squeezed my hand in relief.

Layal said, "And now, for the circumcision ritual. This will allow a more robust growth and signify manhood. We cut off the foreskin as we cut away emotion. This allows for rational

decisions. Officer Ursula, step forward with the ceremonial tools."
Ursula took a scalpel from her belt; it was my scalpel.

"Bring out the slab," Norm said as he struggled for relevance.

Two Vice Patrol officers carried a table with a cement top onto
the stage.

"Place the baby on the slab."

Layal positioned the homunculus in the center of the slab. The
plant appeared to be struggling and thrashing, the formless stem-
penis bobbed about, looking ever so much like a straw. He
motioned to me. "Hold it in place during the procedure."

I obeyed—what else could I do? Ursula stood across from me
as I gripped the waxy doll beneath my hands. Layal stepped back.
Ursula's hand shook as she held the knife above the writhing plant.
The Vice Patrol operated in the realm of blunt force trauma and
electromagnetic beams.

"Can you calm it down?" she asked.

I leaned closer and we spoke between us. "No. Have you had
any experience with sharp objects?"

"I've been practicing on baby corn with the scalpel I
confiscated."

"On cobs?"

"Yes, I've carefully been slicing off the stems. Cobs don't wiggle
around and they are not this large and animated."

"Clever. You're highly capable, more than qualified." I wanted
to flatter but I also felt for her. Like me, she was a hard worker,
asked to go an extra mile during difficult situations but never
feasting at the table so to speak.

"You're the first Cochtonian to give me such a compliment."
Her face was wide and gentle as she said this.

"Hopefully not the last."

"There's no foreskin. It's one seamless shaft."

"Skim lightly over the surface at the tip."

"Get it done," Layal commanded. "Do the deed."

"No," Newton said. "It's a pact with the past. These children
are the future."

"What are you talking about? Officer, get it on!"

Paracelsus leapt forward. "Stop this barbaric practice! I, too, object. These boys are perfect as is." He grabbed Ursula's wrist and held the scalpel, still clutched in her fist, aloft in this manner: his body pressed on hers, their faces nearly touching, their bodies knocking together like box cars in a flooded river. He pushed forward, belly first. She resisted and shoved back. Paracelsus tipped onto his heels and toppled back, then forward onto her.

"Give me this," she said under her breath. "I earned an honor."

"You are so strong," he said, his voice tinged with admiration. Still, he shoved her. She fell back, but a Vice Patrol Agent caught her and pushed her at him.

Isaac leapt in to aid Paracelsus, spouting some seventeenth century obscure quarrel. "These are not descendants of Moses! They arise singularly from the Patriarchs of this modern nation. The knife must be spared."

Ursula waved the blade in his direction. "I don't take orders from Moses and this isn't a knife, it's a scalpel." She held the baby down with one hand, placing hers over mine, and with a flick, she sliced the tip from the organ. It flew off the scalpel and landed, bloodlessly, over her left eye. She moved to wipe it, bringing the scalpel perilously close to her face before wobbling and falling back. The baby hissed, like wind through corn, and waved its tiny arms as the circumcision tool skittered across the cement and into the crowd. Someone yelped and a fight ensued as everyone wanted the scalpel as a souvenir.

"You've hurt him!" Newton called out as I swooped the baby into my arms.

"What about her?" Paracelsus said, leaning over Ursula. She lay with her head flung back, her Stetson askance, one eye glued open by the "foreskin" and the other closed tightly.

"She'll survive. Vice Patrol expect to sacrifice now and then. We're getting these babies to safety," said Layal.

An agent asked us, "Do you have anyone to say goodbye to?"

The alchemists shook their heads. I called out, "Bye, Mom! Bye, Dad! Bye, Sis! Thanks for everything."

More Vice Patrol burst onto the stage. One grabbed me. They led us down the stairs and to the waiting gold limousine.

"Just so you all know, you're checking in with the brothers, but you're not leaving."

CHAPTER EIGHTEEN

We were directed into the Corn Burner, a limo 100% powered by ethanol derived from corn. Clutching a baby while Newton held the other, we sat in the back with Paracelsus. Outside the vehicle, the men in the HumP shirts crowded around, peeking in to see the new heirs and taking knives to the car to scrape a souvenir paint chip.

"Run them over if you must!" Layal told the driver. "Or crush a foot to serve as a warning. I'd hate to create a martyr."

The driver hit the gas and several men shouted and fell to the ground. Unfazed, Layal sat next to the buggy, quizzing us as he gave the fakes a look over. "The citizens seem comfortable with these babies."

"We provided what was demanded of us," Paracelsus replied.

"I notice the shade of green on the skin."

"It's what they are," said Paracelsus.

"Yes. We will see how my uncles react."

"Why did you abandon the loyal officer? Who is checking on her?" Paracelsus asked.

"She isn't abandoned. She's a well-respected agent and used in a multitude of tasks. Being human, she's versatile and less dumb than most other humans. She'll be joining you, if you desire."

"I do desire."

I reached for Newton's warm hand. He didn't pull away. He wrapped his fingers around mine.

Layal grabbed a flask from his jacket pocket and chugged it. "Going to these events scares me. You notice my uncles do not attend in person. I'm the sacrificial lamb. It's my penance for the life of luxury I live. They're looking forward to having you join them at their home. Even better, the ride there is free."

The streets were cleared of people and vehicles for us. We took a detour to ride through the city while most citizens were stuck in traffic. We passed the Pavilion of Agriculture, the bar where I had my Bohemian beer, and Cochton Enterprises itself.

"Drive through the poor section of town," Layal told the driver. "Take the lowliest route you can." The car turned and we went past homes not much shabbier than my own. Since not much was done to help the public infrastructure, gas lines in this part of town would burst and homes would catch fire, leaving the neighborhood punctuated with burned-out buildings, litters of old boards, and lots with simply a basement and no structure. We passed a Vice Patrol barracks, built on a block where all of the homes had been cleared by fires, according to my parents. They'd remarked on how convenient it was to have the genetically created agents, who didn't have families, right in the midst of the poor people. Vice Patrol circled the block, walking alone, as the residents stayed inside.

"It costs so much to keep people poor," the heir remarked.

A bit farther, the homes were small, vinyl-sided, without basements, and on tiny lots. No one was outside. The neighborhoods were deserted.

We traveled through suburbs filled with white houses with many rooms for servants and perhaps a child or two. Sweeping lawns kept the public at arm's length from the Sirs and Icons who lived there.

The road to the Cochton house was ahead, snaking up the only hill for miles around, a pencil mark of a road, made of burned cobs and plastic. Cochtonia was known for its flatness. The Cochton homestead was like pus on a pimple, sitting all white and bulbous on an unimpressive rise. It was surrounded by a trench inhabited by semi-feral pigs. They acted as both guards and sentries. They were bright red with erect ears and, unlike most domestic pigs, tusks. I suspected these pigs ate people, mostly dead people and it gave them the palate for Homo sapiens. We crossed a wooden bridge to the entrance of the opulent home.

The place had a guard house, a shallow tall structure at the far end of the bridge. We stopped and Layal ordered us to get out of the car and bring the homunculi. I cuddled the smaller one, Newton the larger one, and we got out and stood on the planks of the bridge. Two handsome, symmetrical officers came forward, holding out a scanner as if being greeted this way was a form of handshake. A third guard escorted Layal into the mansion. The rest of us were ordered to stand back for scanning.

"Yeah, they're male alright," said a guard passing a scanner over each baby. "But, oink, it's a jumble, not really clear what they are. I guess this smaller one's Baby Bert. I'll call him that."

"You're not paid to be a geneticist. Add neck chips or they can't get in," the other guard said.

He shot a microchip into the smaller baby's waxy neck. It didn't flinch.

"We'll call the fat one Little Clarence. Damn if these don't have the look of stone-faced killers. Like their Dads. Now for the rest of you, come forward."

He scanned the alchemists.

"They're the real deal. Already chipped."

This news of neck chips got me shaking. Mom had told me about them. They tracked you, followed you from scan station to scan station and if you went where you weren't authorized, they heated up, reaching the boiling point of water. The one perk of being meaningless was not having a chip.

"Get over here!" The guard grabbed my arm harshly, nearly making me drop the baby. "You're a super fool for getting mixed up in all of this. I hate to chip the average person. Fortunately, these things are cheap."

He put the cold muzzle to my neck. I instinctively shied away from it.

"If you squirm around, I'll hit the wrong spot, and here's what happens to the wounded..." He gripped my arm and moved me so I got a view of the pigs, tusks thrashing and tiny eyes rolling in their bristly heads.

"Halt! Unhand her. This civilian is not involved in this project. Release her at once!" Newton pressed his luck.

"Redundancy will get you nowhere, Fancy Man. You weren't brought back to life to be bossy. You're here for name recognition, not exposition."

"I should not be here at all, unless you want to turn lead to gold in a process I haven't perfected. Unhand us all."

The other guard shoved Newton. "Oinking fake! How much did we waste creating you? You're ours now. You'll be housed underground. We have a nursery prepared."

"Underground nursery. What could be more pleasant?" Newton said sarcastically.

The sun beat down hellishly. Were the plants reaching toward it? I was pretty sure they were, their chlorophyll cranking into overdrive.

"See this trapdoor on the bridge, Fancy Man? If you leave without permission, it opens and down you go. Oinker food."

I stopped struggling. "If the alchemists have a chip, I'll accept one." The guard moved quickly, resting the barrel on my neck. In my heightened stage of alarm, what was supposed to be a prick felt like being impaled with a nail. I wobbled into Newton's arms and we held each other, trying to quell our fear.

Officer Ursula and her kid came from the house. "Welcome! Welcome! Guards, thank you. I'm taking them from this point."

"You're here?" Paracelsus said in astonishment. "Are you injured?"

"I'm blinded by the light. My eye has been opened, I can see clearly now. Follow us," she said, rubbing her eye. She led us away from the hostile guards and through the walnut doors, opening at the touch of a button. The Cochton house was refreshingly cool and Ursula so welcoming, I blinked back tears. The foyer looked out over Cochtonville, the front walls made of one-way glass. We walked through the white front hall, featuring a light fixture made from hundreds of prisms, arranged in the shape of a boob. Newton stopped to gawk. Had I not been so terrified, I might have been impressed.

"So nice to see a familiar face," Paracelsus said warmly to the officer. "The reception so far was not the welcome these creations deserve."

"I've been moved to house duty," she replied, beaming. "I'll do my best to make you comfortable. Let's take the elevator." Her cheerfulness calmed my anxieties. She walked us through the prismatic foyer, the elevator at the far end opening at her presence. We entered and the elevator dropped us to the next floor.

Newton held his stomach. "Had I experienced an elevator, I may have had new thoughts about gravity."

"It's not gravity, it's your nerves," she said. The door opened. Unlike the bright upstairs, this place was dim, not a great atmosphere for plants. "We're here. Your headquarters."

"Another cellar," said Newton, despondently.

"Sorry, string bean. At least it will be familiar."

The place was the stuff of nightmares—thin halls, dark carpet, and bland doors. I had barely been anywhere besides my own house and my lab. I was discombobulated and could hardly put one foot in front of the other. Nothing was familiar. Newton hovered near me, afraid.

Ursula stopped in front of the room closest to the elevator. "Here's my quarters. I, too, live in the basement with the important workers."

"Mom, you requested this," her kid said.

"I'm keeping an eye out for my friends."

She escorted us down the hall, again stopping in front of a door. "Here's yours," she said to Paracelsus. "Next to mine." She pushed a keypad. "I've set it so your neck chip will open it. You're free to wander this floor and into the courtyard if you care to rendezvous."

"Rendezvous? Ja." Unlike Newton and I, he was all smiles.

His room was a simple rectangle, painted white, with a twin bed and white spread with a yellow and green corn design. Two soft pillows sat at the head. There was no headboard.

Ursula went in. "Here's the bathroom with a shower. There's a toothbrush and paste in the cabinet. Soap and shampoo, too."

"Toothbrush and paste? What are those?" he asked.

"I'd love for you to figure it out," she said. She put paste on the toothbrush "You put this in your mouth and scrub it around on the teeth and tongue. Open up."

He held out his arms.

"Open your *mouth*." She scrubbed his teeth while he stood with his arms out. "Now, come, I'll show you where to spit it."

They went inside for longer than it should have taken to spit out toothpaste. The whole time, the kid, Angel, commented unfavorably on the appearance of the naked babies. Ursula finally came from the bathroom with Paracelsus tagging behind.

"It's all a luxury, one I deeply appreciate, but where's the freedom?" Paracelsus said, toothpaste dripping down his chin. "My duty is done. I delivered the homunculus. Behold, the men. We should all be set free."

"It would be my pleasure to free you, yet I can't do so safely. Your work is not over. This is the floor built for decedents. When it is full, when your room is needed for a child, you'll no longer be essential, and will be allowed to go."

"Go where?" I asked, considering being free to go might not be better.

"To be determined," she said. "But if you're good, there'll be a parade."

"I love a parade," Paracelsus said.

"There must be more homunculi?" Sweat poured onto Newton's forehead from beneath his wig.

"We can't leave these rooms empty now, can we? Science is repeatable. Even I know that much. This gestation took far less than nine months. It's the future."

Newton wiped his forehead with his sleeve "It is, however, alchemy. Alchemy is patchy. On earth as it is above. It's true for laws of motion, but I haven't found alchemy consistent."

Paracelsus added, "It is an art and a science and thus, dependent on the practitioner, his mood, and his insights."

"In that case, it's my job to get you in the mood," she said.

"Good woman, dreams have been known to come true. My skill is conductive to joy, peace, unity, respectability, and to satisfy our needs. It is much like music."

"I'll plan on beautiful music—although it's banned here—from you in the future. Now, how about you shower?" She strode in the shower stall and turned on the shower. The water rumbled from the powerful plumbing. "You take your clothes off and go in there. Till later."

Newton's room looked much the same, although the bedspread featured pink pigs.

He threw up his hands. "I can't sleep here, I might dream of sausages!"

"Tell your dreams to Stella. She'll be right next door and she might appreciate them."

"Am I to have an adequate laboratory or is it more cloistering in a small room? How are we expected to continue and perfect the homunculus or advance science with imperfect tools?"

"It's a shitty situation," said the kid. "Manure in, crap out."

"Angel, why don't you go help out in the kitchen?"

"I'm not hungry."

"Everyone's hungry. Now go!" To Newton, Ursula said, "Get in," hoisting the baby from his arms. "And calm yourself, nervous Nellie."

Newton and I exchanged looks as he complied.

The next room, mine, was larger. It contained two cribs, white with gold gilding, a changing table with a built-in dresser, and a small twin bed with a fringed white spread.

"Welcome to your new home and more importantly, welcome to the nursery. Let's get the darlings dressed and let them rest in these cribs."

I froze. How was I going to do this and keep them from dying?

Ursula went on enthusiastically. "We've got all you need right here. Bottles, formula, diapers. Onesies. Better get some clothes on those babies. Those giant dicks are risqué!"

I hadn't thought of diapers because these were plants. They ate sun and carbon dioxide and pooped out water and oxygen. They probably thought of animals as shit eaters.

Ursula kissed Little Clarence. "I like a robust baby. Hello, Fatty! He's so newborn, he's still waxy. Too bad about his Mama. I guess she wasn't built to last." She put him on the dressing table, picked up his legs with one hand, and scooted a diaper under his bum with the other.

"Let's cover up your little mushroom, okay, sweetie?" she said, fastening the diaper across the belly. The belly button was a flat ring, the kind that forms when a sweating glass meets a table, not a human indentation.

"What's with the lint catcher?" Angel said, pointing. This didn't faze Ursula. She tugged open a drawer and pulled a one-piece legless outfit that read *I'm HumPed*. She slipped it over his head, which I was convinced was a root ball.

"Poor guy looks zonked out." She tenderly put him in his bed. "Stella, your turn to diaper. It takes practice, but you'll get the hang of it. Hope he isn't too tender. I don't think homunculi should be circumcised. Sorry, buddy." I rested Baby Bert on the dressing table while Ursula handed me a diaper. I had never put a diaper on anything before. I unfolded it and stared while the plant quivered.

"I'll show you," she said. She pulled a wipe from a tub on the table and cleaned off Baby Bert's circumcised area.

"Got to keep it clean," she said. She turned him over and wiped his rear where a drop of sap had formed. "A little poopsie." She tossed the wipe in a diaper pail. She lifted his legs and scooted the diaper beneath him. "What outfit do you want, sweetie?" Ursula held up her hand making bunny ears and bobbed it in front of Baby Bert's face. "See the cat, see the cradle." The plant baby did nothing. "Do these guys ever blink?" she asked. "Maybe they're blind?"

"Shit has no eyes," said her kid. "Turds don't blink."

"Angel, get to the kitchen. Now!"

"They're not natural babies," I said. "They're homunculi, which is a whole new world. Please don't call them turds. Their creation took thoughtful crafting, not digestion." Happy I wasn't lying, I took a onesie from the drawer. It had a crown on it. "The Boss," it read. I dressed the baby, pulling the cloth over the waxy body as Ursula scooted her kid out the door.

"I can help feed them," said Ursula. "They look like they're puckering and ready."

"Um, I have them on a schedule suggested by the alchemists. They don't need their bottles. It's time for-for a stroll. Did you mention a courtyard I could sun them in?"

"Sure is and it's open all hours. Your chip gives you access to anywhere the Cochton brothers want you to go. Even better..." She opened a generous closet packed with racks of baby clothes. She reached in and pulled out the old doll buggy. "I figured you lined this with dirt for a reason."

I was surprised and happy to see the old thing. "Yes, to help them acclimate to life on the outside. I fear they'll have a tough go of it."

"They're Cochtons. How hard can it be?"

The courtyard was bound on one side by a high wall constructed from stacked and mortared limestone slabs. Although the west wall threw shade, the yard was wide enough that light shone through the top. The rest of it was bordered by the mansion, towering above. The babies stretched their legs and arms to the sun as I slumped over, pushing them in the doll carriage.

"This ain't prison," Ursula said as we strolled. "We're guests. We might as well be friends! Look at me, I risked my life for this nation and all I get for it is baby duty."

Her negative words had me peeking around for surveillance devices and unsure what to say as her deep, brown eyes frisked me, searching for a reaction.

"My eyes have been opened lately," she said.

"I'm on baby duty as well. Unreasonable. I'm a scientist after all. Or I was."

Dark streaks of deep green, as piney as corn in late July after months of full sun, ran from the babies' fingers and toes to their trunks, or should I be honest with myself and call them stems?

"You'll grow fond of the babies," she said. "I confiscated my child. Her mother died and the kid was bound for the rendering truck. I took her without permission and I suffered no consequences. My girl will be an officer of the law someday, like me, unless it's all Crispers by then. I'll be oinked if she becomes a maid or a nanny." She froze, immediately realizing her mistake with me, scientist turned nanny. "I imagine you were chosen for this job because you can handle that cranky Newton as well as anybody. I notice you two mix well."

"Me and Newton? We don't get along."

"Somebody as nutty as he is might be fun in bed."

"What are you saying?" It was one shock after another with her. I couldn't tell if she was honest or trying to get me to confess to something in this courtyard with high walls and little breeze.

"It's always the crazy ones..."

Sexual activity was regulated here—marriage or with Crisper rental. "How do you know?"

"My mom told me, it's okay. We can talk about such things. Even in the belly of the beast, a person can find love. I haven't given up hope." Her Stetson shaded her eyes. "You might not feel ready for motherhood but trust me, it's a wonderful thing, even if you've got no partner."

A door to the courtyard opened. A man dressed in a dark suit and eating a blood sausage came into the courtyard. Ursula shielded her right eye from the sun. "Oh no, don't look now but here comes the Henchman. We were once friends but I'm seeing more clearly today. He's dangerous. He's trolling in search of a superfluous employee he can dispose of to save some money for the bosses. Act as if the babies can't live without you."

I suspected this was all fabricated. Vice Patrol were taught to lie to gain trust. I was hot with embarrassment. No. My neck got hot in the spot where I'd been chipped. Her belt beeped and she touched it.

"Time to get you back. When your chip heats up, you need to return to your room. It's kind of like an induction oven. It's crude but it works."

"Hello," he said, giving Ursula's eye the eye. "I've been looking for you."

"He's the Most Loyal Henchman," Ursula explained. "He does random *unsavory* tasks."

"Ursula is too complimentary, but yes, I hench at the direction of the brothers. You could call me the Clean-up Man." He bent over to take a peek at the babies. They were both head down. "My, the infants are..."

I covered the babies with the carriage shade. "Sleeping," I said, stopping his hand as he moved to pull back the shade.

"Tell me about their care. Is it the standard fare?"

"He wants to know if anyone can do it," the Ursula warned.

"I see." I gave her my best knowing look—a fake smile and wide eyes.

He took Ursula's arm. "Weren't we having a sincere conversation between us recently? I'd be honored to continue it. I'm here to help you out. Supper's ready. Care to join me?" He bit into his sausage. Grease poured down his arm and splashed onto his leisure suit. The babies rattled in the buggy. They needed watering. He held out the sausage. "Take a bite. What's mine is yours."

Ursula pulled away. "I'm viewing things differently. I can no longer endure your insincere wooing." She rubbed the eye where the circumcised plant material had landed.

Like cleaning up older workers. He woos them.

Paracelsus, his hair soaking wet, wandered into the courtyard. "Hallo! Where's the party? I waited in the shower until my skin became too wrinkled. I came to find you."

"How do you know this alchemist?" The Henchman was angry at Ursula's rebuff.

"He's new here and he's lonely."

"Of course! Or drunk. Smell his breath. Ursula, I don't know what's gotten into you."

"I'm drunk, I admit, and hungry. I hear there is food in the kitchen. You could join me, for two lips are better than one."

"How about I show him out? Excuse me. Stella, I suggest you follow us to the exit."

I dawdled to give them some space. This wasn't my smoothest move. The Henchman approached me. My emotions ran off like a racoon with some trash. A couple of months ago, I might have trusted any male authority figure. No longer.

"I'm not dispensable," I said rudely.

"We won't survive without patriots."

A life form in the buggy rattled like wind through corn during a tornado watch, a cross between bacon sizzling and a hand full of change clanking in a fist. A green-tipped hand thrust from the side of the buggy.

"You're upsetting the heirs," I said.

"The Cochtons decide who remains and who goes. The Cochton hospitality only stretches so far. The alchemists can go back to the entertainment circuit, but you are on borrowed time, unless of course..."

"Of course, what?"

"You take Ursula's place. Let's meet tonight."

"My neck is hot. A hot neck means I am being summoned. Good day!"

He followed me, waving the sausage. "The Cochton hospitality has a short shelf life. Please me and I'll put in a good word."

I went back to my room, slamming the door in his face. I left the babies in their dirt buggy. Should I take off the diapers? What about the rompers? Yes, I might as well free them. First, I stripped down Baby Bert. His circumcision was splitting into two branches. Next, I took the onesie and diaper off of Little Clarence. I put each baby in his crib. My whole life was torn out at the roots. I had no lab. No parents to care for. No income. It was as if I'd died, but I had to go on.

The room had no clock, no window. This place was a big "no." My nose was pressed up against the metaphorical steel shed wall of the future. I was adrift, floating in a tiny boat on a sewage lagoon, metaphorically speaking. "Metaphor" was a word my mother had used in private, telling me not to speak it outside of the home. We didn't want to appear too intellectual. Mom believed in Cochtonia and supported its leaders. Yes, they'd built the empire plundering family farms but it was our empire. And it was doing me in.

There was a knock at the door. I was afraid to answer it.

"Supper's ready." Ursula's kid, with a plate of Porkies in one hand and a glass of carbonated raspberry corn syrup tucked under an arm, pushed her way in before I could invite her to enter. "Got you some grub. Mom said to bring you a plate in case you got busy with the babies. The servants' kitchen's upstairs. You can get meals at seven, noon, and five. Anyone with a chip is free to roam about for an hour before and an hour after meal time. After that, your chip gets hot unless you're in your room."

"Thank you," I said, taking the food.

"That one is deformed," she said, peeking into the buggy. "In a cute way, I mean." She reached her hand in. "Rockabye, baby." She pulled her chubby hand away. "They sleep like the dead."

"Except they aren't dead."

"I want to babysit."

"I'll let you as soon as they are ready."

Thankfully, she scampered off and left me with the Porkies. Even rich people ate these things? I couldn't believe it. Oink, they were everywhere. Why wasn't I rich? I did much of the work on them. Well, they sucked! I didn't want to splorkie, even though I had my own bathroom. I left them on the plate, went to my bathroom and poured out the sugary drink. I filled the glass with water and drained some on each boy's head. They were adorable in their own way.

"Good night, sweet things. What a day it's been, and believe it or not, we're still alive."

I was agitated from the long day but the mattress was buttery soft and I fell right to sleep. I dreamt of Newton. He came to me. He was erect, and I don't mean posture. All three penis chambers were engorged and ready to touch my stars.

CHAPTER NINETEEN

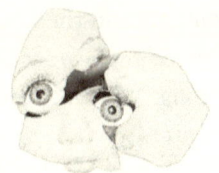

I woke in a sweat to a knock at the door. The realization of where I was, the first time I'd ever been out of my own bed, twisted through me. Fear shrunk the hippocampus, didn't it? My mind was empty of everything but panic. I was chuting for dementia faster than corn transferred from one bin to another.

"What cheer!"

Newton! Emotions cracked out of me—joy, relief, confusion, lust. I flushed, remembering my dream. I'd had an orgasm simply from thinking about him. Virginia Guru hadn't said a thing about this and she had nothing on me.

"Coming," I called out as I rushed toward the door, stumbling over my shoes. I threw it open. Light flooded in from the hallway. There was Newton with a bowl of grits, white with a gold rim, looking like a celestial being rescuing me with ground corn and butter.

"Newton!" I said in astonishment. "What brings you here?"

He shifted the bowl downward, to cover his inflated chambers. "I brought you breakfast. It's served in the kitchen and I noticed you didn't arrive in a timely fashion."

"I, I, was dreaming."

"A dream is the first step toward discovery. You sort through your careworn thoughts, float through a sea of possibilities, and wake with a focus. For example, I couldn't fathom why the moon circled the earth. I fell asleep beneath an apple tree. I dreamed of the moon and earth in a dance together, attracted. Behold, a falling apple fell onto me, straight down. I mused upon the force. It had to be the same as in my dream: two bodies attracted. I started upon a series of measurements and then came up with my laws."

Are you as long lasting in bed as you are in conversation? "Come in," I said, swallowing my yearning. "You've given me a lot to think about before breakfast. Please enter."

He strode in and put the grits on the changing table. He stood over the buggy. "They make me wish these were our babies. In a way they are."

The babies stared up at us with pale green eyes. "Hush, these are fully Cochton. I must admit, they are cute little things." *It looks as if they moved in the night.*

"I was born so small, I fit into a quart pot. I couldn't hold up my head. I was forced into the world early, my mother stressed from the loss of my father."

"Stress is awful! It shrinks your sanity."

"She must have been under unbelievable tension."

"Tension is unhealthy." *Am I flushed yet?*

"I arrived too soon."

"You were ahead of your time. The world is in your debt. Without your insights, superstition would rule over us. People would believe anything, even without evidence."

"I was lonely. My only true affection was for the chemist who took me in and encouraged my penchant for measurement. Scientists have been my only human succor in life."

Pretending to marvel over the babies, I brushed against him. "Is this why you're comfortable with me? My scientific background and results-oriented approach?"

"It is. Look at them, they are a result. Don't you wish for a child?"

"Having one? No."

"True, they can rebel against you. I was a turncoat child and set my house on fire because I abhorred my mother's new husband."

"Attachment disorder?"

"Of course. The babies have more color to them today."

"I took them for a walk in the sun yesterday." *He's getting attached to them and I to him.*

"More hue than green. I detect a reddish tint, it's almost human. They have a meaty quality."

"I don't see it. Perhaps it's the lighting in here." I had to admit, he looked good in the dim light. The harshness of his mouth was softened. His affection for the babies set my heart beating double time.

"I wrote the book on attraction between bodies and yet, I never thought I'd be here. It could be your name or your mind. Or I am not Isaac Newton after all. I longed for a lab and someone to talk with about science. Then I found you. I can't stay away, no matter how much danger we are in."

My dream burned through me like a fire in a grain elevator. Could this really come true? Could I love Isaac Newton and be loved in return? "Science is hope. Science can stand against fear, if we let-let ourselves...experiment."

"I enjoyed experimenting or even re-doing my experiments if circumstances forced it. I had a little dog, her name was Diamond. She was a Pomeranian. In excitement, she knocked into a table and a candle fell on my theory of gravity manuscript and burned it. It took me a year to recover both my mind and my experimental work. Oh, I still did love her, I simply did the experiments again. I miss Diamond. I miss what I was. I long for my lost ability to love."

"You loved?" Oh, those lips of his, like a pink bow, almost feminine in an otherwise masculine face. My heart ached for him and for us. Although I found his dog inexcusable and wasn't sure why he hadn't backed up his notes, I, too, missed my lab. I might never return. My heart was broken and he was mending it. I had to make my move quickly while his universe was open to mine. I plunged my hands into his thick, bushy wig. "I love your dark energy."

He pulled back. He'd told me not to touch him and I'd violated his wish. I jumped away from him.

"I'm so sorry, I didn't mean to abuse you." I backed into my bed and gracelessly tumbled onto it.

"Are you hurt?" he asked, coming near.

"No, unless clumsiness hurts. Forgive me for touching you when you asked me not to."

"I asked you to refrain from touch?"

"Yes, when we met outside the bathrooms."

"Fie! My mood has changed since being set on this impossible task. Forgive my churlishness." He sat next to me on my bed.

With two fingers, I touched his cheek, soft as if he'd never seen the sun. "Let's forgive together."

"In my old life, celibacy pulled me into madness. I was not afraid to love my dog. Why did I fear loving a person?"

I'd read Virginia Guru. I was prepared for the pounding heart and constriction in my genitals. I was not ready for the panicked urgency, as if I would combust if he didn't touch me. "Fear is understandable. People are unpredictable." The tension was pulling me apart. I needed to see his skin, to feel it warm and alive.

"I would steal a kiss but I would need to hang myself for theft after."

I shivered as he came close, his sexy, ancient lips a hair's breadth away. Being so near was standing at the edge of the Milky Way. I put my hands around his neck. "Noose be damned!"

"If this be the rope, I welcome it." He had scant mass but fantastic acceleration, pounding me with kisses. My breath left me and as I fell back, he covered me with a burst of tongue and nibbles. I unbuttoned his vest clumsily while returning his kisses, pawing at his silky ruffled shirt. Giving up at finding a hidden set of buttons in my haste, I freed it from its tuck with frantic pulling. He lifted a hand to his throat and undid the neck button. I moved down across his chest to caress him with my mouth. His silly short pants were buttoned up and with my touch he burst free of his celibate bondage.

"Getting out my bagpipes. Oh, I never dreamed of this."

What did the book say? The woman has all of the power. He was once a powerful man, and I, I had the power.

I knew so much more, thanks to Guru's book. It would be an opportunity to assess his age based on the firmness. I took his penis in my hands. How vulnerable we were together! I squeezed lovingly, he was as firm as a fresh corn cob. Ahh, yes, he was not an old man. We were pulsating like stars, rotating like spiral galaxies, luminous together. My only thought was the power of making him happy. I put my mouth down, down toward the birthplace of his stars. I'd consume them. Down, down over the fresh universe, as ripe as a raspberry, tempting, trembling. Evolution had made penises efficient if not beautiful. I swallowed my own fading apprehension. I took him in my hand and lightly kissed it while it trembled. The fly of his pants flew up and slapped me in the neck; it was like being struck by an errant June beetle.

"Ouch," I said in surprise. I sat up. It hadn't hurt as much as it startled me.

"What's wrong?"

"Your fly attacked me! No problem, where were we?" I began again.

"My fly? I have no fly! Are you injured?"

"Your trouser button was attracted to my neck. How can that be? Like attracts like and my neck isn't a button."

"Ohhh," he groaned. "I know this button, I've worn it before. Yes, it's familiar. Deeply familiar."

"Is it yours from when you were alive before?"

"Yes, clearly. This is my coat, these are my pants. The button is magnetized cast iron. I used it to catch forgers when I worked for the royal mint. I'd put the forgeries near my groin to detect fakes."

"Our neck chips are magnetic! What a revelation! They'll only work at close range, meaning a long-range surveillance detecting device won't find them. We can get far away and not be discovered. Cochtonia does most things cheaply." Knowing the simple way the neck chip was detected gave me hope we'd be able to sneak out of this place, away from the overbearing Cochton brothers. "We should remove these pants. They are hampering our experimentation."

He sat up and I pulled back his pants. Brown seeds scattered on the white bedspread.

"What is this? What did you have in your pockets?" I tried not to be frustrated, but it was as if every moment had an interruption and I was a shaken bottle of CochaCola.

"They are from my apple tree back home in England. These are Flower of Kent apple seeds. Yes, I've saved them all these years. But apple seeds are known to keep vitality for long periods of time." *Like your penis.*

"Apples?"

"Yes, fruit. Round and you eat them, press them for cider. They are crunchy and sweet. Firm but yielding. Juicy but not messy."

"Sounds luscious, I'd like to plant them."

"Let me do the planting."

"I am seeing us together in action."

"And for every action."

"There is an equal and opposite reaction."

I wanted to rub him on my skin like a lotion, sprinkle him all over me. I had such a longing. A craving this powerful, an ache this bad, it had to be punishable by death. And I didn't care. I'd die on this hill if I had to as long as he was holding me. I'd never seen a naked man before. I removed his jacket, which was intricately made with piping. I placed it carefully on the bed. My hands rushed over his frilly shirt. His nipples were hard beneath the gauzy material. He was a great man and I was going to strip him and gaze upon him and take him as mine. For such a bossy male, he was passive beneath my fingers, firm but yielding as I pulled the shirt over his head. He was startlingly white, as white as popped corn. He shivered. Tenderness poured out of me.

"I'll take care of you," I promised. "Don't be afraid. We have each other in this mad world." We drew one another close, our hearts beating together. We rested our heads on each other's shoulders. His smell was timeless—DNA scattered by comets, genetic material in amber. The fear and delight and weight of coming change, from solo to duo, and the buoyancy of affection, pushed my blood through me. If the Henchman rushed in and killed me, I wouldn't die in comfort, but I'd die happy.

I pulled down one stocking and kissed his boney toes. He was the jumpy sort, nothing could be rushed. I dropped the stocking to the floor and removed the other. The babies were dead silent.

He was naked and I was dressed. Power surged through me. I fell on him, kissing his face, his lips, his nipples. There was, however, the wig. He wasn't truly nude.

I put my hands on his false hair. A puff of powder flew out and I sneezed.

"May I see you in your entirety? May I remove the wig?"

"You may have your way with me."

"You honor me."

"The thing cost two months' pay. Society twisted me. I had myself convinced of my superiority and my wig said as much. Take it off and I'll stand uncovered before you. Help me know who I am."

I raised it gently. His ancient, dusty smell lifted with the wig. Unveiled, he had cola-colored hair with cropped waves. "I could drink you in."

"You free me."

"It's what love is."

Again, he fell into me, kissing me with force. He undressed me. We couldn't take our eyes off each other. Blood pounded through him. No matter how he was created, he was alive, and he was mine. My body needed touching, it needed belonging, it sought a new orbit and so did my spirit.

"May I enter, Venus, morning and evening star of my heart?"

"Yes, oh yes." Never had I lived in the moment as I did now. My love for him was intense, doomed, and ideal.

He rubbed his cleft chin on my neck gently and a surge of affection ran through me. How could *he* love *me*? Ready to pop with anticipation, I reached down and held him, guided him. He was a gentle man, sliding in with care, or maybe he was afraid. We had to be silent but we whispered our pleasure to each other and our breath came heavy. His emission was strong, not drizzly, which the book claimed was common with an older man. My small cry of delight was involuntary. I'd wrung myself out.

"You are beautiful," he said, holding me.

"Oh, hush."

"You don't wish to be beautiful?"

"It's so fleeting."

"Wise, then."

"How about resourceful?"

He frowned. Maybe I had stretched things too far. He put his hand to his neck where the chip was. "Ouch! Time to go back to my room. Oh, this place is a prison and yet, our time together was a positive change."

I leapt up, grabbed his pants, and put the button to his neck. "Does this stop the heat? You can't stop magnetism, only redirect it."

"It stops the rise in temperature in my neck."

"Anything iron should be able to give us more time. It's not always easy to find iron here in the land of plastic."

"My pants are special in more ways than one. One moment before I go." His voice broke on the word go. He took my face in his hands and we kissed each other with all of the hunger years and centuries of denial had built up.

"Parting is such sweet sorrow," he said. "I fear parting almost as much as I fear being together."

"I'll visit you next."

He dressed quickly and left me naked in bed. I was happy,

happy to be me. The babies rustled. I went to them. I was high with happiness, nearly floating to check on them.

"How now, sweet things?"

They were all wopsy, falling over each other. I reached in and straightened them so they were parallel to each other. My bare foot touched something cool and sharp. I twitched back. The plate on the nightstand was broken on the floor. The Porkies were gone.

CHAPTER TWENTY

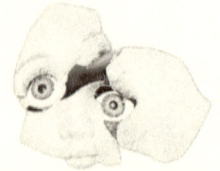

In the late afternoon, I went to him. He was hard, as firm as a young man, and we made love. Yes, that term, put into my head by NezLeigh, was what I was calling this. When we were done and satisfied, we sheltered in each other's arms. I pressed my skin against his, vowing to remember his warmth, for the grave would be cold and lonely. Who was I kidding? I wouldn't have a grave. I'd be eaten by pigs.

"What's being dead like?" I asked.

"It's both peaceful and sad. Peaceful because you are done being a force. Done acting on anything. Sad for the same reason. I imagine I'll return to death when our ruse is discovered. Stella, I'm lost, I'm empty. I don't know my place. I always saw the universe as a grand machine. Right and wrong. Force and counter force. Rulers were lofty and commoners were in their service. These rulers are not divine—they are foolish. I don't wish to be in their service. Nothing is absolute. Now, everything is so relevant."

"I've been trying to figure out a gentle way to tell you as much. Everything *is* relevant. And," I was not sure why I was compelled to say this except that this was a moment of truth telling, "gravity isn't an attraction. It's a wrinkle in the fabric of the universe —spacetime."

"Spacetime?"

"Bodies aren't attracted as much as they fall together in spacetime, like into a dent in this mattress."

"We are wrinkling spacetime, distorting it, and causing ripples together?"

"Yes. Isn't it lovely?"

"I am understanding, but it's too much to fathom. I could possibly have been brought here on a wrinkle?"

"Yes, and mass can become energy and vice versa."

"Mass is not immutable?"

"It can change form. Energy can't be created or destroyed but it can change form. Space, time, and mass are relative. They can change and are dimensions."

"Can time move backwards?" he said. "Can I take you back in time with me?"

I felt tangled in my own limited understanding of relativity. I had been to college but Cochtonia wasn't known for its education. Professors didn't have tenure and could be hauled off to prison for any misstep. "No, accelerating fast can slow time, not reverse it. But light, it appears, is a constant."

"I knew light was special."

"You weren't wrong. Your theory has been expanded upon. Standing on the shoulder of giants is how you put it. *You* are a giant. Science moves forward by co-operation."

"Now that you mention it, a dent in spacetime, occupied together, is most delightful. We've mutually fallen into each other. We've made this dent, so we should be able to return. I believe you. I believe in you. I'm embroiled. It is different from my time before. Yes, poets talked about love, but liaisons were only to create children inside of marriage. I never married because of my fears, and there was a high wedding fee to pay to the government."

"You needed your money to purchase the wig." I laughed and ran my hand through his hair.

"Because of this, I feel as if my life is a new world and you are my guide."

"My life is new as well, it's *our* life now."

"Should we check on the children? Let's."

Hand in hand, we hazarded into the hallway, our feet softly traversing the tile until we reached my door, closed snugly. For a moment, a pang of guilt for leaving the babies flooded over me. I'd left them. Then I remembered with relief, *they're plants*. I turned the knob and pushed the door. It didn't open more than a crack. It was caught on something. I pushed. It bounced back. I pushed again.

"I'll try," Newton said gallantly. He shoved the door. It opened a crack further before it slammed shut.

Officer Ursula came by with her daughter. "I'd ask you what you were doing here together but your neck chips have given you away. Don't worry, I'm all for love."

"I might have a real Dad at last," her minion chimed in. "Thanks to love."

"Hush," said Ursula. "Don't jinx things. What's wrong with the door?"

"It won't open."

"It's blocked," said the kid. "I see fabric under the door."

Paracelsus showed up, his hat askew. "Babies, come to Daddy!"

"Technically, you aren't their father," said the kid. "It's Bert and Clarence."

"Open the damn door!" Ursula shoved the door with her shoulder. It budged a crack.

"Angel, get in there and look around." The daughter slipped through while we bigger people waited nervously outside.

"We'll be needing some pigs," she called.

"Is it the babes?" I cried, half hoping it was.

"Stand away," Ursula said. "I'm busting down the door!" She took a tool from her belt. She pointed it at the door and a pop rang out. The door opened half way. Her daughter peeked out.

"I told you to stand away, kid. You could've been knocked on your ass."

"Mom, you gotta come in here and see this. It's the shits!"

Ursula squeezed through the half open door to get to her daughter.

"Your blast rolled him over," the daughter said as the two stood on the other side.

Rolled him over? I pushed myself through the crack. The victim was not a baby. They lounged in their beds like plants do. A man was face down on the floor, a rag in his hand. A familiar heavy solvent scent, like a grease cleaner, permeated the room.

"It's your ex," Angel said, deadpan.

"The only ex about him is ex-Henchman."

"Oh no. Who is it? Why is he here? What happened to him?" I asked.

"It's the Henchman. He must have fallen," Ursula said.

"Fallen and had his eyes eaten out," said the kid, her voice full of eye roll.

"He fell. Falling is the fifth leading cause of death in Cochtonia after heart failure, farm injuries, being offed by the state, and cancer. I'll need to make a report. Or maybe not. I'll call for help."

"It smells...it smells like chloroform," I said. I bent over, sniffed the rag, and was dizzy. "It *is* chloroform! Move him and throw open the door, before we're all overcome!"

"He was sent here to murder someone," Newton said.

"But the fumes overcame him." I knew this place had bad ventilation. Never did I imagine it was a good thing. I rushed to save the babies, convincing myself they needed saving and indeed, the fumes had turned the tips of their fingers dark, or perhaps I imagined it. Their red veins were in sharp contrast to the pale yellow-green skin and they flapped about in un-plantlike fashion, their legs unusually long.

"Something's wrong with them," I said.

"They are churning like an angry sea," said Paracelsus.

"Or like wrinkles in spacetime," said Newton.

"They need fresh air," I said. "We all do. We need to evacuate until the fumes diffuse. Get out and let me handle this."

"Save his communication device. We'll see who is trying to

contact him," Newton said. He stooped next to the body. He held up the device. "Ahh, here it is."

I scooted them out into the hall, Newton pushing the stroller. Once the rest were out, I picked up the chloroform rag, held it sideways at arm's length, and headed for the courtyard. Once in the courtyard, I wrapped a rock in the rag and tossed it over the wall.

"Stella, your quick thinking sent the foul rag into exile. Do tell, what do you make of this?" Newton showed me the device.

How was Operation Eternal Sleep?

Newton held the device out to me. "It begs for a reply."

"Type back," I said.

"What is type?"

"Here. Let me show you."

Fine, I typed cautiously.

Are they dead?

They will be soon.

The nanny as well?

No. She was absent.

I said to get rid of the babies AND the extraneous woman. We can't have advocates. I thought getting rid of extraneous women was your specialty.

My blood ran cold. I knew we weren't safe, but we'd only been here a day before the first murder attempt.

"What's wrong?" Isaac asked.

"We have to get out of here."

Ursula came out with the body. She held the man's torso and Paracelsus the legs. His face was a ghastly mess of congealed blood. They dropped him on the ground.

"Oink! Take a load off," Ursula said.

"He was there to kill me and the babies!" I said. I held out the device. "Read this."

Ursula read the text.

"Who is it?" I said, panicky. "Who ordered the killing? Why me?"

"That's easily solved," said Newton. "Lure the person here."

"Not before I get more information," said Ursula. She took the phone, typed, and showed me the screen.

The nanny wasn't interested in me. She must hate men.

I'm surprised you failed with your Romeo act. How do you get so much action as ugly as you are?

"Ugh," said Ursula. "I knew it. False romance! If I hadn't gotten the foreskin in the eye, I might not have seen it. The Henchman was hired to woo and dispose of. Glad I got away in time."

"It makes a strong case for limiting who you allow in your space at any time," said Newton, still ruminating over spacetime.

"Are they monitoring our movements?" I asked. "Don't they know he's dead and we're in the courtyard?"

"They could but I'm not sure they understand the technology. For now, I've been put in charge of monitoring this place and all of the Vice Patrol agents in this district. Maybe the next step will be Commissioner." She pushed buttons on her device. "I'll call for a duo. We've got to get rid of this corpse."

Two Crisper patrols appeared. "What do you need?"

"Time to feed the pigs. The Henchman has taken a tumble."

"Pigs are hungry."

As her agents took away the Henchman, Ursula sent another message and showed it to us before sending. *Help. I'm in the courtyard. I've fallen and I can't get up.*

"Brilliant!" said Newton. "The perpetrator or some emissary from the evil one should be here any moment. I'd like to challenge the person who wished for Stella to be sent off!"

"Play it cool, whoever it is," Ursula warned "Angel, keep it zipped."

"Let's take bets on who it is," the kid said.

I said, "It could be a scientist who doesn't want the Homunculus Project to succeed. Clearly, Sir Gotfried had it in for these guys!"

"Face it, someone's got to do something with these babies,"

Angel said. "They have no muscle tone." She grabbed Baby Bert's arms and moved them as if he was doing pull ups.

"Leave it be," Ursula said sharply.

"He's green and he stares. Why isn't he normal?"

"They are not," Paracelsus said. "We did not promise normal infants."

"We promised nothing," said Newton. "We were ordered to produce some fanciful marvel."

"This conversation must stop. We want to identify the perpetrator but not reveal how we lured him here. He's probably dangerous," said Ursula. She heaved the Henchman's device over the courtyard wall.

Layal ran in breathing as heavily as I'd been less than an hour ago. "How can you... What happened? I was just—"

"The Henchman tripped over his own clumsy feet," Ursula said.

"Where is he?"

"He's pig food."

"How unfortunate for the Henchman. He must be replaced. A good Henchman is hard to find. The homunculi?"

I piped up. "Healthy as can be. Take a look in the stroller. What were you asking, Lord Layal?" This jerk had tried to have me killed but I wasn't going to let him know I knew.

Layal's expression was blank. He came over to the stroller and looked askance at the occupants, as if he couldn't bear to see them. "I'm pleased to know they are with us. What wonders they are! Were I the ruler, you would be rewarded. I am, however, not in charge here. I was taken in to peeve my mother, their sister." He allowed himself to get a better look. "I don't know why but it's as if I've known them forever." He lofted his hand over his nose, bringing their smell to his nostrils. "They conjure up all sorts of memories of my life in the wild. Ursula, is it the same with you?"

I was confused. This wasn't the first time someone had commented on the familiarity of the plants, but they'd come from the middle of nowhere.

"I didn't live in the wild but possibly, your Heirship, they carry some tinge of wild," Ursula replied noncommittally.

"Oh, but with these two youngsters among us, I am a distant heir."

"You can't win them all. I am constantly passed over for the Commissioner position."

"Oh Ursula, you have all the power you need." He pointed to me. "How soon can you get ready?"

"Get ready?" Fear enveloped me, like the scent of a hog lot. "F-for what?"

"To present them to the Cochton brothers."

It was unbelievably hot in the courtyard. "What do I need to do?"

"Fix them up and then dress them formally. Make yourselves presentable. Show them to my uncles in their business office. Newton, don't forget the wig. You look like any old rotter without it."

The whole incident with the Henchman had me shook. One thing was clear, Layal had wanted the homunculi dead, and me to the pigs, to secure his status as the only Cochton heir. Little did he know, or perhaps he did, considering his comment about the floral scent, he was indeed the only human heir. Newton hung near as I wheeled the babies back to my bedroom. He followed me in and closed the door behind us.

"Stella, I'm sorry I got you mixed up in this. I only did it because I wanted to get near you. I should have rested in my loneliness. Long ago, I was far too cocky. I saw myself as the greatest, purest mind that ever lived. I sought to unite earth with the heavens through alchemy. Now you tell me that the heavens are filled with these giant sucking holes with gravity tentacles. There's no benevolence anywhere. Some days it feels as if the Enlightenment never happened."

"Of course it did! The way you measure had my heart beating. That's post-Enlightenment lust if ever there was such."

"I marveled at your creativity and the use of, what was it? Enzymes?"

"We can find a way out of here. Now, go back to your room and put on that silly wig. I'll get these little ones ready." I gave him a kiss goodbye, casting my pleas to the messy universe that this wouldn't be our last but even if it was, I regretted nothing. These moments with him were worth death.

CHAPTER TWENTY-ONE

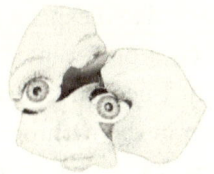

I knew this day would come but not that it would affect my stomach. Despite my brave words to Newton, I went to my room and threw up. In truth, I had no plan. How would I present these gangly things? They'd fooled the public, but the leaders of our nation were much smarter and more ruthless. I'd have to hope for failing eyesight. I opened the drawer beneath the changing table and was overwhelmed with the bloom of onesies, shirts, tiny socks, even shoes. They were designed for real infants, not these dolls. If only someone would have bothered to consult us as to what form and size the homunculi would be.

I had no idea what babies might wear to a special occasion. I'd barely seen a baby in my life. Jelly wore fancy dresses, but these homuncufakes were tributes to masculinity. I riffled through the drawer. At last, I was able to dig out identical white tiny tuxedos with matching green bow ties. The floppy feet would be impossible to keep shoes on. I found some booties, white knit with silky strings to tie them. I grabbed Little Clarence's leg, slipped a bootie over the foot and tied it. The foot dropped and the bootie slid off. I tried again, wrapping the ribbon around the leg and fastening it with a bow at the front.

The heads were growing bushy clumps of pale roots. I had to

admit, these things were cute in a horrible way. Their skin was leathery and waxy, like a succulent. They emitted a pleasant jasmine odor. Like all plants, they were silently sentient. I swore they sent love my way. As I touched them, I grew calmer.

I found two bonnets in the chests of drawers. I tied one on Clarence, another on Bert. They looked so darling. If only there was a place in the word for these sweet things. I arranged them in the buggy. So cute. If only I dared explain to the Cochton brothers how I didn't mean to betray, I only wanted to please.

The babies were ready. I needed to make myself presentable. I washed my face with soap in the bathroom. I brushed my teeth. I looked around my room for a change of clothes. Who was I fooling? There were no extra clothes for me. One way or another, I wouldn't be staying.

Someone rapped on the door. I nearly jumped out of my skin. It was Newton.

"Stella, I had to see you. I want-I want you to flee." He touched the front of his pants. "Take my button and run out of here."

"Your button?"

"Yes, hold it to your neck. It will stop your chip from being sensed. This way, you can escape."

"Isaac, you're going to need that button. You can't go in front of the Cochton brothers with your, er, bagpipes hanging out."

"I have a bad premonition about this presentation."

"I do, too, but we are going to have to show these babies to their Daddies and make a quick exit."

"Stella, if anything happens, I want you to know—and it's more difficult than calculus to admit—but I'm in love with you."

I was overwhelmed and overjoyed. "I love you, too."

Our kiss forged an alloy and was interrupted too soon as a Vice Patrol agent came down the hall. "Newton, I'm here for you."

I grabbed the buggy and tried to follow them out. "Not you," said the Washer. "Wait here."

I closed my door behind Newton. I was giddy from our

revelation and buoyantly optimistic. I observed the babies. They were too green for an infant but too pale for a plant. Their "limbs" were slightly shriveled. They needed water. I filled a baby bottle with water, pulled back the bonnet slightly, and sprinkled some water on Little Clarence. I moved on to Baby Bert but was only half way through the watering when someone knocked on the door. It was Ursula and Angel. Angel rushed in and tickled the babies.

"They're so ugly-cute. Mom, can I have a brother?"

"No, Angel. Get away from them. Stella, follow me. Newton and Paracelsus are being entertained with a buffet. I'll do what I can to make this work but suspension of disbelief only goes so far. Paracelsus is pushing the liquor. I hope it helps."

A chill went through me. I wasn't sure how much Ursula was in on the deception. I did know one thing. She could shoot me on the spot if things went wrong.

We went up to the third floor in the elevator. The door opened to a wide hall. Angel ran down it.

"Angel, get back here. Be respectful!" Angel stopped and danced around instead.

"They're right behind the set of double doors."

The creepy nephew who had sent the Henchman came out of the doors.

"Hellooo! We've been waiting for you. The moment of truth has arrived. The future is now, we are making merry. Join us! Come in as I announce your arrival."

He opened the door and the smell of Porkies wafted out. I peeked around him as he stood in front of me. There they were— Bert in a business suit and Clarence in cowboy boots, a string tie, and buckskin. They were wrinkled beyond belief. Most people here didn't live long enough to boast many skin folds. They gathered at a buffet table including Porkies, blood sausage, corn on the cob, pork rind, and bacon. Newton stood holding a plate with a single cob of corn while Paracelsus and the other men feasted in front of a picture window, all of Cochtonville in their view—

Cochton Enterprises, the town square, the Pavilion, the lazy river winding through town.

I hung back near the door with the babies. They were blank eyed and restless, identically ugly-cute with their puckered lips. Angel poked at them. "Can I babysit them?"

Ursula pulled her away. "Don't touch them," she whispered.

"The tiny outfits..."

"Shhh."

"Uncles!" said Layal. "The moment is here. Prepare to meet your offspring!"

"A toast to the alchemists," Clarence said, holding up a glass. He wasn't drunk enough. He easily clinked his goblet with that of Paracelsus.

"It's been quite a journey, hasn't it?" Bert said to Newton. "We hope you're enjoying your stay. Let's be optimistic it continues. We are grateful for the opportunity to procreate. Trying something new is always exhilarating. What you provided was a once in a lifetime experience."

"If you are not satisfied with the results, we can try again," Newton ventured. "With alchemy, anything is possible."

"Is something wrong?" Clarence asked. "You all seem nervous and apologetic and your wig is crooked."

"Not in the least."

With trembling hand, Paracelsus put his glass on the table. "A homunculus always needs training. Please keep this in mind. You will need a full staff of tutors. They have growing up to do. They still look like frogs."

Newton fidgeted. "You might say they are sprouts. We've been grateful to be in your service. We will present the offspring and if you will, be on our way. No further trouble. We'll be out the door and down the street."

Clarence reddened. "What are you talking about? You are considering leaving? We made you, you're our asset. Aren't you grateful for another chance at life? You go nowhere unless we say so."

"Clarence, it might be true, but we are grateful for their efforts today. Stop the nonsense! Let me see my son," Bert said, with a light hopefulness to his gravelly old voice. "I've been waiting for this all my life. Bring out the babies."

Ursula gave me a shove. The squeaky wheels of the old buggy resonated in the hollow room. The leaders of our nation looked at me eagerly. The babies did their best to nestle their root-ball heads beneath the stroller canopy while flapping their covered toes toward the light from the windows. I walked slowly, step by step, my legs weak as gelatin.

Bert turned to me as I approached. Tears streamed down his face. Clarence adjusted his bolo tie, sweat sparkling on the skin showing through his sparse hair. He put his hands in his pockets, his fleshy cheeks flexing as he breathed nervously. In a few steps, all would be seen. The whole scheme would be revealed. I couldn't do it. I couldn't. I couldn't take one more step pushing these counterfeits. And yet, there was Newton, standing sideways, his eyes on mine, pulling me forward with all the attraction of a superconducting magnet, or maybe, to be old school, the earth toward the moon. The risk, the risk to be at his side was worth it. How lucky I was to be in league with this man. I had to pretend nothing was amiss *for him.*

I walked from the door, across the polished plastic floor, toward the men as they stood near the massive buffet table, as if I was walking down an aisle. The air in here was so fresh, as if they pumped in plenty of oxygen. I gripped the pram's handle. At least I had something to do with my nervous hands. I feared these guys, as well I should, and I walked toward them, nearly fainting.

"Wait!" Layal called out, making me jump out of my skin. "Let me take it from here."

I hardly knew what to think. He had too many tricks up his sleeve.

He brushed up beside me, bumping me. "I'll push. They are my cousins, I'll care for them."

"But you don't know..." My voice trailed off. Why was I concerned if he knew how to care for them? They were frauds.

"It's alright, Stella," Paracelsus said. "We must do what's best for them and what the Cochtons want is what is best."

Bert hugged himself. "Yes, of course. All in the family."

Layal obviously held back any surprise at the babies' appearance. He'd gotten a glimpse of them after all. He held out a finger and ran it across Baby Bert's cool, waxy arm. "Please leave me instructions as to their care. I must get to know them and later, to serve them."

He took the stroller from me and I backed away, my eyes on Newton. I was relieved of the babies but what now? Was this a sudden parting? I would see him again, I had to see him again. I couldn't let the ocean of time and space swallow us. He too, was shocked and almost tearful.

"Come on," Ursula took my arm and moved me to the door. This was it. After all this time. No real chance to say goodbye.

"Let us see our sons!" Bert cried. Ursula paused our exit. Layal propelled the stroller and halted before the buffet table.

"Come to Daddy!" Bert sobbed with open arms.

Clarence held out shaky hands while Ursula wiped away a tear.

Layal tenderly took Baby Bert and placed him in Bert's cradled arms. He grabbed Little Clarence from the buggy and handed him to his father.

The silence was punctuated by Bert's sniffs as he beheld Baby Bert.

Clarence Cochton cleared his throat as he held Little Clarence at arm's length. "This is the ugliest damn baby I've ever seen."

CHAPTER TWENTY-TWO

Little Clarence kicked his legs and waved his tendril arms as his head flopped about. The tiny white silk cap fell to the floor, showing the rootish hair spreading from the head.

"Sir, support his head," I said from afar.

"You've never seen a baby," said Bert. "It's unfair to declare this the ugliest baby you've ever seen."

"The hair is gruesome! This is more uncouth than a Pesto infant."

The baby flopped in his hands and kicked until a booty fell to the polished floor.

"Look at his rosy cheek! He loves you already. He needs you, you're his father," Layal insisted, while Newton and I shared our concern via horrified looks. Clarence Cochton was used to pulling the wool over other people's eyes, not having it placed over his.

Clarence was red in the face. "Alchemists! What is this monstrosity?"

"It's the homunculus you requested," Paracelsus said.

Clarence turned the baby over his arm and spanked it. "It doesn't cry. Don't babies cry?"

"We've added an improvement," said Newton. My heart fluttered at his quick thinking. "They don't blink either. This will be so much better when they are world leaders. No crying, no emotion."

"No, these aren't babies. Where is my Henchman? Guards, call the Henchman!"

Bert held his baby up to his cheek. "Brother, calm down! You're alarming them."

Clarence tossed his baby over one shoulder and sniffed it. "It doesn't smell human. It smells...green."

With his free arm, he wrenched off Bert's baby's hat, tied by a simple ribbon. The bulbous dented head was exposed. "This is not a head!" Clarence pinched off a few strands of hair and held them to Bert's face. "Awfully long for baby hair, and not silky. Shouldn't hair be silky?"

Little Bert stretched out his legs toward Clarence.

"It smells too good," Clarence said, sniffing his baby's diaper.

"Jasmine and poop contain the same fragrance molecule but in different concentrations. It's a metabolic improvement," I said, forgetting my ancillary status. Although deceit sat poorly in my stomach, I was happy to see the plants move arms and legs as if they were animals.

Clarence looked insulted. "Where is the Henchman? This former nanny is overdue for a visit."

"He's on a courtesy call, your greatness," Ursula replied.

"Uncles, please, rely on me for all your needs."

Bert lifted his baby to his nose. Baby Bert wiggled. A bootie fell to the floor. Bert closed his eyes peacefully. "It's a pleasant improvement."

"Brother, you look like a fool, your snout is in a diaper."

"Brother, you are missing the point. Here, sniff." He shoved the baby into his taller brother's face. Baby Bert again stretched out his legs. The other booty dropped off. The ankle was slightly creased where the bootie had been. Clarence slapped the baby. Bert shoved it closer. Baby Bert kicked at Clarence. Clarence shuddered, as if the scent repelled him. It was more than a smell grabbing him. With a gag, Clarence struggled, Baby Bert's legs around his neck right above his tie. The baby was strangling him! Holding Little Clarence above his head, he lurched toward Bert before falling to the polished floor, his baby in his grasp, the legs of Baby Bert around his neck as the homunculus rested on his chest.

"Brother!" cried Bert, falling creakily to his knees beside Clarence.

The guards stepped in, using their strength to tug at Baby Bert whose legs stretched but held fast.

"No," cried Bert. "Do not injure the heir! Life and dynasty must go on."

The Crisper guards, trained to obey, stopped. Red in the face, Clarence, being strangled by Baby Bert, slammed his baby onto Bert in an act of anger. He grabbed for his own neck, tugging helplessly at the baby legs as his cowboy boots rat-tatted on the floor.

Following his plant brother's lead, Little Clarence flapped his legs and latched onto Bert's neck. No matter how much I'd grown to dislike the bros, I couldn't bear to watch them suffer.

The guards moved to help, following Bert's advice, they pulled the tendrils cautiously.

Growing worried, I said, "There's got to be herbicide somewhere. The grass is immaculate. Where's the garden shed?"

"Herbicide?" said Ursula.

"I need herbicide. Now!" I shouted. Who'd have thought working with plants would be dangerous?

"We have a lawncare service," Ursula said. "But they are not on the premises. What are you saying?"

"I can't say what I'm saying."

"The lawn care is privatized. I'll call headquarters to send a team right away." She spoke into her All Things Device. "Another plant incident. It's a doozy! Send a chopper with spray immediately. Yeah, you got the location right."

The leaders of our nation were struggling. There wasn't time for a helicopter rescue. A diversion. A distraction. I ran to the buffet table and grabbed two blood sausages. I flung them next to the babies. "Come on now, you know you like blood." The babies flopped in the direction of the food, as if they were being blown, but didn't release their grasps.

"Damn, they are too young to eat solid foods," Angel said as she hopped over. Squatting, she helped the infants latch on to the meat by shoving sausages onto their bottle-ready mouths. They closed their lips, Little Bert on one sausage and Baby Clarence on another, covering the ends of the meat.

"Come on, little fatty, stop squeezing!" She pulled gently at the tendrils around Bert's neck, tugging them off.

"Let go, little cutie," she said as she removed Little Clarence.

She sat back in triumph. "All they need is love."

We rushed to the brothers kneeling beside them. Bert was on his side and Ursula turned him over.

"Bloody red eye," Newton gasped. "The other one, too! And the necks."

"Ligature marks," said Ursula.

"They wet themselves," Layal observed. "Not dignified."

"They were scared. Get a doctor!" I called.

Paracelsus stepped forward and removed his cap. "I'm a doctor." He bent over and put his ear to Clarence's chest, then Bert's. "Sadly, they are in need of more than a doctor."

"They're dead?" Layal said joyfully.

"Resurrection is the next step. In my day, I believed in using manure for such."

"Shouldn't we do it the way that was done to bring you back to life?" I asked. I wasn't sure what had happened. Had the brothers murdered each other using plants?

"Certainly, they came up with a better process for us. I have no manure after odor." Newton sniffed beneath his arm.

Layal said, "I am the heir, I will supervise the resurrection of my uncles. They were history buffs. How is this done the ancient way? It's what they would have wanted."

"Cut the body into quarters. Bury it in manure," Paracelsus said.

Layal clapped him on the back. "Perfect! You will be in charge of this."

The babies were prone on the sausage, their bottle mouth openings slimy and quivering over the meat. Angel patted them as if they were pets.

Layal walked over and stepped on Baby Bert's sausage. "Now, get rid of the killers. They've done more than I could have imagined."

Obediently, Ursula unholstered her All Things Weapon. "Angel, get your hands off those deadly kids."

"Mom, they're so cute. They didn't mean it!"

"Get away!"

"Come jump on my back," Paracelsus said kindly.

"No, she'll kill them!"

"I do hate children. Guards, grab the brat!" Layal said.

"No need," Ursula said angrily, as Paracelsus peeled Angel from the babies.

Ursula pointed her weapon, pushed a few buttons, and cut the homunculi into pieces. Their tattered outfits flew and the smell of jasmine and sausages filled the room.

"Take them outside and toss these to the pigs," she told Angel, handing her the ratty root balls. The girl grabbed the two severed heads and glumly trudged off.

Layal turned to us. "Sooo, the killer plants were made into babies."

"Killer plants?" Newton and Paracelsus said together.

"It's impossible!" I added. "There's no such thing."

"You're not telling the truth. The folklore about these seeds has floated around in Cochtonia for a while. I saw them myself in the wild when I lived in exile."

Newton, Paracelsus, and I huddled together in fear. We'd ignorantly killed the leaders of our nation? It was preposterous.

Layal went on. "This species pops up now and then. The origin is known. They began as seeds found in the pocket of Thomas Jefferson. My uncles love history, as you are aware, and bought his corduroy pants as a relic of the past. The seeds were revived by scientists at Cochton Enterprises. It was hoped they would be a new crop, one to outshine those found elsewhere. Reports arose about peoples' necks becoming entangled in the vines, so the production was halted. They're weeds and are sprayed periodically when they are discovered. One of you is a skilled insurrectionist, save I'm still alive. You alchemists are much more dangerous and useful than I suspected."

I was flabbergasted. My imposter knees were knocking. I should have known, should have suspected when Sir Gotfried was on the floor with his empty eyes and candy corn drizzle, that the plants had done him in. And the Henchman! They'd killed him, too. No, it was on me. I'd been hasty. NezLeigh had mentioned problems with the plants and so had Gotfried. The veil of truth had been ripped open. The babes were not just a fraud, but a deadly fraud. The heir of Cochtonia couldn't have been happier about it.

Newton put his hand on my back as he addressed Layal. "It's obvious the babies had the vital spirit. It became tainted after their birth. Their gestation was interrupted. We should not have let them be presented as they were. The lions ate the sun so to speak. We fall upon your mercy."

"My uncles demanded it. I have nothing but thanks. Such a clever scheme. I underestimated alchemy."

"Yes, and we obey those who are born to rule. We are humble servants."

"The fools ordered their own doom with their folly. We will not repeat the experiment. We will, however, sell HumP t-shirts for as long as it is profitable. In the short term, we need to release this new information concerning their absence slowly, so as to not inflame the public."

"What do we do in the meantime?" Ursula asked.

"In the meantime? I'm the ruler."

"It will upset the citizens. Upheaval makes room for authoritarians," Newton said.

Paracelsus took Ursula's hand. "There's no room for love when domination is the goal. Love makes a better way."

"On the contrary. Nix to love. It's nothing more than sex wrapped up in glitter. We *will* be authoritarians. My uncles met regularly with historical authoritarians to get tips. An autocracy, an authoritarian regime, isn't built in a day. I won't abandon it, I'm the dictator! Now, Ursula, what shall I do with the three of them?" Layal eyed the alchemists and me.

"They should be useful," she said. "Do you have an immediate need for alchemy?"

Paracelsus swept up the scattered plant parts. He held the double sprout penis of Baby Bert aloft. "Never have I seen such an obviously vital organ. No doubt it will be superior to mandrake. Shall we test it, Officer?" Their intimacy shocked me. I knew they had an attraction, but now was a strange time to talk about it in public.

"Mandrake? Forgive me my modernisms. I don't know what it is. A plant?" said Layal.

"Oh yes, a potent one. Mandrake is of ancient use to alchemists," Paracelsus went on. "These penises are devoid of human blood. They resemble mandrakes, far more than they should. In the right hands, what's left of the killers is valuable. We could make a potion, impart fertility, and allow you to reproduce the old-fashioned way."

"I've read of such lore," Layal said. "I'm well-read. Who here knows about *plants*?" He said the last word slowly, like peeling off a bandage. And there it was, my raw, failed, stupid attempt to appease the Cochton family, openly sore and seditious. A wave of nausea hit me.

"I-I-I do. I work for the foods division."

"Good. I order you to make a potion, as he claims it imparts fertility, and use it on me."

"From the mandrake bits?" Newton said.

"Of course. Guards! Take my uncles away. Prepare them how the alchemist directs. If it fails, I need a potion imparting fertility.

We are keeping Cochtonia in the family at all costs. Alchemists, I appreciate your efforts today, planned or not. Don't think of trying it again. If this fails, there will be a pig farm somewhere."

Newton stepped forward. "She needs the assistance of an alchemist. I will be the one. Paracelsus must stay here and supervise the attempted revival of our former leaders. Where should my work be done? I need a laboratory and the proper chemicals. The potion can't be made just anywhere. We must return to the laboratory and add thoughtful oratory to our labor."

"Oh, fine. How long will it take to make the potion?"

"The moon must be right," Paracelsus said.

"How about a month, or less?" said Layal. "I can't keep this tragedy a secret for much longer. I have to offer an alternative to the homunculi."

At last, Vice Patrol burst in hauling spray tanks with herbicides. These were two older guys, not modified.

"Hold your fire," Layal said, holding up a hand. "I don't need spraying. Oh no, no, no, no. I need unadulterated chromosomes. You're going to take these two brilliant scientists back to their laboratory at Cochton Enterprises to make a fertility potion. They are our future."

"We got a call for herbicide," one said, confused.

"A plant incident," said the other.

"The 'plant incident' is going to be making a fertility potion from a plant," Ursula said. "I'm sure I stated as much. I told you to come quickly and get these scientists to their lab, no questions asked."

"I bestow the vital organs into your care." Paracelsus handed me the double penis. "I suggest a tincture." He bowed to Layal. "Alchemy will extract the pure essence of the mandrake if it be your will. Likewise, your uncles will be risen, or not, according to your desires. In the meantime, let me cast your chart and ask the stars the perfect day to begin the fertility rituals. The potion must be made and consumed when the moon is waxing and the stage must be set for imbibing it. This means at least one full moon cycle so you need to be patient."

"Who will be drinking it?"

"You of course, and anyone you wish to make fertile."

"It's not my policy to drink alone, it's bad for the soul. You'll all be joining me. Agents, take them away."

We went willingly with guards, grateful to be walking out. As we passed through the front doors, I saw the heads, root balls in the dirt near the entrance. Angel had tossed them but they hadn't made it into the moat with the pigs. They lay beside the door, eyes up and mouths open.

CHAPTER TWENTY-THREE

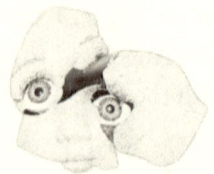

Back in the lab, I put the dick in a beaker and went to examine the growth chamber. It was a cluster of dead plants.

"Sir Gotfried killed them all," I told Newton. "Do you think he knew? Clearly, he didn't trip and neither did the Henchman. The whole scene was ghastly! At least we're free for a while. Making a potion was brilliant thinking on Paracelsus's part. I'm so glad to be away from that place and doing as we please for a month or more."

"The bed was much better there," Newton said.

I flung myself on him and buried my face in his ruffled chest, which smelled vaguely of earth. "I didn't want any of it to happen. I've never seen anything so terrible."

He wrapped his arms around me. "They aren't suffering now and their worries are buried with them."

"What will happen? They were horrible and yet they held this place together."

"We must be careful. If my first life taught me anything about government, one despot often follows another. A point working in our favor—clearly the nephew is pleased to be rid of them."

"And now another pseudoscience on demand is expected. A fertility potion! I shouldn't have propagated those plants. I wanted flowers for salmagundi, not an insurrection. All of this trouble started with a damn salad."

"It started with you doing your best to help us. We were in a predicament. The Cochtons sought immortality. They, I'm ashamed to say it, they sought to breach the bounds of science, to skip steps, using alchemy."

"You are renouncing alchemy?"

"You were right all along. Alchemy and its secrets are wrong. We need science, pure science, to save us."

"It's alright, alchemists wanted to do great things. Big ideas aren't always bad." I went to the lab coats on the hook by the door. I had several and he was close to my size. I slipped one from the hook. "Let's make you a modern scientist now, shall we? It's as wonderful and promising as alchemy. Here, hold out your arms and I'll slip it on."

He looked so cute in his lab coat. I drew Newton into my arms. "It's okay to have big dreams. Who's to say they aren't practical until we try?"

"You are the most caring soul I've ever known. I must meet your father."

"Barnabus? No! You'd hate him. And it didn't start with caring. I wanted a night with a caveman. I, too, had ambitions, shallow, craven, but attainable."

"Your ambitions didn't hurt anyone."

"They did hurt someone. I left the caveman when I should have investigated. His legs were blue. I turned blue. Lady LouOtta thought we had a disease. I did, too. I ran. It turned out to be blue dye from a cheap suit. I washed it off in my shower at home. "

Newton was puzzled by my condensed version of the incident. "You became blue?"

"Yes, blue-gray from touching him. It was dye."

"You assumed it was necrotic?"

"Yes!"

"It was logical."

"But I ran like a coward."

"Would bravery have changed the situation for the better?"

"Not at the time. I didn't know the truth."

"Without the truth, you had no munitions. It would have been foolish."

"I know it now."

"A person can only act with the truth in hand."

I said, "If only I could go back in time, I wouldn't have run. I can't stop wondering what happened to him."

"We must go to the last place you saw him and ask."

"You're the sweetest man alive. Are you sure you're Isaac Newton?" I kissed him on the cheek before handing him a gallon bottle of reagent-grade ethanol. "Did Paracelsus say he wanted to make a tincture? If so, we'll need some alcohol. Pour this over the plant matter. We'll soak it to extract it. Then leave the plant matter in it for effect. I doubt anything will work but it should buy us time. Time together, until...until the end."

I considered what else to add to this tonic. I doubted anything would work but I needed to do my best. I was skeptical but hope wasn't completely dead. The woman in Wowville was pregnant, as Mom had noted. There was a fertility secret out there somewhere.

The plant part stiffened in the tincture.

Newton put a hand to his chin as he observed. "Fascinating! It feels so wonderful to be in the laboratory again. We must give our new leader hope. And keep giving him hope to appease him. We should add representations of the four elements to this solution to give it some alchemical flare. It has liquid, the alcohol, which we can burn, so it's fire and water together. We can ignite it for show. The plant represents the earth. What about air?"

"Carbon dioxide! We'll bubble it in just before we present it. Even if the potion doesn't work, it will be a bubbly alcoholic drink, certain to give a nice buzz. He'll at least feel fertile and attractive." The sunlight dancing and refracting through the beakers gave me my own kind of hope. Science was truth, even in the darkest of times. Technology could be controlled but basic science, no. It was free. It was the cradle of enlightenment.

Newton moved in to embrace me from behind. "You have fine hair and a rump a horse would envy. If only we had time and not trouble! We could spend our days at pasture, and I would give you pleasure." He kissed my neck and put a hand on my inner thigh. "I'm an old-fashioned gentleman. We should make this legal."

I nuzzled into him. "Not much is legal here."

"I'm undaunted by impediments."

Releasing fear of societal pressures allows couples to fully experience intimacy and the complete phases of sexuality, beginning with excitement in which a woman's pelvic area feels expansive, as if it could swallow the world.

I reached out a hand and touched his hip as he pressed close, lifting my hair and kissing the back of my neck.

An alarm went off and the hazard lights flashed as instructions rang out. "Evacuation Drill! Fire! Fire!"

"What now?" Newton said, backing away.

I grabbed his hand. "Come on."

We hurried down the stairs along with the other scientists and engineers, who must have been surprised to see us since we had so recently left with such fanfare. No one took the time to inquire. The alarm was both frightening and irritating as we all had important things we were abandoning to fate. Many people carried their electronic lab notebooks and a few had beakers in hand. We came out in the parking lot, but having no car, we took to the sidewalk, unsure where to go to escape the chaos.

The town was scattered with Agros holding lit plastic bags on pitchforks. Clearly this irritating smoke had been sucked into the Cochton Enterprises ventilation and set off the fire alarm. I tried to weave us through the crowd. We burst onto the sidewalk only to be met by a volley of Vice Patrol. We ran, not sure if anyone was after us or even knew we were there. Lights flashed because we were traversing the sidewalk without paying, but everyone was rushing to either get away from the smell or the enforcers, or both. With each flash, Newton cringed. We turned down a cracked sidewalk, near the town square. We were in the neighborhood of the bar.

"Where are we going?" Newton puffed. We were both winded.

I stopped in front the bar. "This is the place where I had my rental. It's at least familiar. Should we go in? The smoke isn't healthy."

Newton pulled open the heavy door and we entered the darkened bar. The bartender with a long white braid was at the counter. Two tiny-eyed kids were sitting there with her. They ran into the bathroom to hide when we came in, leaving a plate of half-eaten frozen raspberries.

"What brings you here?" the woman asked in a voice mellowed by age.

"The crowds were pressing on me and the smoke is threatening our vitality." Newton bowed. "Sir Isaac Newton, at your service."

"Aren't you a charmer?" she said genuinely. "How may I help you?"

"I seek a place to catch my breath and some answers."

"The kids are innocent. They've been with me the entire time," she said defensively. "They come here for the fruit I add to drinks."

The glittering Tiffany lampshades distracted Newton. He watched one as he spoke. "I'm not here for children. But tell me, why is there so much smoke? What is their peeve?"

"They were cheated out of their land by the Cochtons and they object to the privatized sidewalks. If they can create a chaos, the sensors can't keep up. For a brief moment in time, the sidewalks are free to all."

"I see. They aren't killed by the authorities for their insurrection? The politics of this place baffle me."

"Some were killed when they first tried it, but they sanctify martyrdom and it encouraged them."

"There is nothing like a martyr to stimulate passion and imagination."

"Neither of those fine qualities are appreciated here. You see why more aren't shot on the spot?"

"Indeed. They might gain sympathy."

"Instead, they are reviled, which is what the Cochtons want. Can I get you a drink? Who's the gal?"

I was taking it all in. I hadn't thought to ask the "whys" of this place. "You probably don't recognize me. I've rented from you. The name's Stella Virginia Smithfailed."

"I *do* remember you. The caveman fiasco! He was accused of having a disease."

I blushed. "It turned out to be indigo dye from his cheap suit."

"LouOtta overreacted, as she does."

"And I ran away. What ever happened to the poor guy?" I asked.

"You want a repeat performance? A threesome?"

"It's not for sex. I need to know what happened to him."

"LouOtta had him returned to the State Crisper Facility."

"What became of him?"

"I'm not sure. I put him on my hire list, but he hasn't been released because he's not great for sex—he prefers talking, but he's sweet as all get out."

Newton said, "Stella has a good heart and the betrayal weighs on her. We hope to make it right."

"Our treatment of the Crisper strippers weighs on me as well. It's cruel and we've left no room for romance here in Cochtonia."

"How easy would that be? To bust him out?" I asked.

"Not hard I imagine. Keeping him is expensive, but he won't get sent back unless he's got approved work."

"Stella, he can be part of an experiment."

"Yes!"

"You aren't going to harm him, are you? He's a darling."

"Not at all. Where is this facility?"

"I don't know. The Vice Patrol pick 'em up and bring 'em back."

"The location is known by the Vice Patrol?"

"I imagine it is. Don't they know too much?"

"Thank you," I said. "Newton, it's time to meet my parents after all."

We walked away from town, the smoke and din diminishing as we went. At last, we came to the small white house.

"It's me, I'm home!" I walked in, Newton following, still blinking from the smoke, or perhaps at the starkness of my home's white interior.

Mom and Dad were leaned back in their recliners, flagons of ale on the end tables. They sat up in surprise. Mom nearly cried. "Stella, we're so happy to have you home! Who's this? Is it Isaac Newton? Here?"

"It's Isaac Newton, Mom. He's a friend."

Newton held out his hand and Dad leapt up creakily and shook it with enthusiasm.

"Friend with benefits?" NezLeigh came from her room or should I say, my room with a handful of plastic bags.

"It's an honor, a damn honor." Dad put an arm around Newton and took their picture together. "Where's the other one—the big guy?"

"He's at the Cochton abode. Mom," I said, "Newton and I are on a mission. Did you ever go to the State Crisper Facility?"

"Why yes, but can we sit and have a chat? Why are you home? How are the babies? Are things alright?"

"No, not at all. Nothing is right! I betrayed a man and I have a brief amount of time to rectify it. I *must!* He's at the Facility and I want to bring him back."

"I've been there—not recently, of course. I picked up some releases. The State Crisper Facility is in the country, disguised as a hog facility."

"He's there. How do I get there? How do I get in?"

"Doors sense a magnetic chip. It's like a doggy door."

"Newton will have the chip to unlock since that's where he started out?"

"He should be able to return at any time, but Stella, you've gotten too attached to someone you shouldn't be worrying about. He's a Crisper. They were made to be erotic escorts."

"Mom, how do you find the place?"

"It's marked with a barn quilt, you know, a colorful square pattern painted on a sheet of vinyl and used for an outdoor decoration."

"Where is it?"

"Out where the hills begin to roll. It was a farm once. Lots of the old farm houses and barns are used for clandestine operations now."

"Like my old place," NezLeigh said. "Damn, I bet it's why former Dad got rid of us."

Dad sat back down and scratched his belly. "Where are the homunculus infants? They sure were an amazing feat of science."

"They were, but they're done. Science never sleeps. We came back to make a fertility potion. We have some extra time. Not much, but enough to find this man," I explained.

"Fertility is a thing of the past." Dad took a swig of ale.

I was afraid to reveal too much. "It's a back-up plan. The nephew wants it."

"He's trouble," Dad said. "How about some ice cream?"

NezLeigh asked. "When do you need it?"

"We don't make ice cream. It's at the store," Dad said.

"I'll need the potion in four weeks, maybe less. We've started one but it's all show. If you have one that works--"

"Take me home," said NezLeigh. "We have a fermented drink that pretty much guarantees a knock up. Why do we have so many kids? We've got a liquor made from local plants. Dad's a bootlegger, the son-of-a-bitch. We aren't stupid bumpkins. We know our chemistry."

"Can you get me some of the plants? I'll have to ferment them."

"You've already got them. They're the ones you're growing for salmagundi."

"My plants were killed, for the most part. I have a bit of one but it's not much."

"I'll get you some liquor if we drive out to the old homestead. By the way, how do the Cochtons like those little homunculus monsters?"

"They're inseparable."

CHAPTER TWENTY-FOUR

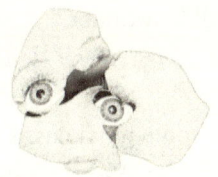

We snuck away in Dad's car, with Mom's permission. NezLeigh was overreacting to Mom's news about facilities built on a farm. She had no evidence it was on her farm. Yet here we were, driving around, headed for her farm, looking for a barn quilt, a caveman, and some liquor. Unfortunately, it was all I had to go on. The corn was knife-edge sharp and taller than a Washer Van.

"Makes you want to cut yourself, don't it?" NezLeigh said. "I'd tell you to stop and let me pick some blades and end it all but you need me too much."

"Who are you kidding? Your life is good!" Gravel hit the side of the car and we powered on, surrounded by white dust. The road was filled up with sameness, as a week must be to a retired person. We drove endlessly. Fifteen minutes passed. I was about to complain about the infinite corn when NezLeigh let out a sob. I imagined it might be from boredom.

"Is it much further?" Newton asked. "This crop is the ugliest I've ever seen. It has hair. It is the nadir of crops."

"It's silk, not hair."

"It looks like a man with short hairs. What's the spout on the top?"

"It's a tassel. You're defiling our national plant."

NezLeigh made another sad sound, a choke crossed with a hiccup.

"It's painful," I said, "painfully dull."

"Damnation! Take me home. Oh, take me home! I want to run up on the porch and open the door again, like I did as a kid. It wasn't the best life, being continually poisoned by farm chemicals, but I held on to my childlike wonder."

Does this mean we're almost there? I need some mercy from this monotony.

"We had a creek and some chickens. I played with my sister all night—she has tiny eyes, too. We see best at dusk, but the dark suits us. We protected the hen house many nights. Raccoons come around and the damn owls. We got good at catching them and eating them, raccoons especially if you sneak up on 'em. They're tough, though. After Mom died of old age at forty, my life was as good as over. Dad tried to get rid of us, but we ran away before he could pull anything over on us. Long story but we ended up at the WasteBin and formed a colony of discarded girls. My sister still lives there, claiming squatter's rights and holding out."

Four towering steel bins surrounded by flat-bed utility trailers with slow-moving vehicle triangles on the back came into view. A white farmhouse sat a ways away, dwarfed by the bins.

"That's it!" NezLeigh said excitedly.

A yellow bi-plane with wheels hanging flew near, the first sign I'd seen of human life for a while.

"The old man's out working," NezLeigh said. "He's a crop duster, or as they call them now, "aerial applicators." He's going the opposite direction so he won't see the car."

We stopped at a crossroad. NezLeigh pointed to the right.

"I'll help you if you help me get my sister. You owe me a favor, remember? The doll? Funny, I haven't heard a whole lot about your craft project."

Certain that it was the State Crisper Facility in disguise,

NezLeigh demanded we walk to her ex-farm, leaving the car behind about a half mile so as not to arouse suspicion. We crunched along the gravel driveway, our feet giving us away. We approached the small white house with the half porch. Behind the house sat a small red barn. Behind that, a long white building. Silver silos with pointed bottoms hovered next to it. And, as if she was gifted with second sight, there it was, the barn quilt, on the white building.

"I told your ass!" she exclaimed.

"It doesn't mean it's here. What are those?" I asked, pointing to the silver structures.

"The mills. It's where they hold and mix the rations. You don't think people slop hogs in this day and age? We've got ethanol by-products to mix in, you know. Holds twelve tons of chow at least. Everything's controlled by technology and life isn't worth much. You need a lot of hogs to make a profit. Economy of scale. He cut me out of all this. He's a damn sell out! Yes, it's a small operation but big enough. He didn't have to toss out his kids. The old farmhouse is still there. Fuck my heart strings, I miss my dysfunctional childhood sometimes."

She pushed some buttons on the mill and put her hand under the hopper. A trickle of tan powder spilled out.

"This isn't hog chow," she said. "I smell the hogs. I see the white building that holds them. How are they being fed? I'd say this is a false front. Somewhere here is the facility."

"Wishful thinking, but it's worth a shot."

Her eyes glowed as if she was high. "Now, listen up. The still is in the basement and there's a trap door leading to the cellar. It's over there to the left side of the house, a little ways from the front porch. It's got two big doors with vertical handles. They're damn heavy. I'll toss one open and run down the stars. They're concrete but the floor in there is dirt. It smells like mildew but the still is there. He's bottling it up. I'll go get the booze, ya dig? It won't take long. Do some looking around."

She scampered off, energized by her return to her farm.

"What is this? What type of farm?" Newton was befuddled.

"It's for pigs. They are confined in buildings so they get fatter."

We walked around the building, its windows darkened, and past the manure shed, toward another confinement building, long with tan vinyl siding and fume fans swirling on the roof.

"How odd," I said. "Does anything look familiar?"

"I was inside most of the time. Perhaps the expanse of field brings back some vague memories."

"The sewage lagoon is massive. Certainly, you saw it?"

"I don't recall."

We neared the building and the sound of hogs snuffling, squealing and grunting grew louder. I could imagine them talking *whatre you whatre you whatre you doing heeeerrrreee?*

"I recall the sound, I think," Newton said.

"It's so accusatory."

whatre you whatre you whatre you doing heeeerrrreee? whatre you whatre you whatre you doing heeeerrrreee?

It didn't sound natural. If I knew one thing about nature, it was the unevenness of living things. Nature sought diversity. The sound recurred over and over in a non-mammalian way. "The squeals repeat. Listen, it's too orderly. It's a recording."

We walked to the edge of the lagoon.

"It smells, but what are you hearing?"

"Besides the pigs? Nothing."

"That's right, the pebbles aren't crunching." I bent over and picked one up. "They're plastic, the same stuff I made the molds for the babies from."

A breeze came up and tossed our hair.

"The water has ripples, but they don't move," Newton observed. "They are the same as they were before the gust. They aren't waves."

I picked up a rock and tossed it at the water. It bounced across the surface.

"It's false," Newton said. "Not water at all."

"It's hiding the headquarters, I'll bet. If we walk around it, will your chip unlock a door?"

He touched his neck. "It's time to test the theory."

NezLeigh rushed to our side. "I got it, I got the hooch. Fertility, here we come!" She showed us a flask sloshing with urine-colored liquid before slipping it into the pocket of her cargo shorts.

"Many thanks. You'll save our necks!" Newton said.

"I got what I came for. Ready to go back or am I spot-on about everything?"

"We think the facility is under this fake sewage lagoon," I told her. "You were probably right."

At the far end of the lagoon, away from the road, the ground dropped.

"I used to sled down this slope, back when it snowed," NezLeigh said. "It's not the same as it was. The bottom's been cut away. Now I understand why Mom, Kola, and I were disposed of. She must have been opposed to this facility. Not Dad though, it was and is his chance to have something he's proud of."

"It's not heavily guarded," Newton observed.

"The regularity of the fake sewage allows for detection of any anomalies easily. It's like dropping something on a uniform floor vs. one with a pattern. Someone can see us," I said. "Even if we don't see them."

"We are coming for the most noble purpose," said Newton.

"To save someone?" I asked.

"Sex?" NezLeigh asked.

"Experimentation and discovery."

We walked down the slope carefully. At the bottom was a set of doors under the lagoon. The phony pond was a roof.

"I recognize it! In here," Newton said. "It's where I come from. It is plain enough to wither a rose and the color of fly specs. Despite this, it's familiar. A port in a storm. My own home, Woolsthorpe Manor, was not fancy. Instead of hogs, it had sheep. Have you ever listened to sheep? The bleating sounds like old men shouting. I was raised in this place much like my first home. Time to go home."

He put an arm around each of us as he held tight to make sure we made it in together, tugging us into the building, its heavy door automatically opening as he approached. It wasn't magic, of course, but for a moment, it seemed like it as we stood, panting, holding each other. We were in a lobby, gray with a set of glass doors, leading to another lobby.

"Where are we?" I asked. "Doors don't open easily in Cochtonia. Is this...a trap?"

"I came from here. I was told I was resurrected. I lived alone but at times met with other created beings to be lectured about the greatness of Cochtonia."

"There are others?" The whole notion made me dizzy.

"Yes, besides Paracelsus, a few more. I did not mix with them much, nor did we speak. I learned about myself. I lived my life again—the prisms and the apple tree. I experienced the boredom of the sheep, the joy of calculus, the encouragement of my teacher, the gut crush of being left behind. I wasn't taught in words. I experienced it. I saw it, heard it, smelled the fireplaces, their ash was on my face. I walked the English streets and witnessed the hangings."

"You always went into the same room, correct?"

"Room? No, I lived in a manor house. I went to school. After a miserable childhood and successful adulthood, I was escorted away through this passageway to enter your world. The people are friendly. The manager could have a record of all created beings. We can inquire about your tawdry tryst. Don't be disappointed, he might be a persona recycled. Through this door lies answers."

Newton walked toward the reflective glass door. It opened. A woman sat at a reception desk. She was wearing drab black and her hair was pulled back harshly in a bun. She drank from a mug decorated with a skull.

"It's Grandma Rhonda, she's still here!" He threw the door

open wider. "How now! Good morrow, Granny Rhonda. You have adopted modern dress since I left."

The whole Granny Rhonda thing was dubious. This woman was doing double duty as a character and an office manager? How cheap was this operation?

"Hello, Isaac! I saw you coming. Welcome back! Do you need rehabilitation? Did I spare the rod?" She put the mug down. What did it read? *Resurrection Inc., Experience The Past.* Maybe I was imagining the whole thing.

"Not at all, I am here for an experiment. I brought my collaborator and guide to help me find what I seek."

"More schemes? What troubles you, Lambkin?" She quickly gained an accent, now that Newton was near.

"I seek a part human for further experimentation. It could be possible to replace the traits from the ancient with the Cochton brothers' genes and to train him to be an heir."

"What are you declaring?"

How brilliant. I took his hand. "He wants a caveman for an experiment."

"What kind of experiment? Aren't the homunculi enough f'r thee?"

"Granny, I speak modern now. No, they are not enough. The Cochton appetite for modifications continues. One project done, another begun. Will you help me, kind Granny?"

"Your request is in our territory here at the facility. Will you be joining our staff? Without my management, you could be stepping too far into what some might call sin."

"How can it be sin if our leaders require it? He is to be our next alchemical transformation. Beast to man! The alchemical aspect is why we must take him to *our* laboratory."

"Mercy! The idea grieves me. If they say so." She pushed a button on her console. "There's one available. He's had low rental volume and he's hard to train. He's possessed by the devil. He's way too explorative and rebellious. He knows nothing of sanctified silence. He needs extra thiamine. The technology was there before the insight. He's a misfit, more than he is a beast."

"I assure you, Gram, he will possess excellent manners after the experiment. Silence will be golden. He will speak only when spoken to. I'm requesting this misfit and will remove him immediately."

"Isaac, you know misfits like nobody else." She poked buttons on her console. "How goes it out in today's world? Did we train you well?"

"I'm learning new things each day and am a diligent pupil."

"You've been making friends, I see." She took a sip and gave me an autocratic stare.

"Yes, this is my lab partner, Stella, and her sister, NezLeigh, who knows the country and served as a guide."

"They've been pleasantly quiet. Have you behaved yourself on the outside?"

Clearly, the news of our malfeasance hadn't reached this place. It was Layal's job to inform the operation, not ours, and after all, our silence was golden.

A guard appeared with Bigg Gib. Yes, he had spots along his pale forehead. Thankfully it was him and not some other misfit caveman. His snake skin was rolled up haphazardly on one side, showing lots of masculine leg. Gib was all smiles, but when he saw me, he shrank back. The guard slapped him on the side of the head for his valid fear, and Gib stood straight to make up for it.

"Will he do?" Granny asked Newton.

"I'll say," said NezLeigh. "Hot damn!"

"Yes," I said. "He's suitable."

"He meets with our approval. Please release him," Newton said. "Duty calls."

The guard shoved Gib forward. "Be friendly."

The Neanderthal ran past me to NezLeigh. He embraced her enthusiastically, enough to make me uncomfortable.

"Aww, he's so loving," she said, delighted.

Not shy, Bigg Gib grabbed NezLeigh's hand and kissed it. "You are truly beautiful. I love your eyes."

NezLeigh turned pink. "I don't come by them naturally. I'm a mutant. Wish I could gaze upon you, your voice is as handsome as a stripper, but it's too bright. I see better in darkness."

"I assure you, I am strong and handsome and a stripper. Like you, I prefer the night. We could be mates. I hope you are not too young."

"It's our lucky day. I just had a birthday. Are you going my way?"

"Am I? I hope so!"

Bigg Gib grabbed her from behind, plunged his face into her hair, and closed his eyes. She arched into him, more peaceful and content than I'd ever seen her.

He quickly moved away. "Too young. You smell like teen spirit."

"I'm not a teen. I've been using cheap shampoo."

"Not a teen but too young to be happy, I hope," said Bigg Gib.

"Most definitely."

"I also am unhappy. I'm plagued. I wasn't created for love, yet I crave it."

"No way! I understand to the depths of my soul."

"Please excuse me while I barf," said Rhonda. "Are you sure he's beast enough for you?"

Newton brightened. "He is the clay and I am the maker. It's been fortunate to see you, Gram. Gramercy. Thank you for the primitive man. We will be on our way. Do we need to sign anything?"

Things were going much more easily than I'd hoped.

Granny Rhonda got off her chair and came toward Newton. "Oh, so sweet. But he's not free of cost. If the Big Men want him for an experiment, where's the payment? Where's my bribe?"

"They will owe it, as any leader. Leaders are not required to pay up front." Newton didn't budge.

"I haven't gotten any orders from them. They are dark on communicating the past few days."

"Alchemy demands secrecy and darkness." Newton wasn't afraid. He was peeved. I loved how his irritations were so reasonable.

"Look, I'll trade you a bottle of hooch for this caveman. It's my final offer. Let us be on our way." NezLeigh held out the flask, trading away the fertility potion.

"Do I know you?" Rhonda said to her.

"I doubt it, bitch."

Rhonda took the flask. "Alright, the three of you are free to go. You, on the other hand." She made a chopping motion and the guard grabbed me. "Stay here! You tricky, wicked thing, being pregnant. Was it nature or alchemy? In any case, we are going to study that cell cluster. It's genetically sound and a girl, so a whole chromosome from Dad, here. With Isaac Newton as the father, we can make it into something interesting, even powerful. A mastermind!"

I was overwhelmed, confused, not sure if this was true or a ruse. If it was true, a scientific mastermind could be a perfect child. "What are you going to do?"

Tossing off the guard's grasp, Rhonda put an arm around me. She was strong for her age, whatever it was. "It wouldn't take much. We'd make the child better looking, taller, and more confident. We'd make sure she isn't sensitive."

I was torn and surprised. I couldn't make a quick decision. It could be an opportunity I never had. Who doesn't want the best for their child? Granny dug her nails into my shoulder.

"Definitively not," Newton said. "Let her go! We will not be having a mastermind. We hast what we came for. Hie and goodbye."

Bigg Gib swooped me from her grasp and tossed me over his shoulder.

"Not so fast," Rhonda said.

"Quick! Rise!" Newton charged the doors. They slammed in front of us.

Bigg Gib put me down and struggled with the door. It had locked. Newton kicked a hinge. The guard drew his weapon. He wouldn't shoot, we were all valuable.

Rhonda laughed. "Tough Daddy. We'll be sure to chip the baby at birth. Technically, it belongs to Cochton Enterprises and they'll control where it goes and doesn't. Isaac, you are the gift that keeps on giving. To think, I'll be a great-grandmother. I'll notify the Cochtons right now."

"Release all of us or their wrath, and mine, will find you."

"I'm awaiting their response, you evil sinner. What would move you to become such a filthy vagabond?" The manager took a drink of the bottle of fertility potion. "Perhaps I understand but your training was to be meticulous. You have strayed from the wishes of your fathers. You need to stay and get retrained." She pushed a button on her console. "Thank you for dropping by. I've set the door to lock you in."

"Forgive me, Granny, and may Heaven and my fathers forgive me as well." Newton yanked the button from his fly and held it to his neck, deactivating his chip. He plunged through the door with all of us following. He and NezLeigh made it out, but I fell back as my neck heated up and the door, apparently set to lock in all beings with a chip, closed on Bigg Gib and me, still chipped. Newton came back, bursting through the doors. I ran to him. He put his button on my neck. It stuck there. "Get out of here."

I ran for the door and made it out, but he fell back. Without the button, his neck grew hot. It was Newton's cradle, one in, one out.

"This petty power grab is the shits!" said NezLeigh as we stood on the outside of the glass door.

"The door is set to sense neck chips. They're magnetic," I said. "It appears she's got it set to lock in anyone with a chip. But Newton had this button, which blocks her detection." I touched the button on my neck.

"Joke's on her. I bet I know how to turn off the electricity. There's a breaker at the house."

"I'll go back in. No one else needs to suffer. How bad could it be to birth a mastermind? It's probably not even true. She enjoys playing with people for spite. Newton hates her. No doubt Layal will tell her to let me go back and make the tonic."

"You're being far too sensible. We didn't come this far for dear Gram to seize you and possibly have you killed, no matter what Layal has to say. He's not going to understand why we're here. That ass won't be as reasonable as you think. Not to mention, do you expect me to drive myself away? You're the only one who can handle the thing your calls a car."

We watched the action inside unfold as Newton grabbed Rhonda's chair and flung it at the door.

"I've got to go back! It's a madhouse in there and it's all because I ran out. You're a country kid, you can figure it out. The engine start code is 747."

Fatigued, I walked toward the door and it opened for me. Only the chipped were locked inside. Rhonda scolded the men as if they were children. "Isaac, I'm going to need to give you a spank on your bare seat. Let's go to the virtual orchard and cut a switch."

The button had caused so much trouble, I had to get rid of it. I wasn't afraid to incubate a mastermind. I was afraid to be without Newton. I took the button from my neck. As Newton rushed toward me, I discretely dropped it into a chalice-shaped urn next to the door. We were going to be stuck together or free together. It hit the interior of the vessel with a faint tick. Yes, of course! I should have known. This wasn't an urn, it was a security device. A strobe light flashed. The button had hit a switch. The glass doors flew open and the hot air from the outside rushed in behind me. Suddenly, a dash for freedom was possible. I grabbed Newton's hand as NezLeigh did the same with Big Gibb.

"Run!"

NezLeigh pulled a weighted plastic bag from her cargo shorts, lit it, and tossed it. The dark smoke filled the reception room. An alarm went off.

We struggled up the slope and stopped at the top of the hill to catch our breath. Rhonda and several guards came out, followed by a man in a buckskin, with flowing locks and a creased tan cowboy hat.

"It's Buffalo Bill!" I said.

A long-nosed man with a swatch of white hair followed.

"And that's Andrew Jackson!" I said. "We had to learn history in school."

A fine-featured Asian man ran out next along with a dark-skinned man, rather tall, and a white man with a mustache and dangling left arm in a military uniform. A troop of Crisper strippers poured out, dressed as gladiators and lions. At last, a woman in a black dress and brown apron with a man in overalls with a pitchfork appeared.

"It's an evacuation, oh crap!" NezLeigh said.

"Good thinking, both of you, to add a wrinkle to the system and to prompt a simple fire drill," Newton said. "Let's not tarry here."

We watched the facility empty. As Crispers sashayed about, something unexpected happened. Several men wavered and fell into piles of dust.

"Holy shit!" NezLeigh said.

"Why?" I wondered aloud. "What happened?"

"It's predestined," Newton explained. "They must not have been designed to live on the outside. Resurrection can have an expiration date."

"Damn creepy," NezLeigh said. "Were they some sort of despots, there to give the brothers advice?"

"Jackson believed in individual rights and forced natives from their lands. It's probably why the brothers resurrected him," I replied. "I'm not sure who the others are, but Layal mentioned the brothers getting advice from some of history's worst dictators."

"No doubt they made sure the dictators wouldn't escape and rival them," Newton said.

"Let's get out of here before Rhonda's buzz wears off and she calls some authorities. Sorry I gave away the tonic but I wanted to save our asses."

"Thank you for saving my ass. I will repay you with whatever your ass desires," said Bigg Gib.

"We've got a back-up for the alcohol," I said. "It's not real but it will buy us some time." Here I was, once again, faking out an autocrat, but if Granny was correct, I'd gotten pregnant somehow. It was possible.

We hurried to the car. As we passed the farmhouse, a rooster came running from the porch, claws out, wings flapping.

"Run like hell!" NezLeigh shouted as the bird pecked and slashed at us with his spurs. He got the back of my leg. I yelped and kicked at it while struggling to get my keys. I couldn't believe something could be so small and yet so vicious. I looked the rooster in the eye and it flapped at me again. Newton landed a hit on the rooster while I dug my keys from my pocket and clicked open the car doors. We piled in, including the rooster. It flapped about in the car and pecked Newton's wig as he held it on his head. With a swoop, NezLeigh managed to grab the bird by the neck and shook it as it flapped in her face.

"It's dead," she said happily, as it continued to flap.

"You could have simply tossed it out. There's no need to be bloodthirsty," Newton said, scolding as Rhonda had done.

"Don't pretend to be mild mannered, you fucker. I saw you toss a chair."

"I overreacted," Newton said. "Tossing the chair was not necessary. However, I had to free you and Stella. The life of a mastermind, set about for whatever purpose the state desires, is not good. This child," he blinked, "will play and sit beneath apple trees."

"What is an apple tree?" Bigg Gib asked.

"I have seeds here in my pocket."

"Damn, pocket seeds from another time. Will they even grow?" NezLeigh asked as she opened the window and tossed out feathers.

I said, "I'm going to grow those seeds, propagate the trees, and plant them all over Cochtonia. We need crop diversity. People are sickly. All we have to do is to pacify Layal enough to give him hope and he'll let us do as we wish. "

"Now you are beginning to understand alchemy," said Newton.

"Very romantic, you turds. How are we going to manufacture this hope?"

"I don't want to be too stupidly positive, but Layal has let his mind fall fallow since his indoctrination into the ruling family. Almost anything will fly past him. We'll use this future baby to convince Layal that our tonic works. We'll barter for our own patch of land. Let's get home and lay out our plan. Just don't tell my parents."

"How long before you get a crop from these trees?"

"Something over five years," Newton said.

"Trouble is, you need the right woman for his fertility treatment, or otherwise, he'll grow impatient," NezLeigh said.

"The right woman to pair with Layal? You think he could have a kid?"

"Damn straight. Look at you. And we need to buy some time."

"What makes time timeless?"

"It's falling in love." Bigg Gib sang a brief song about love.

"We've got to get him to fall in love. Then, take the potion," I said. "There need to be pre-fertilization rituals. This place needs shows. And fertility scans," I said. "We can get them from the InVitro fertility clinic. We'll suggest a pageant and have women get scanned. The winner is his bride." I handed Newton my device. "Send my idea to Ursula, who'll pass it on to Paracelsus, who'll recommend it to Layal."

"Me?"

"You can do it. You're a genius."

"I wonder if there will be any takers?" I mused, as Newton sent his first text.

Bigg Gib said, "Everyone has a heart for love. Someone will love the loveless tyrant."

"Hell yes," NezLeigh said. "I've got the best damn bride for him, someone who's been infatuated with him since the days of his humble, illegitimate beginnings when he was banished to the WasteBin. She's stupid but I don't even need to say it."

"I would like to meet her," Bigg Gib said.

"We're gonna have to. She's off the grid. Head to the colony of Wowville. And Stella, Newton, congratulations!"

CHAPTER TWENTY-FIVE

Again, I turned toward the colony, and again the road narrowed. We were nearly blown off by a truck carrying plastic made from converted hog manure. Bigg Gib and NezLeigh spent the time kissing in the back seat while Newton looked out the window. I hated to imagine what he was thinking after the unbelievable pregnancy announcement. Truth was never easy to find here. Saying I was expecting might have been said for shock value. In any case, the only one of us who was making money at the moment was NezLeigh and once the fate of the homunculi was known, her business would fall short. Perhaps we'd have to reconsider the mastermind idea, if it would support us and pay for my medical care.

We stopped near the bridge and following NezLeigh's directions, walked along the edge of the wooded area. NezLeigh had been correct about the Crisper Facility. I had to trust her on this as well.

"Where are we? Where are we going?" Big Gibb said nervously.

"Someplace ripe for an ambush," said Newton cautiously, holding his fly closed as best he could as we hiked.

"The only one doing the ambushing is us, convincing this person, my sister, to make herself available as a potential mate for

Layal. She persuaded herself that her life is meant to be here in the wild. I need to see her civilized. I used to believe it myself—that Cochtonville was so hateful, I couldn't bear to deal with it. I changed my mind. I'm eating well and the beds are soft. Roofs keep me dry and my pants have pockets. Stella here has helped me find a mate. As for the rest of the citizens, the people aren't as much mean as they are fools, and the fools will be parted from their money."

We came upon an abandoned farm bell, a massive metal thing on top of a wooden post. A rope hung down. NezLeigh pulled the rope and rang the bell as the lonely sound pealed out. We sat on a rock. Fireflies danced in a nearby corn field. The humidity rose.

A girl came from the woods. She was tall with stringy brown hair. She was youngish—a teen, and wore a skirt and sleeveless top made from plastic bags. She and NezLeigh ran toward each other.

"Hot damn!" she said, and she and NezLeigh embraced "Nez, you got fat in the city."

"Sure as hell did. You jealous? You're so skinny, your tits look like two b-bs on a bread board."

"What the hell is a bread board?"

"Shut up!" The girls hugged again and the sister pulled NezLeigh's hair.

"What's this? You found a hair brush. Why're you here? Are you coming back with some company?"

"Hell no! You've got to come with us. We're gonna feed you and make you presentable." NezLeigh tugged the edge of her sister's plastic skirt. "Clothes should breathe, you know. I got money for clothes for you. I even got a rooster, freshly killed."

"I like my freedom," she said, scratching at some bug bites. "I do like chicken though. It's been a while since I raided a farm. Maybe I'm game. I'm gonna be presentable to who?"

"To Layal. H. He needs a fertile woman."

"As in me? Shit, me?"

"It sure as shit isn't gonna be a townie, ya dig? He needs a bride with some oomph when it comes to ovaries."

"Bride? I'm too dumb. He's intellectual with a hot bod and tumbling curly hair. I could never get more than a kiss from him. No more than a kiss."

"He's lost a little luster, and compared to people in town, you're brilliant. They're as gullible as they come and all they care about is if their meat is breaded or stuffed in an intestine."

The sister swirled her hand in front of her face. "I'm too damn ugly. The eyes, the eyes!"

"We'll deal with it. You're coming with us, Kola. Gang, meet my sister. Kola, this is our new sister, Stella, her beau, Isaac Newton, and my hunk, Big Gibb. I'm going to find out what's under his snake skin."

"Damn, it's gonna be another snake."

Bigg Gib picked Kola up and tossed her over his shoulder. She struggled, or pretended to struggle, for she laughed as she pounded his back as he carried her to the car. On the drive home, they talked about the old farm's transformation and cussed their out for tossing them away, arousing Bigg Gib's sympathy. He in turn told of his life raised in a cave followed by his school for strippers and training with pressure-sensitive sex dolls.

"You think Layal's been through the training?" Kola asked nervously. "He was a Crisper escort once."

"Yes, I bet so. Are you chicken?"

"*You* could do it, Nez."

"Except I'm in love with this lug here."

We fell silent. I kept my eyes on the road and my hands upon the wheel. Night fell. The country was dark as nowhere. My mind raced everywhere I couldn't see. Thunder rolled across the corn-filled prairie. Lightning strobed the clouds as they dropped to earth to meet us. It was dark and hard rain hit the car as the wipers frantically beat against it. We needed rain but why now?

"If it hails on the car, Dad's gonna have a fit and fall in it," said NezLeigh.

"It's only rain, not like a chicken in the car." But rain would be enough to bring Dad from his recliner if he noticed the car was gone, and the last thing Newton and I needed right now was a face-off with Dad. We had things to talk about alone.

We pulled into the garage. Dad was standing there.

"I can see this town has a lot of ugly dudes," said Kola from the backseat.

Bigg Gib burst into tears. "Someone's here for me! My honey, forgive me for not consummating our love."

"It's only Dad. Hell or high water, we're doing it, understand, my love?"

"Don't be afraid. He's peeved but harmless," said Newton.

"He can't lift a finger in the house, but in the garage, he's a fly spec inspector," NezLeigh said. "Mom's the one who'll be asking questions."

"Keep Mom busy. Tell her I'm cleaning out the car," I told NezLeigh. "Newton and I will deal with Dad."

"I imagine you have a shit ton to discuss, the two of you."

While the trio went into the house with the nearly plucked chicken, Newton and I faced Dad. Newton was white as a Yorkshire pig.

"Who said you could take my car?"

"Sir," Newton said. "We were serving the Empire."

"You didn't answer my question, Wiggy. Where were you?"

"We were in the country releasing a man from captivity."

"Nothing happened to the car," I added. "Except for a little dirt I can vacuum out."

"The chicken. I saw a chicken."

"And a few feathers."

"Did the chicken shit in my car?"

"It's dead," I said.

"The dead shit and they have erections."

"True," said Newton. "I've seen it on a hanged man."

"Oh, really? What are your thoughts on hanging as opposed to other methods of execution?"

"It isn't a deterrent, as the guilty don't expect to be caught. It simply makes the public more barbaric, as does sausage."

"Nothing wrong with barbarism. Wigs are made from dead people's hair. This why people are called barbers."

"Sir..."

"I need you to get out. You are a corrupting influence." Dad pointed to the pouring rain.

Newton put a hand over his fly. "You are the one being disagreeable, you curmudgeon."

"No, Dad," I said. "This is my home, too. I've been supporting it for over a decade. Get back in the house."

"You take it up with your mother."

As if she heard the commotion, Mom came into the garage. "Barnabus, we need you to cut the head off this chicken. We're having a midnight snack. Stella, would you and your friend like to join us?"

"I need to clean the car," I said. "We'll be there shortly."

As soon as my parents left, I slipped a Ready Charge from the car glove compartment. I pulled down the attic stairs and hurried up, with Newton following. I grabbed Mom's bomber jacket so hard the hanger flew back and almost hit me in the eye. I stooped down and rummaged for the No Regrets in the deep pockets. I seized it and turned it over in my hands.

Newton whispered. "What is it?"

"It's a device that will tell us if your grandmother knew what she was talking about."

I hit it with the Ready Charge, surging electricity through it. The buttons jumped to yellow life. I scanned my abdomen as lights flashed multiple colors. A tiny baby icon appeared in the results window.

Newton bent beside me. I held up the device. "Newton, Rhonda told the truth!"

"It can't be. We are both too old." He sank onto a pile of dusty curtains.

"We can't sit here ruminating. My parents will ask too many questions. Come help me clean out the car. When my parents go to bed, we can consider this unexpected situation."

We hurried down the stairs and hoisted them onto the ceiling. I took a shop vac from the wall and sucked the feathers from the backseat.

"Should you be doing any work? Women in your state should be confined."

"Life moves faster nowadays. No time to sit around."

Mom poked her head into the garage. "Dad and I are hitting the hay. He's getting grouchy. This excitement is too much for him. See you in the morning."

Newton and I crept to the bedroom as the rest made themselves at home in the kitchen. I sat on the bed and kicked off my shoes. Newton sat beside me at a slight distance.

I asked, "Are you scared?"

"I don't like surprises."

"Me neither."

"My reality has been shattered." His voice was harsh. I couldn't tell where he was going with this. I only sensed his frustration.

"It's been a more upsetting day than I planned."

"Am I a real version of myself or a fake? Was my life as it had been before or edited to make me a *version* of who I was in the era 1643 to 1727? And the news! You must understand, I took a vow of celibacy with myself. I've dedicated myself to science, not fatherhood."

"I'll go back. The baby will be modified and taken away. This will allow us to continue our work in science without distraction. It's the proper thing to do. It's responsible. How could I explain it to the kid? 'You could have been perfect but now you're you?' Especially at my age with all the risks, intervention is best."

"Is perfection happiness?" he snapped.

"How would I know? Being imperfect has its problems."

"Who is defining perfection? Do you trust them?"

"I don't trust anyone. And I don't even know who you are exactly." I hadn't meant to voice my fears, but his hesitation had fertilized them.

"That makes us bedfellows twice over." He got up and stood in front of the window, looking out into the darkness. "Clearly, it depends on the imperfections. Should I have been born? I lived a life of frustration with my fellow humans. Yet you tell me, I saved the world from superstition and misinformation."

"You did."

"What I wouldn't have given to be happy. Yet, unhappiness puts the spurs to a person. Our child, although currently hypothetical, when perfected, might not be a mastermind. It might not be unhappy enough."

I didn't answer him. I couldn't bear to voice what I knew was true. *You'll be better off alone in the hermit life you were made for.*

In the kitchen, Bigg Gib sneezed.

"Are you allergic to feathers?" NezLeigh asked, her voice playful. The warm, fatty scent of chicken cooking drifted beneath the bedroom door.

"Your clothes smell tickly," Gib replied.

"Let's go to the basement, where we people wash clothes, and take ours off. We can rinse them in water and show each other how it's done. You got spots in other places?"

"All over."

"Show me your spots."

"Love at first sight. So fucking stupid. Stupid," Kola complained.

I listened to their playful banter, juxtaposing our heavy conversation. I would be safer at the facility, I supposed. I searched his face for a sign. The dim glow from a street light half-illuminated it and highlighted his big chin and wild wig. I studied him, in case, someday, I'd never see him again, at least not up close, and he'd never see me. I needed to remember this light filled moment. A beam twinkled across the purple crystal on my dresser.

"We must do what's best," he said. "For the present, where will you be the safest? In the facility or by my side? I must remain here and go through with the harebrained potion scheme, with or without you."

"Newton..."

I stood up and moved to kiss him, to kiss him goodbye for the present and probably forever. I walked toward him, resolute, with the universe as a judging witness to my biggest fumble yet. Being unromantic, the idea of a life-long, noble heartbreak was as attractive to me as oil to water. The only reason to do this was to save him and maybe me. He could be whatever great man he was supposed to be, or sell trinkets, and I'd be a nobody.

I watched his stony face for any sign he wanted me to stay. If only I understood people better. I hurt more than I knew I could. I rehearsed my line: *I'm so happy we met, but we need to say goodbye so you can go on and do great things.*

"I'm so happy," I said, taking a step forward as his mouth twitched. My eyes on him, I tripped over my shoe and fell forward, sprawling at his feet.

"Stella!" he said in shock. "Stella! Are you injured?" I wasn't hurt, only a clumsy idiot.

He reached down and gently helped me up. "The day has been too fatiguing. We're weary." He folded his arms around me. "What were you saying about happiness?"

I snuggled into his chest. "You make me happy. I'm safer here with you and those I love. Bacteria stick together and we should, too."

"We will protect each other, like the bacteria, whatever it is. You make me happy, an emotion I'm not used to. As long as you understand, I don't know exactly what I am, I am not sure what I remember."

"I don't love the classical Isaac Newton. I love the relative Isaac Newton. In other words, I love you as you exist in this real time."

"I count our time together as a highlight of my life, second only to discovering the laws of motion."

"You are my force."

"A void cannot be acted upon. Thank you for staying with me, saving me from a void. We will protect each other. Our spacetimes crossed before. My second sense tells me as much. This time, I won't lose you." He touched my hair. "Some men would take a mistress due to your condition, but the thought of another is insufferable." We went to shower together, washing the scratches and bruises the rooster caused. His snowy skin, colorless from a life spent indoors, was bruised along his thighs. I had a deep scratches on my legs. We washed each other's wounds.

"Let the water join us in fellowship," he said, as I slathered his hair with conditioner.

"I don't know what that means but thank you," I said, "for risking yourself to free Bigg Gib."

"You took risks for me." He soaped my breasts as the conditioner ran off of his brown, wavy hair. "It might be difficult to comprehend but I dislike risks. I had to be persuaded to publish anything."

"May we hide in time's wrinkle, a secret from trouble."

We held each other, our passions growing until the warm water ran out. We wrapped in towels and together, quietly, we made our way to my bedroom.

He carried me to the bed. He fell upon me, kissing me, taking my breath away and giving me his. I surrendered doubts I might have had—if he was not really Isaac Newton, I cared not.

CHAPTER TWENTY-SIX

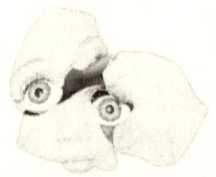

The following morning, I woke to a message blinking frantically on my device.

Attention Stella Smithfailed. Confidential. Our condolences on the loss of your boss, Sir Gotfried. You have been re-allocated. Plan to meet your new boss this morning in your assigned laboratory on Floor 2 of Cochton Enterprises Research Complex. Please forgive the delayed nature of this notification, Your HR Team

I poked Newton, snoozing contentedly next to me, as light poured through the window. "Hey, babe. We've got to get up. It's my lucky day. I have a boss. I have a job. I'm guessing Sir Gotfried never got the paperwork filed to transfer me to the Homunculus Project. Maybe we can get past the tonic making and plant the apple seeds and be real scientists."

Newton stirred. "You are being overly optimistic. I've never known a martinet to abandon a foolish plan."

"Come to work with me and meet my boss. We're a team."

"You're earnest about loving me no matter who I am."

"I am."

"Secretly you hope I am the real thing."

"I'm not sure. What happened to those men yesterday?"

"They were brought back to life but destined to return to dust.

Granny Rhonda mentioned this but I thought it was a religious metaphor."

I blinked back tears, hoping they looked like an allergy. Unless he was a normal guy, hypnotized to think he was Newton, he could be doomed to a brief second life.

"I'll get us breakfast." I went to the kitchen to hide my worries. The rest of the house still slept. Kola was on the couch, a plate of chicken bones on the floor next to her. I grabbed a couple of protein bars and turned to hurry back to the bedroom. Too late, Mom came padding into the kitchen in her socked feet.

"Stella, let's talk." She put three scoops of powered morning drink with caffeine into the drink maker and added a pot of water. "You're up early." She pushed the button.

"I could say the same for you. The sun's up. It's not early, and I need to get to work."

"Work? What is your work these days?"

"I'm back to the laboratory now that I am no longer needed with the homunculi. I'm making a fertility potion, remember? And I have other ideas."

Mom didn't want to hear about my work. "I want to thank you for bringing Kola into the house. She's a delight, and she needs me."

"Don't get too attached, Mom. She's here for a purpose."

The hot water mixed into the powder. A caramelly odor filled the kitchen. "I've been wondering where Jelly is. Kola's still a child and she's had so little. Kola might like the doll."

It was hard to say if this was interrogation or coincidental snoopiness. "I'll look into it after work, err, actually, some kids stole her when I was practicing with the buggy." Darn, I was maxed out on lying. I couldn't manage one more.

Mom poured two cups of beverage. "She was your grandmother's doll and my only grandchild."

"The kids wanted the doll." *Because I paid them.*

She pushed a cup toward me. "You should have told me."

"Things got crazy at work." I took a sip.

"You read my book that I put away in the attic. I put in a magnetic tracking device and it fell out." Of course, she'd been up in the attic. She couldn't stay away from her lube and vibrator.

"I was looking for the buggy and I knocked over a box. The book was in it. And yes, I read it."

"You have a lot to tell me about you and Isaac Newton."

"Stella *Virginia*, Mom? You named me after a sex expert. Put a lid on your curiosity and keep to your own devices."

At last, she launched into the real issue, signaled by a higher pitch to her voice as she whispered. "You are taking too many risks."

"Mom, you're right. This place makes you take risks."

"You and NezLeigh are taking too many chances. We have purity laws here."

"Mom, I had sex with a caveman. Cochtonia isn't pure."

"As a reward! You can't take a lover on a whim, these guys are chipped. They can't be anonymous. There's going to be a knock on the door." She poured a third cup of morning beverage. "And." As I feared, she held out the No Regrets. "This device has a memory. Who used this last? You?"

The whole kitchen was skeleton white. I was having a flashback to the babies killing Bert and Clarence. There were tendrils around my neck. I took a sip from my cup to clear my fear.

"Mom, it's flawed technology. Your device is old and glitchy. I can take care of myself."

She pointed to a blob of toothpaste on my pajama shirt. "Can you? Is he even Isaac Newton or is he a sexual predator? 'Save your innocence. Report at once.' It was the rule back in the day." She walked away, leaving a steaming cup for me to take to Newton.

"Ready to get back to work with me?" I asked, putting our cups on the nightstand.

"I'd like nothing more. I've been fretting. What's this? Tea?"

"You aren't the only one. No, it isn't tea."

"What if I am taken back to the farm because of my sins? I'll be redesigned as a more perfect Isaac Newton. I'll be trained to forget about you, I suppose. No." He picked up the wig on the nightstand and tossed it to the floor. "I won't be Isaac Newton at all. Dress me as a man of today's era. Toddling about in this hot wig and wool jacket is unbearable."

Taking his advice, I dressed Newton in my clothes. We were nearly twins in size. He was handsome as a modern man in my androgynous work clothes.

I rubbed his cheek. "There's no time to shave. I had a run-in with Mom. I'd like to leave before the whole house stirs."

He patted his chest, smoothly unruffled. I put the apple seeds in his pocket. We each grabbed a protein bar and walked back to the lab, over the bridge where Jelly had been "stolen." We watched the light dancing on the water as we munched on our breakfast.

Newton said, "The reflection is as muddy as the water, yet it is reflection as I studied. And behold the sun. The center of the universe, as Galileo proposed, a fire but one with spots and flaws. Stella, science has moved so far beyond me. Did we discover what the sun was made of? And how?"

"A couple hundred years ago. It's the center of the solar system. The universe is much larger. We used spectroscopy to study it. You know, observing the sun through a grating and looking at the colors of lines it produces."

"As light through a prism? The glasses you gave me..."

"Yes, you pioneered it. You helped us learn that the sun was a hydrogen fire. Hydrogen fuses and makes helium. It gives off more energy than a combustion fire."

"Is light made of droplets, as I predicted?"

"No. It's electromagnetic energy."

"Stella, as you cast your lot with me, I want you to grasp, I'm no genius in this era.

I'm no mastermind today."

"Newton, let's not rehash this. I said I love you in real-time, not for who you were in the past. Who you were in the past would not have given me the time of day."

"Hundreds of years ago, I was a product of circumstance. I had something to prove. I was not expected to live. Yet my family had money. The sheep were prosperous. And when the plague hit, I had the luxury of self-study. I was small and strange. I had something to prove. I had to prove I wasn't cut out for sheep.

"Newton, you're right. We can't expect this ball of cells to be a mastermind or to even care about science. Science is not a set of genes, it's a lifestyle."

"True, but what is a ball of cells?"

"It's potential."

"Ahh. There's something I do understand."

We locked hands and walked with scientific optimism to Cochton Enterprises. The research building was a rambling monstrosity next to the Porkie manufacturing plant.

We had no problems entering the building. My lab was beautiful in its brightness.

"It's so good to be back, even though it's a mess," I said. I put my hand in Newton's pocket. "Let's get these apple seeds planted. Is there anything I need to know about them?"

"Like people, they need others to grow to their fullest. A lone tree won't bear fruit. They need nutrients and chilling."

"Nutrients and others. Don't we all need as much? We can propagate more trees and get seeds produced. I want to use science for good, not simply for profit. Your apples are going to save the people from Porkies!"

We donned our lab coats and planted a dozen seeds in growth media cubes with a shot of Awake Dormancy Breaker from some prior project that hadn't worked out. I put them under a grow light. We stood back to admire our latest project. Once we were satisfied no more had to be done, we examined the potion. The plant material floated in an amber liquid.

"Our fate hangs on this solution and on hope," I said.

"Stella, I have a hope."

"Me, too." *I hope you're simply a normal man.*

"I have hope for the seeds but I have a deeper hope, for us."

"What's on your mind?"

"I can't let you keep going around like this."

"What do you mean?"

"In my last life, civil war overthrew the monarchy. The king was beheaded and the new leaders, Puritans, ruled with strictness that I adopted. We have to admit to each other that the disciplined ideals and order found in science are in part, Puritanism. According to my Puritanical values, I did not eat blood sausage. I studied, I was diligent. I believed I was selected by God for great things—it's called predestination."

"The Cochtons spoke similarly, about their inherent greatness. They used it as a rationale to take away farms from the Agros."

"I believed in hard work and discipline. I opposed promiscuity."

"Like here, with exceptions. Sex comes as a reward for hard work. It's becoming clear to me now where our rules came from. Cochtonia is Puritanism run amok."

"Because of such archaic rules from my past, I see you as my wife. A ceremony with a large tax was the English way. Hopefully, it will not be taxed here. I haven't been paid for my services."

"What are you saying?"

"I wish to create a legally binding agreement between us. It will be less easy for life, and your father, to separate us."

"What do you mean?"

"Legally, we must stick together. Our spacetimes crossed before. My second sense tells me as much. This time, I won't lose you."

"Oh, come on! Newton, we call such talk 'corny.' We haven't met in the past." I was touched, although all I could think of was Mom believing she had to get married because she wanted sex. "You've got to get over some of this Puritanism."

An older man in a worn gray suit fluttered in. "Stella Smithfailed? I don't wish to interrupt."

I was immediately comfortable with this plain unassuming guy.

"Come in, we were talking about science and hope."

"Appropriate. I'm your boss, Jester Rana. This is your lab, where you are doing what, exactly?"

Happy to have a boss who didn't have an agenda for me, my words gushed forth as I explained my ideas—to give the nephew a fertility potion and to grow trees as well.

"Golly," he said. "It all sounds useful and harebrained. Who's this guy here?"

"My lab partner, Isaac Newton."

"No, get out! He looks like someone normal. Golly, yes, I can see the resemblance. You're already on to a new project? Science never sleeps! Pleased to meet you." He pulled his hand from a pocket. I thought he was going to pop some candy, but he pulled an electronic lab notebook from his pocket.

"Sir Isaac, will you autograph my lab notes?"

Isaac rocked back on his heels, thinking.

"With your finger on the screen," I said.

He wrote clearly with a well-defined "W". Is. Newton

"Yippy skippy," said my boss. "I'll treasure it." He looked around my lab, pausing in front of the tonic.

"Is it fermenting?"

"It's alcoholic. It's our fertility tincture for his Honor."

"Oh, please! Call him Layal. He views himself as much more swell than he is. You are going to give him this potion?"

"Yes, it's direct orders."

"And we plan to try it ourselves," Newton put his arm around me. "We are dedicated to this experiment and to each other. We must have a marriage license to consummate our plans as soon as possible. Can you help us with this?" Newton's face was stony as he tried to act as if we hadn't copulated.

Our boss smacked his forehead nervously. "Old fashioned. I like it, but, oh, shoot. We don't really have a protocol for marriage these days, having few single men in Cochtonia."

"Newton is a recovering Puritan," I explained. "Any sort of official permission will do. We're results oriented and want to test the tonic on ourselves, but we don't want to be executed."

"Golly. You'd get the royal shaft, wouldn't you? You have high hopes for this tonic. It sounds like a moon shot. On the other hand, I have Puritan leanings myself." He stared at the ceiling, deep in thought while Newton held me tight. "I'll declare you invincible lab partners. It's in my capacity and official enough."

This was a relief to me. Being a lab partner for life sounded absolutely wonderful. Newton was the perfect lab partner—good technique, skilled in mathematics, and eager to shoulder his share of the work. I clapped my hands. "I've always wanted a lab partner for life! Can you join us together immediately?"

"Is there a document to sign? I'd like to make sure this new wrinkle is recognized as binding," Newton added.

"Paper? Golly! No, I'll make a record in your employee files."

"Wonderful," I said. "I've been waiting all my life for the right lab partner to come along."

"I concur." Newton took my hand. "It isn't easy finding someone to share in experiments and data collection."

"Give me a second to write it all up. Let me order you some appropriate clothes and a cake."

"No need, matching lab coats are perfect."

"Keep the coats. Let's get something else as a company expense. There's a little bit of ill fittingness about both of you. I'll send your photo to my wife and have her order something."

The words "company expense" convinced me to accept his offer. The company had barely done anything for me. I had to admit, my clothes were a little worn and tight. And I longed to see Newton in well-fitting clothes.

"Citizens, activate your screens for important information."

We went into the hall where a CA popped from the wall, rudely interrupting my joy.

Layal burst into view. "Hellooo, Citizens. It's me, your leader, with an exciting opportunity."

"Our leader?" said Jester Rana quietly. "I'm getting too old for this caca."

"We are at the dawn of a new breakthrough! Our situation with reproduction here in Cochtonia is untenable. We're on the brink of a cliff, teetering above a fly-infested waste pool. Everything must be done. Everything!" Layal was both serious and flush with excitement.

The errant heir went on. "I have unfortunate news. My uncles are undergoing rehabilitation. The homunculi offspring put a strain on them. The offspring have been removed from the premises. I, on the other hand, am healthy and eager to carry on the family name the traditional way. I am thrilled to announce a Fertility and Vitality Contest, open to all women in Cochtonia. Meet me at the town square tomorrow at four p.m."

Newton and I embraced hearing of the success of our plan.

My boss waited until the screen went dark to speak. "You weren't spoofing me about the fertility tonic, he's into it. The offspring were removed? This place is gonna blow if they're gone for long. People really dig them, and the unnatural idea of male only reproduction has a cult following."

Ursula came through the door, teetering beneath two sacks and a cake box. "This was delivered to the front desk. What's it all about?"

"Ursula! How goes it? We're being united as lab partners. Our boss here wanted us dressed for the occasion." Newton smiled like a kid.

"Make it quick! You've been summoned back. I've been ordered to bring you and the fertility tonic to the festival site at the town square tomorrow. And Newton, is that really you? Get back into your old duds—people expect to see Isaac Newton, not some big-nosed skinny dork."

"Tomorrow's not giving us enough time!" I cried.

"Lord Layal is enthused about the idea and grows impatient." She was understandably irritated with me. I'd suggested this ploy.

"All respects, Officer, but we're having a ceremony first, with photos. Thank you for delivering." Jester took the cake and looked for an open spot on the lab bench to place it before setting it on a chair.

Ursula and I went to the restroom. She unpacked my clothes while I undressed.

"I thought you wanted a contest," she said, annoyed. "I hope you have a way of appeasing him with this stunt."

"I do. Another month would make it more convincing."

"What are you saying? You need to get checked out," she said, eyeing me.

"I checked myself out with Mom's No Regrets."

"And?"

"The inconceivable has happened! It was the plants. I've handled them, even held them to my breast. They gave off estrogen mimics. My fertility was enhanced!"

She scanned me with her own device. "You're right. Is this responsible for the lab partner thingy?"

"In part. He's Puritanical. No matter how old-fashioned he may be, lab partners are equal. Not all men are henchmen."

She held up my new pants with an expandable waist band and stretched them. "None of them go through this."

"I'll take my chances. I've always wanted a lab partner. The rest is pure curiosity."

"Curiosity kills. The again, so does the state."

"My fear exactly. I'm sticking with him. He's all I've got right now. How's your partner?"

"He's a jolly drunk. Angel loves to listen to him talk. I'm not going to have us joined in our personnel file. I don't want a partner telling me how to spend my money, but his companionship is enjoyable. He has no interest in law enforcement. We have the run of the Cochton house. Layal has no desire to see his uncles resurrected, the babies did him a favor. Maybe you can convince him you are fertile and this is his. I can arrange some false genetics scans. I'm in the realm's favor again. It would be easy enough. You might not want a lab partner." She handed me the pants. Vice Patrol agents had such simplistic views. One big lie had nearly done me in—and had done in the brothers. I wasn't able to keep lying. I wouldn't be able to keep track of it all even if I wanted to.

"Me and Layal? No, I believe in Newton and in the potion. Get word to Layal. We must have a presentation and a ritual. This is alchemy after all, and it's mostly show. We will scan women for fertility and have them perform athletics. You need to have it organized."

"He'll love a ritual." She sent a message.

"You can help out at the fertility contest. I can give you a signal when the proper contestant competes." I slipped on the pants. The boss's wife had a good eye, ordering me elastic-waisted pants.

"You've got some kind of set up?"

"There's a woman who is so in love with him, she'd do anything."

"Where did you find her?"

"At the WasteBin. She's an Agro."

"The contest will require masks," she said, saying what I'd feared: Layal would be put off by the eyes.

"Yes, masked contestants! There needs to be some type of physical fitness display."

"Anything else?"

"Be a witness to my ceremony." I put on my shirt and shoes, pulled my lab coat over it all, and went out to meet my partner.

Newton stood among the chaos of my lab, a glowing apple of a man in a crisp yellow shirt and Prussian blue pants covered by his white coat. He had a rugged five o'clock shadow. History had him all wrong. He wasn't a recluse who hated women. He was the sexiest man ever born. My heart beat faster. I involuntarily vasoconstricted, hardening my clitoritis and producing lubrication.

My new boss stood beside him. Ursula grabbed a beaker from the lab bench and a stray bit of dead vine from under a chair and crafted a makeshift bouquet for me.

My boss read the vows he'd hastily written on his device. "We come together in recognition of what it means to be lab partners, working as a team to solve a problem. Lab partners work in tandem to let a crack of the light of verifiable truth into the world. As scientists, I charge you to do good for the world, renouncing selfishness, renouncing violence. Correct each other's errors gently. As scientists, you'll live for the future, imagining it better. You must make sure to give time to the present, enjoy the reality of yourselves together in real-time. I ask you to take the time to be people, to be here and now, enjoying more than the laboratory, no matter how rewarding. Projects end. Experiments fail. Lab partners have no end. Yes, we have something to prove to the world and we want to help it. However, give each other, and life, time to be as rewarding as your work. Do you solemnly swear to stick together, to strive for the goals of Accuracy, Truth, and Precision as you discover and uncover the Order of the Universe?"

"We do."

"You are now Cochton Enterprises's official lab partners, recognized in the nation of Cochtonia and elsewhere."

"And now," Newton said.

"Please excuse us," I finished. "The present is calling."

We planned to visit Newton's room in the basement lab to have time together to celebrate our union, naked and alone on his cot, but the place was back to being a storeroom, filled with broken equipment, as if the homunculus project had never existed.

"They're being dismissed without fanfare," Newton said.

"Lucky for us. We're almost off the hook, as long as people don't ask too many questions."

Undaunted, we hurried home, glowing with excitement.

Kola, freshly showered and in Mom's bathrobe, was at the kitchen table eating Porkies, Mom hovering by her side.

"Isn't she so cute?" Mom said, emoting her newfound relevance. "Now that NezLeigh has someone to keep her company, Kola and I are hitting it off. She needs so much love."

"I damn well do," Kola said, taking a bite of a Porkie.

"Is NezLeigh already in bed?" I asked.

"No, she's out shopping with Gibby. The two of them have been helpful around the house. They are even organizing the basement. Why are you home from work so early and who is this man?"

"It's Newton. Doesn't he look handsome as a modern man? We're lab partners!" I said, happy and energetic. I wanted Mom to share my joy. "We're going to freshen up. Excuse us." My vasoconstriction was bad enough to make me impatient. Newton took my hand and we headed for my bedroom.

"Citizens, activating for important information!" The intrusive call of the Citizen Advisory demanded our attention.

"Everybody get in here for an important message!" Dad called out from his recliner.

We changed direction and went into the living room. An announcement came over the advisory system. Paracelsus appeared with his jaunty cap and ruddy face.

"Paracelsus here. A brief update about the contest. Fertile women, please assemble at the square by four o'clock in the afternoon for instructions. Wear a mask or face covering and dress for athletics. See all of you fertile women and fans tomorrow on the square."

"We'll stay here and avoid the crowds," Mom said.

Dad said, "The events are dangerous. Remember the time that bastard released the ball breaker virus? It's going to take more than a fertility contest to help him or any of us!"

"We have all we need right here," Mom said.

I hated to drop a bomb on Mom's cozy moment, but someone had to.

"Mom, Kola's here to compete in the Fertility Contest."

"The one tomorrow? No! It's too much too soon. No one is leaving this house."

"We'll be in the contest in a fashion," Newton said. "We're providing a tonic."

"We are also providing Kola," I said.

"She is not a thing to be provided," Mom said, embracing the skinny Agro.

She hugged Mom back. "It's okay, Mom, it's okay. I want his love."

"You don't know you want it. You could be having a little

starved-for-love crush." Mom got a plate of cookies from the counter and put them on the kitchen table.

"I want it if it helps people."

"People can help themselves. You are too young to be in such a position."

"Not everyone with tiny eyes can pick up a caveman. If I win, my eyes will be seen and people will get used to them. They'll see them. They might even be beautiful. Beautiful."

Mom held back a sob. "You are beautiful without-without that dirty humper."

"Mom," I said, with growing unease. Mom was right. "Let her make a choice."

Newton chimed in. "Child marriage was common in England in the 1600s and before, especially when land or fortune was involved. However, children were allowed to enjoy their childhoods before entering into the contract."

"Aren't you a fountain of useless old knowledge?" Mom said with irritation.

"History has lessons, Goodwife."

"Barnabus, he's insulting me!"

Nodding off in his recliner, Dad muttered, "Buzz off, Wiggy."

NezLeigh and Big Gibb came through the front door. Big Gibb wore black pants, a button-down shirt, and loafers with a snake skin pattern.

"Hey, look what we did," NezLeigh said proudly. "Never again will he look like a runaway stripper."

"I'm my own man, now." Bigg Gib's baby blue eyes shone with happiness.

"Oh, so glad for you both! Joyous couples," Kola said sarcastically.

"Kola, screw your envy. Tomorrow is the big show. It's your chance! Look what I got you." NezLeigh pulled a glittery black jump suit from a shopping bag. Kola took it from her and rubbed the material on her cheek. NezLeigh pulled a sports bra and matching panty from the bag. "Welcome to civilization. And..."

she pulled a large bottle of hair detangler from the bag, "you can buy anything here in Cochtonville. Time for the makeover. How are you feeling?"

"My guts are hopping like fleas. What do I have to do?"

"You have to show up. Disguised. Ya dig?"

"Like what? Show up where? Where?" Still holding the jump suit to her cheek, Kola shoved a whole cookie in her mouth.

"You'll show up at the town square with something over your face. Come on down, let's try it all on."

As the trio went into the basement to get Kola prepared, Mom cried from the white-upon-bone-white kitchen, "Barnabus, do something! Notify someone. This contest can't go on!"

CHAPTER TWENTY-SEVEN

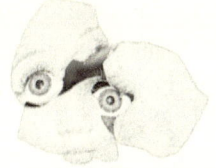

"Bring forth the tincture!" The new ruler of Cochtonia and CEO of Cochton Enterprises, unlike his uncles, was not afraid to take the stage. Wearing a white leisure suit with gold bedazzling, Layal sat on the plastic throne. He clearly craved acceptance of the public, waving to them and having Vice Patrol agents toss out candy corn. My parents had refused to come and watch the exploitation and I encouraged this. The tonic was another act of malfeasance on my part and the fewer witnesses the better.

Some Agros were selling corn liquor, corn dogs, and popcorn to the crowd. After advising Kola, NezLeigh was selling homunculus statues at a discount. Men in HumP shirts hovered around her, cash in hand, while Bigg Gib, appearing nearly human, put purchased items in plastic bags and chatted up the customers. She wore the skirt I'd worn the day I met Bigg Gib. Now and then, he patted her butt playfully. I hadn't told Nez about the fate of the homunculi—I was too uneasy about the misbegotten situation to talk about it, but I'd hinted to her and she was smart enough to understand and scuttle her inventory.

I stood with Newton and Paracelsus behind the curtain on the tower stage in the town square. Newton, in full 1700s garb, but a lab coat over it all, proudly held the potion in a 500 mL beaker.

The penis branch had perked up greatly, surrounded by carbon dioxide bubbles. LouOtta Maliegene was with us, making me burn with embarrassment as before, even as she had no recognition of me. She wasn't dressed in her usual form-fitting clothing. Yes, she had on tight leggings, but they were paired with a loose vest with many pockets. Instead of heels, she wore heavy boots. I tried to avoid eye contact, but she put her hands all over Newton, straightening his already straight wig and fluffing his ruffles.

Ursula stood with us in an official capacity. Finally, she'd had enough and said, "Lady LouOtta, stand back. Alchemy takes concentration."

"I am simply straightening him."

"I am straight enough," Newton said through his teeth.

"Show, don't tell, Newty."

Newton, being the intelligent man he was, ignored her and I swallowed my rage. Fighting with Lady LouOtta wasn't going to get me where I wanted to be, which was back in the lab with Newton at my side.

"I no longer believe in female-based reproduction," she said. "You need to seed the next homunculi. I can afford to sponsor it."

"My reproduction is my own private business and today is not about me." Newton gripped the tonic and looked ahead through the flowing curtains. "Today is about the nephew."

"He's weak and always will be," she said. "Nobody even wants to be his bride."

Clearly, the contest had few entrants. Being the fertile bride of the outcast nephew held little appeal. A platform had been erected in the center of the square a short distance from the tower, surrounded by Vice Patrol agents for protection. Kola stood on the platform in her jump suit. She wore no shoes and a white full-face mask with silver mesh over the eyes—something Mom had confiscated once upon a time when she'd devised a pop-up law saying only the Vice Patrol wore white. Although Mom disapproved of the contest, she gave the mask to Kola, hoping it would be off-putting. It was. However, from what I could discern, there was only one other contestant besides Kola. The challenger wore a yellow leotard with tassels on the breast area and a gold mask. She tossed candy to the people who pulsed around the platform. The performance tower had the three concrete hands, representing each Cochton heir. One hand had been chiseled as if giving the finger. This was the hand representing Layal's mom, who was an outcast and one barrier to his sought for public approval. A rope hung from the middle finger and down to the stage where it sat coiled. I pointed it out to Newton and tried to make a joke.

"Rope be damned!"

As soon as I said it, unease and regret spread through me like a thirst. The tonic was a fake just like the revered homunculi. Mom was right, Kola was too young. What else could go wrong?

"Bring forth the tonic!" Layal's voice was low, like a frog. There was no City Manager announcing this show, no cameras, no microphones, no parade, merely Layal and body guards, a sneak grab at power. Paracelsus put an arm around me and another around Newton.

"The time has come, my friends."

With his escort, Newton and I came out to face Layal and the crowd.

The self-appointed ruler of Cochtonia came from his throne and stood in front of me, his back to the crowd. "How do you know this works?"

I brushed my hands over my belly, pulling my shirt tight. There it was. A swelling. "I tried it on myself. And on him, my legal lab partner."

"It's middle-aged spread."

I shook my head. He held out his hand and ran it across my bump. I grew uneasy at his touch, yet I stood there, well-trained.

"There is so little philosophy about this state of being," he mused. "Was it not once called a mystery in three syllables?"

"Does alchemy have three syllables?" Paracelsus was eager to claim some credit.

Layal motioned to Ursula. "I need a professional opinion."

Ursula had been standing near the curtain. She came forward and ran a No Regrets device over me.

"It's true, your Lordship."

The people at the front of the crowd wore their HumP t-shirts proudly. They voiced their disapproval of my condition with a series of boos.

"This is fully a result of the tonic?" Layal asked. "This miracle could be mine?"

"If the tonic is taken as prescribed, odds are," I assured him, not saying that odds are bad he'll be anything but drunk.

Again, the people in the front of the crowd grumbled. Ursula waved her arm and three agents joined her on the stage. They let their hands, holding weapons, fall casually to their sides. Vice Patrol: one minute a friend, and the next a foe.

Paracelsus stepped forward. "Your highest high Highness and bestower of all that is good, alchemy requires some ancient ways. Allow us to perform the sacred ritual to increase the odds."

He took the beaker from Newton and put it in the center of the stage. In his flowing robes, he bent over it as best he could. He held out his arms and chanted.

"We call on the sun, bringer of gold, help us take this action bold.

The moon, silver in hue, bring a bride who will be due.

Mercury, quicksilver, news of birth, deliver.

Copper, the beauty of Venus, let fertility flow from the penis.

Earth, the dirt to be sowed, an heir is what the nation is owed.

Mars, the Vulcan, to forge the fire, find the best woman to create a pyre.

Jupiter, the staff of life and luck. Visit us tonight, as the will to fuck.

Saturn, with all the wisdom of age, look at us kindly and be a sage."

The alchemist waved his arms over the tincture.

"Thank you for the excellent spell," Layal wiped his eyes. "It brought tears. I hereby lift the ban on poetry that has plagued our country since I can remember."

The crowd murmured, even though none knew exactly what poetry was. Fewer understood why this nephew was making proclamations and having a bride contest. The sun grew hot. Layal went to the front of the stage and addressed the crowd.

"Probably you all wonder why we have come to this—a fertility contest. Today is a sad and happy occasion. We have my uncles and their perfectly formed homunculi—why would I need a fertility potion and fertility contest? I am sorry to tell you, they have all perished, unfortunately perished. The shortness of life makes it all the sweeter. We are all together on the river that flows to the lagoon. My uncles and the homunculi, despite our best attempts, have left the living and joined the dead. I am the heir."

Predictably, the crowd took this news badly.

"Where are they buried?" a man shouted. "We want a shrine."

"You lie!" called another. "They're still alive."

"Bring out Bert!"

A chant rose up "Humper, Humper!"

Sweat dripped from Newton's forehead.

"We want HumP."

They are not pivoting well. He should have known folks here do not like change. It's why they've put up with all the laws. Go along to get along.

Ursula and her troops went to the front of the stage and stood next to Layal. He raised his voice. "Silence as we sing the anthem. Our national treasure, LouOtta Maliegene, will lead us in this revered heritage. We have lost our beloved leaders but we can still join our hearts in song."

Boots clomping, LouOtta came from behind the curtain. Citizens were required to stand at attention while singing the anthem and press their index fingers to their forehead to show they were thinking of Cochtonia. The supporters, instead, waved their caps. One man took out a gun and put it to his forehead instead of his finger.

Surprisingly, LouOtta Maliegene announced, "I dedicate my

rendition to these brave patriots before me. We stand in solidarity with the homunculi. They shall return!" I was shocked. She had nothing to gain by supporting these guys. They advocated for the impossible: life without women. Confused but doing her duty, Ursula held up an image of a green square with yellow silhouettes of an ear of corn and a fat hog. This was our national flag. Immediately, as required, we all pressed our foreheads with our index fingers again to show we were still thinking of Cochtonia.

"Shut up and sing!" Ursula commanded.

"Ohhh." LouOtta held the first note to help the people of Cochtonia get started. This was the only song we sang, we knew no others. Except for the recent alchemical chants, we heard no others. All joined in, finger to forehead, although some in the front made a show of using their middle finger, swinging it around before landing it on the forehead as required. The smell of manure and insecticides drifted on a lazy breeze as LouOtta sang.

"Bombs and tassels, tassels and bombs,
Come father, come brothers,
Hear the sound.
As bombs and corn tassels burst around,
Defend our enterprise.
We will stand against enemies
And favor our friends
As we please.
We are the Cochtonians, right.
Defend. Defend, and fight."

Done singing the brief anthem, she addressed the crowd. "Fight, my men, fight for the right to live free. Fight for the Homunculi, may they return. Take up arms for their homecoming. Patriots, forward march!"

CHAPTER TWENTY-EIGHT

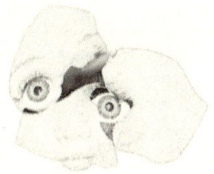

On this last line, the HumPers rushed toward the stage with a barbaric yawp. LouOtta held up a fist in solidarity as she reached into her vest pocket. For what? A weapon? She was dangerous. A dangerous stooge. A traitor to women. Status be dammed. Newton stepped forward to protect me but he didn't make it in time. I leapt forward, my protective hormones surging. I was behind her and she didn't see me. She had her approving gaze on the swell of heaving men. I pushed her with both hands. Down from the stage she tumbled, onto the men, onto the lost cause as the troublemakers fell to the grass, fainting. The Vice Patrol agents were able to detect people who carried concealed weapons and Ursula and her team beamed them with a brain relaxer. I thought everyone knew this but apparently, they'd been left in the dark, with their false sense of security. These guys and LouOtta would wake up with splitting headaches.

Officers moved forward and disarmed LouOtta, holding up a pill bottle.

"It's potassium cyanide!" one said to the crowd.

InVitros were allowed to keep a vial of cyanide and expected to take it when their luster faded. It wasn't clear how she'd planned to use it today. The agents carried her to a Vice Patrol van sitting at the edge of the town square. Bigg Gib hid his face in NezLeigh's hair as LouOtta limply passed by. On the platform, Kola stood with one hand on her hip impatiently. The woman in gold pressed her finger to her forehead. No one in the crowd followed her in the gesture. The crowd was unusually quiet, in shock perhaps. The golden woman did the splits, her finger firmly in place in a gesture of patriotism. It didn't get the attention it deserved. It had seemed as if she might be a clear winner, being more well-dressed and enthusiastic, but attractiveness was all relative at this point. The gesture of patriotism fell flat with both Agros and citizens. Not as many women appreciated no-woman reproduction as I expected. I thought I saw NezLeigh and Big Gibb stuffing the rest of the statues in the nearest trash can.

Layal came forward. "This is a somber moment. Our national treasure, LouOtta Maligene, was a traitor. Let's never sing that mournful dirge of an anthem again." The crowd reacted with a spattering of applause. He held up my arm. "*She* saved our nation with a well-placed push! I'd marry her if I could but she has a lean on her." *All my hard work in the lab and this well-placed push is what I get acclaim for?* "She is the lab partner of Isaac Newton, a man who is not simply an alchemist but a keen scientific mind. Together, this team has made a potion from a mandrake lookalike. Like its namesake, the mandrake, this highly aromatic potion, can restore fertility and vitality to those who imbibe. The homunculi were old science. They could not exist in the modern world. Let us partake of the new chemistry. Let *me* partake! Men and women are in this together. It's time to test the tincture of mandrake."

A Vice Patrol agent carried a decorated table from behind the stage. Another brought four shot glasses. They placed them next to the beaker, still in the middle of the stage.

"Sir Newton, come forward. Pour your creation," Layal ordered.

Newton complied, retrieving the potion and decanting liquid into each glass, but his hand shook and much spilled before he placed the beaker on the table, the "penis" floating in the remaining liquid.

"Who will take the first sips? Alchemist, I invite you."

"Drink it? I don't need fertility. I was the test subject."

"I implore you."

"It needs to be set on fire first."

"We save the fire for later. Drink it!"

Newton downed a shot, then wiped his forehead with his sleeve. "Savory and fragrant. I advocate for it highly."

"And now, the woman." He looked me in the eye with his baby blues and motioned to the shot glass. "Join me."

It was as hot as a cornfield in July on the stage. For the first time, queasiness crept over me. Newton held out his hand to stop me.

"Scared?" Layal asked.

"It's a tincture. Paracelsus said to prepare a tincture. It's soaked in alcohol. And I don't need it, your Greatness," I replied, rubbing my belly for emphasis.

The contestant in gold shouted from the platform, "Don't waste it. Let me at it, baby!"

Ursula jumped forward. "I'll do it." She chugged the shot and slammed the glass on the pedestal. "It's got a kick."

"Now, we wait to make sure there aren't lingering ill-effects. Let's have the competition—for me." He put his hands behind his head and thrust his hips, like the stripper he was bred to be. "It's time for the vitality competition," Layal said. "Let's see how healthy and strong the contestants are. Unleash the Line of Love."

A Vice Patrol agent hustled past us and grabbed the coiled rope hanging from the chiseled hand. He rushed it to the platform and handed it to the woman in gold.

"The most fertile women will make an entrance to illustrate their vitality."

The woman in gold grabbed the rope, swung over the crowd, dropped onto the sleeping HumPers, and walked across them and up to the stage. She stood at attention in front of Layal.

"Reporting for sacrifice, Lord Layal."

"Very vital," he said aloofly. "Sacrifice doesn't impress me. Let's see the next contender!"

A Vice Patrol agent walked the rope back to Kola. Kola tied a knot in the rope, sat on it, kicked herself off the platform, swung to the front of the stage and landed, precariously close to the edge before falling forward onto the cement. She jumped up, brushed herself off, and flipped her thick wavy hair. She took a place next to the other contestant, surreptitiously pinching her on the ass. The woman screamed. A few in the crowd clapped at this show of aggression.

"Let's see who has brains to go with her brawn." Layal went up to the first competitor. "What is your motto in life, Goldie?"

She replied, "Pretty hurts."

"How interesting. Truth is beauty. You are saying Truth hurts?"

"I am saying I'll do anything to please you."

"Pleasure pleases me. Pleasure and intellect."

"Anything you want, I got it."

He went to Kola.

"And your motto?"

"Motto? Motto?"

"A motto is a saying you live by."

"Survival of the fittest. The fittest."

"Meaning?"

"It means the best adapted. Are you stupid? You must have read *Darwin's Book of Bedtime Stories* like I did."

I was stunned. How dare she mention a book of stories? We didn't read such nonsense here, or if we did, we kept it a secret.

"Who are you?" he asked, annoyed. He stared at her naked feet, as if they would tell him.

"I don't read," said Goldie. "And I love Cochtonia."

"I'm beginning to rue the day I decided to save Cochtonia," Layal said. "Why do we have only two contestants?"

"One more than you need, you handsome sucker," said Kola.

"One less than I need," Layal replied.

The crowd chanted, "Kiss the bride! Kiss the bride!" and clanked plastic popcorn buckets together in a most annoying way.

"Ursula, Paracelsus. Help me. Who is more fertile?"

Ursula watched my face as she held her scanner over Goldie, then Kola, then back to Goldie, resting on Kola. "This, our Lord, is the most fertile woman."

Goldie screamed in anger. Two Vice Patrol agents hauled her away while the crowd clapped for Kola.

"Miss, reveal yourself," Layal said.

Kola tossed down her mask, showing her pug-nosed face with small eyes—an Agro. This union would give the Agros more status. He'd been played by NezLeigh, for sure.

The crowd gasped. Some cheered. Others shouted in anger.

Layal put his hand on his heart. "Oh no! Not you! You're the child I saved years ago."

"You think a normal woman would be the most fertile? No, it's me. Me! I'm all yours at last and you are mine."

"It's you! No, oh, no! I protest too much, me thinks."

"Oh, but you'll keep your word! Otherwise, you'll betray yourself. Do you want a baby or not? I won fair and square."

"Are you old enough?"

"It's been a few years since we saw each other last. You are in no position to object to a fertile woman. No position. Hell, no! You are the one I want. We go way back. You saved my life, you handsome fucker. You saved me when I was discarded in the trash. You pulled me from the garbage. You named me. You read books to me, we shared food, and now, I offer life to you, fingers crossed. The potion deserves the best chance, the best."

Layal was conflicted. The woman was fertile—but the eyes and the attitude.

"Kola, I still consider you an abandoned child and..." He paused, struggling. "Yes, you were put into the garbage and abandoned. Yes, I rescued you. Who put you up to this? Does your sister have anything to do with it?"

Layal was self-indulgent but he wasn't dumb. He saw the trap.

"No, my old friend, no, not her, although you saved her, too."

"NezLeigh. NezLeigh!" He shouted at the sky, a man betrayed. He appeared crazed to the crowd many of whom were Agros, who grew agitated at his confusing rejection of the future bride.

"You think my sister put me up to this? I won legitimately. I'm not power hungry. I admit, I'm young and stupid to boot, but power hungry, no. I'll leave it all up to you." She grabbed a shot of tonic and chugged it.

"Now you. Drink up!" She held the beaker to Layal. "Burns like a son of a bitch. I probably don't even need it but you do for sure."

Layal jerked the beaker from her. "The future of Cochtonia depends on us. You say this contains alcohol? Oh, I plead it does. Numb me, oh fermentation and let me serve my country." He drank quickly, his Adam's apple bobbing, until, as he got to the end, the plant dick flopped out on his face. He stumbled back and flung it afar. The crowd of Agros ran away as it flew toward them and landed on the ground.

He wiped his mouth. I expected him to be staggering drunk. Instead, he spoke as if enlightened. "Fertility doesn't mean maturity. I won't have a young bride, even in desperation!"

Kola twirled Layal's long, curly hair. "I'll settle for a kiss on the cheek and a chair beside you, you gorgeous dog. At least for now."

"For now," he said with resignation. "Alchemists, lend me your ears. I need a consult."

Newton and Paracelsus talked with Layal, who folded his arms, looked at the ground, and swayed a little as they offered suggestions. Kola's face went from worried to all smiles. Layal came to the edge of the stage, teetering precariously.

"Citizens, we will have celebratory fireworks, launched from the platform to let the public know that a fertile woman has been located. Consummation might take place after a full year cycle of moons with the option of a second contest or a second year of waiting."

A firetruck parted the crowd and stopped at the platform. The firefighters got a deck box from the truck and carried it to the platform.

"Shouldn't they be wearing safety glasses?" I asked Newton.

"And shirts," Newton replied. "Why are they bare chested?"

"Is this in part why Agro women light fires? I bet they want to see the half-naked firefighters."

The men put a mortar on the platform and lit it with a long lighter. They jumped back as sparks flew and the air popped. The pyrotechnics streaked into the darkening sky and exploded with a dull boom, showering the crowd with sparks falling to earth like a golden shower.

Newton put his arm around me. "At last, something familiar. This place was missing the celebratory exuberance of fire pinwheels, peonies, and chrysanthemums. There is nothing like spectacle. If only an orchestra were playing to accompany the bursting."

"What," I said, "is an orchestra?"

My heart rose as another mortar climbed into the sky and erupted into a green spider with legs reaching toward earth. Things might work out for the best after all. Kola had another year to grow up and Layal had saved face.

Newton squeezed me fondly. "Maybe this place can make some positive changes. Layal appears to be more open than his uncles."

"You've bought at least a year of stability with your solution to the heir problem."

"Admirably, he found the idea of a child bride unappealing, despite their common history."

A pair of golden rings popped above us followed by a crackly heart. The smell of sulfur and perchlorates drifted across the park.

"Your well-placed push quickly ended an escalating situation. I have trouble using the word love but I love you, Stella, and am proud to be your lab partner."

"I love you, too. I'm happier than I've ever been."

The thud of a launch was followed by sizzling as a rocket went sideways, scattering the firemen, shooting over the crowd, and hitting the Pavilion of Agriculture. Another rocket, untended, fell over and shot back toward us on the tower. We yelled and leapt away. Shrapnel from the firework ignited the throne and landed in Layal's lap. He struggled to his feet, screaming and staggering across the stage.

"Shit, no!" His future bride grabbed him and beat the flames out with her mask before rolling him across the concrete as he struggled. "Fire's a bitch," she said, extinguishing him as he screamed in agony.

Heat from the smoldering throne singed my face and the black smoke blew into the milling crowd. A firefighter, his pants seared and smoking, dashed up the stairs to the platform with an extinguisher. He sprayed Layal with powder, making him cough, before squirting the throne. The firefighter collapsed in a cloud of clay, ammonium phosphate and calcium carbonate. I was at a loss as to how to help. A woman around Mom's age, carrying a black shoulder bag, ran from the crowd and up to the stage. She knelt beside Layal. "I'm a medic. Let me examine him." She pulled away the burned pants. "We need ice!" She pointed to NezLeigh and Big Gibb, coming up the stairs. "Get ice from the bar. Hurry!" She made a phone call.

I watched them rush away through the park. Vice Patrol vans were on the grass loading injured firefighters. Two agents came to the stage and Ursula ordered them to take away the man who'd sprayed Layal. The medic removed a syringe and a vial from her bag and injected Layal with a substance.

"Are these injuries fatal?" Newton asked the medic, hovering over our leader.

"They all have disfiguring injuries. Layal's are the most critical. He'll need surgery and prosthetics. We don't have the resources here. I called a medical helicopter from Illinois."

"No, not them," Layal moaned. "Not another country and not Illinois."

Kola threw her arms around him. "Don't take him from me. It's my chance, my chance!"

Ursula said, "You are the chosen one, his bride. You must take the wheel of our tragic nation for the health and safety of the citizens."

"Me? No, I can't! I'm stupid. It's you!" She pointed to me. "It's you, I'm joining my beloved. Goodbye!"

CHAPTER TWENTY-NINE

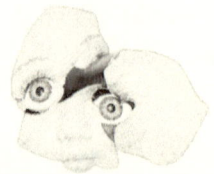

Me? No, I wouldn't. It couldn't be me! I had too many other things I wanted to do. Being a leader of people, flawed, unpredictable people, was not my forte. No, I had a lab partner at last and he and I had a lifetime of being in a lab, ignoring people together, ahead of us. I watched Ursula's face. She tried not to reveal any emotion but she had been passed over again. She wanted it, but it couldn't be her. As much as I cared for her and my parents, the Vice Patrol were raised to think they were always in the right, and infallible leaders telling people what to think had brought us to this point. A leader would need empathy. Did any of us have it?

"Listen to her. It's you!" Layal said through clenched teeth. "The planter. The pusher. You've saved our nation twice!"

It could not be me. I didn't mean to save our nation either time.

Newton put an arm around me. "Please, play along with him. Otherwise, some authoritarian group will fill the void. I know, I lived it."

"I'll do it. Authoritarians have already caused enough trouble for us and for science." Pushing myself through doubt, I addressed the crowd. "I inform the public of yet another tragedy. The heir has been injured. The fire situation is unsafe and unstable. Please disperse quietly. We wait for his recovery." My voice was soft and few heard me.

"Can you disband them?" I asked Ursula. "And move the sleeping HumPers to a safer area?"

"Yes, my Leader," Ursula replied. Her tone was hard to decipher but it wasn't joy. Paracelsus took her hand and kissed it. "I'll be your follower."

"What should I do with the men?" she asked me "Execution is simple."

Execution was extreme. I only wanted to get rid of their stupid HumP slogans. "No, remove their shirts and dump them."

A haze rose over the park

"Is that smoke?" I asked.

Newton blinked. "It appears to be. Did you know that London had a great fire in 1666? It began in a bakery and swept through the entire city. Only a fifth of the metropolis was left standing. Even King Charles II joined the fire brigade. He didn't want to lose his head as had happened to Charles I. The London Bridge was burned. It had been filled with shops and boasted a gatehouse. Miraculously, few lives were lost. It was early autumn after a dry summer, almost as it is now."

NezLeigh and Bigg Gibb returned with the ice.

"The damn Pavilion is smoking like an old man."

"Bits of fire fall like stars."

"We've got to check on the apple trees," I said to Newton. They were my babies, my hope for a more fruitful future for Cochtonia, and my nurturing side was leaping into action. I had to see with my own eyes that they were safe. "Ursula, can you get some firefighters over to the Pavilion and some to Cochton Enterprises?"

"They're more sexy than smart, but I'll try."

The drum of a helicopter came close. The medic packed the ice on Layal's groin. "He's got severe burns. Maybe they can do something for him in Illinois."

The chopper came to rest next to the tower. The emergency

personnel put Layal, sedated, on a stretcher, and took him away with Kola following him to the helicopter.

"Kola," NezLeigh called. "Sister, wait! Don't leave me."

Kola stopped. "I'm going. He'll need a friend in the hell-hole that is Illinois."

As the copter rose, NezLeigh said, "She was always an idiot."

"No," said Bigg Gib. "She knows her heart. I'm sorry your time with your sister was so brief. If things weren't on fire, I'd give you a massage to cheer you."

"Damn, you're so sappy! Being near you might make me a nicer person."

The Pavilion was, indeed, smoking. People rushed toward the fire when they should have been rushing away. After all, the smoke particulates were going to lodge in everyone's lungs and stick there forever.

"Not one person knows what's happening," I said.

"You're in charge," Ursula reminded me.

"Alright. I say call a fire truck, have agents keep people away from the smoke. It's full of soot and carbon monoxide. And Ursula, take over for me. I have to check on my lab."

Newton removed his wig. "I'll leave this fire hazard in the rubbish bin." As we left, he tossed it onto the homunculus statues in the garbage can, a relic of the past. We walked to our future, setting off on a mission and secretly glad to have work as an excuse to leave the people behind. We passed the smoldering pavilion as a firetruck pulled up. We didn't get far before two little Agros stopped us.

"Come help! Fire!"

"There are firemen everywhere, they'll handle it."

"They are at the Pavilion. We need to save the special place ourselves! Come around the corner, please. Come on, move your ass!"

"What special place?"

"The bar."

Hiding out in my lab wasn't going to happen as soon as I'd

wished. Notoriety be damned. Between Newton's advice and my respect for the bar, this was a job I couldn't refuse.

"We've got to lend a hand," I said to Newton. "We need to detour."

"Yes, my Leader." His face was monoculture serious.

"Not you, too?" I said in disappointment.

The corner of his mouth twitched.

"Are you making a joke? Are you kidding me?"

"Yes, I'm being capricious."

I gave him a playful shove. "You'd better obey me."

He put his arms around me. "It depends what you ask, lab partner."

His voice. His breath on my neck. It made me shiver. I was so happy, even with buildings burning around me. This love was something I'd never known I wanted. I'd planned to settle for something less.

"Be my support. Let's put out this fire."

We wove through the crowd. In the haze, Cochtonia looked most unspecial. It was run down and the sidewalks were cracked. There was nothing for the public at all. We joined a makeshift bucket brigade, including bartenders, children, and Agro women. Some Vice Patrol stood by, simply watching as the kids scooped sand from a nearby playground and passed it forward in plastic bags. Newton knew exactly what to do. He took his place in line. I positioned myself near the sandbox, helping to scoop sand into a bag before we grabbed another from the blowing litter of Cochtonville. Down the line, the sand was flung at any flames lapping near the bar. A second line of people passed the bags back. The sand tossing worked to a small extent. As the bits of flaming corn from the Pavilion fire hit the sidewalk, sand was poured on them and they went out. The process was holding its own but not making progress.

I had to do something. I called Mom. "I need you to put the power washer and Dad in the car and meet me in front of the Union Station Bar."

"Stella? Where are you? There's a fire downtown, and rumors of trouble."

"Mom, I'm downtown trying to put out the fire!"

"There are fire fighters for that. Come home, we've been so worried."

"Mom, it's not a big fire here but it could get out of hand. I need you, Dad, and the power washer. Can you come? I'll explain later. And I have news."

"Are you engaged?"

"In a way. Even better, if you want the truth."

"I want the truth, the whole truth."

"I'll tell you in person. Mom, be careful." I hung up, knowing the engagement would bring her running.

The battle with the fire remained at a stalemate, despite the friendly collaboration of the Agros. They were cooperative if something they cared about was at stake. Pops of flame that lit the sidewalk in front of the bar or fell on the building were extinguished and more followed. The task for me was to learn to put out these little fires and to understand who I could depend on here in Cochtonia. Like it or not, my recluse days were over.

At last, my parents showed up in their classic car. Dad unloaded his power washer, wheeling it over to the park while Mom helped him fill it with water from a fountain. Dad pushed it back to the street straight across from the bar. He pressed a button and the old thing roared to life. He raised the nozzle and pulled the trigger. I thought he was going to fall back as the water sprayed from the hose but he had mass and therefore, counterforce. Happily, he squirted the foamy water onto the buildings in front of him, hitting the bar with a direct stream. The Agros cheered as the flames smothered and the building was wetted enough to withstand future sparks.

As Dad playfully extinguished the burning bits of corn falling like snow, Mom turned to me. "What's the news?"

I threw both arms around Newton. "We're a team! We've pledge ourselves to each other."

"Oh," she said. "You've eloped?"

"Yes, and the device didn't lie. You'll be a grandmother!"

"Barnabus, did you hear the news? There are baby clothes in our future!"

"Neither one of us is up to the task."

"No, it's Stella!"

"Is this a joke?" Dad gave the bar an extra squirt.

"No, Dad."

"It's legal?"

"Most legal."

"I'll be damned!" He stopped squirting. "My hose has done its job. This isn't Chicago, we put out fires here. On to the Pavilion."

Happy to see my parents engaged and relevant, Newton and I jogged to Cochton Enterprises, a plume of steam rising behind us.

In my lab, the apple sprouts stood up to greet us, unfazed by the events outside. Their saw-tooth deep green leaves umbrellaed over gangly stems like heavy heads, as awkwardly vulnerable as new piglets.

I thought I might crack open with relief. I embraced Newton. "They're okay! And we'll be okay, too. I know it."

Newton returned my hug. "Sounds superstitious to me."

"Neither one of us believes in superstition. It's hope I'm feeling. Look at them, they're green with promise."

"What do you intend to do with these saplings? Who will plant them?"

"We will plant them. It will be our own outdoor experiment."

"They will take years to bear fruit."

"We'll have years of hope. We'll start a giveaway program—an apple tree in every yard and two dozen in the town square."

"You sound like a leader. Shall we get going? The day has been long. All I want to do is hold you, to become one before we become three."

It was getting dark. A faint smell of burnt corn hung in the air. We walked across the cracked sidewalks. Things in town had settled down. If anyone recognized me as "the pusher" strolling

along with Isaac Newton, no one reacted. We walked onto the
bridge. Newton stopped at the center.

"I need to get some breeze," he said. "Why is it so warm? You
have no seaside and this century is overly hot."

"It's called climate change. You don't have to pretend to be
from another time if you don't want to. You can live in today. I
promise, I love who you are, not who you were." *Or weren't.*

"I imagine if I'm not a genuine being, if I am something
unworldly and raised from the dead, I'll turn to dust when my time
is over."

The thought of him, us, turning to dust was too painful, so I
attempted to change the subject slightly. "Did you know we are all
created from the same chemicals as found in stars and comets and
planets?"

"We're heavenly? You're telling me the alchemists' motto—As
above so is below—is true?"

"Yes, we are space dust. We don't need alchemy when nature
has such delightful pebbles to gather."

"It's true, we are all one. I was never as special and sacred as I
imagined. A man might imagine things that are false but he can
only understand things that are true. I'm free of my notorious
burden, it drove me to madness."

The wind blew our hair as, hand in hand, we watched the river
flow beneath us. The thought of losing him was unbearable. I
stared into the darkness below, the faint moonlight on the water,
and tried to forget his comment about turning to dust. The future
was not going to hold an abyss—it couldn't. We had the trees and
each other. The problem was, the dust was coming. Despite the
promise of this new life in front of us, being in love and caring so
deeply about someone had opened my eyes to the inevitable dust
we'd all be in time.

The end of the season fireflies, the few who escaped the
insecticide barrage here in Cochtonia, twinkled over the water.
There was motion down there. Animals? Wild, white pigs? Pale
figures moved about on the banks, clustering together, large pallid

backs catching the moonlight like Yorkshire hogs. One reared up to show a broad, soft chest. It wasn't pigs. It was people. The HumPer men, their shirts removed, had woken from their device-imposed slumber. I'd meant for Ursula to dump the shirts but I hadn't been clear and she'd dumped the men instead. Some rubbed their sore heads as they struggled up the banks of the Cedar River. Others sat together, some with hands clasped, others on their knees, bowing to something. I swore it was Jelly, although it was no longer light enough to see for sure. The thought of my old doll resurfacing from wherever she'd been tossed gave me the creeps. Would I always be reminded about what I had done with her? Damn, plastic lived forever. I pointed out the men to Newton.

"They look to be partaking in a ritual," he remarked. "They are worshiping something."

"It's the doll I used to make the molds for the homunculi," I ventured.

"A humble doll toppled the autocracy."

"Yes, I'm afraid so, and an errant firework. It wasn't as stable as it appeared."

"They never are. It's why they use so much force to hold themselves together. Our quaint friends here have found a way to keep their beliefs in the homunculi alive." He patted his ruffled shirt. "Am I obvious? I'm glad I'm not wearing my wig. It would catch the moonlight and draw attention to me."

"If they recognize you, they'll probably make you a saint. Let's get out of here."

CHAPTER THIRTY

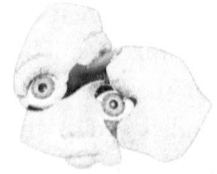

On the other side of the bridge, we approached a group of people, a dozen or so, all carrying pointed objects, thin like a broom handle but clearly sharp. I saw them sauntering toward us, a block away. Most had long prairie skirts and their hair tied up. They were Agro women.

"What do they have?" I asked Newton.

"It looks to be pointed sticks."

"Sticks?"

"Made from tree branches."

"Where would they get those? Are they dangerous?"

"They could be, especially to eyes or if shoved down your throat." His face was worn, as if he'd aged a year in this day.

Now the question was, go toward cocky pointed sticks or toward angry HumPers? I was embarrassed to be scared of the Agros, especially since NezLeigh and I had grown close. They could be allies, but the Agros had some legitimate gripes, so would they be? They approached with menacingly straight walks, swinging the sticks. Where were they going on a night like this, already full of mishaps?

"Caught between the devil and the deep blue sea," Newton said quietly. He looked over his shoulder at the bridge. "Let's go back to the lab."

We turned.

"Hold up," one yelled.

Two had familiar silhouettes in the dark.

"Newton, wait a moment. Doesn't that one look like a Neanderthal?" I said. "Maybe this gang isn't dangerous. I'd recognize the outline anywhere. It's Bigg Gib! And NezLeigh's with him. Look at the hair!"

"I see. Are you sure they aren't being held captive?"

"No, but if they are, perhaps we can help." I got out my device in case I needed to make a quick call

We stood and waited for them to catch up with us. The group surrounded us, sticks out.

"Hey, nerds. How about we poke your eyes out?"

"Don't hurt them," NezLeigh said as the Agros pushed their sticks near our eyes. "She's the new leader. I told you, the Cochtons are gone."

"We don't need her as a leader," said a woman.

"Hell, I don't answer to her type," said another. "New sphincter, same crap."

"NezLeigh, who are these people?" I said, not sure if I was afraid or irritated.

"These people are why I wanted to live in town. I wanted to join up with them. We planned to overthrow the Cochtons, but you've made it all too easy."

"Counter Force is taking the two of you as prisoners," said the woman.

"You call your ragtag assembly Counter Force? You are usurping my term!" Newton said, shoving the stick from his face.

"Would Cunter Force please you, Fancy Man?"

Surprisingly, Newton held himself back. "Possibly."

I scrolled through my phone to call the Vice Patrol to arrest this woman for a Word Crime, but I thought better of it. I wanted their trust. I needed their trust. We had to be in league, but I didn't want my eyes poked out. I asked, "What are you counter to?"

"These days of hegemony must end. We're a league of counter force to push back against the autocratic ways of Cochtonia. The Cochtons used us and abused us. We seek retribution."

"If their force diminishes, so will yours," Newton observed. "If you insist on being a counter force."

"You're right. We'd be free of the burden of force if they are gone."

"The Cochtons are all indisposed. It's a new day," I said.

"It's night, dumb bitch!"

"Your force isn't necessary. The Cochtons are either dead or in Illinois."

"This woman is the newly appointed leader. Please give her respect. She saved me from captivity. How about I give you a massage?" said Bigg Gib.

"Save your guns. She gets respect. So what? Who gives a shit? We still have nothing!"

"I can't make everything right all at once. I'm not smart enough."

"And neither am I," Newton added.

"But we are making progress, which is all any scientist ever asks for," I added.

"Damn eggheads," said a woman. "Who gives a crap?"

"If a wise person is on your side, listen to them," NezLeigh said, poking the woman with her stick.

"Why the fuck would we want your opinion, newbie? We were out here setting fires and disturbing the peace long before you showed up."

"She had a hand in making the homunculus babies and they killed Bert and Clarence," I said.

"Damn."

"Damn."

"Damn."

Three women spoke in sequence. Despite the apparent awe, no one lowered her stick.

"They're gone but the manure remains," one said.

"What do you want from us?" I said to the hostile women.

"You're coming to our headquarters and we will negotiate terms."

Newton took my hand. "History says we should comply."

We walked as they held sticks to our necks. I was pretty sure it wouldn't be difficult to dodge the pokes and get away, but if I was any kind of leader, and I was sure I wasn't one, this confrontation wouldn't end with any sort of battle, fight, or execution.

The homes became smaller and more rectangular. The sidewalk ended and we trod over hardpacked grass. We came to an open area with no lights. Weeds sprouted like haystacks—poke weed and nightshade with their toxic berries were tied up with bindweed—terribly tough to kill with herbicides. Among the clumps of weeds, large-headed figures stood about, their tattered clothing shaking in the wind. They walked not and said nothing, the sentries of this silent place.

"Where are we?" I said.

Newton gripped my hand. "It's the graveyard, a poor man's cemetery at best. These are abandoned wreaths on stands, their faded ribbons blowing."

"This place hasn't been used in at least fifteen years, since dead people are now fed to the pigs."

"Abandoned and unpatrolled."

We entered through an old iron gate, walked along a sidewalk overgrown with plantains, and stopped at a stained-stone mausoleum. Cochton was carved across a white arch. Lichens grew inside of the letters from what I could tell in the darkness. A sad tree hung over it, lonely in this place where grasses reigned. The entrance to the tomb was blocked with a padlocked wrought iron gate but the padlock had been broken and the gate hung open.

"Get in, this in our secret meeting hall."

The opening wasn't large—the size of my bedroom. Granite

blocks sat on one side, engraved with Mother and Father. Below them sat three empty chambers, empty no doubt because the sister wasn't dead—only banished—and the brothers were cut into pieces and awaiting resurrection. Plastic bags and lighters were strewn about. A woman pointed to a pile of bags. "Have a seat."

Newton was wary. He crossed his arms, refusing to sit. "We hold no malice. What do you want from us? Why have you brought us to this place to make merry with worms? You took my words and rob us of our time. It's our wedding night and we are no Romeo and Juliet."

"Stand then, dummy. Hear us out. We are the real Cochtonians, and we belong. We are model citizens."

"Yes," I said. "We recognize as much."

"How will you include us, Pusher? How will we be a part of your new order? How will you keep us from being shit upon?" I thought about ways to change Cochtonia for the better as the women waited for my answer.

"We could start with making the main floor of Cochton mansion a public place for citizens," I suggested. "We'd need someone to manage it. Bigg Gib is wonderful at making people feel at home. How about it, Gib?"

"I was made for the service industry," Bigg Gib said.

"Thanks for the bone," a woman said. "It isn't enough to save your eyes."

"Give us time, and we will make a pact of some sort," Newton said, "similar to the Magna Carta."

"What's the Magna Farta?" someone asked, as others giggled.

"Good woman, the Magna Carta is a document from 1215 England. It's known as the greatest charter ever written. It gave people rights, such as the right to a trial and dictates that leaders must obey the law as everyone else."

"It does?" I asked. This document was something no one in Cochtonia would have mentioned. Certainly, these laws were not held in Cochtonia.

"Damn straight," someone said. "I dig it."

"A trial, as in evidence?" said another.

"Yes," Newton explained. "As free people, you citizens want to know what rights and privileges you receive in exchange for loyalty to the nation. Who will represent you? How will you share in power? How will your representatives be chosen? All of this should be worked out."

A sob rose in my throat. "How do you know this?" No one in Cochtonia would have taught him this. People didn't have rights here and no one shared power. Yes, we complained, we saw the wrong in our leaders, but sharing power? No, we didn't. The idea had merit. The idea wasn't the problem. The problem was, it wouldn't have been taught to him. He *was* a being created from the remains of Isaac Newton, which meant he was pre-aged. He was going to die young.

"I'm pulling it from inside me," he said cheerfully.

"No," I cried. "You learned it from the Puritans. You learned it from Granny Rhonda."

"It's a good idea no matter who came up with it," an Agro said. "Sharing power. This way, we don't have to hurt anyone. Long live the Maggot Farta."

The group laughed childishly.

"We will convene representatives from all aspects of Cochtonia," I said, my voice quivering. I didn't know what else to do other than stick with the task at hand. "Starting with..." I didn't know any of these people. Who should I appoint? Or should I let them hash it out? Thinking about Newton's fate, I wanted to collapse in a sobbing heap, but it wouldn't solve any problems, for me or for society. And wasn't making things better for society the ultimate goal of science? "Starting with someone who has stamina for the task and is in touch with those in town, in the country, and in the wild. And who—"

A woman finished my sentence. "Gets laid enough to be happy. In other words, NezLeigh."

"Yes, she will be your first representative, and now, I just want a bed," I said to Newton. "I'll call Dad for a ride."

"No," said a woman, pulling a plastic bag from a pile. "We'll get a ride for you. It's faster this way. They're only interested in trouble."

She went to the entrance of the mausoleum, lit the bag and tossed it on the ground in front. Another person followed suit. And another. The smoke billowed inside and we all had to rush out, dodging the flames.

"We're smoking the corpses out," someone said.

"Damn plunderers," said another, lighting another bag and tossing it in.

"They think they're better even in death with their fancy carcass house. Now they smell like bag-smoke."

Short-lived smoke poured from the building. The Agros scattered, leaving me with Newton, NezLeigh, and Bigg Gib, as a Vice Patrol van plowed across the weeds, squashed the ancient wreaths, and stopped in front of us. A man got out. I walked forward, eager to get a ride after this long day.

"Grave desecration? It's execution time," said a remarkably handsome Vice Patrolman. He grabbed Bigg Gib. "Did you do it?" He shoved Bigg Gib to the ground. Gib covered his head with his arms and rolled into a ball. NezLeigh ran to his side.

The Washer yanked NezLeigh by the hair. "Get back, jail bait! It doesn't take a scan to know you've overstepped. These dicks are for high-end women who work hard, not scammers like you."

I was at a loss. Did he not know I was the leader? Weren't these new Vice Patrol bred to not have a temper? What advice had Mom given me? Vice Patrol brutality is rooted in insecurity and unfamiliarity, so if in a bad situation, be as familiar as possible. It seemed like incomplete data but it was all I had.

"Thank you for coming," I said. "It's an unintentional fire, it's already burning out. We were hoping for a lift to the Cochton Mansion. I'm Stella Smithfailed."

"Show me your identification."

"This is the Pusher," said Newton, putting an arm around me.

"We'll see about it," said the Vice Patrol Crisper. "We're past due for an execution. Let's see your credentials."

"Scan our neck chips," I said. "Match us to your data base before you talk about executions." I hadn't wanted the neck chip, but our chips meant we could be identified easily. Thankfully, no one made a move to upset him and he was alone with no need to impress anyone.

He scanned my neck, then Newton's. "An employee and Isaac Newton. I have no notification of a pusher." He bent and scanned Bigg Gib. "The ugly guy is property." He turned his device on NezLeigh. "The ugly wench is fair game. The rest of you can go."

I waited for someone to escalate things. It was dead silent. They were waiting for me. The Vice Patrol were my skillset.

"No, call if you want to spare yourself. Better yet, I'll call." I grabbed my device from my pocket and screamed into it, my admission that I needed her. "Ursula!" The Crisper agent came toward me, full speed. Newton stepped in the way to stop him but pulled us away as the agent lunged. The man went sprawling, tripping over his own feet.

"I pioneered inertia." Newton bowed with a flourish of his arm and a glint of moonlit smile.

"Are you having some trouble?" It was Ursula on the phone.

"Yes," I said.

"Yeah, one of your goons," NezLeigh yelled.

"Let me take a look. I see it's a solo agent. What's he want? What do *you* want? He went there in response to smoke."

"Some Agros lit bags but it's nothing, there's no trouble. We want a ride to see you. We've got some great ideas for a society. Where are you?"

"I'm at the mansion. I'll have him give you a lift. I see you're at the graveyard?"

The man got up.

"Yeah and your guy is being unfriendly."

"All apologies."

The man yelled and collapsed, holding his neck.

"I heated his chip remotely using your phone as a hot spot. He'll be more than happy to drive you here to meet me once he cools off."

"Many thanks! See you soon. Ursula, I've got some ideas for a charter, and," my voice broke, "I've got something to tell you about the guys. Ask Paracelsus if he's heard of the Magna Carta."

CHAPTER THIRTY-ONE

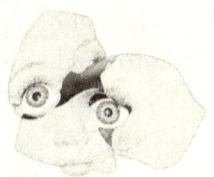

Alone, sitting on faux-stone benches, Ursula and I talked privately in the courtyard. We smelled vaguely like smoke. The moon had set and we were illuminated by lamps with Edison bulbs, an attempt by the late Cochton Brothers to be historical. The neck chip-sensing devices had been turned off along with the cameras in the Roman urns. She removed her hat and her hair tumbled down her back. Her coat was off and her arms bulged from her short sleeves. I wasn't sure what fertility looked like, but perhaps, it looked like this. Ursula was skeptical of my theory that the alchemists were authentic.

"Oink! I don't believe you," she said. "They can't be clones or any form of the real thing. I've seen confidential documents about the historical figures and they were grandiose, superior, especially Newton. He wasn't the friendly guy you hang with. And he was a genius."

"He was resurrected under different conditions. The first time, he was born prematurely to a stressed-out mom."

"Paracelsus lost his mother at age nine. She threw herself into the Sihl River," she said thoughtfully.

"Do you think the Cochtons would have taken such chances— exposing their expensive clones to stress and mania?"

"No, but take heart. Our pals are too average. They're trained monkeys modified to look like the alchemists. Paracelsus knows nothing of the Magna Carta. I admit, he's sympathetic to equality between all people. He doesn't think the Cochtons were inherently better than the rest of us. We argued about it at first but he convinced me. I'm not going to stress about how or where he got those thoughts. He's a mixed bag, but he's my bag."

She had such a goofy smile, full of joy. I should have dropped the matter. But my mind was tossed like a hog shed in a tornado. I couldn't let it go. "They know things they shouldn't know and wouldn't be taught. It's in their DNA."

Even I couldn't bring her down, fortunately. "For a scientist, you don't sound too scientific. In any case, it doesn't matter where he got it. Having a document of rights is a good idea. We've seen how quickly leadership can change. Let's focus on this and not the end of the alchemists. We need to write down the tenants of this equality."

"I don't want to go on without him."

"Cheer up, he's here for the long haul. I've got the document of rights partly drafted. Things are looking bright. What did you text me? I have down 'the right to a trial' and 'leaders must obey the law as everyone else.'"

"Let's add 'Women have the right to motherhood, or non-motherhood, as they desire.'"

"Good. How about 'sidewalks and streets belong to the public'?" she said.

"The public needs to be free of assault and violence, too, and they have a right to privacy, which means no more neck chips," I added, a little afraid she'd take it as an affront. She tensed, knowing what I meant, but she wrote it down. "And 'citizens have the right to be educated.'"

"Maybe we'll have fewer people who long for a homunculus with that last one. But you don't know people like I do. They lie. In any case, we can give it a shot. Any other ideas?"

"I'd like Virginia Guru's *How-To Guide to Human Sexual Response* to be recommended reading for all over eighteen and available in paper."

"Because?"

"Sex is a normal part of life. It shouldn't be a commodity. I nearly missed out on a full life because of the taboo."

"We can have some copies of it, and other books people think they're hiding, in the Community Center. We should leave some room for people who don't want to hear about it at all."

"Celibates. Yes, Newton was a celibate intellectual in the past."

"Maybe the guy you're with now isn't him after all."

"I hope you're right."

NezLeigh came to join us, walking slowly, her hands in tight balls. I'd introduced NezLeigh and Ursula and I'd asked Nez to meet us after I'd had a moment with Ursula. She was here but with obvious trepidation.

As a chemist, I knew strength could be increased when substances were mixed, and I was sure this would be the way of our new society. Alloys, composites, formulations—they all multiplied the positive aspects of a sole material. I needed NezLeigh and Ursula to get along for my own psyche and for the good of the people.

"NezLeigh," I said. "Come mix in. Share your thoughts."

"Only if you're gonna listen to them."

Ursula made the first move. "NezLeigh, I need to apologize for the rogue agent. Clearly we need to make changes at the top to prevent such a lack of training and such an unfamiliarity with the people they are meant to serve."

NezLeigh stood near the wall of the courtyard, arms folded, looking much like Newton when I'd first seen him.

"We need your contribution to our charter. We're making a list of things we hold true for our society. Come give us your thoughts," I said as warmly as I could. I understood her fears.

She came and stood looking over my shoulder at the document we were working on. "Add 'Crispers have the same rights as others. Agros are full members of society.'"

"Natural addition. What else?"

"We need a way for all citizens to give input, and citizens need to accept the responsibility to be informed, ya dig? We got to where we are by allowing a lack of information."

"Great idea," I said. "We need to be a flexible society."

"Yes, and another thing." Ursula pulled up her shirt. "Unhook me. These contraptions have got to go."

She pulled her arms out of her black bra. Her breasts fell forward, free. She walked to the edge of the courtyard, swung the bra over her head, and winged it over the wall.

"Me next." I took off my lab coat and my bra.

"Damn, I never understood those things," NezLeigh said.

It took two tries but I also tossed my bra over the courtyard wall.

"The boob chandelier at the entrance has new meaning now—freedom for breasts."

NezLeigh clapped. "Ban the bra! Shit, we are rapidly finding common ground as a society."

"I'm utopiaed out now," Ursula said. "We can get back to this tomorrow."

"Me, too. Utopia is a messy business."

Our partners entered the courtyard. Paracelsus had invited the men to have a tour of the mansion and a Cochlite beer with him. My heart skipped a beat when I saw Newton. He was so handsome, rocking on his heels, his beautiful brown locks flowing like a lion's mane.

"Aha, we don't need surveillance to find you," said Bigg Gib. "Our souls call to each other."

"I heed the call from the bottom of my sappy heart. We need to head out and head for bed. I'm not at all sleepy," said NezLeigh. "It's a great night for walking. I assume we won't be detained."

"Would you like to give the rude agent another try? I can summon him to give you a lift."

"I'll take you up on it. I believe in second chances. Stella, I'll handle the folks. I'll explain it all. Don't come home, stay here and rest. I imagine the questions will last until daybreak."

"I've put Angel to sleep," Paracelsus added. "Shall we celebrate this day as only two can, Ursula? Bert's king-sized bed is all yours, Stella and Newton."

"Come on, lab partner," I said to Newton.

The bedroom of Bert Cochton was as large as my entire house. The walls were decorated with images in frames, some had a rural theme and others were abstract.

"What is this decoration? Where are the slogans?"

"It's a gallery," said Newton. "These are paintings. They're art."

"Art is banned here."

"For the regular folks but not for them. No doubt it was plundered."

"This one looks like the people who ran out of the Crisper Facility during the fire alarm." I stood in front of a painting of a woman in a black dress and a man in overalls holding a pitch fork in front of an old house with an arched window.

"It has a tag. 'American Gothic.' Taken from the Art Institute of Chicago."

"This one is 'Alchemistic Egg' and was seized from the University of Iowa." Newton stood in front of a green-hued painting featuring birds and contraptions.

The most obvious painting took up an entire wall. It danced with black, blue, and yellow figures. The tag said it was 'Mural' taken the University of Iowa.

"We should return it," I said. "If the school is still there."

"Yes. I could look at it forever," said Newton, "except you are here beside me."

"At last," I said. "We have all the time and space we need."

We put our lab coats on a leather chair, so soft it must have been pigskin and fell on the bed together. We let our fingers mingle as we sunk into the marshmallow-soft mattress. We touched foreheads.

I said, "Together we make a great mind, even if we fall short of being a mastermind, although I must say, the Magna Carta memory was brilliant."

"Don't thank me, thank King John and the threat of Civil War. Stella, I've never been happier. I'm free of my former self's anger. There's no need for the act."

"Is this why you didn't throw things when the Counter Force accosted us?"

"Yes, and I knew you could handle it. I was free to be rational, not irritated, as my reputation demanded." He stroked my hair.

My finger grazed his lips. "You are such a sensitive soul and you've been so across time. And you're kissable."

We increased the force of our embrace. His kisses were sweet, warm, and slightly beery. We melted into the soft bed, falling into spacetime together.

"If only we could be here like this forever. Ah Newton, the world is turning too fast."

"It turns?"

"Yes, it does."

"No wonder my head is spinning."

I took his face in my hands and kissed him. We undressed each other. He cupped me to his naked body. We laid together, skin to skin. It was the two of us alone on our own island of shared time. The ripples of who we were together rocked us to the core.

How did it go after? Well, nothing's perfect, but perfect is the enemy of the good, unless you are making precise scientific measurements. And things were good enough.

As expected, the Cochton brothers never revived and Kola and Layal never returned. With his share of the profits from Cochton Enterprises, Layal went to the university and became a philosophy professor at a small, private college. Kola, too, got an education and became a park ranger. They remained friends but never became a couple as she'd hoped. Instead, she fell in love with a lighthouse tour guide and he with his books.

NezLeigh and Ursula weren't fast friends, but they kept each other in check. Bigg Gib and NezLeigh turned out to be best in touch with the people and gradually grew into leadership positions, leaving Newton and me time to run Cochton Enterprises and to work in the lab. Perhaps most importantly, we began a school, which was free for anyone who wanted to learn. We distributed apple trees at the annual Festival of Trees, and although Cochtonia never gave up Porkies, we were able to move to a more varied plant-based diet.

The first floor of the Cochton mansion became a community center with two large vines growing on either side of the door and a warning sign at the entrance: *No Porkies, no blood sausage, and no candy beyond this point. Fruits and vegetables only.* We also posted a warning of traits of autocratic leaders, in case any of us got too big headed:

Leaders pretend to be masterminds and insist only they are capable of saving the nation.

Only those loyal to the leaders have positions of influence.

Information is censored and tightly controlled.

Exploitation of invented outside or internal threats to justify mistreatment; often involves scapegoating groups.

Tight control of all facets of society government, including romantic and reproductive freedom.

Seizing of property for private gain.

And as for the guard pigs, we crossed them with lactating pigs to produce a strain with all of the milk and none of the smell. The State Crisper Facility needed to do something besides engineer people to be exploited. Cochtonia came to be known as the land of pig milk and apple trees. A tranquility fell over our nation. It was the calm that comes from believing you are one together, with science working toward the improvement of life not just for the few but for many, as it should, to bring enlightenment and happiness to all.

THE END

EPILOGUE

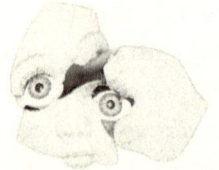

Apple, our eldest, showed no indications of being a mastermind. Slender with her father's pale complexion, she preferred assisting Angel with the milk pig development program, playing with the piglets to tame them.

Fig, the second male born naturally—after Ursula's son, Fritz—arrived when his sister was barely two. He was a plump newborn with broad shoulders. I gave up all romantic notions of childbirth upon his delivery. It was an ordeal. I feared he resembled my dad, but he learned to count at the age of eighteen months, which indicated he was smarter than Barnabus by a long shot. However, when he was five, he and Barnabus snuck across the river on a clandestine apple raid. The stolen apples were good contributors to the hybrid vigor of the Apples of Kent. We crossed them and I developed an apple-filled biscuit that became a popular treat.

We were the happy family Newton never had. Yes, we experimented. Yes, we learned. But we also played. We'd put on diffraction grating glasses, take to the street, and dance in rainbows beneath the streetlights.

Many evenings, Newton and I sat in the courtyard looking at the stars with Apple and Fig. We told them about forces, counter forces, attraction, spacetime, and alchemy.

One night, we watched the sky in wonder with Angel, Paracelsus, Ursula, and Fritz. The moon rose.

Newton said, "Did I tell you all how I discovered the moon was in love with Earth?"

"Yes," said Paracelsus, "many times. Did I tell you how I cured wounds, leprosy, gout, and dropsy?"

"Yes. No..." Newton raised his hand to point to a falling star.

He never finished his sentence. He reached for my hand. His was cold. Our eyes met and his grew dim. He and Paracelsus crumbled into dust.

"No!" Ursula uttered, a sob in her throat. "No, what's happening? It can't be true! Don't go. Don't go!" She got out her device and beamed it at the falling shower of etherical particles.

I'd almost forgotten about the prediction. We'd initially gone back to look at the records of the resurrection, but all we could decipher was a mention of graverobbing. I fell forward onto the powder, grasping for what was left of the man I loved. Yes, of course he had been the true Newton, for I understood him and he understood me.

Crying, the children rushed into the dust as it ran through their outstretched fingers and blew in the wind.

"What should we do?" Ursula asked desperately.

"Nothing," I said. "Nothing, we need to leave it for the universe."

The ashes swirled around us. We blinked, our eyes filling with dust and tears. The strange thing was: Newton was still with me. I felt so close to him. I saw the future. I saw myself running into his arms. What was broken by time would be reunited in space. We'd fall into the wrinkle again.

With hope, I wait until we'll be united. And we will be. Because with science, much is possible, but with alchemy, everything is possible. And sometimes, if the attraction is strong enough, the two wrinkle together in time.

Thank you for reading! Did you enjoy? Please add your review because nothing helps an author more and encourages readers to take a chance on a book than a review.

Don't miss more sci-fi fun like ANDROMEDA'S REBEL by City Owl Author, Debra Jess. Turn the page for a sneak peek!

And discover more from author Catherine Haustein at www.catherinehaustein.com

Also be sure to sign up for the City Owl Press newsletter to receive notice of all book releases!

SNEAK PEEK OF ANDROMEDA'S REBEL

By Debra Jess

Tamarja Chase scraped the last chunk of frost from her nose with the back of her sleeve just as the door to her first appointment dissolved. She'd been frozen in cryo for who knew how long, and she'd come out soaking wet because some damn tech hadn't released enough antifrost into the tube. Defrost and dump was Manitac Corporation's policy for its prisoner population, with no explanation as to where the company had assigned her. Now she had to meet the parole officer in charge of her entire future looking like a beached walhoon. Without thinking, she stepped forward, but instead of entering the office, she slammed into the guy exiting, sending a rain of droplets from her curly hair all over her already ugly brown jumpsuit.

"I'm so sorry." She stepped back, knowing she should lower her eyes, but she didn't. She never had before, which had gotten her locked in solitary more times than she could count.

The guy exiting the office also stepped back with an automatic, "No, it's okay. My..."

He didn't finish. Instead, he stared at her, his blue eyes widening with shock and recognition.

Tamarja stared back. How could she not? Manitac Corporation might have kept her in the deep freeze, but the ice hadn't cooled her libido. This guy sent waves of heat through her by doing nothing more than standing there.

He was tall, with a powerful build that made her wonder why she hadn't broken her nose when she ran into his broad chest. His short-clipped blond hair was slicked back, but with a few rebellious strands escaping in the opposite direction. Sharp cheekbones and pale eyebrows accented those blue eyes that now raked over her in a most unprofessional manner, which didn't help her unwelcomed instinct to return the favor.

To her disappointment, his brief flare of pleased recognition settled back into standard Manitac arrogance and superiority.

"What are *you* doing here?" The sharpness of his baritone voice said more than the words.

Oh boy. His mood dissolved further into anger and judgment, if the vein pulsing at his temple was any indication. Not out of cryo for—she checked the clock projected into her vision—ten minutes and forty seconds, and already she'd managed to piss off a guard. He had to be a guard, given that he wore an all-black uniform with multiple weapons clipped to his belt.

But he wasn't Manitac. The gold epaulets had three stripes, so he had some authority, but the swirling circles of his insignia didn't ping any memories. Manitac flunkies wore all gray all the time for everything.

"Do I know you?" she asked without considering the consequences. Who was she to question him? She had no memory of this guy, but he sure recognized her, which could only mean one thing: he knew she was a puppet—a mind-wiped prisoner—even if she wasn't wearing the bright-orange jumpsuit of one. Her memories consisted of the aching fear resulting from her mind-wipe and not remembering anything—family, friends, her birthdate —followed by two years of flight school and being forcibly shoved into a cryo tube until someone needed a pilot.

The guy didn't yell at her, though he sure wanted to from the look of things.

Before he could say anything else, another voice rose from inside the office. "It's okay, Daeven. Let her in. We'll talk later. Promise."

Daeven. It must be his first name since the nameplate on his uniform said "Blayde." He looked over his shoulder at the speaker but didn't step away from the door. The voice from the background said something else, but Tamarja didn't hear it. Fog enveloped her vision, and her head started to spin. She reached up to rub her temples to ease the pain as unobtrusively as possible, but she couldn't complete the action before Daeven Blayde turned his attention back to her.

It dawned on her that even as he blocked her from getting into the office, she also obstructed his exit. She was the prisoner here, the lowest creature on the social ladder, and he was...well, she wasn't sure what authority he had, but whatever it was, it was higher than her.

She stepped away from the door and lowered her hands back to her sides, but she still didn't lower her eyes. Daeven Blayde stormed past her and didn't look back.

"Come in, come in, come in," the cheerful voice called from inside the office.

She had no choice, so she made one last attempt to tame her curls before putting on her game face.

The Manitac officer waiting for her leaned back in his chair, balancing it precariously on two legs. Manitac must have an abundance of hot-looking officers in the upper ranks, because Yohzad Cyrek could challenge the guard in the sexy department. His smile, warm and inviting, soothed her nerves, and her thoughts of that Blayde guy dribbled away. Cyrek's hair, black and curling over his ears, nearly hid the ear jack that projected Tamarja's file.

Manitac operated an extensive civilian fleet, but the company demanded military-style grooming from all its officers. Her breath hitched at a new thought. Was Cyrek another rebellious spirit?

Cool it. You're a damned puppet. Lusting after Manitac officers is a guaranteed trip back into the deep freeze.

She couldn't remember her crimes, but she could remember the prison flunkies dragging her into the medical center of the flight school on graduation day, using high-energy restraints to keep her strapped in the cryo tube until the freeze sequence silenced her.

It had all been read and recorded at her sentencing hearing.

"Tamarja Chase." Cyrek motioned for her to sit in the utilitarian guest chair on the other side of his desk. "You are one lucky woman."

"Why is that, First Officer?" she asked.

He dropped his own chair back onto four legs with a thump. The noise startled her, but she folded her hands on the desk to hide her jumpiness. Casual, but respectful—that was her goal.

"There's an overabundance of corporate pilots, all of them looking for a berth." He removed the ear jack and tossed it onto the conference room desk. Disrespect for Manitac property? Her opinion of this Cyrek increased.

"Placing a sentenced laborer, and a partially mind-wiped one at that, should have been impossible." He laced his fingers across his flat stomach, self-satisfaction oozing from each pore. "I, however, have not only placed you in less than four standard years but also found you a world considered to be near paradise. With the new slipstream terminus here at Jarvis Station, travel time from the Unity Homeport has been cut in half. Dawn's Landing promises to become one of the most productive Manitac colonies in existence. But it needs pilots, and I just supplied them with one of the best."

The name of the colony meant nothing to her. Less than four years in cryo? She clutched her hands tighter. She had feared that she had lost twenty, thirty, maybe even fifty years. Less than four years meant the family she no longer remembered might still be alive. The friends she couldn't name might find her, if they were looking. She bit and then released the inside of her lip to better hide her hope. "A wonderful opportunity."

"One not to be squandered on foolish attempts to seek the past." Cyrek's tone scolded her, his smile tightening for a moment.

She'd thought she had mastered the art of masking her feelings. Cyrek was more perceptive than most Manitac officers.

"Your past isn't something you want to live through again." He took a sip of something clear from a cup, offered her some, but she shook her head. "Best if you move forward and focus on your future. As the Manitac liaison between corporate headquarters and its AuRaKaz subsidiary, I'm the only one who knows of your prisoner status and your sentence. To everyone else, you're a Manitac pilot on loan."

"Then you know who I am? What I did?" Never mind if that Blayde guy knew who she was. She no longer cared if her hope showed.

Cyrek retreated, swiveling about, his dark eyes leaving hers and seeking the stars crossing the view pane. He had answers, she could see that, but would he share?

"I believe..." He stopped and shook his head, clearing away his indecisiveness before turning back to her. "I believe you got a raw deal, Chase. As your legal rep at the time, I successfully argued that your charges fell more along the lines of corporate espionage against Manitac, rather than treason against the Unity government. Though Unity mostly relies on Manitac to oversee the peaceful settlement of both the Calypso and Callisto arms of the Andromeda Galaxy, once in a while they like to remind us of who's in charge."

Her hope halted its slow retreat and pulsed again. Cyrek clearly wouldn't cross the line by giving her a past, but if he had fought to give her this second chance at life, then she had an unexpected ally out here. She needed all the allies she could find.

"But where exactly am I?" she asked. She remembered the basics: the Unity Homeport was located in the Callisto arm of Andromeda Galaxy, the most core ward of life-sustaining solar systems and where humanity had originated. It had colonies scattered along the trailing edge of both arms.

"My apologies." Cyrek shook his head and made a note using his stylus. "I would have thought the medics would have told you. Jarvis Station is in a geosynchronous orbit around Dawn's Landing, the fourth planet of the Dawn solar system located midway along a minor spur between the Callisto and Calypso arms of Andromeda."

His description helped a little, but she couldn't remember the system or the spur. Until she could access a navigational system, she wouldn't really know how much had changed while she was in cryo.

"You're a unique entity," Cyrek continued. "The only partially wiped prisoner in the whole galaxy. You aren't preprogrammed with loyalty to either Manitac or the Unity government. That's a choice you will have to make."

That meant she wouldn't devolve into a full-blown puppet. Manitac meant to keep her this way. "But why?" she couldn't help but ask, not sure if she wanted to know. "What did I do to deserve this?"

Cyrek just shrugged. "Right before your arrest, Manitac Medical had tried to find a way of educating the puppet population to take on more complex tasks than the usual manual labor they're given. Our early experiments proved, shall we say, unsuccessful. The Unity government ethics overseers started to balk about a few deaths that had occurred. So to prevent an entire shutdown of the program, Manitac Medical decided to try a partial wipe on a prisoner. When the call went out, I submitted your name. I knew you would survive the operation with your sanity intact. So far you've exceeded all expectations and proved me correct. All it took was a two-year refresher course, and you are now the owner of a Class III pilot's license."

She looked down at her folded fingers. Refresher course, huh? That could only mean that she'd been a pilot before her wipe. She had never made the connection, but now that she knew she was an admin's experiment, she didn't know what to do with the information. Unique in the universe? Given a second chance with her personality and independent thoughts intact? She wouldn't become a mindless drone? She should be grateful, but somehow her gratitude couldn't claw its way past her disgust.

How do you thank someone for giving you a second chance when you're not if sure you wanted one? Her hands started to shake, so she pulled them closer to her body, grinding her nails into the back of her hands. There was no escape. Her head had known that, even if her heart hadn't.

If Cyrek noticed her struggle, he didn't indicate it. Instead, he busied himself by hooking his ear jack back over his left ear and pulling a stylus from his pocket.

Flipping through pages of projected data, he entered information into the data prompt. "I've arranged transportation for you on the first morning shuttle. You'll have an early call for a four-level decon. Will you be ready on time?" The stylus hesitated, and he looked up, his concern giving his eyes a warm fire within their darkness.

"You mean Manitac still hasn't figure out how to make compressors work in space?"

Before her big freeze, there'd been rumors of large developments in the area of space compressors. Compressors already allowed near instantaneous travel across short distances by compressing gas into plasma inside one window and then propelled small quantities of solid and liquid matter through the space in-between, delivering the load through the opposite window. The tech worked on people and had already replaced the elevators and slidewalks at the flight school, but Manitac hadn't quite figured out how to compress a vacuum. When it did, the corporation's dominance of space travel would increase exponentially.

Cyrek raised an eyebrow but didn't take the bait. "If we had, we wouldn't need pilots at all, and you would still be frozen."

Ouch. She really needed to tone down the snark. Cyrek appeared to like her, despite her crimes. She couldn't afford to have him turn against her. "I'll be ready."

He shook his head, evidently not convinced and dismissing her misstep, letting the warmth return to his eyes. "Look, I understand this is a lot to take in, and you've only been out of cryo for less than an hour. Sleep sickness often throws your emotional equilibrium out of balance. The medical team here on Jarvis can treat the nausea and dizziness, but Manitac hasn't equipped them with a psych team to deal with the emotional backlash." He gave her a sympathetic look. "Why don't I take you to your quarters, and we'll finish this up tomorrow morning after decon? I can't shuttle down with you, but there's no reason why I can't brief you after you've had a good night's sleep."

His stylus danced again before she could agree. Considering she was now an indentured servant for all intents and purposes, it hadn't really been a question anyway. One by one, she uncurled her fingers from their death grip. Maybe her relief was as obvious as her hope.

"You're all set." He stood up and moved around the desk, holding out a hand to help her stand. "Ready?"

Tamarja hesitated and then accepted Cyrek's assistance.

She nodded. "I'm ready."

Don't stop now. Keep reading with your copy of ANDROMEDA'S REBEL by City Owl Author, Debra Jess, available now.

Want even more sci-fi fun? Try **ANDROMEDA'S REBEL** by City Owl Author, Debra Jess, and discover more from author Catherine Haustein at www.catherinehaustein.com

---

They took the sky from her, and her memory, but no one could take away her rebellious spirit.

Mind-wiped and implanted with a death collar in case she should get out of line, Manitac's corporate flunkies told Tamarja Chase that love could never be a part of her new life. However, working on a paradise planet as the director's personal shuttle pilot does have its perks and Tamarja intends to take advantage of both.

Perk number one: dark and sensuous Yohzad Cyrek, her parole officer and personal champion.

Perk number two: Daeven Blayde, a blond and brooding badass, who can't decide if he wants to throttle her, kiss her, or both.

Falling for Yohzad would scratch all her rebellious itches by breaking the rules about prisoner and officer relationships, but not even he has the power to set her free.

Pursuing Daeven would be like loving a lightning strike: powerful, explosive, and deadly.

But, when other mind-wiped slaves start disappearing, her love life quickly becomes the least of her worries. Death collar or not, Tamarja takes a stand—one that could not only kill her but lose her the man who truly loves her and force her to kill the other.

Please sign up for the City Owl Press newsletter for chances to win special subscriber-only contests and giveaways as well as receiving information on upcoming releases and special excerpts.

All reviews are **welcome** and **appreciated**. Please consider leaving one on your favorite social media and book buying sites.

For books in the world of romance and speculative fiction that embody Innovation, Creativity, and Affordability, check out City Owl Press at www.cityowlpress.com.

ACKNOWLEDGMENTS

I'd like to thank those who believed in this series including my friends, family, and coworkers. My infinite praise flows to Tina Moss and the dedicated team at City Owl Press. Many thanks to my talented editor, Christie Stratos, for making this an enjoyable journey. To my dogs, Daphne and Apollo, who spent hours snoozing by my side as I wrote this tale, let's go for a walk.

ABOUT THE AUTHOR

Born under a half-illuminated quarter moon, Catherine Haustein is never sure if she favors light or shadow. Her *Unstable States* series contains ample portions of both. The author and chemist lives and teaches in a tidy town in Iowa on the shores of a lake which sometimes is cited for elevated fecal coliform levels. A graduate of the Iowa Writers' Workshop, Catherine weaves the passions and optimism of science with the absurdities of  the present and dark possibilities of the future throughout her books.

www.catherinehaustein.com

 twitter.com/hausteincɪ
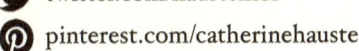 pinterest.com/catherinehauste

ABOUT THE PUBLISHER

City Owl Press is a cutting edge indie publishing company, bringing the world of romance and speculative fiction to discerning readers.

Escape Your World. Get Lost in Ours!

www.cityowlpress.com

facebook.com/CityOwlPress

twitter.com/cityowlpress

instagram.com/cityowlbooks

pinterest.com/cityowlpress

tiktok.com/@cityowlpress